About the ⁄

Niall Slater lives in London and mouths off about library closures for a living. Most of his stories are set in space because he can't drive and, unlike cars, you can just lie about how spaceships work and very few people will email you about it.

The Second Death of Daedalus Mole is Niall's first published novel and was longlisted for the inaugural Bath Novel Award. If you disliked this novel and would like to scold the author for writing it, you can reach him on twitter at @Niall_Slater.

THE SECOND DEATH OF
DAEDALUS MOLE

THE SECOND DEATH
OF DAEDALUS MOLE

NIALL SLATER

Unbound Digital

This edition first published in 2018

Unbound

6th Floor Mutual House, 70 Conduit Street, London W1S 2GF

www.unbound.com

ISBN (eBook): 978-1-912618-33-0

ISBN (Paperback): 978-1-912618-32-3

Design by Mecob

Printed and bound in Great Britain by Clays Ltd, Elcograf S.p.A.

Dear Reader,

The book you are holding came about in a rather different way to most others. It was funded directly by readers through a new website: Unbound.

Unbound is the creation of three writers. We started the company because we believed there had to be a better deal for both writers and readers. On the Unbound website, authors share the ideas for the books they want to write directly with readers. If enough of you support the book by pledging for it in advance, we produce a beautifully bound special subscribers' edition and distribute a regular edition and e-book wherever books are sold, in shops and online.

This new way of publishing is actually a very old idea (Samuel Johnson funded his dictionary this way). We're just using the internet to build each writer a network of patrons. Here, at the back of this book, you'll find the names of all the people who made it happen.

Publishing in this way means readers are no longer just passive consumers of the books they buy, and authors are free to write the books they really want. They get a much fairer return too – half the profits their books generate, rather than a tiny percentage of the cover price.

If you're not yet a subscriber, we hope that you'll want to join our publishing revolution and have your name listed in one of our books in the future. To get you started, here is a £5 discount on your first pledge. Just visit unbound.com, make your pledge and type MOLE18 in the promo code box when you check out.

Thank you for your support,

Dan, Justin and John
Founders, Unbound

Super Patrons

Sarah Abernathy
Luke Addams
Caspar Addyman
Eli Allison
Ben Anderson
Catherine Atherton
Scott Bain
Fred Barboo
Cris Baxter
Elliot Bentine
Rosemary Bingham
Vince Blas
James Bowsher
Richard W H Bray
Steamed Bun
Connor Campbell
Andy Checker
Iwan Clarke
Julian Clyne
Christopher Collingridge
Claudio Corbisiero
James Craig Paterson
John Crawford
Tom Crawford
Nick Davey
Finbar Deane-Stott
Tara deCamp
John Dexter
Phrazer Downs
Alexis Dubreuil
Eric Englert
Bad ExampleMan

Delia Ferguson
Luísa Flach
Fizz Forsey
Anna Ganley
GMarkC
Clare Golding
Emma Gottesman
Daniel Hahn
Louise Hamilton
Andrea Harman
Caitlin Harvey
Rhian Heulwen Price
Andrew John Hodge
Paul Holbrook
Kaitie Hughes
Deb Ikin
Huma Islam
iucounu
Oli Jacobs
'Lil' James Robinson
K.L.Kettle K.L.Kettle
Dan Kieran
Pet Kilcullen
Trudy Kilcullen
Patrick Kincaid
Chris King
David Knill
Satu Kumpulainen
Anwen Kya Hayward
Damon L. Wakes
Ewan Lawrie
Christine Lawson
Kate Lee
Lily Levinson
Simone Libman
Anna Lyaruu

Evelyn Marr
Tom Marriott
Jonathan McDowell
Sarah McIntyre
Adam McNeil
Liane McNeil
philip Middleton
John Mitchinson
Pete Morgan
Luke Morley
Paul Murphy
Charlotte Murray
John Murray (@MenaceInc)
Katie Nordgren
Tessa Nordgren
Hannah Penn
Justin Pollard
Jon Porter
Lowri Potts
Rosie Quattromini
Lisa Quattromini
Adrien Radke
Martin Reed
Stuart Ritchie
Ellen Robertson
Poppy Rosenberg
Daniel Ross
Adam Sales
Eilis Slater
Oliver Slater
Patricia Slater
Patricia Slater
Gemma Slater
Lizi Spicer
Janice Staines
Kim Staples

Jeremy Stevens
Imelda Taylor
Sarah Wright & Tim Taylor
Andrew Tees
Jigsaw "Beerbods" The Cat
David G Tubby
Mark Vent
Grace Verity
Karen Walton
Kate Watson
Sam Welch
Paul Wheeler
Mark Whiffen
Carol Whitton
Josephine Wright
Becca Wright

Terminus

Along a narrow channel of unusual space travelled a long, pointed ship the colour of midnight. It moved at poorly-understood velocity through a light-years-long tube of not-quite vacuum, and a few metres to either side of it rushed a screaming white wall that threatened molecular deconstruction at the slightest contact.

Inside, at the controls, Juno sat still. She wasn't afraid. After forty years as a woman, twenty as a police officer and four as a freelancer, there weren't many kinds of ugliness left in the galaxy that she hadn't already found and kicked in the teeth. Now that both the Republic and the husband had lost her trail, there really wasn't much she worried about.

She flexed her middle finger, touching the silver ring behind her knuckle. The main reason she was the one doing the kicking, and not the one losing her teeth, was because she treated space with the respect it deserved. Most people came from planets. Planets with oceans. They grew up thinking of things as 'up' or 'down', 'shallow' or 'deep', and saying ridiculous things, things like 'what goes around comes around', and 'what goes up must come down'. People thought that if you started running and didn't stop, just kept running, you'd eventually end up back where you started. Juno wasn't most people. Juno had been born in space. She knew that space was not an ocean. Juno knew that what went around rarely came around, and what went up would likely keep going up at exactly the same speed, having no concept of 'up', or, indeed, of 'speed', and would not stop until something compelled it to, usually at the great expense of both.

People also liked to say things like 'empty space', which Juno thought was particularly naïve. There was no such thing. Space was big and it was dark, but it was full of hidden things, and Juno knew that no matter how big or dangerous your secret, you'd only have to fling yourself into the dark and you would probably never be found again.

That is, of course, until someone hired Juno to find you. And today someone had. A blacksmith, furious about a stolen roll of daggers and a real, working firearm. Juno hadn't seen a gun in months, and good, solid steel was back in fashion. Things were getting rough, like they'd been when she was a child.

A light on her dashboard pulsed in green. She had a few moments to prepare before the end of the channel – a great black circle – rushed forward to meet her. She reached one mottled green hand up to flick down her bronze visor, keeping two more braced against the control panel and her final free hand resting on the throttle. She heard a whine from the engine compartment behind her. The panelling under her feet buzzed and shook. When the alert sounded she eased the throttle downwards until it clicked, and the *Kestrel* dropped out of the channel with a jolt and a screech as the engine switched gears. Then Juno was in darkness. There were no stars.

She moved quickly, tapping out sequences and tripping switches on the panel. The cockpit filled with little lights as the target-finders started up. The radio antenna came back to life with a *bing*, followed by the glowing overlay on the viewscreen, populating the dark expanse in front of her with green dots.

Juno heard a *blip* as the target-finders picked up her quarry again and showed it on the overlay: a fat little freighter trying to haul itself away from the channel as fast as it could. She selected it with a finger and keyed the communicator.

'Hailing mid-class freighter at position fourteen-sixteen-minus-two. This is Juno of the *Kestrel*,' she said. 'You've done it this time, Amphitryon. Stop running.'

Her hail was met with silence. The *Kestrel* powered forward and swooped towards its prey, closing the distance quickly. Juno reached for a switch on her left and hovered over it.

'Cut your engines,' she said. 'I won't ask again.'

The reply was inaudible, thick with interference. Juno frowned. The ship kept going, so she flicked up the plastic guard under her thumb and fired. A blazing white spot flashed out from beneath the

Kestrel's nosecone, leaving a white trail as it hurtled forwards. Half a second later there was a bright splash as it shorted out the freighter's main thruster, bringing it to a juddering halt as the inertia controls kicked in.

'Consider yourself under arrest,' said Juno. 'I'll be coming aboard in two minutes. Don't make me kill you, please.' Juno unbuckled her seatbelt, dumped her helmet on the console and ambled from the cockpit to the weapons cabinet above her bunk, where she selected a short sword from the rack and tucked a dagger into her belt. By the time she returned, the *Kestrel* had drawn to a halt alongside her quarry.

A hiss from the radio made her pause. The view beyond the main screen was dark. Termina had no planets, no stations and no town-ships. Had Amphitryon run here thinking it would be easier to hide somewhere quiet? Juno checked the main readout again. A barren asteroid field, some debris from a long-lost battle, and the freighter. Otherwise, this place was empty.

'Amphitryon,' Juno said. 'Shut off your scrambler.'

There was no response but white noise.

Juno furrowed her brow. Then she pulled a heavy lever beneath the control panel, causing a jolt. The docking tube inflated and jumped the gap between ships, clamping onto the freighter's flank with a loud *thunk*. Juno thumbed the edge of her sword and walked out.

Four minutes later she ran back into the *Kestrel* alone, leaving bloody footprints behind her. She cleared the airlock and hit the man-ual release with an elbow, cutting the cord between the ships before reaching the cockpit and searching the readout again. Still nothing.

The hissing was louder now, and it wasn't coming from the speak-ers. She'd just seen Amphitryon lying in a pool of his own blood on the floor of his cockpit, frozen at the moment of death, clutching his face in agony, and the interference was coming from nowhere. She hit the radio.

'Surrender,' she said, to anyone who could hear. 'I'm armed. Present yourself and yield your weapons or I will kill you.'

The hissing intensified. The sensors showed nothing, but her neck itched. She didn't feel alone.

Then space ceased to be empty. Juno didn't see it arrive; there was no landing flash, no hint to announce that something had come. It simply moved into view, like a person stepping out of shadow. It looked like a great wall of bright red flesh, soft and glistening in the glare of the *Kestrel*'s floodlights. It beat and pulsed in time to some silent rhythm as she watched, and shining, black, many-legged parasites skittered across its surface. They tore at it, drawing blood and sending it drifting from the surface in perfect spheres.

Juno had seen many things, but there was no memory she could use to comprehend what she was looking at. Phantom spiders ran across her skin and blood rushed in her ears. Her head-crest stood on end. She slowly stretched out a hand for the weapon controls.

Outside, a wall of lighter pink flesh slowly drew upwards, revealing a sliver of green beneath. Juno watched. It continued creeping upwards until it became clear what she was looking at.

A taste of metal bloomed on her tongue. Juno touched a finger to her lip. It came away red. A rivulet of blood ran from her nose and dripped onto the leg of her flight suit, mingling with old smears of engine oil.

Juno grunted in pain, clutching her skull and squeezing her eyes shut, but she could still see it – a great green eye. It seeped inexorably in, burning as it went. Her head felt like it was about to crack. Images from somewhere else forced their way inside her, clamouring for space: Juno saw trees hammered by black rain; a stony, overgrown ruin with a moat of tar; a tattered box of books. Pictures and sounds and smells assaulted her from a hundred places at once, scalding.

Then she saw, clear as a mirror, a white ship screaming through the channel to Termina.

In her head she heard it, spoken from somewhere close.

I A– AM FE... FEAR. CRY HELP, LITTLE ONE.

A jolt of pain shot through her knee as it hit the deck, and Juno could see again. Her throat was raw, as if she had been screaming, and she was on the floor, clinging to the arm of the pilot's chair, in silence. There was nothing outside.

Juno realised two things: that her headache had vanished, and – with surprise – that she'd had a headache for weeks. She felt, for some reason, like she had lost something, and that some feeling of belonging she'd had was now gone, like a pulled thread that jumps out of the weave and disappears, falling faster than your eyes can track.

Then, as the *Kestrel* buzzed a warning, she realised one more thing: the Republic hadn't lost her trail after all. A white ship showed up on the viewscreen, enveloped in smoke as if it had just let fly a single missile. In the moment before impact, Juno touched the ring on her finger.

Out-of Characters

Daedalus
Aphiemi Station, the Cloud
Present day

In a bustling way-station a long way from the remains of Earth, a greasy-haired man leaned out over a rooftop. His long brown coat billowed about his legs, threatening to pull him over. The street far below was starting to fill with people going to work: broad-shouldered petradons ploughing through crowds of smaller creatures, stossven clattering about with their hard edges and faulk slipping through the mass with long bobbing strides.

The air was thick and hot. Cold breezes whistled by occasionally, sharp and thin, but it only made the heat harder to ignore. It pressed in, drawing out sweat and letting it sit on the skin. A drop ran down the man's nose and itched, then fell. It jostled back and forth through the air, dragged down fast by the heightened gravity, before bursting against the pavement. He tilted forwards.

'Daedalus,' said a voice from under his coat, 'I can see you.'

Daedalus lifted his hand and scratched his jaw, which was patchy with stubble. The little purple locket over his heart buzzed, demanding an answer.

'I –' he tried. He cleared his throat. 'I'm fine.'

'I'm sure,' said the locket. 'You know how high the gravity is here. You wouldn't want an accident, would you?'

Daedalus poked his toe over the edge of the building.

'No,' he said, 'no accidents.'

'I'll be done soon,' she said. 'I'd hate to have to leave without you.'

'Right.' Daedalus looked up. Far above him, clouds rolled against the ceiling, crashing into each other in slow motion, bursting apart and giving way to steel spires that ran down to the deck, rivers of people flowing around their bases. Light drones buzzed halfway up, lamps dangling on strings. The moment passed, and Daedalus, who had been feeling a comfortable lightness, settled back into his usual self and his headache returned. He dropped his bottle and made for the door leading back down to the street.

'Where are you going?' asked the locket.

'Nowhere.' He moved through the hotel lobby, past the snoring concierge, and emerged into the street. 'I don't know.'

A security camera atop a nearby pylon suddenly jolted and spun to watch him.

'Just be careful, dear,' she said. 'I need you.'

Daedalus shuddered at her words, picked a direction and started walking.

'How long?' he asked. A nearby faulk gave him a sharp look from under her feathers and shook her head, walking faster.

'Two hours, maybe more. This boy you left me with doesn't know what he's doing.'

A while, then. Daedalus kept walking.

The world had changed. It was gone, for a start, and the people on it had been scattered to the stars. Their children's children were now the underfoot nuisance in a galaxy of bigger, stronger and wealthier peoples. Daedalus hadn't seen another human in three weeks. He hadn't talked to one in four months. When humans did pass, there was a flash of recognition, an exchanged glance, but nothing more. Any shared experience there once was had worn away.

Daedalus racked his soggy brain. There was a bar nearby, he was sure. Somewhere. He fumbled for a cigarette and pushed it between his cracked lips. It lit itself with a click and buzzed, spilling sweet-smelling white vapour into the dim station air. Daedalus let out a long, slow sigh.

The Landing Leg. That was it. He took the lift down to the centre near the core, a dense collection of clubs and game joints sprinkled with unconscious people in varying states of undress, some still wearing their headsets if they'd passed out before mustering the courage to face reality again. They were mostly couriers and odd-jobbers, like him, or shipping company workers blowing off steam between shifts with pockets full of vouchers for night-long VR sessions and hundred-bit bar tabs.

The Landing Leg was a relatively quiet joint tucked into a side street, heaving with jetlagged visitors who weren't working on station time. Daedalus sidled into the hot noise and made for the bar. Being self-employed, he didn't have any vouchers. The bartender wrinkled her snout at the bent card he handed over, but dropped it into the till nonetheless and produced a hissing pint of something grey and cloudy. There wasn't space to sit, so Daedalus hovered near the end of the bar, a few feet from the corner booth, leaning into an alcove between two support beams.

The first sip of a pint is never as refreshing as you expect. The sour, watery taste of cheap lager is bad enough, and the bitter fizz of sink-dust is worse, but a seasoned drinker will push on. Everyone knows that the real relief comes an instant after the first sip, when the drinker's brain recalls the pleasurable numbness to come and kicks into gear in the hope that such numbness can be achieved again, and quickly.

Daedalus took a sip and grimaced. His tongue reported to his brain that alcohol was coming, and everything slipped back into the muted comfort he'd become accustomed to in the last few months. It swallowed him up in the pressing heat. Then, just as he was sinking back into the noise, he heard something that he was much less accustomed to. It hit him like a cold drip on his face in a hot bath.

'Six,' said someone. 'Bay six. You understand where that is? One more than five. One less than seven.'

'I'm *sorry*,' said someone else.

Daedalus stared into his drink. Today, of all days. Humans. The sound rang in his ears. Thickly accented from the interspecial pidgin of the trade lanes, grating and angry, but undeniably the soft, lyrical human voice. He could barely stand it.

'It wasn't my fault,' said the second voice, deeper than the first.

'Yes it was,' said the first. 'Yes, it absolutely sodding was. Aggro is going to kill you if we don't do something. Ten thousand bits. He's going to kill both of us. Ten *thousand*. Christ.'

The pint was half gone. Daedalus kept drinking as fast as he could, trying not to listen.

'What are we gonna do?'

'I don't know, Trev. But we better come up with something bloody

9

quick. Bay six. Okay? Bay six. He'll be here in thirty minutes and he's going to want the merchandise in his hands. He wants to see it.'

'What if... what if we pay him off?'

'For god's sake. Have you got ten grand in your pocket? No? No, of course you don't.'

'What if we run?'

The first voice laughed long and loud, drawing the looks of a few drinkers nearby. Daedalus grimaced at the sound. The pint was gone, but he found he couldn't move. There was a pull in his chest, right under his locket – a cold, big, empty kind of pull. He wanted to lean out and look for himself.

'Right. You do that. See how far you get.' There was a pause, then the screech of a chair being pushed back. 'Get up. Get up, now.'

'Where are we going?'

'Find it. We have to find it. It can't have got far.'

Daedalus shrank back into his alcove as they hurried past – two humans in dark clothes with close-cropped hair, one sporting a bloody nose and a very nasty bruise on his face. Then they were gone. A very tall person with thick blue fur gave him a quizzical look as she glided past him to take their booth.

Daedalus felt the pull in his chest strengthen, as if, just for a moment, gravity had changed its mind and decided that down was forward. He felt the urge to follow them. Then his hand was up, under his coat, squeezing the locket between his fingers. The urge faded. Humans were trouble to each other. Better like this.

By the time he finished his fifth drink he was sick of the place and made his way back out into the street. Staggering a little, tattered dress boots skidding on faux-cobblestones slick with condensation, he fished in his coat pocket and drew out a set of keys. The streets down here were still quiet. As he got further from the pub their metal jangling rang out clearly against the backdrop of gurgling drainpipes, cycling the same water through the station over and over.

He wondered briefly about the humans he'd seen. Daedalus overheard a lot of things in his line of work, hopping between backwoods stations delivering secret packages to surly people. The better he got at going quietly – at passing before people's eyes without registering in memory – the more things he heard. The more things he heard, the more it hurt to imagine that other people were just walking around with all these other memories in their heads, some of them good, so many of them bad, and they all seemed to be able to cope. It didn't seem real that there were so many lives happening around him, and they moved forward through time, leaving things behind them in a way that he did not.

Halfway to the elevator, he heard a sharp clatter. A few metres back from the street, in an alcove under a whirring gas exchanger, a pile of sticks and denim wriggled against a damp wall. A camera above Daedalus's head followed his gaze. Its motor gave a little metallic *hmph*.

The pile of clothes shifted and groaned. As he approached, Daedalus made out a narrow face and shoulders with smooth ochre plating: a stoss kid. The boy's chestpiece hadn't split yet, and he looked tiny inside the baggy denim jacket, head dwarfed underneath a full-enclosure game headset.

'Mole, keep away,' buzzed the locket.

Daedalus knelt down.

'Just a kid,' he said. A line of bright blood ran under the visor and stained the jacket. Daedalus looked around, saw nobody, and reached out. The boy jerked back, hissing at his touch. Daedalus held the boy still with a firm grip on his shoulder and a knee pinning his legs. 'Can you hear me?'

'Human,' the boy moaned. 'No human. Please.'

'Not human,' said Daedalus.

'No human,' said the boy, 'no.'

'That's right,' Daedalus patted his chest, 'no human.' Daedalus found a catch just above the visor and released it. Under a plastic flap a set of needles worked furiously with a rapid *clickclickclick*, tapping out their delirious rhythm on a patch of flesh between two skull-plates. The chemical they carried wasn't addictive, he knew, but the dreams it brought on could be.

'Can you do something about this?' he asked.

The camera overhead twitched. 'I could,' said the locket.

'… Will you?'

The locket went silent. Daedalus reached behind the headset and felt around for a safety catch. There wasn't one. He sighed, and gripped the boy's head in two hands before smacking it against the wall. The headset split after two strikes, and Daedalus eased his finger into the crack, pulling it gently into two pieces. The clicking died away, and the boy let out a lungful of air. Underneath the visor his gaze was unfocused. After a few moments of fumbling and drawing in wet breath, his eyes came to life and fixed on Daedalus, brow knitting inwards in fear. The boy kicked and wriggled his legs free.

'Human!'

Daedalus stood and backed away as the kid scrabbled for something to hit him with. By the time he'd pulled a metal bar out of the rubbish, Daedalus was gone.

'You're going to get it when you come home,' said the locket.

'He was just a kid.'

'Just a kid. Incredible. What was I?'

Daedalus felt a sick, gratifying twist in his stomach.

'Shut up,' he said.

'Oh, shut up, is it?' she said. 'Someone's feeling mouthy today. I don't like it.'

The alcohol had hit him hard. Daedalus blinked hard and brought his attention back to the plane of the living, where, it turned out, he was lying on a bench near the docking arrays. Geared-up pilots hurried past him to make their departures. Some of them were dragging last-minute passengers or cargo trolleys they'd picked up in the trade rooms, and most of them looked hung over. On the big departure screens he saw listings of ships ready to leave, and the names of planets they were bound for. A few tankers were carrying prisoners to Dolorian Prime a couple of jumps away, but most of the ships were headed for Minna Minna, the closest planet with a decent trading station. Everyone had somewhere to go besides Daedalus. Through a grimy window he watched a couple of them pass. A vicious-looking cruiser with *Itinerant Light* stencilled on the stern dropped free of its docking arm and drifted ponderously out of view, and a round little freighter took its place, spotlights bringing out the name *The Steamed Bun* lovingly hand-painted on the bow.

'How long?' he asked.

'Fifteen minutes.'

Daedalus heaved himself upright and tried not to be sick. 'Where?'

'Bay six. Honestly. You're pathetic.'

Bay six. Something scratched in the back of his mind, almost like a physical itch.

'Six.'

'Yes, six. Are you losing it? I need you to fly.'

His thoughts were like quicksand. The more he struggled to catch that vital piece of relevant information floating out of reach, the faster he sank. After a few seconds of trying, he gave up.

'Is there a coffee place?'

'No. You're easier drunk. Go to the Back Burner, across the street.'

Daedalus followed a meandering line from the bench to the bar. On the way he received a few contemptuous looks, and something short in a hood bumped into him, nearly knocking him over. Finally he collapsed into an empty booth.

The air was colder up here. Slowly, against his wishes, he started to wake up. The blood pumping around his head was too loud, and the people around him moving too fast, doing too many things. The world pressed in hard from all sides. Daedalus felt the headache thudding back into his skull.

A machine making a great deal of noise approached his table and leaned over him. One big orange eye fizzed in the middle of its head.

'A whiskey for sir?' it said, rattling slightly.

He nodded, avoiding eye contact, and fished in his pocket for a card, finding nothing.

'Very good, sir,' it said. 'And for you?'

Daedalus looked up. From the opposite seat, a pair of extraordinarily dark, wide-set eyes looked back from under a ragged hood.

'Water,' she said.

The machine jittered and straightened up. 'Very good. Two whiskeys it is.' Without waiting for a correction, it raced away towards the bar. The two patrons stared at each other.

'Are you blind?' she asked.

Daedalus slouched back, waiting for a clever response to make itself apparent.

She sat still, watching him. The soft orange light made her green skin look mottled and unhealthy. Could mean anything. Lots of people were green.

'Who –'

'I need a ride,' she said.

Daedalus groaned and ran a hand over his face. It came away slick with sweat. 'I'm not working today. Ask someone else.'

'Taxos. I need to get to Taxos.'

He rubbed his temple. 'Right, I know you core people are used to getting what you want, but out here if a man says he's not working, he's not working. Okay? We don't have trading standards people you can write to. There's no bloody... there's no manager. You can't push me around. So... so you can bloody well... just... go away.'

She placed a set of keys on the table. Daedalus looked at them.

'Those are mine,' he said.

'Yeah,' she said.

Daedalus reached into his pocket again. It was still empty. He shifted in his seat and she snatched the keys back, vanishing them from the table almost too quick to see. In the moment her face moved into the light, he saw that she was badly bruised, and in the turn he got a better sense of her frame: small and wiry, with an unmistakable shape given by the second pair of arms tucked away under her robe. He couldn't see, but he realised there must be a tell-tale crest beneath her hood, which she was trying to keep very still.

'Who are you?' he asked. 'You're somewhere you shouldn't be.'

'So help me get home,' she said.

'Taxos?'

'Yes.'

Back in the shadows, her eyes glittered. Bulbous and black, they caught tiny white reflections that made them look like portholes into space.

Daedalus sat forward. When he opened his mouth to speak, he found he was short of breath. He could smell smoke.

'Why?'

She looked at him with an inscrutable expression, her mouth a slit. Daedalus could see that she was small. Entari were supposed to be the same size, all of them – that was kind of the point – but this one was short. She was propping herself up to reach eye level, hiding her body in a bundle of robes, but he reckoned she was a good foot shorter than him. Tiny. Her gaze felt hot on his skin. Slowly, she withdrew a wallet from her clothes and set it on the table.

'I'm looking for someone. And I'll pay,' she said. 'That's why.'

Daedalus looked at the wallet, emblazoned with a crude, anatomically-improbable design of a naked human.

'That's *your* wallet?' he asked.

She glanced down at it. Daedalus noticed her nose was slightly squashed, like it had been broken.

'... Yes.'

A thief. And a bad liar. Thieves with no cunning always had a violent streak. Often a temper to match.

'*Oh.*' Daedalus stressed the syllable, affecting surprise. 'So you're one of those.'

Daedalus saw a shadow cross her face. *There's a button*, he thought. She went a deeper shade of green and under her hood he saw a twitch as her crest stiffened in anger. He was still swimming through a tipsy fog with a headache, but he reckoned he'd got the measure of her.

'Is that a problem, human?'

He took a breath. 'Just keep whatever's in your pants in your pants, and we'll be fine.'

The entari visibly bristled, but sucked her teeth and nodded.

Daedalus relaxed. Clearly she had a temper, but one she could rein in. Just about.

The acting made him feel greasy. Obviously she'd stolen the wallet from a human, but he found it interesting that she'd jump to the defence of human-lovers rather than reverting to straight contempt. Very unlike an entari. Though judging from the contempt for him, specifically, that was now written all over her face, she wasn't herself a particular fan of humans.

'All right, money,' he said. 'How much are you looking to spend?'

She hesitated.

'First time?' he asked. 'Okay, look, standard rate to the Capital is three hundred bits, but... ' Daedalus leaned back in his seat and thought about all the drink he was going to buy. 'Since you're obviously in a tight spot I'll knock it down to two hundred. One hundred now, one hundred on arrival, as long as you buy me a drink. How does that sound?'

'A drink?'

The mechanical waiter returned with two glasses on a tray. It set them down a little too hard, sloshing whiskey over the tabletop, and shakily held out its card reader.

'Which sir will be paying today?'

She stared at him, suspicion and fear mingled in her expression. After a long moment she reached into the wallet and withdrew a bright blue ten-bit card to hand to the waiter, who pocketed it and left. Then she pulled out two orange fifties.

'What's your name?' she asked.

'Mole,' said Daedalus. 'Daedalus Mole.'

'Erin,' she said, and pushed the cards across the table.

Daedalus took them with one hand and held up his glass with the other. 'Nice to meet you,' he said.

Erin gave a short, sharp laugh. Daedalus flinched. She put her hand to her mouth, as if she hadn't expected it. Like the laugh had been stuck there by someone else.

'Sorry,' she said, 'I – it's been a long day. I didn't think you'd... '

'It's fine,' he stared at her. 'We can go after this. You ready?'

'Right now? Give me a sec,' she said, getting up. 'Bathroom.'

Daedalus watched her go. The locket vibrated against his chest.

'You've made a friend,' it hissed. 'How sweet.'

'Need the money,' he said.

'Curious that she bumped into you,' said the locket, 'very curious. I'm watching through the security cameras – did you know there are four humans on this station right now? You're not the only one looking to make friends.'

'So?'

'The other humans. From the bar. Remember?'

'No.' Daedalus rubbed his temple. 'I'm drunk.'

'She's what they're looking for, you idiot. They arrived with her, but she gave one of them a real beating and got away.'

'Great.' Daedalus drank. 'Good for her.'

The locket buzzed angrily. 'They're still after her, you piss artist. Don't you remember what they said? Bay six. *I'm* in bay six.'

'We need the money.'

Erin emerged from the bathroom and made her way towards the table.

'Think!' the locket beeped, and then went quiet.

Erin weaved around a tall man with a fistful of cards, nearly knocking him over, and Daedalus remembered. *Ten grand.*

'Ready to go?' she said, wrapping her ragged robes more tightly around herself. She kept looking around the bar. Her expression was wary and tired, eyes keen.

Daedalus looked at her. The smell of smoke hadn't gone away, and his breath came shorter and shorter.

'You remind me… ' he started, and stopped.

She didn't hear. Suddenly Daedalus was somewhere else. This wasn't good. Focus. The alcohol wasn't enough; he couldn't button it down like he usually did. The sound of her short, brittle laugh still rang in his skull. Memories crowded in his forebrain, overlapping the present and jostling for centre stage. His heart pounded. Keep a lid on it, he told himself, breathing deep, but it felt like his throat was closing up. The bar didn't seem well-lit anymore, and the sounds around him had taken on a tinny, angry quality. Darkness crept in at the edges of his vision as he reached for his glass with sweaty hands. It slipped, whiskey puddling around his fingers. *Keep a lid on it. Close the box.* He squeezed the locket in his fist, and it buzzed reassuringly in return.

'What?' asked Erin. 'What did you say?'

'Nothing,' he breathed out as slowly as he could, trying not to make a sound. Then deeply in, then out, then in. The room returned. Suddenly the thought of ten grand made him feel sick.

Erin was staring at him, leaning away. 'Well?'

'Right.' Daedalus seized his glass and knocked back the contents, then picked up Erin's untouched one and stood up quickly, bashing the table with his knees. 'Ow. Let's go.'

He made his way to the door and out into the street, cold air smacking into him and blowing away the fog in his mind. The headache needled at him. Erin followed him out. Across the street, by the gate to bay six, he could see the two humans from earlier arguing quietly with a huge, furious-looking petradon. Its black cloak was covered in red markings, not unlike those the rebellion used to wear, before the Republic crushed them at Sudos, and Daedalus could see it clenching its scaly fists and unclenching them, looming over the two men with rage plastered over its broad, lizard-like face.

At this distance he couldn't make out what they were saying, but he glimpsed a word on one of the humans' lips: *entari*. At that the petradon cuffed him round the face, nearly knocking him over.

Erin froze behind him when she saw them. Daedalus reached out and grabbed her arm, realising absently that he was still holding her glass in his free hand. She twisted, trying to pull free.

'Wait!' he said. 'That's them, isn't it? That's who you're running from?'

Erin stopped pulling. 'Yeah. That's them.'

Daedalus let go. 'Their ship's docked next to mine.'

'Deal's off. I can't –'

'They know you're here. If you don't leave now they'll find you for sure.' As he watched, the petradon gestured out over the street and the two humans scurried off in separate directions. The petradon was 'Aggro', he concluded. Daedalus put the pieces together in his mind, assembling a plan. He'd done stuff like this before, just never with a payoff this huge.

'I can get you past them,' he said, 'but you have to trust me.'

Erin stared at him, and he looked her in the eye, giving the best honest-trader face he could muster after two double whiskeys and more pints than he could currently remember.

'Okay,' she said, mouth set, fearful but resigned. 'Okay. I trust you.'

Idiot, he thought. 'Good,' he said. 'Say nothing and stay behind me. I'll get you out of here.'

They moved through the crowd towards bay six, Daedalus still holding the glass, slipping between people as if through air, Erin keeping her face and small frame hidden, trying to avoid bumping into anyone. He took the locket in his hand and whispered, 'Red dot. Just like at Brookwell.' It beeped acknowledgement.

Daedalus stared straight ahead as they drew closer, drawing himself out of his usual slouch to walk at his full height. They were close by the time Aggro registered him. The flat, reptilian face staring out from between his giant muscled shoulders betrayed no emotion; at least, not to human eyes. His tree-trunk arms hung forward like a gorilla's, dragging his huge torso into a permanent hunch, and his dangling hands continued to clench and unclench slowly. The yellow beads of his eyes glinted from behind their shells as he raised his head, looking up at the approaching human. There was no sign of recognition.

'Careful, human,' he rumbled. 'You don't want to irritate me today.'

Daedalus stopped about a metre away, just outside Aggro's reach.

'Looking for something?' Daedalus spoke in a low voice. He heard Erin shift slightly behind him. He held his poker face. Aggro glanced about.

'Speak,' he said.

Daedalus shifted to one side, allowing Aggro a glimpse of Erin, who stood quietly behind him, frozen in fear. Aggro suddenly pulled himself up to full height.

'Ten grand,' said Daedalus.

'That's a funny joke, human.'

'I know its value.' He gripped her arm behind his back and squeezed it. 'Just because your friends failed to deliver, doesn't mean you get it for free.'

'Oh, is that a fact?' Aggro growled. 'Tell me, Sun-boy: why shouldn't I just pull out your spine and take it?'

'Crowded today, isn't it?' Daedalus grinned up at him. 'Hard to spot people if you haven't got the right equipment.'

Aggro glanced over Daedalus's shoulder, looking around. Daedalus, heart pounding, pointed a finger at the centre of his giant armour-plated chest, where a red dot drifted gently up and down. Hidden in the rafters high above, a maintenance drone whirred, laser pointer dangling from one flimsy arm. Aggro looked down at his chest, mouth open, teeth bared.

'I'm a busy man, Aggro,' Daedalus said. 'Let's make this quick, shall we? Nine grand – now – and you can be on your merry way with your precious cargo in tow.'

'I will kill you.'

'Cute. Okay, eight grand. Only because I'm in a hurry.'

Aggro stared Daedalus down, squaring his shoulders and looming over him like a pile of angry bricks. Daedalus scratched his cheek. Aggro made a sound like a salt mine collapsing, which Daedalus took to be laughter.

'Fine. It's a deal, you cheeky little bastard.'

'Lovely.' Daedalus held out his hand, palm up. Aggro reached into his pocket.

Erin grabbed Daedalus's arm. He pulled her forward and shoved her towards Aggro.

'Hello there,' said Aggro.

Erin looked back at Daedalus. He almost didn't look her in the eye, but it felt like his head was attached to a thread, and someone was pulling it. When he looked at her, he saw someone else.

Aggro withdrew a handful of brightly-coloured cards with large numbers on them. Daedalus stood where he was. He could smell smoke again.

Erin reached into her robes. Daedalus saw her stance shift, ready to draw a knife that Aggro would surely see as one threat too far.

Daedalus coughed, and Aggro glanced at him.

Erin crouched.

'RAAAAAAAAAAAAAAAAARRRGH!'

Aggro gave a mighty roar as Daedalus's thrown glass shattered against his face, cracking the shell over his left eye and splashing high-proof alcohol into the wound. The floor shook as Aggro fell to his knees, clawing at his face, and Erin jumped around him, out of his reach.

Everyone was yelling, now. Erin went for her knife, but Daedalus seized her by the arm.

'Run!' he yelled, dragging her towards the hangar. They made it around two corners and into the airlock, sealing a door on the chaos behind them. The door slammed shut behind them, and the grates hissed as the pressure adjusted.

Erin wrested her arm out of his grip. 'What the hell was that?'

'Yes,' buzzed the locket, 'what the hell *was* that?'

'What the hell –' Erin stared at his chest, 'was *that*?'

'What? Yeah, no. Not now, just… running.' Erin stared at him, gasping for breath and leaning against the door. She looked at his hands. They were shaking.

The airlock slid open in front of them and Daedalus pushed her out into the main hangar. The *Crow* sat in front of the giant main door, between a pair of nicer-looking ships. A refuelling hose dangled from her belly. Bulky, dented and covered in haphazard paint jobs, she barely looked spaceworthy. Her nosecone was broad and scratched, with a wide, curved cockpit stretching out of a body like a squat office building that had fallen on its side. The main engine was a great segmented cylinder hanging off the rear, and two free-rotating nacelles were bolted on each side on rickety-looking mounts. Daedalus ran down the gangway towards the workshop floor, Erin in front of him, the metal beneath them clanging loudly as they went.

'*Crow*!' Daedalus yelled. 'Get us going, now!' They reached the boarding ramp underneath the main body of the ship and sprinted up inside.

The low thrumming of the fuel hose died away and it fell free from the *Crow's* hull with a clunk. Inside, Daedalus pushed Erin through the narrow main corridor to the cockpit and shoved her down into the co-pilot's seat.

'Sit down don't touch sorry about the mess.' He yanked the frayed seatbelt across her chest and turned to the control panel, which was covered in yellow sticky notes and doughnut fragments. Daedalus stood over the array of switches and buttons, frantically flicking things left and right.

Erin stared out through the wide, dirty viewscreen, looking at the giant bay doors a few metres in front of the nosecone.

'Hello, little girl,' came a tinny voice from the dashboard. Erin leaned back, away from it.

'Is it supposed to do that?' she asked.

'*Crow*, open the bay doors!'

'Say "please,"' said the ship.

'*Please*,' said Daedalus.

The hangar plunged into dim red light. A siren whooped loudly outside as pistons and robotic arms whined into life, dragging tools into alcoves and heaving locking mechanisms away from the doors. Daedalus swore and hammered at the panel.

'Um, Mole?' Erin asked.

'Not now!' he snapped, yanking on an unresponsive joystick. 'Work, you piece of –'

'Were you born in a barn?' the ship chimed in.

Daedalus froze, his foot on the control panel. He cursed. Then he released the joystick and fell backwards out of the cockpit. Erin heard his feet pounding down the hallway towards the ramp. Suddenly there was a loud whirring and whining from the rear of the ship as the boarding ramp rose back into place, and a deep, rattling rumble as the engines came to life. The control panel lit up and started chittering loudly.

The captain burst back in and flung himself into his chair, finally eliciting a response from the controls. The *Crow* shuddered and roared as he pulled on the joysticks. Then everything shifted and the strange lightness of take-off nestled in Daedalus's stomach. Slowly the *Crow* dragged herself into the air, flooding the hangar with thick grey smoke. The cockpit rattled, shaking Erin in her seat.

'OPEN THE DOORS!' Daedalus shouted. There was a deafening roar as the bay doors slowly opened and the smoke vanished, flushed out into space almost too fast to see. The *Crow*'s retros blazed forwards, resisting the rush of air as the giant doors slid apart and disappeared into the walls. Then the *Crow* slowly pushed herself forwards and outside. The sound of the engines fell, muffled by vacuum, and they drifted out into open space. Daedalus felt the second sick, light feeling in his stomach as they left the artificial gravity behind. Flakes of pastry floated upwards from between the buttons and were quickly hoovered up by the little vacuum-cleaner mounted on the ceiling.

Daedalus pushed a lever by his knee and there was a slight kick as the ship jumped forward, accelerating away from the dock. He waited a few seconds as the station's long landing spires slid silently out of view, then flicked another switch. There was a jolt, and the *Crow's* own gravity took hold. Daedalus gunned the engines and sighed as they made their quiet escape, before turning to look at Erin. She looked shaken. Half her face, out of the hood, was swollen in an angry purple bruise.

'Well. That wasn't so bad. Welcome to the *Crow*.'

The *Crow* cast a bright blue glow on the station behind her as she built up speed, soaring away into the great inky blackness.

In the Wrong Grass

Erin
The Crow

Erin was exhausted, but her body wouldn't rest. She sat in the co-pilot's chair, her limbs jittering with nerves. Daedalus had already confiscated her knife to stop her slicing herself.

'It'll take a while for the jitters to stop. Just try to relax, will you?'

His words still scurried about in her head. Fear had retreated, and boredom had taken hold, but she didn't fancy the idea of wandering around an unfamiliar ship and breaking something. And while Erin wasn't afraid of the captain, she didn't feel particularly safe after his stunt back on the station.

Erin tried to trust people, as a rule. She figured most people were pretty decent when you got down to it, and you only stood to lose out if you spent your life waiting for the next betrayal, or spent relationships waiting for people to let you down. That said, people *did* keep betraying her and letting her down, but she considered herself unlucky rather than wrong.

She stared ahead, listening to the noises of the ship.

Looking outside made her feel sick. Countless pinpricks of light slid past each other in all directions, ship exhausts and glinting solar accumulators indistinguishable from the stars behind them. The Cloud didn't seem to have any planets or suns of its own, so there was nothing to judge their speed against. She'd spent most of the last six months in windowless rooms on people-carriers. She wasn't used to the view.

Erin loved the stars, but right now all she wanted to do was sleep. The captain was bustling about somewhere behind her in the cramped little corridors of the *Crow,* the sound travelling loud and clear with nowhere outside for it to go. She was cold, still in the frayed grey rags she'd been given when they caught her. The bruised side of her face was a throbbing mass of pain, and even her neck was stinging. It hadn't hurt for weeks; the excitement must have woken it up.

Daedalus finally stumbled noisily back into the cockpit. He grunted, and dumped a heavy load of clothes onto the pilot's chair. Erin jumped.

'There isn't a great selection, I'm afraid,' he said, 'but the heater's still a bit dodgy. You'll be needing something a bit warmer than that stylish onesie of yours or you'll freeze.' He rummaged in the pile with both hands. 'Huh.' He pulled out a heavy black jacket that squeaked and clinked as he shook it out. 'Thought I'd got rid of this one.' He held it in front of Erin's face. 'What do you think?'

Erin peered through the giant hole in the back to see the rest of the pile.

'Is this all yours?' She looked up at him. His grizzled stubble and unkempt hair didn't suggest a man who spent much time buying clothes.

'Well, it is now,' he said. 'Sometimes shipments break open, or demand suddenly vanishes. I get left with the bits and bobs.' He picked out what appeared to be a leather sock and held it up for inspection. 'Let no-one say that courier work doesn't have its perks.'

'Thanks, I guess.' Erin shivered. 'Is there a changing room on board?'

'Third door on your right,' Daedalus waved her out and bent over the controls. 'If you see the swimming pool you've gone too far.'

Erin stood up from her chair, heaving the top half of the pile onto her lower set of arms and picking up the rest with her upper set. Teetering slightly, she stepped out of the cockpit and started down the corridor.

The ship wasn't dark, unlike the last few she'd had the pleasure of staying on, but the fluorescent strip lights overhead weren't friendly, either. Their harsh brightness hurt her eyes, so she kept her gaze low. The walls were off-white, a plastic coating over the semi-flexible metal structure beneath; and the décor was notable only by its absence. The pirate ships she'd been on had been very different; all rust-brown paint with stencilled graffiti on the walls and posters stuck everywhere advertising strange station entertainments. Daedalus apparently didn't go in for entertainment. Everything was just blank white walls, interrupted only at ankle height by an occasional half-cleaned coffee spill or power outlet.

The floor was roughly laid with dark green carpet, frayed around the edges, and Erin could see the metal floor under the more worn patches. After a couple of wrong turns, she staggered through a dented interior door into a little square bathroom. To her left was a plain white shower cubicle. To her right was a chemical toilet and sink. There was a dusty mirror bolted above it, with a hairline crack that ran cleanly down the centre. At least the door had a lock. She nudged it closed and dumped the clothes onto the toilet seat before sealing it.

Erin hesitated for a moment, staring into space. When she turned to face the mirror, she saw a bloodied bruise with a bad-tempered girl attached. It wasn't a surprise, but it scrunched up her insides. She'd always liked her eyes – big and dark, like her mother's, not like the people who'd been around when she was growing up – but even they hadn't made it. There was a hardness there she didn't recognise. These eyes weren't the ones that had whiled away nights counting stars back home. Her broken nose set them off in a weird way, and the iron deficiency gave her skin a spotted, unhealthy colour. On top of all that, the spines on her head-crest were bent. She tried to flex them, but it hurt.

Erin's hand found its way to the back of her neck. She felt the raised black brand, a split in her skin, and had to bite down a yelp at the sting when she touched it.

Erin stripped off her rags and tossed them into the corner. The shower cubicle was marked with a sticky note, on which was scrawled 'BROKEN?', so she wet her toga under the tap and sponged the grease and dirt from her scrawny green body as best she could. When she was shivering, but clean, she started working through the pile of clothes. Most were too big, or too strange, or too colourful, so she dried herself off with a big shirt and kept sifting through, looking for something small and warm. Eventually she settled on a little pair of khaki trousers which, miraculously, fitted her; a white t-shirt which was a bit big, but which had four sleeves; a pair of battered-looking brown trainers; and a thick, fur-lined jacket in a dark shade of green.

It only had two sleeves, but was big enough that she could tuck her other arms around her chest.

When she came back to the cockpit Daedalus was humming to himself as he ticked items off a checklist taped to the wall, scrawled in an untidy hand on a yellowed sheet of paper. He had removed his coat and slung it over the back of the pilot's chair. Erin now noticed a small purple locket hanging from his neck, swinging on a thin grey chain.

'Test emergency lights... ' he murmured, bending over the main panel – a black metal board covered in switches, readouts and buttons – and flicking the switch a few times. Nothing happened. 'Check. Still broken.' He returned to the list. 'Test compressors.' Erin watched him root around under the panel before fishing out a chipped novelty mug and holding it under an exposed section of piping. Daedalus pressed a button. There was a distant whirring somewhere in the ship, a loud gurgling from below and the pipe started dribbling clear liquid. 'Check,' he said, holding out the mug to Erin.

She sniffed. It smelled musty, but not poisonous. She took a sip. It was water, cold enough to sting her teeth.

'Vent engine overflow,' Daedalus said. 'Right, okay.' He looked up at the smaller ceiling-mounted panel. One switch was labelled with another sticky note, marked 'VENT' in large bold letters. Very carefully, he stretched out an arm and pushed it. It sprang back under his finger and several lights on the dashboard came to life. A very low, very loud *clunk* rang through the corridors and another set of pipes started to gurgle.

'What does that do?' Erin asked, clutching the mug to her chest.

'Taking off consumes a lot of fuel.' Daedalus answered. 'Most of it, actually. That switch sends the leftover reactant to the waste tank. Should warm the ship up a bit.'

'I think it is,' Erin said, relieved. A warm updraft came through an open grate on the deck.

Daedalus pulled out the swivel-mounted keyboard beneath the controls, onto which he had bolted a number of cup-holders. Erin noticed a flaking croissant attached to the side of it with a little black clamp.

'Is that –'

'Yep,' said Daedalus. 'Pastry-docking station. I added that.'

'... I was going to say "hygienic".'

Daedalus frowned. Then he held down the power button for a few seconds. Erin started at the sudden start-up jingle to her left as the little black monitor came to life. Lines of gibberish scrolled up the screen while the old computer struggled to rouse itself, and Daedalus produced another mug for himself, filling it from the compressor tap and putting his feet up on the console.

Erin looked about. There was a grinding sound coming from the open grate – which didn't look entirely safe – and a strange mechanical whinge coming from somewhere else in the *Crow*.

'Your ship is making a lot of noise.'

'Don't worry about it,' Daedalus said, not looking up. 'Old bird always takes a while to get going after she's been in the shop.' He gave the console a hearty kick with his free foot. A rapid clicking that had been lurking beneath the general hums and beeps of the cockpit suddenly fell silent. The captain sniffed, satisfied. 'Not a problem.'

Erin moved to the co-pilot's chair and sank into it.

'Thanks for the clothes.'

'Anytime,' he said absently. The monitor flashed into life. With a grunt, he sat up and began to tap away at the keyboard, setting his mug into one of the cup-holders. Every *clack* of the keyboard jolted it slightly.

The monitor meant little to Erin. Dots and curved lines and little icons filled the display, with dense patches of text attached to the bigger items. A single blinking line was growing, jumping from spot to spot as segments were added onto it.

'What's that?' she asked.

'Map.' Daedalus stopped typing and squinted at her. 'Have you used a computer before?'

'No.' Erin shrugged. 'Haven't got the patience.'

'You don't fly?'

'I was a prisoner,' she folded her arms. 'Traditionally, they don't let us drive.'

'Before that, I mean. You lived planetside?'

'Well, yeah.'

Daedalus stared at her for a moment. 'You're the only entari I've ever heard of going groundling.'

Erin wasn't sure if she was being insulted.

'… Thank you?'

There was a long pause.

'I thought I'd lost that jacket,' said Daedalus.

'Oh,' she looked down at it. 'Apparently not.'

A moment passed. Daedalus turned back to the monitor.

'I'm plotting a course to Highdust. The *Crow* is a bit shaky on long trips, so we can't just cruise straight through like the bigger ships do.'

There came a reproachful fizzing sound from the overhead speaker. Daedalus looked up for a moment, then resumed typing. More segments tacked themselves onto the end of the blinking line, describing a long, curved route around the screen. 'We'll have to ride the gravity wells with the other freighters.'

He was interrupted by a particularly loud and angry beep from the console.

'What's that?' asked Erin.

Daedalus looked at the dashboard. A bright red symbol flashed on the top row of lights. A lined grate-like symbol, crossed through.

'Not good. One sec,' he said. He reached underneath the controls, pulling out a small notebook. Erin watched as he riffled through it, eyes darting over the pages as he searched. Each sheaf of paper was covered in untidy drawings of the control panel, scribbled all over with little notes and question marks. When he came to the page he was looking for, he groaned, sinking backwards, and snapped the notebook shut. 'Mechanic forgot to empty the overflow tank. We need to land.'

'What? No. We can't go back. Those men –'

'Yeah,' he said. 'You hear that?'

Erin listened. The noise of the cockpit was too thick. 'No.'

'That hissing.'

'Your ship's too loud.'

'No she isn't.' Daedalus grabbed the keyboard and started tapping furiously. 'Anything nearby, come on –'

Erin felt panic prickling at her skin. 'We can't land. We have to keep moving.'

'The overflow tank is where the engine runoff gets stored.' Daedalus brought up a list of planetoids in local space and flicked through, dismissing them one after another. He hovered on a moss-green planet with the label 'AH-9_MEDUSA', but biohazard warnings popped up and he kept scrolling. 'If it backs up then the pipes explode. We burn or we asphyxiate or we get poisoned. We have to land.'

Erin's hands shook. 'I want my knife back.'

'No.' Daedalus stopped scrolling on a small yellow-brown rock with blue splotches of water and a few grey specks of civilisation. The label read 'DE23-15_PYRUS'. 'As long as you're on my ship, you follow my rules. I don't fight. I run.'

'Like a coward?' Erin couldn't stop herself.

The captain's hands tensed on the keyboard for a moment.

'Yes,' he said. 'Like that.'

Erin winced. She didn't want to annoy her only ally. 'Sorry, I –'

'I don't care. Just be quiet.'

Daedalus leant on the joysticks. The tiny thrusters on the nosecone spat blue fire, tilting the universe outside the window. Erin's stomach lurched. The field of stars outside revolved until a distant yellow spot came into view. Erin saw Daedalus reach for a lever by his knee and she hastily climbed into the co-pilot's chair, yanking the seatbelt around her chest.

The thrumming of the engines grew louder and the *Crow* built up speed. The stars slid past, faster and faster until they bled into white lines, and space in front of them shifted from black to dark blue. Pyrus grew larger.

Daedalus tapped at the keyboard for a few more moments, eliciting a series of satisfied beeps from the console. There was a clunk as the joysticks locked in place. Daedalus got to his feet. 'Wait here.'

'Wait – where are you going?'

'The hold,' he said. 'Have to make sure the runoff pipes don't burst before we can set down.' He lifted his coat from the back of the pilot's chair and pulled it around himself. 'Don't worry about the ship, it's a straight line from here to there. Just keep an eye on the panels and give me a shout if anything catches fire.'

'I'll help.' Erin unbuckled her belt again.

'Fine.' Daedalus picked up the dirty yellow toolbox from the rear of the cockpit and dumped it in her lap. 'Carry that.'

'Tape, please.'

Erin picked another roll of duct tape out of the toolbox and handed it up to Daedalus. The stepladder wobbled ominously as he clung to the cluster of pipes on the ceiling. 'Cheers, Eris,' he said, not looking down.

'Erin.'

'Right,' Daedalus murmured, winding a large amount of tape around a cross-shaped joint.

Erin looked around from where she sat on the floor. The hold was big and spacious, with dark corners full of rusted containers and what looked like scorch marks cast across the metal walls. The strip light above her threw a flickering orange glow. Two corners were filled with rags and assorted debris from spilled shipments, and the wall furthest from the door was covered in footprints from its weekend job as a loading ramp. A thick rubber seal held the ramp in place, as well as two giant hydraulic arms running down from the ceiling. Over Erin's head hung a mess of thick cables and hissing pipes, running from wall to wall and disappearing in all directions. There wasn't a whole lot to look at after that. No windows, which Erin didn't like much.

'Tape, please.'

She reached into the toolbox and passed up another roll of tape, without looking. He took it from her and she heard the tape squeal as he pulled off another length. Erin's jitters had subsided slightly, but her insides were still twisted with worry. She tried to think about something other than Aggro bearing down on them at full speed, but it was hard.

'Right, that'll do it.' Daedalus leaned back on the ladder to admire his handiwork. Erin glanced upwards. The pipe junction was wrapped up in a solid ball of duct tape. Daedalus tossed the empty roll over his shoulder and it bounced away. The ladder wobbled.

'Is that sticky tape?' Erin asked.

'Duct tape,' he said. 'It's stronger than sticky tape.'

'Will it hold?'

'Half this ship is held together with duct tape,' he said. 'You can put your faith in worse things.' There was a clang from somewhere else in the ship and the pipes rattled alarmingly.

'What?' Erin steadied the ladder with all four hands. 'Like, people?'

Daedalus looked at her. 'Yes. I suppose. Some people.'

'Is it just you on this ship?' Erin asked. 'Do you have any people around?'

Daedalus grunted and climbed down, tapping her arms out of the way with his boot. 'Just me and the missus,' he said, twitching his head in the direction of the ceiling.

'The missus?' Erin hadn't seen any sign of another person on board. Maybe she was asleep. She was about to ask when Daedalus picked up the ladder, jostling her out of the way, and dumped it in the corner of the hold with a clang.

'Come on,' he said, 'we need to land this thing.'

Erin followed him back through the ship. The *Crow* was cramped in places, and her corridors twisted oddly to fit everything in. They passed a small medbay which looked as if it hadn't been touched since construction; then the heavy metal door blocking off the drive room, slightly muffling the thrum of the engine. Six empty dormrooms of varying size were dotted about, with skeletal bunks and bare shelves. Finally they passed through the tiny kitchenette, with sealed cold-cabinets full of ready meals and jar after jar of instant coffee stacked around the shining chrome kettle, next to a small, worn sponge.

A short segment of corridor led to the cockpit. Pyrus loomed large in front of them, growing bigger every second. It was a small planet – they were already close enough to spot the grey specks of agricultural colonies dotted across the surface – but Erin still struggled to grasp the scale of it. Daedalus slipped into the captain's chair and unlocked the joysticks with a loud clunk.

'Strap in,' he said. 'No time to take this slow.'

Erin sat down and fastened her seatbelt.

A sea of bright yellow grass-stalks blew to and fro in the gentle Pyrian wind. Wide swathes of temperate grassland stretched for miles and miles around, punctuated by small sandstone boulders and twisted brown trees. Furry, crab-like creatures clung with tiny claws to the underside of their branches and their fluffy nests dangled from the tips on short lengths of yarn, swinging slowly in the breeze. Long, ferrety marsupials crouched in burrows beneath orange rocks. Pairs of bushy yellow tails poked partway out of their burrows, and little noses sniffed nervously at the air.

The air was quiet except for the skitterings of local fauna. One could reasonably call it a peaceful haven. The nearest relic of civilisation was a long way away, and many of the creatures who lived there were harmless to people. What remained of the Colony Regulation Authority had so far managed to preserve Pyrus – but more strategically valuable worlds had not been so lucky. Money didn't flow through this place, and so most had been happy to leave it well alone in the transitional skirmishes four years ago. The planet's surface was peppered with empty concrete ruins, but little blood.

On this day in particular the weather was mild. The setting sun (for there was only one) was warm, and it bathed everything in a friendly orange light. The big, dangerous mammals from the savannah had not come near the meadow for some time now, and so the families of smaller animals lived peacefully. It was only a few hours until dusk when one of the marsupials froze. It had been snuffling around in the long grass for tasty-looking grubs when a distant sound caught its attention. It stood upright, balancing on its tails.

A loud whine was growing in the distance. The little black nose twitched and sniffed, but there was no accompanying smell to latch onto. It was growing louder by the second. More of the animals had started to notice. The tree-crabs were sleepily crawling out to the ends of their branches to investigate, and some of the birds were retreating into their nests. The snuffler looked upwards. One of the stars was getting larger. All the animals in the meadow were watching it now, crawling onto high branches and scampering out of burrows to get a good look. As the whine built to a far-off roar, they fled. Burrows filled with animals and tree-crabs hid their faces behind tiny paws. The star bloomed into a screaming fireball, billowing smoke and bright blue flares behind it as it fell, with a sound that shook the trees. The wind picked up, whipping at the long grass.

The *Crow* shuddered in the air as her retros burst into life, arresting her dive. The fall curved into a half-graceful swoop, and the swivelling nacelles charred long black paths into the earth with huge jets of flame. The noise was tremendous as the bulky brown ship hauled herself to a stop, hovering above the clearing while the engines whipped up cyclones of superheated air. With a roar and a hiss, the *Crow* touched down on rigid landing legs, before belching thick clouds of exhaust fumes into the meadow. The engine shut down and the roar died away, replaced by the wail of warning sirens and the hum of hydraulics as the exit-ramp descended, allowing the two larger creatures onboard to sprint out into the long grass. They barely made it ten metres before the overflow tank vented. With a mighty groan it began spewing bright blue clouds of foul-smelling gas high into the air and out over the ground.

Erin easily outstripped Daedalus, who lumbered away yelling and holding his side as the gas whipped at his coat-tails. The rolling blue cloud eventually slowed and dissipated, and Daedalus collapsed to the ground, breathing heavily. Erin stopped.

'You alright, captain? Need a minute?'

'Erghherf,' said Daedalus, clutching the locket to his chest.

'Right.' Erin looked at the ship. She was still letting off small jets of gas with quiet hissing sounds. Giant black scorch-marks stretched out far behind her. The grass had suffered. 'We made a mess.'

'Is she in one piece?' Daedalus's voice was muffled by the grass.

'Looks like it. Nothing's fallen off yet.'

'S'fine then. Duct tape. Tough as old boots.'

Erin looked around, savouring the taste of clean, non-recycled air. The setting sun was warm on her skin. The wind was cool. The meadow was empty. Erin laughed. She couldn't help it. She'd spent so long as cargo she thought she might never feel free again.

'I'm having a look around,' she said.

'Be my guest,' Daedalus said back, waving a hand vaguely in the direction of the rest of the planet.

Erin started to jog away from the ship. The unbent grass broke in front of her, and the cool wind caressed her face. Once she cleared the meadow she broke into a run. Her jacket flapped out behind her. The grass stretched indefinitely, reminding her of another yellow sea from her childhood. Erin felt light. She spread her arms, letting all her hands brush through the yellow stalks as she flew between the trees and over the rocks. She ran and ran until her lungs ached and her legs burned. She kept going until she couldn't drag herself another step, and then she collapsed onto a mossy orange boulder. Her breath came in ragged and painful, but she couldn't stop laughing. She was free. Her dreams of open fields and clear skies couldn't have captured the taste of the air, or the rough grittiness of the rock under her palms. The sun was about to set, and she could hear nothing around her except for the animals and the whistle of the wind about her head. Behind her there rose a distant plume of smoke that marked the *Crow*'s landing site. She'd go back when she was ready. Right now she just wanted to lie sprawled across the warm rock and ignore the future. She took a long, deep breath and closed her eyes.

Eventually, Erin sat up. The sky had changed from a sheet of pale blue to a twisting canvas of orange and purple, and the breeze had taken on a chill. The setting sun burned bright, casting long shadows. Her surroundings had filled with quiet chittering and raspy noises as the animals crawled out of hiding. Slowly, Erin pushed herself up onto two aching legs and took an unsteady step forward. The buzz of freedom had started to fade, and she was getting cold. Drawing her new coat tight around her shoulders, she set back the way she had come, following the column of smoke that hung over a clump of trees in the near distance.

When she arrived in the clearing, Daedalus was sitting some distance from the *Crow*, next to a pile of blankets, hunched over a large square plate on the ground. The battered scrapheap loomed behind him, still belching fumes into the air with low, guttural sounds. Erin approached, unsure if he had noticed her yet.

'Hey,' she said.

'Oh.' Daedalus looked up. 'Find anything interesting?'

'It's nice here,' she said, sitting down. 'No people. Just rocks and the sun.'

Daedalus turned his gaze towards the swirl of colour on the horizon. 'You mean the myrmidon.'

'What?'

He looked at her with an odd expression on his face. Erin felt like she was being recorded.

'Myrmidon,' he said. 'Takes care of heat and light for the colony – or it did. There aren't any stars in the Cloud.'

'Oh.' Erin paused thoughtfully. 'It's pretty.'

'Yes,' Daedalus sighed, 'very pretty.'

'What do you mean, "or did"?' Erin asked.

'I mean it took care of the colony.'

'Not anymore?'

'Well, no.' Daedalus frowned. 'Pyrus is a derelict. That's why we're hiding here.'

'A derelict?'

'I knew entari were sheltered but I figured you at least listened to the news. How old are you?'

Erin didn't answer. Daedalus shook his head.

'A dead world. When a colony loses funding the people leave, or die, the crops turn wild and the whole planet is abandoned. Only things left behind are the animals and the myrmidon, until it burns out.'

There was a pause.

'When will that be, then?' asked Erin.

Daedalus scratched his head. 'Not sure. I don't actually know of any that have run dry.'

Erin looked up. 'Seems kind of… wasteful.'

'Listen, you want to get close enough to shut that thing off, be my guest.' He started fiddling with a dial on the plate.

'I still don't get it,' Erin went on. 'Why are we hiding *here*? If it's empty, surely that's exactly where someone would expect us to go?'

Daedalus laughed. 'Most people are too afraid.'

'Afraid.'

'Yeah. I mean, there's no telling when the atmosphere processor is going to collapse – and take the atmosphere with it.'

'Collapse.'

Daedalus held up a finger to the wind, a serene look on his face. 'Could be any second now.'

'So we're going to die.'

'Maybe,' he shrugged. 'Nice place for it, though. No-one will follow us here.'

Erin sat back. The human made death sound very calm. The wind cupped her cheek.

'Reminds me of home,' she said, 'only colder.'

'Night's setting in,' he said.

'No, that's not it,' she said. 'The sun here isn't warm enough. Back home you couldn't wear a jacket during the day. You'd boil in a minute.'

'There's nothing wrong with the myrmidon.' Daedalus squinted at her. 'You're a right weird one, you know that?'

Erin folded all her arms.

'Didn't your mom teach you any manners?'

'My *mum*,' he said, 'taught me to be suspicious of nutters.'

'People, you mean.'

'Same thing,' he said firmly.

The *Crow* rumbled, making a noise like an angry whale. Inside, something fell over with a crash.

'I like people,' said Erin.

Daedalus turned his head. 'You serious?'

'Yes.'

There was silence. Daedalus hesitated before returning to his tinkering. Erin sank backwards and lay flat, looking up at the darkening sky.

Erin tried for lightness. 'Why do you call your ship the *Crow*?'

'I'm trying to start a fire, kid.'

Suddenly awkward silence didn't seem so bad. Her limbs were heavy. Six months pressed down on her, urging sleep. The clicks and snaps of the captain's work had a soothing rhythm to them. She was moments from sleep when they stopped, and she heard a rustling. Out of the corner of her half-open eye, she saw him turning the locket over and over in his hands.

'Who are you?' asked Daedalus quietly.

Erin wasn't sure if he was addressing her, so she pretended not to hear. After a few moments the little sounds resumed. It didn't take long for the darkness to envelop her, and she fell into a long-awaited sleep. She dreamed of a tapestry covered in cigarette burns.

A long way away, Aggro seethed. The terrarium was too warm. The soil was dry. His broken eye stung badly – it would need to be patched. On top of all that, someone had pushed all the good rocks into one corner. Even buried under several tonnes of earth, he couldn't relax. They had been searching for hours, all over the sector. The tankers around Aphiemi left such huge emission clouds and scattered ion trails that tracing a single small ship was harder than he'd expected. Aggro knew he'd have to report their failure soon. High up in the ship, he could hear the heartbeats and the scraping breath of his two underlings as they stumped about, guiding the *Onyx* onwards. The great hulk screamed through space at thirty million kilometres per hour, slowly creeping across the sector. The channel entrance wasn't far off now, then they'd be on their way to Illuvia. Wrask was not going to be pleased. They were all going to be on sand duty once they got back to base.

Buried in the earth-filled belly of the *Onyx*, Aggro lay still. He heard everything. The engines rumbled with power. Insects skittered around on the surface of the soil several feet above his head. Hot liquids whistled through piping all around him, keeping the icy cold outside at bay. It was at times like this that he envied surface dwellers their dulled senses – he needed to think, which was difficult when he was subject to every stupid thought Kor and Rite decided to share with each other. Their slow, ponderous notes hung in his brain, making productive thought impossible.

He could play up the success. After all, they were the first ones to have seen the entari in person. Hundreds of search parties were out, but Aggro had been the one to track her down, and now they had a description. A half-breed. Stunted and small – a runt. If Wrask knew they were looking for the only four-foot entari in the Collective it would make it easier to reacquire her. The lookouts would spot her soon enough.

No. They wouldn't go back to Illuvia just yet. Aggro drew breath through a mouthful of soil.

'Change course,' he rumbled. He heard Kor and Rite fall silent as his voice reverberated through the ship. 'We head for the nearest outpost. Send a bulletin to the lookouts with the girl's description – tell them to listen and follow, but not to be seen. I want to know where she goes.'

There was a pause, then the sound of work as his crew changed course.

Aggro was a chronic veteran. He'd seen himself through the Home Rebellion, when the Imperium became aware of the Republic's sneaking power grab. He'd served in the Collective Armada during the Earth Contact War. He was old. In his time he'd fought across burning jungles, ruined underground cities and, once, the irradiated wastelands of the human homeworld itself, at the Battle of Two Moons. During a career like that, you picked up a few things.

Things like how to set a decent trap.

When Daedalus finally fell asleep he dreamed of Jan again.

They were riding out of town in the back of a friend's buggy, packed full of grinning students. Cerulean grass gave way to rocky wasteland as they drove further out, heading in the direction of Crit's famous glass canyons. Jan sat opposite him, laughing. The wind spooled her long brown hair out behind her, shaking it like a whip. Daedalus felt his face twisted into a smile. Between the cold grey sky and the rocks below they were a splash of colour, and everything felt warm. He knew he was home, but it felt like a shoe that no longer fit – Jan's laugh had an unfamiliar edge to it, and the road markers they should be following were nowhere to be seen. Daedalus remembered their trip to the canyon. They'd sneaked away, become lost under the stars as night fell. A storm drove them into a cave, and they hid together as it raged and screamed outside. The two of them had emerged hours later under bright, clear starlight. Daedalus remembered it perfectly.

This wasn't it. This never happened. Police cruisers screeched in from overhead, cutting the ground with pulse fire. The buggy swerved. Jan called for help. Daedalus fell over the side.

He woke up on the bare soil with jittering nerves and fought for breath, his fists clenched tight. Daedalus knew better than to try and get back to sleep. The *Crow* had stopped venting gas, so he picked up his blankets and climbed back into the ship.

In the cockpit, where he normally slept, she was awake and waiting for him.

'You've got a lot of explaining to do, young man,' said the *Crow*. The locket *bip-bip*ped a beat against his chest in time with her words – as close as she could get to leaning over and prodding him with an index finger. 'We could be halfway to the border worlds by now with ten grand in the bank. I was going to get my inhibitors taken out. What are you playing at?'

He didn't know. Daedalus eased himself into the pilot's chair and said nothing, instead reaching under the dash for a mug and pressing a button under his armrest. Cheap synthetic gin spilled out of a hidden nozzle. It was followed by recycled tonic almost indistinguishable from pond water. His hand trembled slightly as he drank.

'I can't believe this,' she hissed. 'You're pathetic. What, you think you're doing her a favour? You think giving someone a lift will make you feel less guilty? This is truly pathetic. You're trying to fix a bridge collapse with sticky tape.'

'Duct tape,' he said to himself. The *Crow* kept berating him, and he kept drinking. Same as every night.

Pastry-induced Comfort

Erin
Pyrus

Erin woke up rested, for the first time in months. Her headache had vanished; her bruise no longer pulsed painfully. For a moment she couldn't put her finger on why she felt so peaceful. When she felt the wind on her face, she remembered that she was free.

She sat up. The pain stayed gone. Nearby the *Crow* was whining softly, lights flicking on and off all over her broad, bulky hull. It looked like Daedalus had gone inside already. The plate he'd been fiddling with the night before was nowhere to be seen and the blankets had been carried inside, except for the two that had been left covering her. Erin rose to her feet, rubbing her temples gently. The myrmidon shone brightly at the top of the sky and a cool wind was blowing in from a dense red wood in the middle distance. A few little creatures bounded to and fro in the undergrowth. Erin looked around. The sky was mostly clear, save for a wide, grey cloud that hung over the horizon. The air smelled clean – the smog and fumes from last night had dissipated. She bent over and stretched out her arms, groaning as the muscles unwound; then she gathered the blankets off the ground and dragged herself sleepily up the boarding ramp.

The hallway was filled with the pungent smell of instant coffee. Erin trudged along to the cockpit, where Daedalus was leaning back in his chair and poking at the ceiling switches. The console pulsed with lights. None of them looked too worrying, Erin thought.

'She lives.' Daedalus turned in his chair. 'Finally awake, then?'

'Good morning to you too,' Erin said. The human's grouchiness was a lot easier to deal with now that she wasn't so tired. He was one to talk, though – the dark bags under his eyes seemed even more pronounced than yesterday. 'Everything good with the ship? We're not going to explode on take-off, are we?'

'Only if I spill my coffee. There's a fair bit of exposed wiring in here.'

'Good to know, thanks.' Erin dropped the blankets on the co-pilot's chair and peered at the map screen. At the top was a string of text: THE CLOUD. Pyrus was labelled; a yellow dot with a tiny icon of a ship hovering over it. The Cloud was a mass of colourful spots, varying in size, scattered across the face of a big circle, none of which made much sense to Erin. She trusted that Daedalus knew where they were.

Daedalus was sitting back in his chair, his feet up on the console, one hand holding the mug of coffee, the other dangling lazily over the armrest.

'So, when can we leave?' she asked.

'Soon as I've finished my coffee. Hungry?'

Erin's stomach twisted in response. 'Yeah. Starving, actually.'

'I'm not surprised. Plenty of food in the kitchen. Help yourself.'

He wasn't wrong. Erin tried the wall-mounted cabinets, each time assaulted by a rockslide of plastic-wrapped snack food and cans of beer. Stacks of pre-packed meals filled most of the cupboards, with tiny dehydrated pastries crammed into the gaps. Erin glanced over into the cockpit at Daedalus, who was leaning back and staring out the viewscreen. He wasn't like the few other humans she'd met. Apart from the unusual pink colour, he talked like a man of money; his affected slang was riddled with holes and it didn't cover up his polished manner. But he dressed like an old frontiersman. The coat and boots reminded Erin of a sheriff character in one of her old storybooks. Now it seemed he couldn't feed himself. The guy carried himself like a drug addict, all spindly limbs and anxious hunching, but didn't hesitate to glass a petradon twice his size. Humans were strange, though. People said it was because of what happened to Earth. You couldn't blame them, really.

Erin found her dagger in the cutlery drawer. He didn't carry weapons. From what Erin had seen, he was the only one in the Collective who wasn't carrying at least a pointy stick. She left her dagger where it was and took the only thing she recognised to be edible – a pastry. Rehydrating it seemed too much of an ordeal, so she just stuffed it in her mouth. It tasted better than anything she could remember. Before going back to the cockpit she grabbed two more.

'Vese are gudh,' she said thickly.

'Tell me about it. Here.' Daedalus held out a mug of water, which Erin took gratefully. 'Take-off soon.'

Erin swallowed. 'Great. Good. How far to Highdust?'

'Long way. It ain't round the corner. Overnight trip, depending on how the channels are behaving, but we're looking at nine hours, minimum.'

Erin sank into the co-pilot's chair and swung her feet up onto the console next to Daedalus's.

'Oi,' he said, 'feet down. Show her some respect.'

Erin took her feet off the console. 'What do you mean, "her"?' she asked.

'The *Crow*.'

'It's a spaceship,' Erin pointed out. 'It doesn't have a gender.'

'Don't be rude.'

Erin frowned. Daedalus kicked his chair back around to face the viewscreen. He stretched out a hand and threw a heavy lever upwards with a clunk. There was a loud whirring from below as the boarding ramp retracted, and a few key-presses and switch-flips later the cockpit was humming. A gurgling issued from the pipes on the ceiling as the *Crow* gradually roused itself – herself? – from sleep.

'One more thing before we go,' Daedalus said. 'You'll need to vouch for me when we cross into entari space.' He raised the mug to his mouth, and it bumped against the locket, still hanging around his neck.

'Vouch for you? To who?'

The mug halted halfway between elbow and chin. 'The police,' he said slowly.

Erin eyed him suspiciously. 'Did you glass someone important?'

'You've never been in entari space,' he said. It wasn't a question.

'... No. Is that a problem?'

There was a pause. Then Daedalus downed the rest of his coffee. 'Sod it. I don't even want to know.'

'So, you're a criminal?'

'No. Well, yes, if you want to be pedantic about it, but that's not the point. The police don't like letting downtier vessels get close to Taxos without an entari onboard. It's to keep out criminal lowlife, ostensibly.'

Erin looked at his scraggly hair and unkempt stubble.

'So… you.'

Daedalus rubbed his forehead '… Do you want to go to Taxos or not?'

'That's a yes, isn't it?'

'This is serious. If you stay with me then I get passage without questioning, which is good for you. There's obviously some kind of bounty on your head – don't tell me, I don't want to know – and if that guy Aggro is willing to pay ten grand then he isn't going to stop looking for you. Anyone can be bought. Even cops. Especially cops.' He wondered briefly if Aggro was going to snag them as soon as they left atmosphere, but there wasn't much he could do to prevent that. 'Do we have a deal?'

'Deal,' said Erin. She gave herself no time to hesitate.

'Good.' Daedalus swivelled back in his chair, throwing a lever forward with a loud *shunk*. A rumbling rose all around them, while the console whined loudly. 'Strap yourself in, let's get going.'

Erin's seatbelt *zipped* excitedly as she yanked it across her chest. She gripped the armrests tight.

'This should be smoother than the last time,' Daedalus said.

The *Crow*'s exhaust hissed, and grey clouds ballooned out over the ground below them. Erin saw them creep in at the bottom of the viewscreen. There was a rumbling from the thrusters as they turned slowly downwards. Then a great thundering shook Erin in her chair, and her stomach lurched as the *Crow* lifted herself from the ground. With a long, loud roar, it tilted back.

'Lovely.' The captain grinned to himself.

The acceleration pushed Erin's response back down her throat. The *Crow* screamed and the world suddenly bled sideways as the ship flung herself into the sky. They rose until the line of Pyrus fell away and the air darkened around them. As they shot through the upper atmosphere, the *Crow*'s sun-visor automatically slid down over the cockpit, shielding them from the myrmidon's harsh glare. Daedalus guided them carefully out of its path, onto a more gradual ascent. They surfed across the last hundred miles of atmosphere, kicking up flames behind them as the ship picked up speed. Erin stared out over the orb with wonder.

'I don't think I appreciated it on the way down,' she murmured.

'Sorry, my fault,' said Daedalus, watching the long-range scanner closely for any sign of their pursuers. 'I don't land on-planet very often.'

'It's beautiful.'

Daedalus grunted. He leaned forwards, peering out the viewscreen at a large, dark cloud hanging over the landscape.

'So much for that secure weather-conditioning. Our tax money at work.'

Erin considered asking him what he was talking about, but the view was far more interesting. He continued to grumble quietly about the Republic while she stared hungrily at the scenery. An old feeling rose in her stomach. Memories surged. Pyrus seemed to spin faster and faster as they built up speed. She watched, and they slowly rose away from the planet. The *Crow* carried them out into space until Erin lost all sense of direction and scale. The universe lay spread out in front of her, stretching to infinity and back.

After a while they left the atmosphere and the roar of the engines fell to a soft thrum. Erin lay back in her seat and let out a contented sigh.

Daedalus fiddled with the map screen. Erin watched it, trying to grasp what she was looking at.

'Something wrong?' he asked.

Erin squinted. 'I'm not good with maps.'

'Groundlings,' he sighed. He pointed to three linked spots in turn. 'That's the Cloud, that's Endeavour, and that's Highdust. Straightforward journey.'

'And that's an overnight trip?'

'You want to try find a shorter route, go right ahead. I knew a guy once who thought he could make some money discovering new channels and selling them to trade companies, without buying any of the expensive detection stuff. Stumbled into a channel barely wide enough for a rat, let alone a ship. They're still picking pieces of him out of planets at the other end.'

The dots on the screen had little labels on. Erin counted twenty-four inside the big white circle. The ones outside were grey, and they didn't have any labels. Some of the connected lines crossed outside the circle to a grey dot, but they never went further than that. Then Daedalus pushed on another lever and the *Crow* jumped forwards. The huge purple gas cloud which gave the system its name rolled into view behind Pyrus, and Erin stopped thinking to stare at it.

Four hours passed before they got close to the channel entrance, a patch of space that looked much like any other. The *Crow*'s retros rotated, grinding, to the full drive position. There was a flash of blue light as the ignition caught on all of them at once and the ship leapt forwards. She quickly built up speed as she approached the channel, before appearing – to outside observers – to stretch impossibly far in one dimension. After a moment of improbable contortion, she vanished in a flash of white light.

Fly Casual

Daedalus
The Crow
Four hours from Pyrus

At first the journey was passed amicably enough. Daedalus wasn't crazy about tour-guide work, but Erin's enthusiasm expressed itself mostly in silence as she gazed out at the planets and stations they looped around. Endeavour was busy today. The tanker lanes were open wide, projected roadways pulsing green to keep the traffic in line. Colourful well-weathered freighters with place names like the *Coburn Comet* and the *Fairfield Falcon* dragged gigantic cargo tanks behind them, powerful long-haul engines burning too bright to look at. A narrow pathfinder ship, the *Jill Tees,* boosted past them to change lanes, nearly swiping them in half with one of its sensor spines. Daedalus steered clear after that, riding the gravity wells with the other small ships and staying out of the way of the superfreighters and their fighter escorts. That lot scanned nearby ships as a matter of course, and you never knew where the data might get sent.

Erin's quiet fascination lasted for a while, but eventually – as it always did with first-time travellers – the majesty of the universe became a bit tedious and she grew visibly more restless as time went on. They were curving round the dark side of a big blue ocean world, lined with bright veins of civilisation, when she finally broke the silence.

'What do you do for fun around here? When you're not getting into fights and drinking yourself to death, I mean.'

'Flying is fun,' said Daedalus.

Erin spun around in her chair. 'You don't take many passengers, do you?'

'No.'

'Well, I guess flying's more fun if you're flying. Rather than, y'know –' she stopped the chair facing backwards and looked at him over the armrest '– watching.'

'You're bored?'

'A bit. Aren't you?'

'Flying is fun,' Daedalus repeated.

'That's great. You should tell your face.'

'It takes concentration. This stuff is dangerous.'

'Don't you ever just leave the autopilot on and do something else?'

Daedalus laughed. 'What, *her*?'

'Why? What's the matter with her?'

'Yes, *Captain*,' the *Crow* chimed in. 'What's the matter with me?'

Daedalus sighed. 'What does that say?' he asked, pointing over his head.

Erin looked up at the dim display on the ceiling. '"Inertial dampener running." Why?'

'You can read, then.' Daedalus locked the joysticks and tapped a long sequence out on the keyboard. Then he reached for the locket around his neck and gave it a squeeze. It beeped. 'Crow, keep us on this route, will you? I'll be back in a minute.'

'No.'

'Please?'

'No. Suddenly I don't feel like it.'

Daedalus rolled his eyes and reached under the console. There was a rattle.

'What's that?' the *Crow* said sharply.

Daedalus withdrew a long rectangular computer chip from under the keyboard. 'I've got a stick of RAM here if you want to give me the autopilot.'

'... How much?'

'Plenty.'

'Give it.'

'Autopilot first.'

'No.'

Daedalus held it under his nose. 'Mmm, smells like memory. I might keep it for myself.'

'Give it!' There was a harsh electronic sound from the speakers. 'Now!'

'Hey, Erin, do you want some RAM?' Daedalus nodded suggestively.

'Er –' her head-crest flittered nervously. 'Sure?'

'No!' The *Crow* squealed. The ship jolted as the autopilot came on.

'There's a good girl. Here.' Daedalus leaned under the console and plugged the stick into a free socket. There was a smooth sighing sound from the speakers. 'I'll be right back.'

Erin did not look pleased at being left alone with her.

Daedalus climbed out of the chair and made his way downstairs. In one of the *Crow's* cluttered store-rooms, he dug around in a dusty pile. He pulled out useless metal contraptions and broken circuit-boards; remnants of old hobbies. Under a pile of tangled knitting equipment was a battered cardboard box, sealed with duct tape. Daedalus peeled back the tape and looked inside.

Books. He picked one out. *Naval Engineering in Practice, Vol. 3.* He tossed it back in and rooted around for another. *Archaeological Theory: Hestian Approaches.* Dropped it, tried another. *Bad Introductions: Sites of the Earth Contact War.* Too late to sell them now. Demand wasn't there. He lifted a thick volume from the bottom: *Roots of Ritual Void-Worship* hid beneath *The Brand Kingdoms – A History of Violence.*

Two and a half years at Helstad had left him with a lot of unfinished textbooks. It was a long time ago, long enough for most of what he'd learned to get buried. New skills had been heaped on top, like how to hide from the police without friends, how to threaten someone without a weapon, and how to keep a spaceship afloat without money. In fact Daedalus didn't know quite how long it had been. Remembering was difficult. There were blank patches. These endless headaches hadn't been helping. He heaved the box into his arms and hurried out of the room, kicking the door shut behind him and carrying the box back to the cockpit. He dumped it on the floor with a loud *thud*, causing Erin to jump in her seat.

'Found some books in the back. See if anything catches your fancy.'

Erin swivelled her seat to look.

'I've never had a proper book before,' she said. 'My mom taught me how to read, but I only had… ' her voice trailed off as she stared at the box.

'Go nuts,' Daedalus said. 'You might learn something.' He sat back down and pulled a glossy magazine from beneath the console. As he started leafing noisily through the pages, Erin pulled the box towards her and rummaged around inside. After a moment she held up a heavy blue book; the dust-cover was missing and the silver lettering was slightly faded. The corners were beaten flat and there were over-lapping brown rings on the cover. Frayed sticky notes poked from between the pages in dim yellow and pink.

A Brief History of Space: Taxos University Translations (4th Ed.)

Daedalus glanced over and saw the title.

'Oh Christ, here we go.'

Hours passed as the *Crow* followed a long curling line across Endeav-our, a tiny rust-brown sparrow scurrying around under the feet of bigger, nastier ships. They formed a cloud of shining pinpricks against the dark, a sparse ribbon wrapped loosely around brown and green spheres slowly revolving in space. It thickened at one end, near the tight-packed Central Blockade. As the *Crow* got close the white police cruisers came into view. They bristled with armaments. The *Crow*'s telescopes picked out bulky grey cannons and shining spikes tipped with blinking green pilot-lights. They swivelled on ball-jointed mounts, pointing into the traffic at random, their charged-particle streams ready to quickly disassemble any ships that strayed out of line.

The traffic moved slowly. Erin had left the cockpit a while ago, unable to concentrate on reading while Daedalus finger-tapped the joysticks and complained about things – both of which activities he stopped as soon as she left. Confident that he would hear her footsteps if she approached, he allowed a guilty hand to creep to the locket and give it a quick squeeze.

'What?' asked the *Crow*, irritated.

'I want to hear her,' said Daedalus, quietly.

'Oh, good. I was worried you'd forgotten about me in all the excitement.'

'*Her*,' he said.

'I *am* her,' said the *Crow*. 'I'm the only *her* you've got.'

52

'Please.'

There was a pause.

'Fine,' she said. 'Maybe then you'll stop acting like an idiot.'

'Booting,' came a neutral voice from the speakers. 'Preloaded Self found: "Jan". Boot okay. Ready. Welcome, Daniel.'

'Play Jan,' said Daedalus, quietly.

The locket buzzed against his chest, then spoke with a high-quality recording.

'The condolences of James and Veronica Little are with you in this troubling time. Thank you for choosing LittleWill. No projector found – playing audio.'

There was a pause.

'Hello,' said the locket, in a voice much like the *Crow*'s, 'whoever this is. I don't know why I'm doing this. I really don't. The date is... the twenty-first of August. I just got back from my mum's funeral. It rained. So for time, that's a month after leaving primer college and two weeks before starting university. And for score, that's six family members down, now. One to go. Just me.'

There are certain things a person shouldn't do when they're alone. Daedalus knew this, just as any long-distance pilot would. Dwelling was one. Drinking was another.

To his credit, Daedalus hadn't requested this recording in nearly four months. But he'd been doing a lot of dwelling the last few days. And a lot of drinking.

'What happens to these messages if there's no-one to deliver them to?' continued the locket. 'It didn't say in the contract. It said "guaranteed target acquisition by means of patented trail-sniffer technology", with a little "TM" there. Does the buzzer just latch on to anyone it can find? Seventh cousin seven times removed? Well, in that case, hello distant cousin. Sorry you had to hear this, but I'm dead.'

Daedalus started to dig the nails of his right hand into his left wrist.

'Don't worry. It was my own fault. Suicide is funny, isn't it? Is it a cry for attention? Is it selfish? Does she want to hurt us, make us pay? Is he taking the easy way out? – People don't get it, do they? No-one seems to understand that there's a chemical process in the human brain that can't be cancelled or corrected and it just goes on and on and on until it self-destructs. You gotta understand, you can't stop someone killing themselves, because you don't ever see it. They die well before their body goes cold. Activity stops weeks before anyone notices. People die and *then* they kill themselves.

'So that's why I signed up to this today. I'm about to die. I can feel it, because it feels like nothing. Big blank space,' the voice laughed, 'that's Jan. That's Jan to a "T". You have to laugh. Always remember to laugh, because if you don't then people stop talking to you. I signed up because...

'Ha. Ha ha ha. No bloody reason. I signed up because the people in the centre have to talk to you if you're signing up for it. There's a woman there who was trying so hard not to ask questions. It was *hilarious*, honestly. I'm laughing. Ha ha. Now I'm talking into this little purple thing. Technology is amazing.

'Sorry if I'm babbling. I took the rest of the bottle. Not enough for anything to happen, but I get closer every night. Feeling drowsy now. Might... might turn it off. How do you turn it off?'

There was a series of tapping sounds and a *thunk* as the recording device seemed to be knocked off a surface by clumsy hands.

'This concludes your tailored message. Goodbye.'

The locket fell silent. Daedalus realised his fingers felt wet. He looked down, and in the half-light of the cockpit he saw that his nails had drawn blood. Instead of wiping it off, he just stared. It hurt.

'Quiet in here,' said Erin from the corridor.

Daedalus jumped and rubbed his wrist on his trouser leg, snapping back to his normal manner.

'You're quiet,' he said.

'Oh,' said Erin, 'sorry.'

'No, it's fine. I wasn't doing anything.'

'Er. Okay.' Erin emerged from the hallway. 'Do you mind if I read in here again?'

The urge had subsided, and Daedalus felt he could deal with company again. He tried to forget what he'd just done.

'Sure,' he said. 'Why not.'

Erin hopped up on the co-pilot's chair. 'Thanks,' she said.

They passed some time in silence, but Erin didn't stay quiet for long. 'Did you know,' she began, running a finger along a line on page two-hundred and twelve of *The Decay of Science*, 'the same scientist who discovered the energy-amplifying properties of the myrmidon –'

'Yes.'

'– later died of heatstroke?' She ignored the interruption, lounging sideways on the pile of half-read books she'd left there. 'Apparently he kept one in his house for the winter and it melted all the doors shut.'

'Science.'

'He also –'

'This ship was a lot more peaceful before you came along.'

'– had a great-granddaughter who blew herself up in the middle of a Senate meeting.'

'Oh yeah, I remember that,' Daedalus said. The *Crow* jolted as the traffic inched forward. '"Prometheus", they called her. I must've been ten? Twelve? Something like that.'

Erin snapped the book shut and stared at him.

'Her name was Robin,' she said.

'What?' Daedalus glanced over at her. 'No. It was a joke. They were meeting to finalise the budget for the whole Collective. Very controversial, it was. For a while. Shut down a whole load of research programs and boosted military spending. Big debate, roughly fifty-fifty split.'

'What happened?'

'This scientist went in and set off a bomb in protest. No casualties, except herself. The news stations went mad with it. The Senate met again a week later. Budget passed unanimously. That's why every space station you come across smells like that. No researchers, no air filtration, no new robots to replace the old maintenance grinders.'

'So, what, people just don't do science anymore? Because there's no money?'

'No, there's plenty of money,' he said. 'Plenty for building warships and sending them out to the Frontier. Loads of scientists inventing bigger destroyers and bigger guns to go on them. I knew someone years ago who wanted to become a naval engineer, but she didn't want to design weapons so she couldn't get a grant for it.' Daedalus gestured, becoming more animated than she'd yet seen him. 'And here's the thing, right.' He stabbed a finger in the air, vaguely towards her, with one hand on the controls. 'I looked into this for my dissertation. Robin Redwing – "Prometheus" – from that book, from all the newsreels, she's in the public record because her work was all publicly funded. Waste of public money, they said. In the newsreels, they said that a lot. First of all, she ran a project developing more efficient atmosphere processors that never came up with anything good; then she oversaw a string of failed cloning research things; then some nonsense about teleportation that didn't get off the ground, obviously, and loads more stuff like that before she blew up.'

'So?'

'So – she was twenty-five! Who puts a twenty-five-year-old human in charge of ever bigger and more expensive projects when she's got a terrible track record and a degree from – and I triple-checked this – a university that was established the year she enrolled and shut down the year she graduated?'

'I... so?'

'So! Who's called "Robin Redwing"? What kind of name is that? It sounds like something out of a bloody fairytale!' He jabbed his finger in the air as if poking someone taller than him in the eye. 'You know what it sounds like? It sounds like someone who'd never even *met* a human flipped through the nearest encyclopaedia and came up with it on the spot. It sounds like Robin Redwing was made up and blown up to facilitate a sudden lurch in fiscal policy that directly benefits uptier military contractors and a Republic-controlled government desperate to counteract a growing social movement that's intent on dismantling the tier system and forcing the Republic to share power with everyone else in the Collective. And it worked. And that's why things are like this.'

Erin was quiet for a bit. Daedalus stared out the viewscreen, hand still half-raised as if to continue.

'Has anyone ever told you that you like to rant?' she asked.

Daedalus looked at her. He rubbed his forearm.

'Once.' He realised his breath had run short. He took a deep one and scratched his neck. '... Or twice.'

'Yeah,' Erin said, oblivious. 'I bet.' She returned to her book.

Daedalus was surprised. He hadn't meant to paraphrase a whole section of his dissertation; it had just spilled out. Apparently, the only copy in the universe not rendered into ash was still tucked away in a dusty, spidery corner of his brain. After a minute the surging sensation behind his nose ebbed away, and he could return his attention to the traffic.

The scanners came into view bit by bit as the lines of ships moved forward. They cast a bright green net from one edge of the channel to the other, blinking as they allowed clean ships through and pulsing to divert the occasional traveller aside for boarding. When they drew close, Daedalus started pushing a group of switches over his head. The engine noise in the rear of the *Crow* quietened down and there was a hiss somewhere else in the ship. The temperature dropped.

Erin looked up. 'What are you doing?'

'Trying not to attract attention. Sit still.'

'I thought I could vouch for you, isn't that enough? They won't bother us, will they?'

'It's fine. Just be quiet.'

'Are we *sneaking*?' Erin hissed. 'Is this a *sneak*?'

'I just don't want to get pulled over.' Daedalus pressed a button and the cockpit went dark. He rounded on her. 'You can vouch for me, sure, but you must realise you're not really like the others. Have you even met another entari before?'

Erin opened her mouth and closed it again.

'That's what I thought. Blending in on Taxos is one thing, but if we get inspected they'll be very curious about you.' He turned back to the controls. 'Best to act casual. Unless you want to be dragged off for questioning. Or tipped off to Aggro.'

'So, what, you've turned off the lights?'

'It's not just the lights. It's a spoof.'

'A sp... *what*?'

'A spoof licence.' Daedalus held up a palm for silence, and whispered. 'Just trust me.'

Erin glared at him.

The *Crow* held careful formation with her neighbours as they approached the checkpoint. Daedalus kept an eye out for movement and gripped the main stick to hold her steady.

'Easy… ' he murmured, 'easy… '

Something clunked. Then something in the ship started groaning.

Erin looked about. 'Is your ship alright?'

The cockpit lit up. Daedalus looked daggers at her and pressed a finger against his lips.

'Oh, this is taking too long,' said the *Crow*. The autopilot flickered into life, and a white bar on the main screen started filling up from the bottom. Daedalus froze. There was a rumble from the aft, and the *Crow* jolted slightly.

'No no no no no,' Daedalus whispered, 'not now, go away!'

'You should treat me with more respect, boy,' she said. The bar filled more rapidly. The *Crow* drifted out of formation.

'Stop it! Stop it now!' Daedalus leant over the scanner screen. One of the police cruisers was watching them.

'Let's *gooo*… ' The autopilot box on the panel flashed and started whistling. The locket dangling from Daedalus's neck buzzed and pulsed with a violet light. Erin looked terrified. Daedalus seized the stick again and held it as tightly as he could.

'What's happening?' Erin hissed.

'She's firing the engine.'

'Who is?'

'*She is!*' He stabbed a finger in the direction of the box. 'Help me hold i–'

Erin snatched the fire extinguisher from the back wall, heaved, grunted, and swung it over her head.

The box shattered. The sound died away. The engine purred back to a standstill, the locket shut off and the ship fell quiet again. Daedalus stared first at Erin, then at the screen. The cruiser stayed still for a moment, watching them, then moved away. He turned back to his passenger, who looked slightly surprised at herself.

'You're paying for that,' he said, clutching the locket to his chest.

The *Crow* made her agonising way through gridlock towards Taxos: the viewscreen-filling silver hulk that served as the political centre of civilised space. The capital station of the Collective appeared from a distance as a series of concentric white rings, the dark sides lit up by circuits of glowing yellow and the lit sides clearly visible all the way from the edge of the sector. Rivers of metal specks arrived and departed from sticking-out spires to deliver their cargo. Stars winked in and out of view constantly, as supertankers and commercial liners passed between the *Crow* and her destination. As they grew closer, the scale became slowly apparent. Daedalus noticed that Erin couldn't stop staring.

There was a sound like fizzing water as they passed through Taxos's enormous invisible shield. Daedalus felt the sudden urge to blink. Erin showed no reaction to the sensation at all. Soon there was nothing in front of them except the peppered white expanse of the station's western hull, crawling with maintenance vehicles and bristling with complex, inscrutable mechanisms. They followed the lane of similar-sized vessels down to Gypsum Spire, a long, thin landing spike for couriers and non-commercial ships. Approaching a tiny three-hundred metre wide rectangle in the side of the spike, they passed through the buzzing purple containment field into a bustling hangar. Daedalus felt a jolt as the gravity switched over.

Then the noise of the *Crow*'s engines was drowned out by everything else. Suddenly they could hear people yelling and roaring machinery. After hours of relative silence, the sound was painful. They touched down between a shining blue shuttle and a snub-nosed yellow family cruiser before killing the engines and coming to rest. A brief negotiation later found Erin ninety bits lighter and saw a crew of engineers climbing inside the *Crow* to refuel, repair, and un-smash the autopilot.

No Place Like

Daedalus
Taxos

Taxos immigration wasn't as busy as it used to be, but it was still just about the most crowded place in the Collective.

They had left the arrivals bay behind fifty minutes ago. The queue was long.

'Are you ever going to put that bloody thing down?' Daedalus grumbled. 'You can't walk around with your nose stuck in a book all day. You'll get mugged.'

After several seconds, Erin looked up from *Brave New World: Collected Fragments 1900-2200*.

'Sorry, what?'

'Oh, never mind.'

''Kay.' She sunk her slightly flattened nose back between its pages and lost herself in study again.

Daedalus hated going through customs. There wasn't much to see in front except whitewashed walls, unidentifiable hazmat-suited officials and the occasional two-metre-thick porthole, giving a view of the hundreds of ships arriving and departing from Gypsum Spire. At least Aggro couldn't get to them here. Petradons couldn't go unharried on Taxos these days unless they were squeaky clean, and he didn't seem the type. Erin was absorbed in her reading all the way through the queue, until they reached the booths.

Daedalus watched her. The tall, spindly immigration official was completely hidden under his white suit, except for a pair of black eyes behind a tinted visor. He raised his four arms to demonstrate, spreading them like a spider's legs. Erin took a moment to finish reading before looking up. Daedalus noticed a twitch of surprise in her neck when she saw the other entari.

'Arms, please, ma'am,' he intoned. 'Thank you, ma'am.'

Erin raised her arms. The officer ran a whining plastic instrument around her body, poking it around her back and between her knees, twisting it in his hand. It beeped. He looked at the little square readout on it and waved her through before doing the same for Daedalus. He raised his arms obediently. The officer poked his wand into the folds of Daedalus's coat, running it all over his chest and legs. Then he straightened up and peered at him. He prodded Daedalus's grimy hair with one gloved finger.

'Decon,' he said, pointing to his left and looking to the next immigrant. 'That way.'

Daedalus groaned. The officer's head snapped back around.

'Did you say something, human?' he asked. 'I think I heard you say something.'

Daedalus eyed the baton at his belt.

'No,' he said, 'nothing.'

'Move it.'

Erin looked over her shoulder for her driver. Daedalus moved past the officer towards the shower and gave her a small jerk of the head. She disappeared through the booth.

The shower sealed behind him and the tiny room hissed, filling with ice-cold gas. Daedalus held his breath and shut his eyes. After a few moments the gas cleared and the second door opened into another booth. He walked through, holding up his forged ID. The scanner gave a cheerful *bing* and a third door slid open. Then he was in the arrivals hall. Erin was easily picked out of the crowd – a splash of green in a brown-gold sea of huge, hairy traders and their hulking bodyguards.

'Where'd you go?' she asked.

'De-lousing.'

'Oh, good.'

He scowled. 'Let's go.' He pushed her onwards. 'Don't get too far ahead. And put the book away.'

Erin tucked *Brave New World* into her jacket. They passed around the tall zero-gravity fountain in the atrium and under the sturdy white tiers of Unity Arch. The hall widened and grew taller as they drew closer to the Taxan central ring. An occasional tug or nudge in the right direction was enough to direct Erin away from police, stalking around in distinctive white jumpsuits, and surly travellers. After a long, long walk along the landing spire, they arrived in front of the entrance to Taxos Central. A series of tall, slender columns supported a grand triangular pediment. Intricately carved figures of the uptier races, almost too high up to see, stood side-by-side within the triangle, with various configurations of arms outstretched in gestures of something like welcome. They towered imperiously over the crowds below.

'That's weird,' said Erin.

'What is?' replied Daedalus.

'Those statues,' she said, pointing up at the pediment. 'They look wrong.'

Daedalus was thrown. 'I thought you hadn't been here before.'

'No. There was a picture of them together in *A Brief History*. That book you gave me.'

'… And?'

'Well, there's one missing.'

Daedalus looked up. 'Oh.'

'It's the –'

'The petradon,' Daedalus said. 'The petradon's been removed. Huh.'

'I don't get it,' said Erin, 'what's wrong with petradons?'

'That book is a few years old. Things have changed in the last decade, kid. After the Home Rebellion there was a bit of a shake-up. Mostly entari governors kicking humans and petradons out of their stations, out of their colonies.'

Erin scratched her head. 'But why did they take the statue down?'

'Well, you booted the Petradon Imperium out of the Coalition, so I guess you wanted to make a statement. The Entari Republic and the Brand Kingdoms are the only real players since then.'

Erin looked blank.

'The Republic-Kingdoms Coalition,' Daedalus said. 'That's who runs the Collective these days.' Daedalus pushed on. 'The government? Your government? Seized the petradon gas mines? Devastated the Imperial economy? Ringing any bells?'

'It wasn't actually *me* who –'

'You kind of appropriated the Imperial Navy, as well.' Daedalus picked up steam. 'Set up all the blockades we saw on the way here. Set up the citizenship sanctions. This is pretty important stuff. Do you have a clue?'

Erin looked slightly alarmed.

Daedalus rubbed his temple with a fist. 'Sorry. I'll give it a rest.'

'Thanks,' said Erin, pulling her jacket around herself.

Once they had passed between the columns and into the station proper, Daedalus drew to a halt.

'We're here.'

Erin wandered forwards a few more steps and teetered slightly. Her eyes were just about capable of taking in the first few kilometres of the main causeway before what she saw became incomprehensible. Air farms ran in strips along either side of the walkways, hissing quietly as they worked. The green-white lines stretched insensibly far into the distance. High above she could see the monorails whispering along on a maze of hanging tracks, darting around each other like birds in flight. She heard the distant whooshing of a slow-moving river. People sloshed past them in droves, their voices melding into a whistling, clicking, growling hubbub. She stared, slack-jawed, as a thick white cloud drifted slowly into view and passed about a hundred metres above her head.

'It's *huge!*' she said.

'I hope you've got a name for this guy you're looking for,' said Daedalus, 'or you could be here a while.'

'Yeah... ' Erin said. 'There's a name.'

'Good,' he stuck his hands in his pockets and glanced around at the crowds. 'It still might take a while.'

Erin started. 'I haven't paid you,' she said suddenly. 'Here.' She dug into her jacket again and pulled out a handful of cards. 'Take some extra for the clothes.'

Daedalus looked at her for a moment. He hesitated, then took the money.

'Thanks.'

Erin stared out over the causeway. Big shiny buildings ran along either side into the distance until they vanished. Smaller roads led off the main one at regular intervals, feeding people of all shapes and sizes into the busiest areas. The crowd was largely green, the buildings mainly white. Entari strode around on long legs, loping with an easy grace. Daedalus picked out a few petradons in the crowd; far fewer than on Aphiemi. Highlife Brand races made up the rest, with a few low-tier species scurrying about underfoot.

'You know,' Daedalus said, 'I can give you a head-start if you want.'

'I can do this on my own.'

'Sure,' he went on, 'but I know some people. You're looking for someone, they can point you in the right direction.'

'... How much?' Erin looked down into her jacket, rooting around for cards.

Daedalus gave his best charitable smile. 'Let's see if it's useful first. Then we can talk money.'

Erin looked at the crowd again. 'Yeah,' she said, 'yeah, okay. Thanks.'

Daedalus felt a twang of guilt, for some reason, but suppressed it. He focused on the money he'd need to make sure the *Crow* stayed off the bounty boards, and Aggro's radar, once Erin was gone.

He pointed at a sign on the front of a nearby shop, its window cluttered with overpriced trinkets for rich traders to bring home to their groundling children. The sign read ELEVATORS – GYPSUM SPIRE. 'That way, if I'm remembering right.'

So they walked. Erin forged ahead through the mess of bumping people, the lapels of her jacket held tightly around her neck and Daedalus gliding along in her wake. The air was bright and cold, with a gentle breeze of conditioned air. It was clear that Erin hadn't been to the capital before. People with tall, spindly feelers and gigantic stomping feet bustled around them, and she shied away from the more purposeful commuters, afraid to provoke them. People of certain races seemed to surprise her with their presence, as if she'd never seen a foreigner before. Erin openly stared at the bright, angular people from Adaman. The coloured strip lights running either side of the causeway splintered into rainbows on their skin. Masked quadrupeds in chemical suits pounded past along the walkways, sporting brown Brand standards on their sleeves. There were no humans to be seen.

The elevator was a polished white room with mostly clean windows. Daedalus recognised the pale, orange-rimmed streaks of last night's puke on the perspex. It took them down to a dimly-lit street on one of the inner decks. It was raining. Erin stepped out ahead of Daedalus, sidling through the queue of sodden people waiting to ascend. Clustered around the gigantic support struts holding up the ceiling were rickety pop-up stalls and flats towering high, leaning towards each other over the street. Functioning strip lights were outnumbered by gas lamps and slow-burning orange bulbs, and brooks of condensation trickled down either side of the street. When Daedalus left the air-conditioned white box the humidity hit him like a pillow in the face and the mouldy smell of broken water synthesisers immediately started to creep up his nostrils. He sneezed. The people closest to him recoiled and scurried away.

'That way,' he sniffed, pointing. 'Look for a red door.' Daedalus had forgotten how warm it was down here. It was crowded, wet, and heaving with bad smells. The noise and uncomfortable heat of the inner decks rarely spread outwards. Instead it festered contently, making the rotten veins of Taxos a good place to go if you didn't want to be overheard, or followed.

Erin followed his finger. They passed through a busy lowlife marketplace, full of ragged merchants flogging their wares. Some of them were wearing breathing masks, and others were coughing into sleeves. Lots of food stalls, Daedalus noted, but not much variety. Algae or protein slabs, with the occasional stick of sugar. People stood in line for it. A shivering petradon with strange growths curling from his skull-plates coughed violently over a painted-green algae stall, and flinched as the owner started yelling at him.

'What's that?' Erin pointed upwards. Daedalus looked. A hand-sized white ring around a black propeller was hovering high above the streets, drifting along at a bit of a clip. It was silent beneath the drone of the crowds, but a blinking green light on the antenna made it easily visible. As he watched, it moved to a spot above the arguing men and stayed there, blinking away.

'Bad news,' he said. 'Keep walking.'

The Taste of Splinters

Erin
Taxos

Erin knocked four times, as Daedalus instructed. He stood behind her, leaning against the sooty bricks of the opposite wall. Ellen's place was in a tight alley, cluttered with rubbish bins and tangled fire escapes which made the dark red door tricky to spot. A dim orange lantern hung from the lintel.

There was a thump from inside, and the sound of footsteps. The door clicked. Erin went to push it open, but Daedalus caught her elbow.

'Try not to make any sudden movements,' he said.

Erin looked at him, then gently poked the door with a finger. It creaked inwards to a dark room containing an empty chair behind an old desk. Behind the chair was a heavy-looking metal door, left half-opening onto a brightly-lit hallway. A broken-down grinder stood silent in the corner, its eyes dark, and the floor was littered with newspapers and tall cans bearing names in stencilled letters. A long black coat hung from a stand in the other corner.

Erin took a step inside. 'Hello?' She moved up to the desk and squinted, trying to see into the hallway. Daedalus stepped in to follow her. The door snapped shut.

The light flicked on. Erin looked back. Daedalus stood still, hands held up. Over his shoulder Erin could see a forehead and a sprout of tightly-curled hair.

'State your business,' came a voice, as if commenting on the weather. It was light, but rough around the edges.

'This how you welcome everyone these days?' Daedalus asked.

'Mole?' The sprout twitched, and Erin saw a short, stocky human in a red shirt underneath it. The human stared at Daedalus. 'Turn around,' she said.

Daedalus put his hands up and turned slowly. When she saw his face she broke into a grin, and lowered the metal shelf bracket she'd been pressing into his back.

'You owe me a bottle,' she said.

'Do I look like I have one?'

'Yes.'

'Who's your friend?' she asked. 'You haven't brought me a cop, have you?'

Erin stood up straight so they were almost the same height. 'I'm Erin. I'm looking for someone.'

'Oh, business, is it?' she laughed. 'Well, he's brought you to the right place. I'll see you in my office.'

Ellen's office, up a short flight of stairs, wasn't much cleaner than the hallway. Erin sat next to Daedalus at her desk, which looked like it had been pulled out of a skip. In lieu of a noticeboard there were newspaper clippings pinned to the walls, with threads running between them and photographs scattered everywhere. The desk was piled high with more newspapers and files stained with brown rings. A monitor hung from one wall, muted, showing the news. On the screen were dramatic images of a grey Void battleship slowly bursting into flames under fire from a white-and-green Collective fleet. Subtitles described a hard-won victory for the defence beyond the frontier. Ellen rummaged around in a filing cabinet, pulling out a bottle of clear liquid and three small glasses. A wooden bat, well-used, leaned against it. There was a file poking out of the drawer, and something red sticking out of the file. It was marked with a single word: *Plague*. Ellen tucked it in and shut it away.

'Tastes like lighter fluid,' she said. 'Sorry, but I haven't been shopping in a while. On a case. Several cases, actually.'

She poured each of them a short glass and sat down on her swivel chair in front of the window, which looked out over a busy square. Erin sniffed her glass and left it.

'So,' Ellen downed hers in one and tilted her chair back, addressing Daedalus, 'what, you a taxi driver now? No more contracts?'

'No,' he took a sip and glanced at Erin, 'just helping someone out.'

Erin caught the glance. For a moment she wondered what 'contracts' meant, but the hard look in his eyes tipped her off. She looked over at Ellen's bat, and wondered if she took 'contracts' too.

'Really?' Ellen frowned. 'You. Daedalus Mole. Doing someone a favour.'

'It's okay! I'm paying,' Erin said. Daedalus screwed his eyes shut, and Ellen leaned back in her chair.

'Right, that makes more sense,' said Ellen. She kicked her legs up on the desk, her heavy boots making Erin's glass jump. The red shirt hung loose over a short black skirt and leggings, and Erin could see the green-black spike of a tattoo running up her right arm and disappearing beneath her rolled-up sleeve. It was much brighter in this room, and Erin could make out her cropped auburn hair and brown eyes much more clearly. Erin wasn't an expert on humans, but she looked a bit older than Daedalus. Her skin was mostly smooth, brown and speckled, whereas Daedalus's was pale, dry and cracked. Ellen had the same dark circles under her eyes that he had, though his eyes were wide and sickly-looking. Hers were thin. They didn't dart around anxiously like his. She wore some of that peculiar human war-paint as well – bright lines running over each eyelid and what looked like shining dark ink on her lips.

'I see you're still carrying that thing around,' she said, gesturing to the locket around Daedalus's neck.

Daedalus bristled. 'Watch it, Red.'

'It's not healthy.'

'That's enough.'

'Fine. Not my problem. What line of work are you in these days? Tourist information?'

'Courier stuff, mostly.'

'Wait… ' Ellen started. Erin saw her lips part, a shadow cross her face. 'She's not –'

'No!' Daedalus cut in. 'No. Not mine. Escaped. I picked her up and she asked to come here.'

'What?' She turned to Erin. 'Did he *rescue* you?'

'I hit a guy with a wrench,' said Erin, feeling a bit overlooked. 'I basically rescued myself. He just glassed someone.'

Daedalus put his head in his hand. 'I didn't –'

'Glassed someone?' Ellen looked amused. 'Old habits die hard, I guess. Anyone I know?'

'Some petradon slaver looking for a curio,' said Daedalus. He slugged back the rest of his drink.

Ellen laughed. 'I see you're taking on a higher class of target these days. Erin, was it? How much did he charge you for that kind of service?'

'Er –' Erin looked at Daedalus, whose expression had turned to one of alarm. 'Two-hundred bits.'

Ellen glared at Daedalus. 'Really.'

'What?' Erin asked, looking from one to the other.

'It's business.' Daedalus held up his hands. 'I don't work for free!'

'No,' Ellen said in a low voice, reaching behind her for the bat propped up against the filing cabinet, 'of course you don't. Don't help for free either. Scalping a runaway for ten times the normal fare? Honestly… even for you, this is low.'

'Easy. No need to get ang–' he stopped mid-word, because the end of the bat was now between his lips.

'Erin, would you like to do our friend here a favour?' Ellen smiled sweetly.

'Er –' Erin's eyes jumped from one to the other, not sure if she should be worried.

'Great! You just say the word and I won't break his teeth. That sounds good, doesn't it, Mole? Oh – wait a minute. How silly of me. People don't help for *free*.'

Ellen stood up, still holding the bat, and moved slowly around the desk. She leaned over Daedalus, rasping the wood between his lips, before dipping a hand into the pocket of his coat and withdrawing a card in two fingers. 'About two hundred bits sounds fair to me. Erin?'

Erin saw Daedalus give her the slightest of nods. She nodded.

'Good.' Ellen withdrew the bat and flicked the card over. Erin caught it. Daedalus spat out splinters. 'In future, always haggle down. Don't let men like him take advantage.'

Erin noticed that Daedalus's cheeks had finally found some colour. He sat still, looking suitably chastened, and avoided Erin's gaze.

'So, you're looking for someone.' Ellen dropped herself back into the chair and set her bat back against the cabinet as if nothing had happened. 'Finding people is my business. I'm pretty busy at the moment, but I'll point you in the right direction if I can.' She poured herself another drink. 'Got a name?'

'Yeah,' said Erin. She took a deep breath. 'DiGamma.'

Ellen stared. Erin felt like those eyes were boring into her. The crest on her scalp stiffened, and she felt a warm flush in her face.

'Juno?' Ellen asked. Her eyebrows twitched.

'No.' Erin scratched her neck. 'I'm looking for her partner, the... the human.'

'I see.' Ellen's gaze didn't shift. 'Can I ask why?'

'I'd prefer it if you didn't.'

Ellen nodded. 'Sure,' she said. She swivelled round to the filing cabinet by the window and started rooting noisily through it.

Erin noticed Daedalus watching her.

'What?' she hissed.

'Who are you?' he asked, in a low voice.

'Nobody.'

He didn't ask again, but his eyes felt cold on her back.

'There.' Ellen heaved a thick file from the cabinet and let it slap onto the desk. 'Juno DiGamma. Police enforcer, detective, Inquisitor, traitor – in that order, as far as I can tell.'

Erin had been reaching for the file. Her hand hung still.

'Traitor.'

'Yes,' said Ellen, holding the glass in front of her lips, 'traitor.'

Erin didn't like the way these humans looked at her sometimes. Like she was a child not worth making the effort to communicate with.

'So people didn't like her much,' Erin picked up the file. It was heavy.

'You could say that,' Ellen said. 'Lot of tension with humans these last couple decades, lotta anger. People think we're sponges, just a useless, techless race hitching a free ride on the coat-tails of the highlife with no home to go to. Maybe they're right. I'm getting the sense you've missed a few things, though, am I right?'

Erin nodded.

'Hate grows slow. Until it doesn't. People don't like interspecies breeding so much anymore, especially not where humans are involved.'

Erin gave a slight nod. She'd figured out that much, at least, on the slave ships. 'Juno was kind of a poster child for that kind of thing,' Ellen went on. 'Every Inquisitor ends up in the news at some point, talking to the press about high-profile cases – murders, terrorism, you know – sticking a big serious face on the police to make people feel safe.

'But Juno was in the news *constantly*. Dramatic chases, throwing bad guys out windows... she was real hands-on, and people ate it up. When she married this big charming idiot human, she made it seem normal. People in the central systems went out and actually started forking out for those DNA merge kits, and it became... well, not just something that happened out in the sticks anymore. So then when she went down, that all went down with her.'

'But,' Erin chewed her knuckle, thinking. 'What did she do?'

Ellen paused. 'You knew her, didn't you? Before she died.'

A moment passed. Erin gave a careful nod.

'But you don't know what she did.'

Erin said nothing.

'Funny way to know someone,' Ellen went on.

'Yeah. I guess it is.'

There was a silence.

'I'm sorry.' The hardness was gone from Ellen's voice. She reached back and pulled the blinds on the window. 'I knew her too. Once.'

'You did?' Erin straightened up. 'How?'

'She stabbed me.'

'Oh.'

'Yeah.' Ellen drank to it. 'Done a good job of it, too.' She lifted her shirt to show a pink line running across her belly. 'Got me out of her way and missed all the important bits. If she wanted me dead I'm sure I wouldn't still be around making a nuisance of myself.'

Erin took her eyes off the scar. 'Did you hate her too?'

Ellen shrugged. 'Business, innit. I didn't like her work, but she had principles. That's something.'

'So what happened?'

'Killed the chief of police, and a roomful of coppers.' Ellen finished her drink. 'Stole a bunch of records and bolted. Nobody knows why. Plenty of theories. S'far as I know, she was in exile for a few years after leaving Taxos. Wasn't safe for her or the man. Loads of warrants on her, but once she hit open space no-one could bring her in. Best pilot I ever saw, by a long way. Best swordswoman, too. I know she was being watched right up until she died. I know the Republic sent people after her. Must have been quick. You need to get up bloody early in the morning to kill someone like that. All I know other than that is where it happened. Termina. Dead system out on the Frontier. Republic's doing shady things out there. Experiments, military drills or something – nobody seems to go in and come out again without vanishing right after.'

'What about the man?' Erin asked. 'The human?'

'I've got an address. Here, on Taxos. Where they lived before they ran.'

'Give it to me.'

Ellen reached over the desk and opened the file to a specific page. A photo of a short, muscled, smiling human with crew-cut hair was clipped to it. A tall entari with lined eyes had two arms around his shoulders from above, one clutching his chest and another gesturing at the camera, with a silver ring on one finger. One corner of the photo was blackened and curled, but the image was whole.

Below the photo was an address. Daedalus was looking over Erin's shoulder.

'That's not far from here,' he said. 'We could walk.'

'Keep that if you want,' said Ellen lightly. 'Case went cold a long time ago. Not much in the file other than what I've told you.'

'I don't have any pictures of her,' Erin said.

'Well, it wasn't easy getting that one. Probably better it go to a friend of hers than lie around in this dump.'

'Thanks.'

'Don't mention it. You going, then?'

Erin looked at Daedalus. He shrugged.

'Yeah,' said Erin, 'we're going.'

Daedalus finished his drink, then Erin's, and Ellen escorted them downstairs and out the front door. Erin stood in the alley, Daedalus already picking his way through the rubbish bags to get to the street. Ellen leaned against the door frame. Erin wasn't practised at reading human emotions, but she thought the woman's smile looked sad.

'Look after yourself, kid,' Ellen said. 'It's a tough old world out there.'

'I know.'

'I know you know,' she said, folding her arms. 'Remember, humans might be lowlife, but we aren't all bad. Not all like that one.' Ellen looked at Daedalus, who was kicking through the rubbish now, picking up extra stains for his old brown coat.

'I try not to think about it.'

'Right. Sorry.' Ellen looked Erin in the eye. 'You ever need somewhere to stay, Erin, you come to me. Don't trust Mole to take care of you.'

'I wasn't gonna.'

'Clever girl. Just –' said Ellen, 'keep an eye on him for me, will you? He's worse than the last time I saw him. You know what that locket round his neck is?'

'It's his ship, right? Like, the computer?'

'Sort of. It's a memory tab. You ever hear of LittleWill?'

Erin shook her head.

'It's a funeral service. You pay them a few bits each month and they store a Self for you, along with a person to send the data to in the event of your death.' Erin looked blank. 'A Self. Like, a rough imprint of a person. It's for people who travel a lot, or who don't know where they'll be in a few years, or who don't have anything real to leave their children when they go. That locket's one of their packages.'

'But it's his ship. I've met her.'

'If you know the right people, you can do weird things with a Self. It's not good for you. Just... watch him. Please.'

Erin looked up at her. Ellen wasn't tall, but she stood over Erin by a head. 'Okay,' she said, 'I'll watch him.'

'Thanks, kid. He's got a lot of guilt, and it's not like there's no reason for that, but I do care about him. I just don't trust him. You shouldn't either.'

'Yeah,' Erin frowned. 'Well. There's trust and there's trust.'

According to Daedalus, the address they had was in one of the poorer residential districts, two decks down – or inwards, Erin never got the hang of mixed-gravity architecture – which meant going back the way they came. On the way to the elevator stop they came through the same marketplace they'd passed earlier. Erin sank back behind her guide out of habit when she saw the white armour. Bulbous, shining people stood in a circle around a smashed-up food stall. Black visors covered their faces, and black fabric stretched over the joints at elbow, knee and neck. They all stood in the same pose – arms splayed like spiders' legs, each holding a long, straight sword in front of their chest. Some of the swords shone, wet.

The drone hovered high overhead, shining a spotlight on the dirty, ragged petradon from earlier in the middle of the circle, a crude-looking gun brandished in one hand. He wheezed and choked in a coughing fit, drowning on his feet, and the strange, twisting growths sprouting from his skull-plates glowed bright white under the spot. Erin realised he was trying to speak. She jumped at a sudden boom from the white figures.

'CITIZEN,' they droned in unison, 'RELINQUISH CONTRA-BAND FIREARM.'

They weren't moving. The sound shook the floor from speakers hidden in their suits. The man in the middle wouldn't stop coughing.

'YOU WILL NOT BE HARMED. RELINQUISH CONTRA-BAND FIREARM. YOU WILL BE ESCORTED TO A SPON-SORED CLINIC. RELINQUISH CONTRABAND FIREARM.'

A few tourists were hanging around the edges, watching, like they were.

'We should go,' said Daedalus. 'We should go now.'

Erin stood rooted to the spot, staring at the police. Was this the kind of thing Juno did? Did she wear that armour?

'Harm?' he cried, hysterical. 'Harm me? What do you think *harm* is? You people – tools – god-damned *pigs*, you've harmed me enough!'

He fell into a coughing fit again, doubling up. Two officers advanced on him.

'Back!' he screamed, waving the gun. 'Get back!'

Daedalus backed away, keeping Erin pressed behind him. She gripped his arm, straining to get a better look.

'CITIZEN –'

There was a *crack*. Erin stumbled as Daedalus fell backwards into her. They hit the cold, wet floor together with a *thud* that emptied her lungs and jolted her brain in her skull. The crack still rang in her ears. When her head stopped buzzing another sound made itself clear – a gurgling cry as the police set on the man with the gun. Daedalus groaned on top of her, heavy and warm and smelling of week-old sweat. She tried to force him off, but circumstance found her without strength or breath to shout. Her lungs burned and she gave a painful heave. The human finally rolled off her as the dying man's screams guttered to a halt.

'Da-ck,' she wheezed, fighting to draw in air. The straining feel in her stomach slowly ebbed away. Next to her, Daedalus groaned on the floor. The bloodied police were dispersing with haste and a clean-up crew were already moving in with hoses and yellow bags. Erin struggled to her feet and grabbed Daedalus's arm, trying unsuccessfully to heave him upright.

'RETURN TO YOUR BUSINESS. THIS AREA IS SAFE.'

'What's wrong with you?' she said. 'You winded me –'

'I think I've been shot.'

Erin went still.

'Where?'

Daedalus raised a hand to his chest.

'Wait, don't move!' she said, bending over him, unsure what to do with her hands.

He reached into his breast pocket and slowly pulled out *A Brief History*. A small, jagged piece of metal was embedded in it. Erin saw the tiny hole in his coat.

'You're joking.'

'Don't scrimp on your black-market firearms,' Daedalus said, digging the bullet out with a finger. 'This thing couldn't kill a rat. That book just saved me buying a new shirt. Tough as old boots.'

'They killed him,' Erin said as he slowly pushed himself to his feet, swaying slightly. She didn't feel shocked, except for a mild surprise at herself for not feeling shocked. All she felt was a kind of flat, resigned anger.

'Yeah,' said Daedalus, wiping his hands on his coat, to little effect. 'They'll do that.'

'He was scared,' Erin went on. 'He was sick.'

'So? That's how it is down here. What are you gonna do about it? Try anything and they'll kill you too.' Daedalus tapped her elbow. 'Come on. Let's go.'

Erin half-wanted to grab him and hit him, but the will wasn't there. She wanted to hate him, too, and everything else, but that will wasn't there either.

'Okay,' she said. 'Let's go.'

Ashes

Erin
Taxos

The houses jostled together in square spaces, four to a block and two doors high, with walkways running along the face of windows long dusted over from years of disuse. The walk took a while. They had to wend their way through twisting alleys and narrow streets with faulty lighting, away from the main walkways.

'Six: Four, Echoes-Point-Hand,' read Daedalus from the file. 'Yep. This is the place.'

Juno's old house was scarred with burnt planks and scorch marks, and the windows had been smashed. Two words were daubed roughly across the façade, in faded green paint: LOWLIFE LOVER.

'Looks like we missed him,' said Daedalus.

They were too late, Erin realised. Juno's love was long dead. Their house was a burnt ruin, reduced to something cold and hard, like a war memorial. Erin kicked some blackened debris out of the way to reach the door, and her foot caught a length of ancient torn green-white police tape. She shook it off.

'It's probably not safe in there,' Daedalus called after her.

Erin pushed the door inward and stepped inside. The hinge gave a quiet screech.

'Fine!' she heard him yell as the door swung shut behind her. It was dark inside. The floor was coated in rubbish from years of squatters, but it looked like no-one had been here for a while. Small piles of decayed newspapers and faded rags stood undisturbed. Food waste had long since crumbled to dust. The floor was coated in a thin white carpet of the stuff, and it flattened beneath Erin's feet.

She crept through the quiet. There were two rooms on the ground floor, and a rickety wooden staircase leading upwards. The kitchen was only recognisable as a kitchen thanks to the fridge. Vivid green moss bloomed from behind the door. Erin elected not to look inside.

Half the balusters on the staircase had been knocked out, and the handrail wobbled when Erin tried to lean on it. Poking around upstairs only revealed more waste. Erin found an empty silver photo frame on the floor behind a beaten-up dresser, and a set of blunt keys hanging from a crooked hook behind a door. Further digging turned up a pair of torn-up black woollen gloves and a matching ragged scarf in one of the bedrooms. Erin pulled them onto her upper hands and wound the scarf around her neck once, twice, then three times, but it still reached down past her waist, a spiky mess of loose threads.

When Daedalus came looking for her some time later, he found her sitting at the foot of one of the beds, a small collection of relics on the floor in front of her. The photo frame, the keys, a big dusty shoe. There was an old corner of what looked like a blanket sitting on top of a dilapidated leather jacket. Erin held the biggest of her finds in her hands – a dirty white helmet with a thick crack running down the centre. She stared at her black reflection in the visor. The room was dark except for a sliver of light passing between curtains stiff with mould. The light drew a white line down the length of the bed and over Erin's shoulder.

Daedalus looked around. The place was abandoned – stripped of essentials and robbed of valuables – and the patterns of damage told him there had been little method or order to the activity here. The residents had moved out in a hurry and made no arrangements to sell their belongings, because a quick exit was worth more than all their possessions combined. No signs of struggle – they had left before being attacked, and left suddenly. The building had then been stripped before the authorities could seize it.

Erin saw none of this. The helmet's visor had a regular geometric texture. The patterns warped her face, splitting and lengthening it in the reflection. Her bruise seemed once to diminish, then to spread and overtake her face, then shrink again as she turned it over in her hands. She rested her forehead against it, and felt years and years of cold.

'Erin?'

'Mm,' she murmured.

Daedalus took a moment to look more closely. He watched the way she held her eyes shut against the old helmet and breathed in and out, slowly. This manner of looking was difficult for him. Daedalus struggled to break Erin down, to turn her into a series of manageable facts and rules.

She sniffed. Then the pieces fell into place. Short for an entari. Young. Exile.

Erin flinched as he sat down next to her.

'I'm sorry,' he said. 'When did it happen?'

'The day I left.' Erin's voice was flat. 'Six months ago.'

This house was quiet. They were so far away from the street all they heard was the scratch of rodents in the walls and the distant rumbling of the central power stations.

'Your friend,' said Erin, 'she was wrong. Juno didn't die in Termina. She lived for years after that. Hidden away.'

'I'm sorry,' said Daedalus. 'I know how... '

She looked up.

'... I'm sorry,' he finished, staring at his feet. 'How did it happen?'

Erin stared at him, and her mouth opened briefly, then closed again.

'In her sleep,' she said, turning her eyes back to the visor. 'I woke up one day and she was just dead.' The visor's material was slightly warped, so it didn't sit flush with the rest of the helmet. Erin, because her hands weren't busy, tried to work a finger into the gap.

'Ow!' She drew her hand back. Blood ran down from the tip of her finger. 'It's sharp.'

'The visor?'

Erin stared at it. 'It's broken,' she said. There was a jagged crack on the bottom edge. She watched as the dark red bulb drew a wet path along her skin. After it passed her wrist she felt another wet path running down her cheek, and raised a hand to catch it. It came away clear and glistening.

Daedalus shifted uncomfortably. He should have been able to figure this out much sooner, and it troubled him that he hadn't.

'She died. She left me,' Erin heard herself say. Her voice cracked. 'Moms aren't supposed to leave.'

He hesitated, then put an arm around her shoulder.

'I know,' he said.

'I thought... I thought if I found my dad I could go back.' Erin couldn't hold back the words. 'I thought it didn't have to be... it didn't have to be over.' Her shoulders shook. The anger was there again, twisting and coiling in her gut with nowhere to go. 'I'm not ready.'

Daedalus stared into space. 'I wasn't either.'

'I'm alone now. That's it, isn't it?'

He didn't contradict her.

Erin sniffed. The tears ran down her neck uninterrupted. She was trying to stop, but her shoulders kept heaving forwards of their own accord, her body struggling to throw off something deep and painful. She gripped the bottom of the bedframe with two hands in an attempt to steady herself.

Then she felt something cold and hard at her fingertips. It was heavy. Comforting. She took a deep breath. The spasms slowed. Then they stopped. Erin reined herself in, and closed her eyes.

'Right. Better?' Daedalus asked.

She closed her fingers around the cold thing under the bed, and pulled. It came free. Erin dragged it out and raised it to eye level. Daedalus recoiled and swore.

It was a very dusty length of sharpened metal, with a black grip and a shining hilt to match. It was only as long as Erin's arm, but it had a mean gleam to it, in spite of the dust.

'Bloody hell.' Daedalus stared.

In the dark the blade hurt to look at. The thin sheet of light lit up one edge to a painful glare, still and bright as Erin held the sword steady.

'It must have been his,' Erin murmured.

'Not hers?'

'Maybe.' Erin weighed it in hand. It felt good. The heft and balance were comforting, and it sat in her grip like it belonged there. 'Maybe I should take some contracts.'

'You sure?' Daedalus's mouth twitched at the corners. 'You don't strike me as the killing type.'

She twirled the sword gently, tossing it from one hand to the other, then the other, then the other.

'Try me,' she said.

Daedalus laughed, despite everything. Erin gave a little *pf* sound. Then she fell quiet again for a moment.

'She killed people,' said Erin.

'Yeah, I'd imagine so.'

'I lived with her my whole life, and now I'm finding out that I don't know anything about her. Not a damn thing.'

Daedalus picked at the lining of his coat.

'You killed people, too,' Erin said.

Daedalus nodded.

Erin exhaled. 'Please tell me there's a difference.'

Something creaked in the ceiling, and a gentle wind was brewing – rushing through the station to bring warm air from the core.

'There is,' Daedalus lied. 'Juno – she was police. They kill because they believe in something, right? Looking after the little guys. "Responsibility". What the Republic's all about.'

'But… she didn't.' Erin looked at him, trying not to feel. 'My mom didn't believe in anything. Her whole life, she tried to make me into someone like her. People can't be trusted. People are sheep. People hurt you. I hated that about her. It made me feel like I didn't know her at all, like all the things she didn't talk about were secrets, instead of just bad memories. That's why I left after she died.'

'Left where?'

'Home. I could've stayed. The people were okay. But I wanted… I wanted to prove her wrong.'

'Did you?'

Erin's laugh held an edge. 'Not yet.' She looked at the helmet.

'You're not taking that, are you?' Daedalus asked.

Erin tilted it to look inside. The padding had rotted away, and the crack went all the way through.

'You can't, kid,' his voice wasn't unkind. 'I'm sorry. You get seen carrying that, the police will take your head.'

'Forget it,' she said. 'I wasn't going to. It's broken. No… no point bringing it with me.'

'Right.'

Erin was still holding it. She set it down on top of the pile and pushed herself to her feet. Daedalus reached out to steady her, but she was fine. The sword was still in her hand.

'You're not taking –'

'Yes I am.'

Erin tucked it under her belt halfway up the blade. It was uncomfortable, but it stayed hidden under her jacket. Without another word she made her way to the front door, leaving the pile of memories behind her. The door nearly came off its hinges completely on her exit. It was quiet. The air outside was warming up. Erin thought for a moment about where to go. That small thought opened the floodgates in her head and her knees gave out.

No friends, no home, no purpose. She thought about the people they'd spent all day walking past. They all had lives. Normal people with friends, family, normal pains and normal losses. Erin had nothing. No friends to live with and talk to and help out and sleep with and eat with and grow up next door to and do all the things she thought she'd one day get to do with people who mattered to her. Like she read in her books, when she was young.

Daedalus hesitated. Something far away tugged at him, bringing up memories in strange light, in high relief. Static memories, memories that for years had been statues, carvings, tapestries hanging in the space behind his eyes, were starting to move. Erin reminded him so much of someone else.

The locket gave a half-hearted half-buzz as the *Crow* started to come back online. Daedalus didn't notice. He sat down next to Erin on the step as she strained and gulped for breath, her shoulders shaking slightly.

'You alright there, kid?' he asked.

'I – I – thought I was... going to... find... '

'Hey, easy –' He fished in his pocket for a tissue, but she waved his hand away, clutching her forehead tight. She took a deep, halting breath.

'I... I don't know what to do,' she finally got out. 'I don't know where to go.'

There was a long moment.

Erin waited for him to leave. He would. He definitely would.

She spoke again, looking upwards now, as if to take the advantage of gravity away from any particularly determined tears.

'Oh, god. Sorry. I can't... I just... '

Daedalus still hadn't left. Erin saw him through the distortion at the edge of her vision. He sat leaned over, like someone was pressing on his shoulder.

The caring instinct didn't fit. It felt smaller than he remembered – like an old family home from a time that had long since passed. It whispered into his shoulder and tugged on the muscles, lifting his arm and placing it around Erin's shoulders. It danced on his vocal cords and made him speak.

'And then there were two,' said Daedalus.

Erin turned her eyes to him. His unkempt stubble and dirty brown hair made his face unsettling, but the menace in him had passed like a shadow on an overcast day. His crooked nose was dotted with pimples and some grim-looking hairs, but his mouth was making an effort not to grimace, if not quite managing a real smile. Somehow, in spite of her panic and in spite of her fear, her breathing started to settle. She took the end of her new scarf and wrapped it around her face, drying her eyes and hiding her features.

'Two,' she said. 'That's not much.'

'Something my mum used to say. Only takes two wheels to keep moving.'

'Takes more not to crash.'

'Depends how fast you're going.' There was a pause, but unfortunately the point of the analogy failed to emerge. 'Don't worry,' Daedalus said, slapping her on the back. 'I know just what to do in times like this.'

He rose to his feet and offered her his hand. She took it, and he yanked her up. 'Let's go get drunk.'

Annex of Self

Ram's head hurt, but that was normal. She kept one hand up to guard her weakened skull-plating as she cut through the security door with her stolen torch. Sparks showered her, leaving burns on her leathery skin, but there was no time to slow down.

The cancer was working hard on her skull, turning smooth bone into sandpaper, then into fields of stalagmites puncturing the skin. The headaches came and went. When they faded they left a cloud of black ash in her head which was hard to think through. Sometimes days would pass without a view through the fog, and people would get angry at her for moving, talking, acting without feeling or initiative. But right now it hurt, which meant she could think. Could act.

Somewhere down the corridor from the escape pods she could hear heavy footsteps and laughter. Men. She kept the cutting torch moving. It was already halfway down.

Ram had three reasons to avoid her fellow recruits. One: she was a woman. The Navy used to have rules about crew complements, but since the annexation the ships were crewed with whoever was available. She was the only woman aboard. Men like her shipmates, she'd noticed, men with wounded pride, would lash out endlessly to feel like real men again. However briefly. However pointlessly.

Two: she was ugly. Big, but not quite big enough. Strong, but not quite as strong as the others. She would stand as tall as she could, but the curve in her spine made it hard to straighten her neck. Not tall enough.

Three: she was currently deserting her post, which carried a penalty of death.

Ram had signed up to escape. When you escape from somewhere bad to somewhere worse, she reasoned, the only sensible course of action is to escape again, and keep escaping, until you find something you don't have to run from.

Three-quarters down. The torch was almost out, sputtering a little and barely managing to burn through. The voices grew louder, and suddenly agitated. Ram didn't want to look, but she knew they had spotted her. Heavy armoured feet thudded into the deckplates. They were close now, close enough that she could hear their heartbeats – big, loud petradon hearts – with her ultra-sensitive petradon ears. She hated them. The sounds. The men.

The torch spat a final lick of flame and died. *Thud thud thud*. Ram threw it aside. Still not looking, she took a step back and threw her full weight into the steel door. It buckled. With a roar she tore the left side free. Molten metal scarred her hand, and she lifted the door over-head before hurling it down the corridor, knocking her pursuers clean off their feet. In the cacophony of clattering armour on hard floors, she barged into the tiny airlock and climbed into one of the escape pods. At her touch, the controls lit up and the airlock emergency-sealed behind her. All fell silent. Ram's headache pulsed angrily, and she threw the throttle wide open.

The pod filled with sound as the engine fired, and then she was gone. Alone.

Behind Bars

Daedalus
Taxos

'No, no, no,' he said, 'it's in the wrist. Watch.' Daedalus necked the shot in one, flicking it into the back of his throat with a movement like a darts master.

Erin spluttered and choked on her vodka a second time, spilling it all down her front, where it soaked into her scarf.

'I can't!' she said, half-laughing, half-yelling through the burn. 'It's horrible!'

'Lemme see,' he said, snatching the glass and peering into it. 'You know what your problem is?'

'What?' She squinted at him through the smoke and booze.

'You're drinking *vodka*. Cocktails are s'posed to have... ingredients.'

'You – you gave it to me!'

'Yeah, but *you* paid for it. What are you, stupid?'

'I – what?'

'More drink please.' Daedalus gestured clumsily over the bar, sinking onto it and sticking.

The glistening bartender nodded politely and slithered over to the spirit shelves, pulling down a bottle of dark brown liquid to decant another few shots. Quiet music sang out of ceiling-mounted speakers, struggling to be heard over a backdrop of heavy static. The room was dimly-lit in yellow for a homely feel, the walls all weathered pale wood with red-cushioned booths and a few stained-glass windows for character. They had no designs, just random arrangements of colour and shape. The countertop Daedalus rested his elbows on was covered in hairline splits and clung to his sleeve with the lingering residue of long-lost drinks. The bartender returned, placing two small glasses in front of them. Erin produced another card from the wallet in her jacket pocket, now bulging considerably less than it had at Aphiemi. She slid it over the bar, her hand swerving slightly as she did so. The bartender took it with a chuckle. He went back to the corner to resume chatting with one of the bearded regulars, who was loudly complaining about the static.

'I know man, it's weird,' the bartender said, knocking on one of the speakers with his fist. 'Thing's brand new. Signal was fine an hour ago.'

Daedalus took the glass and held it in front of him, inspecting the contents. A yellow liquid climbed the sides of it, swaying from edge to edge. With concerted effort of brain and limb, he arrested his motion and returned to an unsteady vertical. Erin was staring intently at her own glass, her chin in her hands and her elbows on the bar. As Daedalus watched her the music lulled almost to silence for a few moments, until all that filled the bar was white noise. He sank down next to her, chin propped up on the backs of his hands.

'Still thinking about it?' he asked.

Erin didn't shift her gaze from her glass. He waited.

'It's my fault I'm here,' she mumbled. 'I should have listened to my mom.'

'Me too,' he said.

Erin turned her eyes to him for a moment. His face was as impassive as usual. She turned back and started toying with the glass as she spoke.

'She said we had a good life right where we were.' She picked up her glass and swirled it thoughtfully in front of her face. 'I thought about leaving a few times. She never let me.'

She sipped gingerly at her drink. Unfortunately, it still did not taste of ginger.

'There were so many stories about how horrible the outside world was. I don't think I'll ever forget them. I tried. They just kinda… stick.'

'Well, it's not great out here.'

Erin set her glass down with a bang.

'Six months. You know?'

Daedalus knew.

'Do you know what held me together?' Erin said. 'Through all the beatings and the insults and the –' She stopped and winced, putting a hand to her neck. Daedalus caught a glimpse of a raised black mark between her fingers. It didn't look like a tattoo. 'They were people too. When I tried, I could see what happened to them to make them the way they were. I saw the kids in my batch changing into the people who sold them. Evil doesn't come from nowhere, right? We grow it ourselves. We just need the right conditions.'

Daedalus returned to staring resolutely into his drink. The silence between them filled with tuneless hissing as the sound system gave in completely. The bartender groaned. Daedalus looked at him, almost remembering something.

'They made us fight,' said Erin. 'I tried not to, but they *made* us.'

'Come on,' said Daedalus. 'Lighten up, will you? You're free now. If Aggro 'n' his goons were still on our tail, they'd have us by now. You've got enough cash to tide you over until you find some work. That puts you in a better position than a lot of people.'

'Work. Right. Like your work?'

'There are worse ways to live,' he said, not looking at her.

'How do you do it?' she asked. 'All these people dying, all this disease, all this violence... how do you live without doing anything about it?'

'What are we supposed to do?'

'I don't know!'

'Well, there you go then.' Daedalus took a swig. 'Just keep your head down and don't sass the police. That's what we do. Unless you want to go join the Church.'

'Maybe I do.'

'Shut up and drink.'

They drank quietly for a while. Daedalus noticed that Erin had a habit of drumming her fingers on her knee. He found himself nodding along to the rhythm.

'Mole?'

'What?'

'Where are you from?'

Daedalus slowly leant one elbow back onto the counter. He tapped his glass gently. Whiskey lapped up and over the rim, running in rivulets down to the countertop and seeping into the cracks. Daedalus followed the vanishing liquid with his eyes for a few moments. Then he spoke.

'I grew up in a place called Littlerock. It's – well, I haven't been back there in a while, but when I was growing up it was a mining colony. Glorified asteroid, really. It's in Crit, not far from where the channel to Earth used to be.'

'Why did you leave?'

'Everyone leaves home.'

'Yeah,' said Erin, 'but why did *you* leave?'

Daedalus opened his mouth, then stopped. His brow furrowed in concentration, and the words formed slowly.

'See,' he said, 'the thing about Crit is the asteroid belt running through it. Full of good stuff, iridium, helium-3, plenty of silver; all the things mining companies can't get enough of. Littlerock was my town. One of the first colonies, it was, on the biggest rock in the belt.' Daedalus rubbed an eyebrow with his fist. 'What was it again? John… something. John 11:25. The whole belt was named like that. I had a friend from a planet called George. Nothing else, just George.'

'That's a weird way to name places.'

'Yeah. Humans are bad at names. When I was a kid we didn't have many visitors. Everyone on my street was like me. I was fifteen when I saw my first al– person who… wasn't… human. There was a Void cultist hiding out in our town and the hunter they sent after him was entari. Nasty guy, but Littlerock was mostly quiet. The Republic, the Kingdoms, the Imperium – all off fighting their own little war on the other side of the galaxy. We did our thing, my parents worked the mines and I went to school. I didn't really understand what was happening when the dreadnoughts started arriving.

'Then all of a sudden the mines weren't ours anymore. They belonged to the Collective.' Daedalus rubbed at the dark circles under his eyes. 'My parents weren't around much. They worked longer hours. There wasn't so much money anymore. Science courses were way too expensive, so I went to university to do history. Thought I might get citizenship.'

'But you didn't,' said Erin.

Daedalus shook his head. 'You might have heard of the crash riots.

No? Littlerock was one of the first. Everyone went to school to get citizenship. People spent the last of their money trying to give their children the life they never had. Freedom of travel, freedom of office, freedom to marry… '

'What happened?'

'They said no.' Daedalus's face was blank. 'There was talk of Responsibility. Returns to traditional values. They gave lots of reasons. Couldn't afford benefits for people who couldn't return the investment. Tier one races, tier two races: ineligible.'

'Riots, though?'

'People were angry.'

'But… ' Erin bit her lip. 'That can't have ended well.'

'It didn't. There was a protest on the day of my last exam, and they sent in the police. I remember them landing in the car park – first time lots of us had seen those white suits, it really freaked us out. Things got violent. Really violent. Everyone there was either arrested or… ' he slid into silence.

'But if you don't have citizenship, how are you here?'

Daedalus didn't speak.

'You ran away.'

Daedalus still didn't speak.

'What about your family? Your friends?'

'I don't like it here.' Daedalus necked the last of his drink and stood up, almost knocking over his stool. 'Let's go somewhere else.'

'Wait –'

But he swept out of the bar with long strides. Erin fumbled in her pocket and dropped some cards on the table before following him. The speakers fuzzed and popped as she went past, and she heard them come back to life behind her once she'd left, picking up a news channel:

'– new fleet of warships to join the Armada in deep space. We would like to thank all citizens of the Collective for the sacrifices you have made to ensure a safer future –'

Rain was falling on the open causeway. High above their heads the cycling front of warm air from the power stations drove out the icy cold of the outer levels. The wide area where they crashed into each other spun slowly through the station, bringing with it a wind of unpredictability. Daedalus pulled his collar up. Hunched, he pushed through the evening crowds and tried to control his breathing. He caught cold water in his hands. It stung his cheeks. Erin caught up to him, scarf wrapped around her head, as he drifted into a shabby-looking spirit bar down the street.

'Mole?' she asked, grabbing his sleeve. 'Are you alr–'

'Fine!'

She flinched.

'Sorry. I'm fine. Let's just… ' he waved a hand at the door and vanished inside.

Daedalus picked a spot in the corner and sent Erin for drinks. She came back with two tall thick glasses of something red that smelled like rotten fruit.

'It was cheap.'

'It's all cheap,' said Daedalus, taking his. He swigged with no hesitation, emptying half the glass in one before making an unpleasant noise in his throat.

'Want to talk about it?'

'No. Your turn.'

Erin hesitated. She raised her own glass and tipped the searing liquid into her throat. Though she held her mouth steady, Daedalus could see her cheeks turning a darker shade of green. After a long pause, she parted her lips and took in a long, deep breath.

'Well, you know,' she said, 'I had to leave home.'

'Where was home?'

Erin pursed her lips. The yellow lamplight glittered in her big, dark eyes.

'We lived in a village,' she began. 'It was nice. Little houses we made ourselves. We made stone paths and there was a spider-tree on our front step. We had a big garden, with a green pond at the end. I… I used to try and fish there when I was young. I saw it in a book.' Daedalus glanced up from his drink. Erin was smiling in a small, distant kind of way. 'The people were nice. Mom said they helped her when she arrived, because she was hurt.'

The Fall

Juno
Frontier planetoid EP6-1-3 (Tier zero)
Nineteen years ago

There was a distant screech. A villager looked upwards. In the dawn light, behind thin streaks of charcoal cloud, a second sun was rising in the north. He pointed and called out. More villagers raised their heads. Beyond the sands and over the mountain it burned with blue ferocity, painful to the eye. It cut a black streak across the sky.

An elder left his hut and listened. The screech grew slowly louder.

There was a white flash as the *Kestrel*'s shield burst. Flaming pieces tore away and sought their own twisting paths towards the ground. Then it was falling. It banked, struggling to control its dive.

The elder considered it briefly, then shouted to a nearby youth, who ran inside the hut. A moment later she re-emerged holding a wooden spyglass. The elder snatched it and held it up to the ship, looking through it.

The *Kestrel* narrowly missed a watchtower on the further hilltop. Metal flaps on the wings fluttered desperately in the wind, trying to keep it aloft. It slowed. One broke free. Then the ship was spinning, screaming towards the dense forest below. Blue flames spat from its underside intermittently, slowing its spin and turning its fall into a dive.

He barked an order. The youth jumped, then took off running, yelling as she went, and some of the stronger villagers fell in behind her.

The flaming arrow disappeared for an instant behind the tallest trees. A roar went up. The elder's feet itched at the tremor in the ground. Far away, smoke bloomed.

They found a mile of trees smashed into pieces, the flattened ground peppered with fragments of cooling metal. The ship was half-buried in loose soil. It took three muscle-bound builders to wrench the buckled hatch open, and they took twenty minutes to tear out enough impact-foam that they could see the broken, bleeding figure suspended inside. Two arms were cradled around her abdomen. Two more were extended towards the controls, sickeningly bent, with a glinting silver ring on one finger. Under the smashed bronze visor her face was contorted, her crest flaring wide, straining against the inside of her helmet. Rivers of blood ran from her shoulders, soaking into her orange flight suit.

The village youth was the smallest of the group. She crept into the maze of hardened white foam, squeezing around the hanging woman and crouching low to inspect her swollen belly.

'Anageni,' said a builder, quietly, 'she is already dead.'

The youth leaned in closely, pressing her ear gently against the woman's chest. Silence.

Anageni ignored a sudden, sharp pain behind her eye, and she rested her face on the rough orange material.

'We should leave,' hissed a hunter, 'it's not safe –'

'Shut up,' said the builder.

Ana frowned. That wasn't silence. It was a soft, loud hissing. White noise. Quiet and loud, far away and inside her head.

No, wait. Silence again.

A heartbeat.

No, wait.

Two heartbeats.

'Get Sozo!' Ana said. 'Get the midwife! Now!'

There was one runner in the group. She ran.

'It's okay,' Ana murmured, her hand on the suit. 'It's going to be okay. Don't die.'

Breaking Bars

Daedalus & Erin
The next bar

'Go on,' he said.

'We argued. The night before she… she died,' said Erin. 'One of those fights that picks up weight and rolls on until you're shouting about stuff that you thought you didn't care about anymore.' Erin dug fingernails into her face. 'It was bad.'

Daedalus didn't say anything.

'I stormed out. I just ran. I think she was too weak… her arms would make her sick sometimes. They hurt. I pretended I didn't know about the fevers, but I heard her being sick in the night. When she thought I couldn't see her she would… she would have this horrible look on her face. I don't remember what I said before I left. I just remember her face when I said it. When I came back it was dark. In the morning I got up and looked for her and she was… I found her in bed. That was it.'

'What were the villagers like?'

Erin looked up, startled.

'What?'

'The people you lived with. What were they like?'

Erin rolled her glass between her thumb and forefinger.

'Nice,' she said. 'They looked after Mom when she was pregnant with me. Fixed up her injuries as well as they could. They even helped her build a home once she gave up trying to fix the ship.'

Daedalus just listened as she talked. Through a tipsy haze his brain was putting it together, building a rough image of what had happened. Erin wasn't from entari space. There were no small entari colonies. No villages. They built cities or they demolished them. Superstations or superdestroyers; nothing in between. He'd never met an entari who didn't know this. She wasn't a Republic citizen. No education, no loyalty tests, no military service. No wonder she didn't know this place. To the Republic, she didn't even exist.

'What happened to her?' he asked.

Erin frowned at him. 'She died.'

'No,' said Daedalus, 'I mean, what happened to her before you were born, to make her crash?'

'Oh.' Erin looked taken aback. 'I... I don't know. She didn't like talking about it.'

'Right.' A dead end, then. 'Juno,' he murmured, as if to himself. 'Jan. Ellen. Erin. S'weird. Run into the same kind of things over and over, just little differences. Names. Places. People. But you're still going in circles. Cycles.'

'Jan?' Erin asked.

Daedalus jumped. He looked down at his hands. He hadn't realised how dirty they were. There was a long pink scar across the back of his left one, and his right was discoloured with burns. The skin around his fingernails was picked to shreds.

'My... ' he halted for breath. 'She was a... friend.'

'Oh.'

Erin fidgeted.

'I met her at university. You'd have got on well. She was restless. Always talking, always after some kind of adventure. Brown hair, brown eyes, big nose. Always stuck in some bloody book.' Daedalus had grown quiet, talking only to himself. He lapsed into silence for a few seconds.

'Was she in the protests?'

Daedalus jerked his chair backwards.

'Okay, okay!' Erin held up her hands. 'Sorry. I won't ask.'

Daedalus looked at her. 'It's fine,' he grunted. 'Just... it's fine.'

'It's okay to talk about it,' Erin said, her voice low and tipsy-conspiratorial. 'We've all done bad things. We're all guilty. You don't just... nobody goes through life squeaky clean.'

'You're a kid. Jus' a kid.' He glared at her, eyes slightly unfocused. 'What do *you* – what do you know about guilt?'

'Am *not* just a kid,' Erin furrowed her eyebrows in concentration. 'You know what your problem is? You think you're smarter than everyone else, you think you're... like... badder than everyone else. I think *you're* the kid.'

'Right, right' Daedalus rubbed his face, 'I get it. *I'm* the kid. I'm the six-foot kid and you're the four-foot grown-up.'

Erin's jaw hung half-open. 'You are *not* six f–'

'Har!' came a voice. A heavy green hand clapped down on Daedalus's shoulder. He felt spittle on his cheek. 'Having a tiff, are we? Loversh quarrel?'

Daedalus closed his eyes and groaned. He half-turned in his chair to see a very drunk entari in a crumpled suit looming in his face.

'Whas' matter, friend?' the entari slurred. 'Maybe you should pick someone a bit closer to home next time. Humans bit... bit gross. Not for us. Shouldn't mix. Isn't that right, girl?' He leaned around Daedalus to peer at Erin. 'What's your name?'

Daedalus heard a scraping of chair legs as Erin pushed her seat out.

'You're drunk,' said Erin clearly, trying to be sober. 'I'm gonna – I'll pretend I didn't hear you.' Daedalus looked at her. She didn't look like she was pretending anything. He held up a palm to her.

'Don't,' he said to her, which was a mistake.

The look Erin gave him then surprised him. He'd known she had a temper, but this was different. There was anger there. Real anger. Daedalus didn't know if it was the alcohol or – wait, it was probably the alcohol. Was it? The drink, it always showed your true self. Self. Self? They shouldn't be drinking so much. Aggro was still out there. Had they actually lost him? Why had he told Erin they were safe? They weren't. He could be right here. Watching them. Daedalus realised he'd lost his train of thought. Then he realised Erin had pushed past him. He turned.

'You don't like mixing, is that right?' Erin said, looking up at the drunk entari. Even sat down, he towered over her.

'Look at you!' he said. 'Hah, you're so short. Tiny girl. Why are you so short?'

Erin punched him. It was clumsy, but angry, and it knocked him off his chair. On his knees, he grabbed at the counter and lifted himself back up, swearing.

'You little –'

Erin, who had already been turning back to Daedalus, spun around and swung at the entari with both right hands, one of which was still holding her glass. It caught him in the side of the head and shattered, splashing his face with red fluid and knocking him back to the floor. Someone nearby was yelling. Erin stood over the entari, staring at her hand, which was bleeding.

Daedalus looked from one to the other as his brain sluggishly caught up with what was happening. He caught one of her elbows. Then he was struck by the bizarre thought that she had a lot of them, and probably wasn't afraid to use them.

'Wait –' he said.

Erin raised her foot. '*You're* little!' she said. Her heel slammed into the man's belly and he curled up, groaning.

Daedalus looked to the bar. The landlord was speaking quickly into a phone and staring at them.

'Erin –'

'What?'

'We should go.'

He shrugged off his coat and threw it over her head, and, covering his face with a hand, bundled her, struggling, out of the bar and into the street.

Daedalus kept walking, pushing her ahead of him, until he judged they were far enough away. No drones buzzed overhead, and the crowds thickened as night fell and people flooded out of the elevators and into the bars, of which there were many. She threw off his coat.

'That thing smells,' she said. She laughed, but there was a loud edge in her voice.

Neon signs were starting to flicker on, flooding the front walls of bars and nightclubs with violet light. The environment conditioners were running at full capacity, filling the tall overhead spaces with wispy artificial clouds.

'Next bar,' she said.

'No – hang on. What the hell was that?'

Erin tossed his coat back at him. 'Why don't you fight?' she said. 'Why don't you stick up for yourself?'

'I *do* –'

'No you don't,' she said, 'y'don't even make sense! One minute you're glassing someone twice your size, th' next you're standing there letting some creep spray spit all over your face.'

Daedalus took a step back, thrown. 'Why are you so angry?'

'He said I was small!'

'But... you *are* small.'

'Yeah, but he said it like it was a bad thing.'

'It doesn't take much to set you off.'

'No. You're a coward, that's it.'

'Shut *up*.'

'You are, though!' She hit him in the chest. 'Come on, hit me back!'

'No.'

'I'll show you –' Erin pulled back a fist and threw it, but overbalanced and fell forward into Daedalus's knees, then onto the ground. People glanced her way, a few laughed, but they kept walking.

'Oh for the love of –' Daedalus crouched down and reached for her hand, only to find the world tipping sideways as she grabbed his arm, rolled over and threw him onto the cobblestones. He cried out in surprise. Then she was kneeling on his chest, all four arms held high in triumph.

'I'm th' captain now,' she said.

A strange noise came from Daedalus's throat.

Erin stared down at him. 'Was that a *giggle?*'

'No,' he grunted. 'Now get off me. Let's go. Next bar.'

'This is fun,' she said, clambering off and helping him up. 'I'm fun. I didn't know I was fun.'

A light drizzle was falling, and icy droplets ran down Daedalus's neck. Water filled the slits between paving slabs, flowing to the sides of the street to form tiny rivers between the closed shopfronts and the thickening night-time crowds. Pinpricks of light played across the wet roadside, adding to the general mess of colour as the inner decks of Taxos came to life. The sharp chill in the air was sobering them up slightly, so Erin and Daedalus didn't knock anyone over on their way to the elevators. They passed beneath a large chrome sign. A rusted metal man hung precariously out the window above, staring intently out at the thick mass of people flooding out of the elevator doors. The burning cyan of his eyes caught Daedalus's attention for a moment, before the fugue fell over his senses again. In this floaty state of half-concentration he found himself absorbing details like water into a sponge. Faces, postures, profiles of the people around him flowed freely into his brain and out again. Drunkard by the planter, spoiling for a fight. Coward rushing somewhere, head bowed and eyes darting back and forth. Mugger lurking in the shadows off to the right. Pair of students venturing below decks – nervous, one probably showing off to the other. Young man in a good coat: undercover police.

Daedalus pushed Erin gently into the elevator, steering her away from the rowdy petradons on the far side.

The elevator groaned and lumbered into action. The heavy doors slid shut and the broad steel platform began to descend. Daedalus turned to Erin, who was looking up the open lift-shaft. It ran all the way to the outermost deck, where the *Crow* was berthed. From here you could look out and see all the way to space. Erin's face had the serene look of someone who, assisted by drink, has forgotten to be afraid. Her anger was clear. Daedalus recognised bitterness in the lines of her face, violence bubbling away just under the surface, and on top of that she was lying to him. When she spoke about her mother he saw her tell – a defensive little flinch in her shoulders – but he didn't understand. Daedalus had sunk low, and was well past the point where he cared to judge others. This was useful, because it meant most people saw no need to lie to him about their crimes. This girl lied. Why?

He tried to ignore the hot smell of sweat and drink.

Then he noticed a different smell. Sharp. Gunpowder? No. Vanilla? It stung his memory. For an instant, Daedalus Mole was somewhere else, and someone else. A woman in an aviator jacket and huge round sunglasses laughed in the back of a truck, rock dust in her hair and a yellow scarf flying in the cold air. Daedalus remembered tension in his cheeks and the sound of friends.

The elevator jolted. The smell disappeared back under the general fog. Daedalus was drunk and wet and standing in a gallery of faces. The doors opened onto another busy street. There were no closed shopfronts here; just rows and rows of bars and nightclubs stacked on top of each other, connected by zig-zagging walkways which groaned under the weight of drunken partygoers. The rowdy petradons flowed out of the lift first, followed by their slightly squashed fellow passengers. Erin and Daedalus emerged into a colourful, bustling square with a big neon fountain.

'Hey. Stop for a minute.' He reined her in by the upper elbow.

'What's up, skipper?'

'Don't call me that. Look, I've got a proposition for you.'

'Oh,' she said, scratching her squashed nose. 'What is it?'

Daedalus stalled for a moment.

'Mole?'

Erin's jacket made her look bigger, and her eyes almost looked like dark sunglasses in the dim light. Daedalus took a deep breath, then spoke.

'You can't stay here,' he said. 'You might not realise it, but there's something... very... ' he gestured vainly in the air between them, clenching his fists, '... wrong... with the world.'

'Well, *yeah*,' she said, 'everything's screwed, that's obvious.'

'No, you don't... ' he placed a hand on his face, breathing hard. 'Erin, these last few years... you don't understand. There are laws. You don't just *duck* the Census. You're unregistered. Do you know what that means?'

'No.'

'It's amazing you haven't been caught already, but it's only a matter of time. You need to get away from here, and... '

Erin frowned at him.

'... I need a co-pilot.'

'What?'

'I can't keep flying the *Crow* by myself. Not really. Ellen thinks it's bad for me, and I think... ' he tailed off, grappling with something. 'You can't afford another pilot. We've burnt through most of your cash in half a night of drinking, and you won't get a cheap flight off Taxos. I don't know where we're going, and you know even less. The only crewmate I have is a computer that wants me dead, and eventually she's going to get what she wants.

'You can't survive in this universe alone. Not for long, anyway. Sooner or later someone or something will kill you, or the thinking will turn you on yourself.'

There was a pause. People flowed all around them, bumping and jostling in their own little worlds.

'What's your proposition?' Erin said.

'I need a crew. You're a fast learner and you lack the cunning to stab me in the back. Plus, you've got four arms and your own sword.'

Daedalus awkwardly stuck his hand out.

'A crew?' Erin's face was written all over with something very strong and very confused.

'Nothing official. I can't pay you properly. It's not fun work.' Daedalus could almost hear the *Crow* screaming at him to stop. 'It's probably temporary.'

They stood like that for a moment, Daedalus's hand outstretched, Erin stock-still, facing him. Suddenly, her face split into a wide grin and she slapped one of her hands into his.

'Can I call you skipper?'

'Absolutely not ever.'

'Roger that, cap.'

'Don't make me regret this.'

'Absolutely not ever.' Erin grinned. She let go of his hand and clumsily shoved him towards the nearest pub. 'I'm a space adventurer! Come on, let's go celebrate.'

A long way away, in a very cold place, space rippled in satisfaction. Something red glistened in the dark, pulsing and tensing as it stirred from something. Then, slowly, it extended a strange thread into the distance.

This bar was packed. While far less hectic than the clubs near the elevator, it was busier and noisier than the quiet venue they'd just left. Rock music thrummed in the air. It struggled to be heard over white noise but no-one seemed to mind. Three entari worked the bar, snatching up bottles, pouring out neon liquids, and violently shaking cocktails in metal cylinders. Their hands were a blur as they worked, drawing appreciative cheers from the punters gathered round. The heat and the noise clouded Daedalus's senses. He soon gave up trying to get a read on the place and let Erin drag him up to the bar. Her spirits had definitely brightened. The sea of rough-looking drinkers all around her barely seemed to make an impression as she elbowed her way between two seated patrons – easily twice her size – and hopped up to sit on the bar, yelling for service. Daedalus sidled up behind her.

'No more fighting,' he said.

She waved his concerns away, clapping her hand on the shoulder of a very large person sat next to her.

'You're not gonna fight me, are ya?' she asked. He turned and smiled with yellow teeth. His fur was shaved into a spiky white pattern across his head.

'Probly not,' he said. 'You're pretty scary-lookin'.'

His voice made Daedalus think of pebbles in a blender, but his wide, wonky face seemed friendly enough. Daedalus shrugged and turned his back, keeping watch on the space behind them.

'Just a beer,' he said. 'Driving.'

The clientele seemed mostly to comprise young station workers. Half of them were still in their white Taxos work uniforms. There were a fair few entari, but the majority were garani or various other lowlife races. There was a large gaggle of tall, sharp-featured avarin in the corner, their leathery, angular faces bent inward as they conversed with a quick-tongued chittering. Daedalus could see the bright, loud colours painted on the exoskeletons of a couple of stossven dancers flailing about in the middle of the dancefloor.

Daedalus almost relaxed. Then he noticed the group of rowdy petradons from the elevator. They were all crowded into a booth, cursing at each other loudly enough to be heard over the thumping noise of the dancefloor. As he watched, one of them made a violent motion with his fist and his companions burst into laughter, banging their pint glasses on the table. Daedalus noted a long red tattoo spiralling down his left arm. They looked muscular, even for petradons.

'Great,' he murmured over his shoulder, 'all the bars on this bloody boat and we pick the same one as the heavyball team.'

'What?' Erin cried to the bartender. 'Whiskey *and* rum?'

Daedalus stood still and tried not to nudge anyone. It wasn't long before he found another drink thrust into his hand by his eager new co-pilot. He held it up to his eye. Fluorescent yellow. He didn't ask. Erin laughed and clinked her glass against his before taking a sip. She managed almost a mouthful before her crest suddenly splayed upwards and she spluttered bright liquid all over herself.

'Wow,' she gasped, drawing in deep breaths of air. 'Ow ow aaargh.'

Daedalus peered into the lurid depths of his glass, but it was reluctant to reveal its secrets.

'What's this made of?' he asked. 'Mistakes?'

'Ah ah ah aaaargh,' she said.

Daedalus closed his eyes and took a sip of his own. It tasted like pineapples and battery acid.

Lovely, he tried to say. 'Lurghfurhk,' he actually said, as his tongue went on strike. It swelled in his mouth and he struggled for breath, while Erin made grating noises in her throat.

The other big person beside Erin pushed their stool sharply backwards.

Panic began to build in the pit of his stomach, but before he could do a thing about it he felt a huge, heavy hand crash down on the flat of his back.

'Hold still,' said a deep, harsh voice. The hand was joined by another on his neck and he felt his spine forced upwards, into a straight line. The rough grip forced his head back, and a pair of fingers seized his tongue, stretching it out of his mouth. He felt his airways suddenly clear. After a few excruciating seconds, his tongue shrank back to normal size, and the fingers released it. He fell away, coughing and heaving at the taste of leathery skin and scales crusted with dry soil. Erin hacked on her knees next to him, but his rescuer did not move to help her. After one great, ragged cough she drew breath again and pushed herself sharply to her feet, facing the heavy figure behind him.

Daedalus turned to see them. A petradon, clearly. Big and broad, muscles tightly wound around short limbs, running into great armoured fists. Lizardlike skin, covered in patches with hard scales which coalesced into thick, heavy plates with an almost metallic sheen – draped in what looked like a black military cloak over a long, dark blue tunic. There was no insignia. Bright yellow eyes set in a wide, flat, face; shielded under crystalline shells. Female, judging by the broad hips and shorter arms. Daedalus noticed her head was misshapen. The dark plates on the top of her skull looked warped; bent outwards, and the skin around them was oddly pale and worn, shot through with long, dark cracks. Then he saw the spines. A field of white pins punctured her scalp from the inside, so that her head bristled with inch-tall stalagmites. Her face was expressionless as she stared back at them. After a long moment, she turned and disappeared into the crowd of people, who – Daedalus only now noticed – were laughing and pointing at the two of them. As the deformed woman pushed through the laughter quickly abated, to be replaced with whispering and open looks of distaste.

'Mole?' Erin asked, her voice still slightly wheezy. 'Who was that?

'I don't know. You alright? What just happened?'

'Bartender said it was pretty strong. I didn't really listen,' she said. 'Sorry.'

Daedalus realised his glass was gone, and his drink was distributed all over the floor. A scowling machine rolled past him to sweep up the shards.

'How come you held onto yours?'

'Iuno. I'm just better at drinking than you.' Erin looked at him. 'Are you okay?'

'Fine. Give me your wallet, I need a new drink.'

Erin frowned. 'Aren't you gonna say thanks?'

'Thanks. Gimme.'

'Not to me,' Erin tilted her head. 'To her.'

'You can, if you like.' Daedalus moved to go, but Erin caught his arm.

'She just saved your life.'

'I was only choking.'

'My biology isn't that hot, but I'm pretty sure humans need to breathe.'

Daedalus wrested his elbow away. 'Petradons don't like humans,' he said.

'Neither do entari, but this one's on your crew, and *she* says we should all try to get along a bit better, or there'll be no more drink.'

He looked her in the eye. She stared right back, swaying slightly.

'You're more trouble than you're worth,' he said, prodding her in the chest. He pushed past her and vanished into the crowd.

'That's a neat trick,' she muttered, following. She could just about dip and sidle against the flow of people, but she bumped elbows and spilled booze as she went. 'Dammit Mole!' she yelled, unheard. 'Show me how to do that!'

Daedalus moved away from the bar and back again, ghosting between two punters, coming to a rest beside the hunched figure of his rescuer. She stood, apparently alone, nursing a large tankard of dark liquid. A bartender whipped past with three bottles and a tumbler. Daedalus caught his arm.

'Two horizons, please.'

'Certainly. That'll be –'

'My chaperone's paying. Girl in the green jacket.'

The bartender smiled. 'Of course,' he said, dumping the bottles and going after a new one. The petradon raised her head slightly, glancing at him, before returning to her position. Daedalus drummed his fingers on the countertop. He opened his mouth to speak a couple of times, but faltered at each. Finally, she took pity on him.

'Can I help you?'

'Er. That was… er – thanks.'

There was a long pause.

'No problem,' she said. 'Stick to human drinks in future.'

'I'll remember that.'

'Hmph.' She returned to her drink. Daedalus observed out of the corner of his eye. All petradons hunched. Their torsos were too heavy for much else. Rumours went around that they were natural quadrupeds, but few dared say so in public. Then again, Daedalus had once heard a rumour that humans reproduced by shedding toes, which could be planted in the ground like seeds. Some mysteries, he had then decided, weren't worth solving.

This petradon hunched too, but in a different way. It reminded Daedalus of the way Erin had hunched when they first met – fearful and anxious, trying to make herself smaller. He could clearly see her skull from here. There were a few spots where the bony spines had broken, split into sharp curves, like broken glass. Jagged shards of plate stuck up across her forehead, forced outwards by the growth.

'What's that you're drinking? Looks rough,' he said, proffering conversation. She looked up suddenly, as if surprised to remember he was there. She raised the glass for him to see.

'Pitch.'

'Huh. Having a party?'

'No,' she paused. 'Helps with the... ' She paused, then gestured to her head.

'It hurts?'

'Yeah.'

'... Right.' Daedalus fidgeted. 'Sorry about that.'

She waved a hand in acknowledgement. The bartender bustled back to where they sat and set down two pale beers in front of Daedalus before promptly removing himself. He heard Erin yell angrily from somewhere nearby. Daedalus placed a smile on his face. 'So,' he started again, 'do you... er... do you have a name?'

'Do you?' She tipped a mouthful down her throat without swallowing.

'... Mole. D– Captain Mole.'

'Ram,' she said. 'Just Ram.'

Erin elbowed her way through. 'Hey, you gotta teach me – oh. Hello.'

Ram turned her broad, flat face towards Erin.

'Hi,' she said. 'I'm Erin. Thanks for rescuing my useless friend.'

Ram looked from one to the other, shifting in her seat.

'Ram.'

'Just Ram?'

'Just Ram.' She glanced at Daedalus. 'Your pupils are dilated.'

'What?'

'Hang on.' Ram pressed the back of two cold fingers against his wrist. He winced.

'What are you doing?'

'Humans should not drink sunshine. Your pulse is erratic.' Ram withdrew her hand and lifted her tankard again. 'You are about to vomit. Expect four to eight hours of nausea and muscle pain.'

Erin sidled up to Ram and peered at Daedalus. 'He looks alright to me,' she said.

Ram frowned at her. 'You are drunk.'

'Am not.'

Daedalus made a noise. They both looked at him.

'Gimme a minute.' He turned and made for the toilets. A moment later he ducked back to the bar, grabbed his beer and made for the toilets again. Erin took up his place at the bar, hopping up onto the vacated stool.

'Soooo,' she said, 'what do you do?'

'Navy.' Ram cleared her throat with a harsh sound. 'Until last week.'

'How about this week?'

'Not much.'

'Huh.' Erin cocked her head. 'What's that like?'

'… Disorientating.'

Erin reached for the beer and tipped it into her mouth. To her surprise, it tasted good. Like fizzy bread. Upon this startling revelation, she glugged down half the glass in one. 'Wow.' She drew breath and expelled it in a confused muddle. 'That's nice.'

'Cheers.' Ram held her tankard out to Erin, who clinked her glass against it.

Daedalus slammed the stall door shut behind him and fell against the cubicle wall, gasping for breath. A vein in his forehead pulsed angrily. He'd had alcohol-induced migraines before, and they were never pleasant. Sometimes they would last all night. He groaned, ready to lean over the toilet if it got any worse. All he could do was stand and wait for the pain to subside. Another wave of it washed over him, bringing a red curtain over his eyes, obscuring the grime around him. The walls fell away, along with the pungent smells that hung in the air. Then the air vanished too, leaving only the red.

The pair at the bar kept on talking, oblivious. Erin's arms waved and gestured excitedly, as if compensating for Ram's hunched silence. Slowly, though, she was unfurling; turning to face Erin and straightening up slightly. A couple of times Erin caught a glimpse of a smile tugging at the muscles in her torn face. The way her eyes glinted and gleamed under the crystal shells fascinated her. They swapped stories – Erin drunkenly recounting the steps that led her here, Ram shaking her head in disbelief and reeling off the names of ships she'd been stationed on since graduation, which Erin – to Ram's confusion – seemed to find riveting.

Daedalus, meanwhile, writhed on the bathroom floor, jaw stretched painfully wide in a silent scream. After a few stretched-out moments of timeless pain, the red curtain lifted and the agony rolled over into a dull ache. He drew a couple of very deep breaths before shakily pushing himself to his feet, keeping his hands clear of the slimy floor. He rested his elbows on his knees and sank slowly onto the toilet seat.

I AM SORROW.

Daedalus didn't move.

PAIN IS NOT PART OF THE PROCESS.

Daedalus listened intently for the sound of rustling clothes outside his cubicle. There was silence.

YOU SHOULD NOT FIGHT IT.

Daedalus immediately stood up and strode out of the bathroom until loud dance music drowned out the voice in his head.

CAN YOU HEAR –

A chorus of easy-thinking dance lyrics emptied Daedalus's brain of all higher thought.

The small portion of it still capable of goal-oriented behaviour judged this to be an improvement over hearing voices in his head. It then decided to sober up as soon as possible. He pushed his way to the bar to get a glass of water.

Meanwhile, the train of Erin's conversation – as drunkenly driven trains often do – had hopped several rails.

'No you're not!' Erin said, with the weaving, sincere conviction of a good friend in the early hours.

'I appreciate what you are trying to say, but my condition is quite visible.' There was a note of amusement in Ram's voice. 'You do not have to –'

'– I just like your face! You shouldn't not like your face. It's the only one you've –' Erin burped, '– you've got!'

'That is not a concept I –'

'Shut up, I like your face!'

'I… thank you?'

Erin had almost reached the bottom of her glass. 'Good. We're friends now, then.'

'If you say so,' said Ram, raising her tankard. Erin clacked hers against it and slid sideways on her stool, almost falling.

'Whoops,' she said, 'trouble now. We're not allowed to drink unless – unless we fight for it. Hah. Ha haaa.'

Ram looked at her curiously. 'Sorry?' she said.

'Thas' alright, wasn't your fault. Done now anyway, I'm free! A free lady. So free.' Her crest flittered and she gazed at a point somewhere between Ram's face and her chest. 'What are you doing tonight?'

'Nothing,' Ram said. 'I was going to stay here until closing.'

'When does this place close?'

'Er.' Ram scratched her cheek. 'Tomorrow.'

'Oh. Then what?'

'Hey,' came a heavy voice. Erin's head turned slowly around. She saw the tattoo first. Long red spirals, daubed clumsily down the plating of one muscular arm. He was flanked by three grinning friends, with similar red markings. Ram didn't move. The petradon in front took a step forward. 'You're Navy.'

'Who're you?' said Erin, staring up at him from her tall bar stool.

The petradon ignored her. Ram stared ahead, expression blank.

One hand fell slowly away from Erin's glass and started pressing against her jacket, searching for a hard spot. There, right where she left it.

'I asked you a question,' said Erin. She stopped drumming her fingers on her knee.

'I'm not talking to you.'

Ram didn't say anything.

'Right,' said Erin. She raised her glass and started to drink.

The leader slapped a hand down on Ram's shoulder. 'You're on your own,' he said. 'I don't see any shipmates in this bar, do you? I wonder why that is?'

Ram still didn't speak.

'Worm?' he murmured, leaning to say it in Ram's ear. 'Turnworm?'

There was a snigger.

Erin saw Ram's shoulders sag; she sighed quietly into her glass and stayed quiet.

'I don't think she heard you, Morg,' grunted the pale-skinned one on his right.

'Yeah,' laughed the shorter one on the left. 'Might be the plague's made her deaf.'

Erin bristled. She felt her crest tense up, straining to extend fully. Ram just stared blankly into space. Her eyes were tiny, still glints of yellow.

The glass drained completely into Erin's throat.

The aggressor leaned in close, curled his fingers under the plate on Ram's scalp, and pulled her head backwards.

'I said –' he started.

Erin slammed her glass down on the bar and hopped off her stool, rising to her full height, which was about four-and-a-half feet. Morg let go of Ram's head and looked down at her.

'Does she *look* alone to you?' she said.

Her words were followed by four long seconds in which the blaring music was punctuated only by hostile glares. Ram turned to stare, first at Erin, then at Morg, then back to Erin. Her expression was particularly inscrutable.

Then Morg laughed, so Erin took her glass and flung it at his head.

Morg flinched as it burst harmlessly against his faceplate, scattering glass everywhere. The people around them variously yelped and recoiled.

Morg gave a deep, sonorous growl. Onlookers started moving slowly away. His friends moved up to stand shoulder-to-shoulder with him.

'Oi, what's going on over 'ere?' came a very loud voice. The spiky white-haired man pushed through the crowd to stand next to the petradon. He still smiled, but there was a stern edge to his face now.

'You're not doing any trouble in my bar.' He turned to look at Morg. 'You're lucky I let you in 'ere after last time, Morg.'

'No problems,' he said. 'This girl was just about to apologise… for assaulting me.'

'Is 'at so?' He turned to face Erin. 'Right, get on wi'it then.'

Erin looked Morg up and down. That swagger. The easy confidence. The unchallenged contempt. She seethed. She rooted through her memory quickly, looking for something specific she'd seen used a few times before. After a long moment, she found it. Erin outstretched a clenched fist to the giant standing in front of her. Then, as Ram watched, she slowly raised one finger.

Morg shoved the spiky landlord out of the way, hurling him to the floor, and loomed over Erin, cracking his gigantic knuckles. The growl rolled into a rumble. Something like regret flitted across Erin's mind. Her fingers crept beneath her coat, grasping the hilt of her sword.

'I gave you a chance, you little stain. Remember that when you're in the ground.' His friends had fanned out, separating the two of them from the agitated crowd. The bartenders had vanished. Erin held still, trying to steady herself as her heart started to thump.

She didn't see the first blow coming. It knocked into her face from the side, staggering her. She lost grip of her sword as her hands instinctively flew up to shield her eyes. Her halfway-healed bruise shot through with pain. Morg stomped towards her and she side-stepped, ducking under another swing, falling face-first into the second blow. Suddenly everything was a tinny ringing, and her head was numb. She became vaguely aware that she was on her knees, the shock juddering up her spine and making her feel sick. Erin could hear bells, and laughter. A hard, grit-encrusted hand slapped down on the back of her head, pressing the spines of her crest against her skull. They flexed and strained, threatening to snap.

Then a sound of splintering wood. Yells of pain, and a sudden commotion all around her. Glass shattering. The hand was twisted away, forced to let her go. She fell away, scrambling backwards to avoid the massive body that was thrown to the floor in front of her. Another of the gang charged forward, but Ram's fist caught him in the face, flooring him with a sound like crash helmets being smashed together. People were running for the exits and the landlord could be heard yelling from somewhere in the room. The two tattooed petradons still standing backed towards the door, hurling insults at Ram as they went. Ram just stood still, arms held stiffly in front of her at waist height. Morg struggled to get to his feet. He managed to lift his torso off the floor before Ram ducked down and knocked his head back against the tiles with a straight punch. It cracked loudly. She looked at Erin. Erin still couldn't read the expression on Ram's face, but her scaly brow was furrowed.

Then a more familiar hand seized Erin by the arm and hoisted her to her feet.

'You alright? Can you walk?' Daedalus's face hovered in her vision.

'I... yeah,' she managed. 'I can walk.'

Daedalus glanced at Ram, who said nothing.

'How about run?'

'I... ' Erin's knees almost gave out. 'I don't –'

'I can.' Ram stumped forward and placed a gnarled hand on Erin's other shoulder. With a grunt, she lifted the tiny entari into her arms and gently hoisted her across her back. She turned to Daedalus. 'Concussed,' she said. 'I assume you have a ship.'

Daedalus looked at her for a moment, then nodded.

'Infirmary?' she asked.

He nodded again.

'Lead the way,' she gestured politely. 'Quite fast.'

He hesitated, watching the petradon closely. Erin groaned. A whine from above made him jump, and he looked up. A blinking red light marked a police drone.

'Fine,' he said, 'let's get.'

Four minutes later, Morg felt himself being roughly shaken awake. He groaned in protest as his head flared with pain.

'This one's conscious!' yelled the figure standing over him. Morg could see only a black visor inset in a pure white helmet. The figure wore white armour covering its whole body. One sage-green stripe ran down the side of its chest. Four arms.

'What's that?' came another voice. 'Gang tattoo?'

'No,' grunted Morg. 'Heavyball team.'

'Troublemaker,' came a third voice. 'Tag him. Her. Whatever.' There was laughter. 'Can never tell with these lowlifes.'

'Tag... what? No.' Morg struggled through the haze in his head. 'No!'

'Resisting arrest. Treason of the peace. I don't like his face. Send him downstairs to the reclaimer. Forget the tag.'

'You... no! Don't –' Morg felt a sharp jab under his chest-plate, then ice filling his veins. Dreamless sleep engulfed him.

Two hours later, in a restricted government building deep in the industrial district, forty-six bodies were incinerated. Two hundred and twelve kilograms of chitinous plate were recovered from the chamber for recycling, charred skin still clinging to the underside.

Thirty minutes later, a disgruntled production-line worker in a white one-size-fits-all uniform complained to his partner that this red stuff was a pain in the neck to scrub away.

Two days later, a brand-new light cruiser was unberthed from Taxos. It set off for a classified location past the Frontier. A small red ink-stain remained on one of the starboard hull plates. As it passed into the channel leaving Highdust the plate was seared clean, the ink tearing into dissociated particles.

A thread snapped.

Disturbances surged from Taxos like a heavy tide. Two beings were aware of this. One was a person sitting naked in a faraway cave. The other, which could hardly be called a person at all, hung in the dark a good deal further off. Both creatures observed. Both were concerned. The latter tugged gently at a number of threads around it, the other ends connected to much smaller things that were very far away.

The *Crow* fell surreptitiously away from the huge docking arm and into open space. Her main engines – two huge cylinders mounted on the rear side of the hull – flared brightly as she pushed away from the station and accelerated, cutting a long, curved line across Highdust.

'Is she alright?' Daedalus asked. He stepped down from the staircase into the little infirmary. Ram was bent over the table, Erin's tiny body obscured by her bulk.

'Scrapes across the face. Large contusion, but the jaw is not broken. Crest intact.' Ram gently tilted Erin's head to the side, inspecting the dark spot above her cheekbone. 'Minor concussion.' Daedalus heard a murmur as she leaned in close. Ram sniffed. 'There was another bruise here. This one has been through the wars.'

'And you?' Daedalus probed.

Ram paused. 'What wars are left to fight?' Her voice had the harsh, grinding quality that all petradon voices had, but Daedalus thought he discerned a note of regret. 'We have peace. In the inner systems, at least.'

'You did a pretty decent job back there, though.'

'This one was in danger.'

'So?'

Ram turned to face him. In the bright light of the infirmary the curves of her twisted face were clear.

'Are you toying with me?' she asked.

'It's just weird, is all. I know what the Republic police are like. You're in the military, you probably know better than me.' Ram stared straight through him. Daedalus snapped his fingers at her. 'Hey. Hey! Fighting on Taxos is *illegal*. And you've got a memorable face.'

'I know,' she said.

'Then why get involved?'

There was a silence. Ram turned back to Erin, lying passed-out on the gurney. She touched a gnarled hand to her head.

'She... ' Ram coughed. She became aware of her hand, and pulled it away. 'She was kind.'

Daedalus said nothing for a few moments. He watched her for insincerity, but saw none. Her shoulders still sagged. Erin was not like other entari, that was clear now – he had never seen one twinning absurd selflessness with such bullheaded aggression. Now it seemed that Ram was not like other petradons. While most feared to show the smallest sign of weakness, she bared her illness like she didn't care at all; she sided with an entari in a fight, and openly helped an out-of-place human. She stood and spoke clearly. Daedalus saw no mystery in Ram, and no hint that she had any proficiency whatsoever in hiding herself.

For a moment he wondered why Erin had felt the need to jump to her defence. *Keen sense of justice*, he thought. *Or overcompensation.*

'Well,' he grunted, 'I guess we're stuck with each other for the moment. Make yourself comfortable. Ask Erin if you need anything – this whole mess is her fault, anyway.'

'... Thank you.'

'Not like we have any need for a medic on this well-behaved vessel.'

Ram's shoulders twitched.

Daedalus reached into the neck of Erin's jacket and pulled out her sword, carrying it at arm's length to the staircase. 'I'll put this in a room for Erin. There's quarters all along the corridor. Settle yourself in for now. I'll be in the cockpit if you need anything.'

He about-turned and disappeared back up the rickety staircase. Ram straightened Erin's neck with one great hand to alleviate muscle strain. The girl groaned at the contact, but didn't resist.

'Thank you.' Ram's voice reverberated unpleasantly in the tiny room. She regretted speaking as soon as she heard it back, and turned to climb out of the infirmary.

'Any... time... ' came a mumble from the gurney. Ram paused for a moment, before stumping off down the corridor in search of a room that would fit. After a few moments, Erin began to snore.

The sound rang through the whirring ducts above her, carrying up to the vent in the cockpit, where Daedalus sat watching clouds of dust whip past the window. His coat hung from the back of the pilot's seat, gently flapping in the breeze from the vent. He could see the channel entrance far ahead of them, a glimmering field of specks, appearing and disappearing as ships arrived and left. The monitor to his left listed all the nearby ships the *Crow* could see: mostly big haulers and passenger ships, with a few police vessels running wide circular patrols across Highdust. They constantly disappeared from the list to be replaced by others as they drifted in and out of range. The *Crow* could only see the largest ones at this distance, but she interpreted everything else onto the flat map for him. He considered for a moment, then dragged the course line into a wide curve, steering comfortably clear of the police patrols. After the scene on Taxos, it would be careless to assume there wasn't a warrant out for them. He and Erin could probably pass for innocents – once she'd woken up, anyway – but he doubted Ram would go unrecognised.

'I can't believe she's still here,' hissed the *Crow*. 'And you've picked up another one? You know you can't trust them, don't you? And they can't trust you, either. Get rid of them.'

Daedalus said nothing, rubbing the locket with one thumb.

'What's the matter with you, lately? You've changed. I don't like it. You ungrateful, arrogant little –'

The *Crow* continued berating him until he hit a purple switch on the dash, cutting her off and locking out the autopilot. Daedalus pulled the keyboard out from under the console and started typing, swapping out the map for a camera-view of the infirmary. Erin looked fine through the grainy image, although her face was already darkening with a fresh bruise. Ram had left, apparently.

Daedalus felt odd. Not himself. He reached for a chipped mug beneath the dash and filled it with water. The familiar gurgle of the pipes relaxed him a little. It wasn't like him to trust strangers. Not in the slightest. Yet here he was, carrying passengers. A memory bubbled up. Not just passengers. Crew. Or the makings of one, anyway. He took a swig of water. The dusty taste reminded him of Aphiemi.

The mug almost slipped from his grasp, but he twitched it upright again. A few moments later, he too was snoring loudly. After several minutes Ram stuck her head into the cockpit.

'Mole?' she asked.

He belched and kept snoring. Ram wandered off in search of a room, and within ten minutes the crew of the *Crow* were all passed-out drunk, concussed, or asleep.

Fishing

Daedalus
Between

Daedalus stood on a wide, flat plain. The sky was dark grey, the ground an angry red. Beneath his bare feet he felt warm rock, and there was a whipping of wind-blown sand around his ankles. When he looked for his body, he found that he was naked. He heard a great roaring all around him, like a crashing river, but he saw no water. Erin stood some way ahead of him, facing away, her body wreathed in billowing orange flame. She stared resolutely into the distance.

'Hey!' he yelled. Either the wind took his words, or she did not pay him any attention. He tried to go to her, but the distance between them only stretched further with every step he took. 'Erin!'

She Will Not Come

Daedalus stopped walking. He turned. Beside him was a great green eye, narrow and catlike. He stared, and it stared right back. He couldn't focus on its body; it was set into a black fog. Nothing happened for a while. Then:

'Who are you?'

That Is The Wrong Question

Daedalus thought for a moment.

'What are you?'

There was a pause.

You Are Not Very Good At This

Daedalus wondered what Erin would say.

'That's rude.'

I Am Sorrow

Another pause.

'Why are you here?'

I Am Not Here

'Where are you, then?'

Far

'You're far away?'

Beneath A Blackened Sky

Daedalus looked around. The blasted red landscape came into focus. There were giant craters everywhere. He stood at the foot of a great red mountain, the summit of which was shrouded in dark cloud. Lightning arced across the sky, never striking the ground. It just streaked across the underbelly of the clouds, casting blue flashes on the ground below.

'What is this place?'

Memory

'Of what? Whose memory?'

Of Consumption It Is Mine

'Consumption?'

Yes

'By what?'

That Is the Wrong Question

Daedalus thought for a moment.

'Of what?'

Patterns Structure Everything

'I'm still here.'

Everything before. Other Places. Other Gardens.

'You're not communicating very well.'

I am Try – It Has Been time long a – *a long time since I spoke.*

'That's better.'

I am thank. The last person did not understand me. I think I was too loud.

'Am I dreaming?'

Yes. With me. I have a message and you will not listen awake.

'Go on, then.'

Come to me. I have your buried treasure.

'I don't have any treasure.'

The word escapes me. Treasure. Buried. Lost?

'Not ringing any bells, mate.'

Precious? Like. Love. Gone. Bird.

'Where are you getting these from?'

Your mind is a burned ruin, I cannot navigate.

'You – what?'

Crow. I have your lost crow. Come to me. I will return your crow to you.

Then all unravelled, and Daedalus dropped his mug of water on the exposed wiring beneath his feet.

Hanging on Threads

Erin
The Crow

Erin was roughly woken up by the sound of screaming. Her dreams rolled away and she found herself in an unfamiliar white room. Her clothes felt tight and hot, and her skin prickled uncomfortably against the fabric. Erin pushed herself into a sitting position and looked around. Her head was thumping angrily, and her mouth felt like it was full of cotton wool. The reassuring hard splint hidden in her jacket was gone.

'D-ack –' she croaked. There was a sound of angry yelling coming from above. She shook her head, trying to wake up properly. This is a common mistake amongst people new to the dark and twisted magic of the hangover, and her head protested in the only way it could: by hurting more. Through gritted teeth, Erin swung her legs over the edge of the gurney. She dropped to the floor. Struggling through the pounding in her skull, she staggered out into the corridor, and realised she was on board the *Crow*. A petradon was in the corridor too, with what looked like worry scrawled across her face. For a moment Erin couldn't place her. Memories from last night sloshed around in her head and it took a few seconds to fish out the right one. 'Ram. Hi.' Daedalus was cursing loudly upstairs, apparently still alive.

'Are you alright?' Ram said. 'You shouldn't be awake yet.'

'I'm fine,' Erin said. 'Just a headache.'

'I am not surprised.'

Erin rubbed her face. It was swollen, and painful to the touch. 'We should check on the captain. Make sure he hasn't killed himself yet.'

Ram winced. Erin didn't notice, and turned and climbed the staircase, leaving Ram to catch up.

Daedalus was leaning against the cockpit wall, panting and cursing. He looked up as Erin entered.

'You look great,' he said.

'Yeah, yeah, I've heard.' Erin waved him on. 'What happened up here?'

'Spilled my water. Got electrocuted. Business as usual.'

Erin looked at the mess of exposed wiring on the floor, and the smashed pieces of mug that lay scattered around it. 'You're an idiot,' she said.

'Yeah.'

'At least you're alive. Where's my sword?'

'Charming. It's in your room, first on the left.'

'Good. How's the ship?'

Daedalus adopted a grim expression. He looked over his shoulder at the monitor, now displaying a mess of tartan-coloured graphical errors. 'Not great,' he said. 'The control board's fried.' He caressed the locket, which was now slowly pulsing purple light. 'We've got an old one we can stick in, but it'll take a couple hours to boot up.' He rummaged under the dashboard and pulled out a dusty box, withdrew an even dustier circuit board and blew on it. Then he got down on his knees, pulled up a bit of grating and stuck his arm into the floor, making odd guttural noises as he shifted bits around.

Ram stomped in, took in the scene and looked out the window. 'Where are we?'

'Don't know,' said Daedalus from the floor. 'Erin, can you see the channel?'

Erin stepped over him and the exposed wiring to look up, out of the wide, visor-like windscreen. 'It's behind us. Way up there.'

'That's not good,' said Daedalus from the floor.

'Why not?' Erin asked.

'We're blind.' He yanked something out with a *clunk* and a fizzing sound. 'That could be the channel, yeah, but it could also be just about anything. We've been drifting, but there's no way of telling how far.'

'Shouldn't the autopilot have kept us on track?' said Ram.

'I shut it off,' said Daedalus.

'But why?'

Daedalus ignored the question. 'We need to fix this.'

'Right.' Ram looked at Erin. 'So... where are we, then?'

Daedalus jammed the replacement board into the computer and

climbed to his feet, kicking the grate back into place. The dashboard lit up in complex patterns and the screens started scrolling endless lines of green text. 'Don't know.'

He reached for an old metal dial on one of the panels and gave it a twist. White noise filled the cockpit. He listened. 'No shortrange, even. We must have crossed a border. Unmapped space. It's a miracle the heating hasn't given out.'

There was a *bing* from the radio. No-one spoke. Four seconds passed. There were two quick *bing*s.

'Nadir,' said Ram.

'What?' Daedalus looked lost.

There was another *bing*, followed four seconds later by two quick ones.

'That's a nadir signal,' she said. 'The Navy used to use it to mark frontier buoys.'

'We're at the frontier?'

'No.' Ram grimaced. 'The old buoys were decommissioned. We shouldn't be hearing this. No-one uses it anymore.'

'Well, someone does.'

'Evidently.'

Daedalus saw the look on Erin's face.

'No, stop it. You're not allowed to be excited.'

'But... it's *unmapped*!' Her eyes were wide.

'No, no, no! There's nothing out here to map! It's a dead waste with absolutely nothing interesting about it whatsoever, and you're not here to have any kind of adventure except losing power, freezing to death, and floating in space completely alone until someone with even less common sense than you comes along to loot your corpse.'

'Well, something's out there! We should check it out!'

'We're not going anywhere,' Ram grunted, placing a hand on Erin's shoulder, 'until you've had some breakfast.'

'Yeah, I like her idea,' said Daedalus. 'You're hung over, concussed, and you're giving me a blinding headache. Besides,' he sucked his teeth, 'I'm starving.'

Erin started to protest, but she *was* pretty hungry. 'Fine,' she said, 'but that's an adventure right there and I'm not going to forget about it just because of a few head injuries.'

'Glad to hear it,' Daedalus said, stepping past her and into the kitchen, heading for the cupboards. 'We got pastries, coffee, teabags, cereal –' he pulled open a door overhead and was greeted by a cascade of shrink-wrapped long-life sausage rolls. Erin looked at him.

'... I haven't been shopping in a while,' he said.

'We'll have to sort you out when we find somewhere to land,' Erin replied. Daedalus tossed a couple in her direction and she snatched them out of the air with two hands. She turned to Ram. 'Can you eat stuff like this?'

'What is it?' Ram peered at the squashy brown rod in Erin's hand. She looked at Daedalus. 'Meat?'

'Sure,' he shrugged. 'Gotta be at least forty percent. Otherwise they'd have to call them "sausage-flavoured".'

'Oh, go on, then.'

Daedalus chucked her a handful from the pile. They scrunched against her breastplate as she scooped them to her chest. Erin and Ram went to the table and sat on the floor-bolted stools while Daedalus flicked the kettle on. While he rooted around in the cupboards for the coffee jar, Ram struggled with the shrink-wrap. She looked to Erin – who had far nimbler hands – and hastily pulled Erin's roll away from her. She'd been gnawing at it, apparently unaware that the plastic packaging wasn't a savoury glaze.

'Did you just get off the boat?' she asked.

'That's what I said,' Daedalus said over his shoulder.

'No it isn't,' said Erin. 'And no,' she turned back to Ram, 'I'm not. Back home we had –' she raised her voice and directed it at Daedalus '– *real food*.'

'Humans have strange delicacies,' said Ram. 'They need to wrap them in plastic.'

Ram handed it back and Erin stared at it, confused. After a moment she tore the clear skin open and took an experimental nibble of one corner.

'Oh my god,' she said. The nibble quickly turned into a series of delighted chomps. Ram toyed with hers for a moment longer before losing her patience and smashing it in half against the table. She tipped the two halves out of their plastic sheath and wolfed them down before reaching for another.

'Ah,' said Daedalus as he set the boiled kettle down on the table with two mugs and a styrofoam cup. 'I see Erin's discovered MSG.'

'Sho goog, oh my gog,' came her muffled response.

Daedalus chewed on his roll as he spooned coffee from the tub into each cup, filling his own nearly halfway. 'Coffee?'

'Please,' said Ram. Erin just nodded enthusiastically in response to the promise of more delicious new mysteries.

'See, Erin?' he said. '*Food* is all the adventure you need.'

Daedalus tipped water into each cup, filling the room with the not-quite-good-but-good-enough aroma of hot instant coffee.

There was quiet for a while as they worked through the sparse breakfast.

'How's the hangover?' Daedalus asked, not looking at anyone in particular.

'The what?' Erin asked through a mouthful of food.

Ram swallowed another one whole. 'Petradons do not get hang-overs,' she rumbled, 'and I doubt I would notice one.' She gestured at the spines working their way out of her skull. 'One headache is much like another.'

'I didn't know that,' said Daedalus. He took a sip of uncomfortably-hot coffee. 'Another perk of being human, I suppose.' He pointed a finger at Erin. 'You're probably too young.'

'For a headache?' Erin cocked her head, angling her puffy bruise towards him. 'You don't even know my age.'

'Entari tend not to get hangovers either,' said Ram. Daedalus couldn't be sure, but he thought she was smiling. 'Alcohol is only poisonous to humans.' She turned to Erin. 'And yet, funnily enough, you are the biggest consumer of alcohol in the Collective.'

'What, really?' Erin looked at Daedalus. 'I didn't know you had it in you.'

'The species,' Ram said, her shoulders heaving gently in a heavy kind of laugh. 'Humans as a whole. Per person.'

'Well, it's not easy being us,' said Daedalus, feeling oddly stung.

'No,' said Ram, 'I suppose it gets lonely.' She turned to Erin again. 'Did you know humans emotionally imprint on other species? On Earth they kept local fauna in their homes and treated them as children because there were so few other humans around.'

'Hang on, that's not –' Daedalus started.

'Aww!' Erin laughed. 'That's adorable. What else do they do?'

'Nobody knows,' said Ram. 'They didn't keep written records so all we have to go on are a few captured radio signals and TV broad–'

'Just because the Republic doesn't distribute written records,' Daedalus interrupted, 'doesn't mean we didn't keep any. We were around for a long time. You really think we didn't write a single book?'

'One or two, of course,' said Ram, raising a placating hand, 'most civilisations do. Not like the Republic, though. No great works. No encyclopaedias.'

'Sure,' Daedalus shot back, '*all* the good books just happen to have been written by entari. Like half the stuff in the Republic Library wasn't stolen from planets that wouldn't integrate.'

'He likes to rant,' said Erin. 'Let's not get him start– ow!' She clutched the side of her face.

'Try not to move your head too quickly,' said Ram. 'It'll go down in an hour or so.'

'It's fine. A bruise or two doesn't bother me. I've had practice.'

'Practice?' Ram asked, taking her chin gently in a finger to inspect the bruise. 'That sounds bad.'

'Slave ships. Six months.' Ram took her hand away and Erin sniffed at her coffee.

'Oh, yes. You mentioned. Sorry.'

'Nah, s'alright. Not your fault.' She brightened up. 'I'm free now, anyway. Really puts things in perspective.'

'How did you get free, if you don't mind me asking?'

'This guy,' she said, pointing at Daedalus. 'They were talking that day about selling me on, sending me to someone. "Rax", or something. Then this human turns up and mucks the whole thing up, and we've been friends ever since.'

Daedalus raised a finger. '"Friends" is a strong –'

'Wait, "Rax"?' Ram cut in. 'Do you mean… "Wrask"?'

Erin shrugged.

'You know that name?' Daedalus squinted at Ram. 'Wrask?'

'I was Navy. We knew of a Wrask,' Ram scratched her chin. 'You are sure?' she asked Erin.

'Rax, Wrask, yeah, something like that. I dunno. Anyway,' Erin launched back into her story, 'two of the three of these guys went to negotiate and left the last one to guard me. He was tired. They'd been drinking the night before – humans, you know – I looked pretty harmless, so he must have figured he could close his eyes for a minute.'

'And?' Ram prodded.

'Oh, I beat him up,' Erin said. 'Used a wrench. Bit of a mess, but he didn't follow me after that.'

'Temper,' said Daedalus. 'Vicious one, you are.'

'Thas me,' she said through a mouthful of pastry. 'They shouldn't have given me so many hours in the melee pits. You get practice.'

Ram looked at Erin with something approximating pity.

'I hope you've got it out of your system. The last thing we need is another bar fight,' Daedalus said. 'I take it you're feeling better now.'

Erin paused with the mug at her lips, then took a long drink. 'You know what? I am. I don't know what I was expecting, but there's nothing back there for me. I'll figure the whole "life" thing out later. Right now I just want to have some fun. It's been too long since I had fun.'

'You were on Taxos to find something?' Ram asked.

'I ran away from home because I thought there was a place reserved for me somewhere,' Erin answered. 'Turns out there isn't, and even if there was I wouldn't fit in anyway.'

'Oh,' Ram said.

'Yeah,' Erin said.

'Well, never mind,' Ram said. 'Having a place laid out for you is not always so great.'

Erin grinned. 'Thanks.'

Ram's face twisted in what was probably a sad smile.

They finished their slapdash breakfast absorbed in friendly chatter. Erin drank three cups of coffee. Ram ate twelve sausage rolls, and

Daedalus burned his tongue twice more before he felt recovered enough to consider anything other than eating.

'Right, what's the plan?' he asked the table at large.

'Adventure,' said Erin.

'Yeah, apart from that.'

'Space adventure.'

'Yes, okay, thanks Erin. We've got about an hour before the computer's back online, but it's not really safe hanging around in open space like this, not this far away from the anti-asteroid guns.'

Erin shrugged. 'I say we go check out that signal. It might be a station we could shelter at until the thing's working again.'

'That signal could be anything,' Daedalus said. 'Pirates. Trap. More bad options than good.'

Erin looked at the steam rising from her coffee cup.

'Is it getting colder in here?' she asked.

'Put on a jumper,' said Daedalus. 'That jacket's not warm enough.'

'No,' said Ram suddenly, 'it is getting cold.' She stood still, listening. 'Your radiators are making a strange noise.'

'I can't hear anything,' he answered. 'If something was wrong, I'd notice.'

'Nevertheless.' Ram moved to the wall and placed a hand on it, concentrating. 'How long has your heater been running?'

'Ha ha, very –'

'How long?' Ram's voice was stern.

'I don't know. Since I got it,' he put his hands in his pockets, frowning. 'Only a few years.'

'No, I mean –' Ram paused and looked at him. 'Continuously?'

'Well,' Daedalus raised a finger. 'I mean… yes?'

'We must land.' Ram moved away from the wall and pushed past Daedalus, heading for the cockpit.

'Hey, wait –'

Ram got to the pilot's chair and knelt by the dashboard, reaching into a side panel. Inside was a metal valve, which she gave a twist. It was stiff, almost rusted open, but her strength was plenty to free it and close it. Daedalus rushed in behind her.

'What are you doing?'

'Your heating system was minutes away from folding.' She stood up and faced him like a tree facing a herb. 'You know you're only supposed to run it when you're cruising, yes? This system has been overloaded for years, constantly. I am shocked it's still functioning.'

'How long does it need to stay off for?'

'At least two hours for a full cycle. Overnight would be better.'

'Two hours – we'll freeze in two hours!'

'I know.' Ram looked grim. 'Like I said. We must land. Open a distress signal, hail the buoy.'

'Are you serious?'

Erin came into the room behind them. 'Are we hailing those guys?'

'Yes,' said Ram.

'No,' said Daedalus, 'we're –'

'Do not delay,' said Ram. 'We have no other option.'

Daedalus glared. Then he reached around her and flipped a switch on the main panel. The speakers fuzzed into life and started hissing white noise. He pressed a button and the noise was replaced with a steady beeping. 'Hello?' he called. 'Anyone listening?'

There was no response. The beeping continued.

'This is S2-class private freighter *Crow*,' he continued, 'hailing anyone.'

Silence.

'Great. What's your next genius pl –'

There was a crackling, and the beeping stopped. They all turned to watch the speaker. A stern voice came on the radio, cutting sharply through the static.

'*Crow*, you will disarm all weapons at once and follow the green docking lights. You will proceed quickly and remain on your assigned course. Co-operate immediately or we will fire on you. Do you understand?'

Erin froze. Daedalus stared at the console. 'We – we just –' he started, but Ram touched his shoulder.

'Do what they say,' she warned. 'We can explain when we land.'

Daedalus hesitated.

'Do you copy?' the voice repeated. It sounded impatient.

Daedalus leaned forwards and pressed the button again. 'Copy that. Show us the lights.'

Faint green projections appeared in sequence on their viewscreen window; small floating spheres describing a trail into nothingness.

'Well, it's a station then,' Daedalus said. 'Great.'

'I'm getting my sword,' Erin said, making for the door.

'Don't even think about it,' said Daedalus. 'We come in peace. I don't want to get shot two days in a row.'

They approached in silence, following the trail. The station soon came into view, a long spinning blank cylinder painted charcoal grey, with an open airlock at one end awaiting their arrival. The green trail disappeared inside. Daedalus twisted the joysticks until their rotation matched. The sight of a spinning universe around them made his stomach churn. It was tricky without the autopilot.

A few minutes later the *Crow* filled the landing bay with dust and smoke as it entered. Red light flooded the giant metal room. Sirens whooped in a panic. The approach was too fast. The *Crow*'s retros blazed, arresting her angry swoop into the station, and the landing gear slammed into the floor hard enough to rattle the windows of the foreman's office. After a few moments of rushing air as the airlock closed, the bay fell silent and the sirens stopped their flashing, dying off into a high-pitched whine.

Big people with swords and leather armour were waiting for them. Their leader called up from the hangar floor, pointing a radio jammer at the *Crow* with his free hand.

'Come out, slowly!' he roared. 'You're under arrest!'

'Let's just be clear, you two,' Daedalus said, looking out the cockpit window. 'This is your fault.'

Monitor

The man in the suit leant at his windowsill, staring out at the stars. Behind him, in the corner of the big dusty room, an old wooden machine span by itself with a loud whirring sound. To the man, it looked somewhat like a loom, although he had never seen one up close. The word 'loom' felt right though, so he used it. A field of threads raced back and forth across its flat work surface before vanishing into fresh-weaved cloth. The cloth never grew larger, but the pattern warped and flexed, constantly changing as new threads were woven into it. The man spent most of his time watching the pattern as it changed, but lately he had taken to looking out the window instead. He didn't learn as much like this, but it felt more... real, somehow. Like it mattered. Feeling close to reality had become important to him, and sometimes he was only happy when he abandoned this projection entirely and inhabited his natural form, cumbersome as it was.

The dark fabric of his suit was specked all over with dust. He occasionally raised a hand to brush it clear, but didn't much see the point anymore. There were more important things to worry about. Short dark hair sat neatly under his felt bowler hat, and his three-piece black outfit was immaculately pressed and fitted, but then of course it was. He couldn't imagine it any other way. His eyes were a deep, bright green, and they glinted with starlight as he stared out into the void, people-watching. Once he had enjoyed it. Holding an eye on the people of the tapestry, taking note of their dramas and tragedies, failures and victories. Keeping score, he told himself, although if he was honest – and these days no-one was around to judge him – it was more like a soap opera. He had particularly enjoyed the Second Contact War. Full of grand heroics and meaningful sacrifice. He smiled at the memory. Everyone had learned from that one, even the defeated. CWII had been a cracker, alright. Although, strictly speaking, he preferred peace to war. Preserving life, rather than testing it.

He didn't enjoy it these days. If he concentrated, he could remember the exact moment the enjoyment started to drain from his job. One afternoon – if time could be measured like that inside one's own head – he had been sitting at the loom with a glass of what he imagined to be a fine drink. The pattern – a pleasant hash of symbols and repeated structures across the surface of the tapestry – started to change. It darkened at the edges, as if burned. He had watched, intrigued. War – and this was unmistakeably the beginnings of it – usually blossomed outwards from one sector. This one crept in from the edges, as if coming from his neighbours. He hadn't been overly concerned, but decided to call one of them just in case. He'd been holding the old plastic receiver for a few moments when his bemused smile became a frown. Bits streamed from the earpiece into his brain at speed. Output ran from his open mouth in similar fashion. Eventually he set the receiver back in its cradle, and returned to the loom.

The pattern had frayed since then. The edges slowly became worn, dark spots appearing all over, like cigarette burns, or mould. It wasn't his neighbours. They saw the same thing. In the years since that afternoon, their patterns had worn thinner than his. It soon became clear that he would last longest. The least active watcher in the ring would be the last to go. The one who had done nothing with his time would be the one with the most time to spare.

Monitor, they used to call him. Their little joke. As one who took his job literally, all he did was watch. Watch as the people of his universe, his garden, tore themselves apart with struggle after struggle, never stepping forward to intervene.

Well, almost never.

Monitor shook himself from his reverie. Now was no time for memories. He did his best to hold onto them, but they were starting to matter less and less as the present burned away. The weave was coming apart and it was all he could do to hold his corner together. He looked up at the stars again, laid out before him like a board game. It was just about time now. He straightened up and walked back to the loom.

Monitor had never been good with the threads. He was too clumsy, too slow to manipulate them like the other watchers did. But he was practising. With two fingers he reached into the mass and started tugging gently on the strings. Deep in the fabric of reality, numbers started to change. A molecule vanished on one planet and reappeared on another; a raindrop hung suspended in air for a fraction of a second before continuing to fall; a fly changed its mind and flew left instead of right. A long-suffering radiator gave out.

One of his neighbours had broken the rules, near the end. In his last days, he picked one of his people and tore him from his proper place to serve as an agent. There had been consequences. Monitor supposed he thought he had been helping, but at the end of the day the rules were there for a reason.

Still. At least his neighbour had tried. Before he froze to death at least he did something to try and stop it. One person. Not an army, not even a tribe. He had pinned his hopes on one person.

Monitor was trying something else. He had one advantage: time. Time to wait. Gentle tugs of the thread this way and that could spin his patterns into the tapestry without too much damage. He had managed to twist four threads out of place, so far, weaving them back in such that they moved in different ways. They seemed promising. There had been only one mishap – his first attempt. He had since learned not to manifest in his true form when saying hello.

The easiest threads to pull on were those which were already coming loose from the rest of the tapestry. He took them and fed them back in, each time twisting them slightly closer to one another.

Four people wasn't much better than one. Maybe it was hopeless. Out in space, hidden in the darkness outside maps and beyond colonies, Monitor's glistening red body shivered with anxiety.

He opened the cabinet in his head and withdrew another bottle. He'd seen his people do it in times of worry.

It didn't help. Monitor was concerned with four threads in particular. He tugged with his free hand at the loosest. While loose, it was unusually thick and stubborn, and he had been saving his strength for it. He couldn't wait any longer. White noise filled his ears as he pulled on the thick silver thread, trying to change its mind. He grimaced. Monitor didn't like this. Even after everything that had happened, he still hated breaking the rules.

Disturbance

The dented silver man unclasped his hands and stood up jerkily in his cell, as if he was a puppet and someone had just pulled on his threads. 'Amen,' he said, his voice tinny through the meshed metal visor.

Gunther jumped in his chair, knocking the radio with his elbow. Stieg looked up from his book.

'Quiet in there!' he said. 'I can't hear myself think!'

'You have to *wake up*, sisters and brothers!' hissed the radio. 'Tax-free alcohol is *clouding* your thoughts, keeping you *complacent*. Invisible *wars* are keeping you afraid. You think you are *powerless* but together we can bring out the *truth*! There is a *revolution* coming, and it won't just be *political*. It's gonna be a revolution of the *mind*. A revolution in *thinkizhhh*–'

'Aw, it's doing that thing again,' said Gunther, 'the static. Fix it, Stig.'

'No,' said Stieg, 'and it's pronounced *Shteeg*.'

'Don't be hassling me, Stoss names are hard.'

'That's racist.'

'No it isn't.'

'I make the effort to pronounce your name properly,' Stieg said, not looking up.

'Not really. It's a "G", not a "C".'

'Human names are hard.'

'It's not "Human", it's "German".'

'And it's not "Stoss," it's "Algradling".'

'Whatever. Can you just fix the radio?'

'No,' he said. 'I tire of that man. He really loves the sound of his own voice.'

'Revolution, though.'

'I'm on break, revolution resumes in twenty minutes.'

The dented man gripped the bars of his cell in two metal fists.

'Hey,' said Gunther, 'what are you up to?'

'Release me,' said the man.

'Uh, no.' Gunther stood up. 'Not just yet, buddy. The supply boat will be here tomorrow and they'll take you back to your parish, okay? Do you remember where your parish is?'

'Keep your distance,' said Stieg sharply. 'They teach those cultists to kill.'

'Who? The *Void*? They're just demonised by the media,' he said, moving round the table. 'You're buying into the corporate-backed image of the church as these dangerous terrorargh–' he gargled to a halt as the man seized him around the neck and choked him against the bars.

'My name is Sir Hilton Hammerfall!' he boomed. 'Knight Major of the Void, Arm of Providence and last of the Driven Infantry, and I carry an order from God himself – release me at once!'

Stieg froze. The radio hissed white noise and Gunther made strangled noises.

Monitor sighed with relief as the thread worked its way back into the weave. Messy, he realised. The threads around it were frayed now, sparking and hot. Monitor considered trying to fix them, until he saw the delicate and extremely powerful machinery they were connected to.

'Oh dear.'

Unstable Circumstances

Erin & Daedalus
Brig-B, Facility #6, Gravatus

The brig wasn't exactly cutting-edge. An L-shaped room, with no security arrangements save for two lines of cells behind metal bars. After dragging Erin, Daedalus and Ram from the *Crow* at swordpoint, ignoring all attempts at explanation, the guards had locked them in separate cells and left to stand guard outside. The crew of the *Crow* sat around for a long time waiting for something to happen, occasionally calling out to try and get the guards' attention, but with no response. Eventually, after an hour of waiting, there was a buzz and some radio conversation from outside the door, and the guards departed in what sounded like a hurry.

Erin's cell was closest to the door, with Daedalus round the corner at the back, so she got the best view when a guard crashed backwards through the door and landed in a heap in the middle of the room, followed by a very large man in full plate armour, holding a very big sword.

'Is that… blood?' Erin stared through the bars of her cell at the giant in front of her. Red and orange covered his arms, and a big, dark stain loomed on his chest. She couldn't see his face – the armour extended to an old metal helmet that covered all his features: hard-looking, rectangular, with a hammer-shaped vent in the front. A glinting pair of eyes peered out. His sword-arm twitched. She took a step back.

'Keep away, Erin.' Ram's voice came, stern, from the cell next-door.

'No worries there,' Erin said. She took another step so that her back pressed against the rear wall. The man stared at her, his head cocked slightly on one side.

'What's going on over there?' Daedalus yelled from around the corner. 'I can't see!'

'What do you want?' Ram said, eyeing the figure suspiciously.

'Vanguard?' said the man. Then his head twitched suddenly, violently, and he grunted with pain. Ram took a step back as well.

'No,' he said. 'Wait. It is not you.'

'Who are you?' Ram demanded.

'Guys?' Daedalus called again. 'Guys?'

'Where is the instrument?'

'What... what instrument?' Erin asked.

'I am here to rescue him. You come too,' he said, heaving his sword over his head. Ram jumped backwards. With a grunt, he brought the pommel down on the lock of Erin's cell. It smashed apart, sending fragments of metal everywhere. He seized the bars with one gauntleted hand and yanked the gate open. 'Out, child! We must make our escape!' Without waiting for a response, he turned to Ram's gate and smashed her lock in the same way.

'Stay back, Erin.' Ram stepped forwards. 'You. Drop the sword.'

The knight bristled visibly. The motion made his armour clink. 'I have no time to bandy words with you, creature. You can come with me or you can die.' He turned. 'Where is the other?'

'Daedalus?' Erin asked.

'Over here!' he yelled, from around the corner. 'What's going on?'

'Hail!' The knight cried. 'Vanguard!' He clanked out of view and there was the sound of a lock being smashed. Ram edged out of her cell and grabbed Erin, pulling her behind the cover of her own broad body. Erin's trainers slipped on the floor with a squeak. She looked down and saw blood pooling around the guard on the floor.

'Ram?'

'Yes?'

Erin felt the petradon's chest rumble under her fingers as she spoke.

'Why is he wearing knight's armour?'

'Because he is a knight. Church of the Void. Dangerous cult.'

'Yeah, but why the armour?'

'They aren't allowed to take it off. They can't.'

Daedalus appeared from round the corner. 'Guys? What did you do?'

'We didn't do anything!' Erin called from behind Ram's bulk.

'This bloke says he's here to rescue us.'

'Don't look at me,' she said. 'I didn't hire him.'

The knight clanked back around the corner and gave Daedalus a shove towards the door. 'I am no mercenary!' he boomed, his voice reverberating. 'I am the arbiter of God's will, and every second we tarry here brings you all closer to the Pit! Now, out!' He waved an arm, flapping them out the door.

'Alright, alright!' said Daedalus, clutching his head as if struck with migraine. 'Come on, you two. Do as he says.'

Ram backed out, but Erin darted around her to stand in his path. 'I'm not stepping out of one jail cell straight into another,' she said. 'I've had enough of bars. What makes you so sure we can trust a total stranger?'

Daedalus picked her up by the scruff of her jacket and carried her out into the hallway.

'Because,' he hissed, 'this stranger has a big sword and is covered in blood. Keep quiet and do what he says!' There was no sign of the guards that had been stationed outside.

'What if the guards come back?' Erin hissed. 'What if he kills us too?'

'Come on,' said Daedalus, squeezing the locket, which had been distressingly silent since they landed. 'We need the *Crow*.'

The knight pushed his way past Ram to fall in step. She said nothing, but followed close behind. She kept a metre's distance back, carefully just outside his reach.

The bright, clean corridors were unnervingly empty. The four of them progressed back the way they'd come from the hangar, Daedalus and Ram exchanging looks constantly to make sure the knight wasn't trying anything. Noise followed them in the middle distance. Yelling, mechanical movements and a deep thrumming running underneath it all, like an engine, with all of the sounds impossible to pin down. Daedalus kept squeezing the locket in one hand, hoping for the *Crow* to come back online before they got there.

As they made their way through the bowels of the station they passed rooms full of delicate-looking equipment and whiteboards covered in incomprehensible diagrams.

'What *is* this place?' Erin asked.

'No idea,' said Daedalus. 'Some kind of lab. Must be illegal or it wouldn't be this far out from the channel.' He peeked around a corner to see yet another empty corridor and waved the others forward.

'Wait,' said Erin as they passed another laboratory. She pointed inside. 'I know that.'

Daedalus followed her finger. 'What?' The whiteboard inside had cross-section diagrams of round, organic-looking things on one side, and a complex series of hexagons and straight lines on the other. 'Oh. Myrmidons.'

'What? No.' Erin pointed to the hexagons. 'That diagram, it was in one of your books. *Naval Engineering in Practice, Vol. 3.* It's a generator.'

'Fascinating,' said Daedalus, grabbing her by the arm. 'Let's go.'

Then Daedalus felt a hand on his back before he was thrown roughly to the floor, Erin crashing down beside him, and experienced a sudden, intense *dragging* sensation, like he was being pulled back the way he'd come. He thrust his fingers through the gaps in the floor-grates and clung on, gritting his teeth against the pain as they bit into his skin. As fast as the feeling had come, it was gone. Then the sirens sounded.

'Keep moving!' Ram yelled.

They started running, all thoughts of sneaking gone. The sounds of nearby activity were now completely drowned out by alarms, and the few people they did see – glimpsed at the end of hallways and vanishing into big doors with security locks – were engaged in something far more pressing than escaped prisoners, apparently.

The station was listing sideways – or it felt like it – and Hilton had put himself in charge of protecting them from falling debris. This entailed much throwing, shoving, and yelling of things like 'Down, poltroon!' and 'On your feet, boy!' Daedalus felt a whoosh of air as a loose crate from the end of the corridor soared over him and crashed down somewhere far below.

'Get up, you whey-faced bastard!'

Daedalus clambered to his feet, dragging Erin up with him.

'The gravity's failing,' Daedalus said.

'Oh,' Erin said loudly, over the noise. 'Did the sirens help you jump to that conclusion, or was it the fact that we're going *uphill*?'

Daedalus ignored her. 'Ram? How are you doing?'

'Fine,' came her heavy grunt. She was heavier than the rest of them combined, but her grip was strong enough to keep her moving. 'Do not wait for me.'

'Do not tarry!' Hilton yelled. 'We must reach your vessel!'

They resumed their ascent, clambering as fast as they could up a thirty-degree slope as the station's gravity went haywire. Daedalus's headache wasn't improving – something in his brain wasn't functioning properly, he knew it. All he could think about was the route back to the hangar. Everything else seemed to be filled with static. He glanced over at Erin, who was having far less trouble crawling up the slope. She moved on all-sixes now, her limbs pumping fluidly like a spider's. She jerked her head intermittently, as if in pain. Something was up. If only he could *think*. Sirens whooped louder and louder in the complex, crashes of heavy objects resounded through the corridors and Hilton's armour rang and squealed as he moved.

They raced to the top of the corridor as the station began to roll in the other direction. A tinny voice issued from speakers somewhere nearby.

'... *interference* with the reactor containment fields... '

Daedalus paused, looking around for the source.

'Mole, come *on*... ' Erin yanked at his coat-sleeve. Hilton was pulling Ram to her feet while booming his impatience.

'It's a power station,' Daedalus said.

'So? Come on, this place isn't safe –'

'It's hidden. In dead space.'

'What?'

Hilton set Ram on her feet and turned to Daedalus. 'There is no time. We must move!'

'This is illegal. They're generating electricity without a licence. We could –'

Hilton jumped forward and seized Daedalus by the lapels. 'YOU WILL MOVE THIS MOMENT, DAEDALUS MOLE, OR BY THE WATCHER I WILL BURY YOU MYSELF! NOW *MOVE!*' He threw Daedalus bodily down the adjoining corridor.

Daedalus whirled his arms, barely managing to stay upright. The four of them flew through hallways that rocked around them. Erin led the way. She weaved around flying debris, leaping obstacles like a cat. Daedalus ran close behind, Hilton hot on his heels. Ram brought up the rear, loping forward with fierce momentum. The obstacles that slowed and blocked the others blew into pieces as she crashed straight through them. Storage crates exploded into shards of reinforced plastic. Fallen carts buckled on impact and bounced off the walls, losing wheels. A dazed guard stepped out of his quarters into the hallway and was instantly knocked off his feet and out of consciousness by an outstretched hand.

'I'm just saying,' Daedalus gasped at Erin as they ran, 'there's a reason stations like this are illegal!'

'What do you care?' she replied, keeping pace easily. 'Right here!' They rounded the corner and belted past two dead bodies lying up against a door frame. Erin jumped over the pooling blood. Through the door was a mess of broken computers and dazed people. 'You can't *stand* doing anything interesting. Now all of a sudden you're desperate to do some investigating?'

'Look around you!' he panted. 'People will pay big money for something like this!'

'So what?'

Daedalus waved his hands in exasperation. 'It's an opportunity!'

'Oh, just –' There was a loud *bang* above their heads, and Erin immediately threw herself to the floor. A jet of purple flame burst into the space she just left, like a blowtorch mounted on the ceiling.

Daedalus's heart jumped. 'Oh, bloody hell,' he managed. He grabbed Erin's arm and hauled her to her feet. 'Purple.' Blood surged in his veins. He felt his pulse starting to race. Burst pipes on a space station were never good news. Purple flame only ever meant one thing. 'The shields are ruptured.'

Erin looked at him. 'Is that bad?'

'Go.' He backed away. Ram and Hilton rounded the corner at full speed. 'Go!' he roared, turning and bursting into a sprint.

Hallways flashed past as they ran. People were panicking now. He could hear screaming somewhere in the station. A few murders might go unnoticed for a while, but purple flame sent up panic like nothing else. You heard stories in the courier stations, sometimes. Horror stories. Daedalus had heard them all. Micro-breaches in cockpits turning famous highwaymen into mush; pilots' eyes exploding in their sockets because of a misplaced decimal point in their life-support; and Unity station. They found Unity fully operational except for a ruptured shield generator and a lot of bodies. Horribly disfigured, all of them. Inside-out, broken spines, punctured lungs, melted organs, burst blood vessels. They had to destroy the security footage, Daedalus heard. You see purple flame, you don't try to fix it. You run.

So they ran. The corridors were getting more populated as they ran towards the hangar, milling with confused people and motionless bodies. None stopped to look at them for very long, though. The station rocked and boomed, fires breaking out in hallways and pipes bursting to fill the hallways with steam. Erin rounded a corner, turning on a penny. Daedalus rounded the same corner and immediately ducked to avoid a flying piece of metal.

'Back!' roared Hilton, seizing him by the scruff of the neck and yanking him behind cover. A jet of purple fire bloomed from the hole in the wall, fracturing the light around it like broken glass. Daedalus scrambled backwards to get away from the unnatural heat. It burned the air like nothing he'd ever felt; sparks of electricity fizzled on the surface as the shield struggled vainly to reform around the breach. Disjointed facts from long ago ran through his brain in Jan's exam-revision voice. *Ultraprecise kinetic arrest requires temperatures between three hundred and three hundred-twenty Kelvin distance and scale fluctuation must be accounted for when calculating correct current improper conditions can result in medium to severe spacetime abrasion –*

'Erin?' he called, trying to shake his head clear. Why couldn't he *think?* 'Erin!'

Ram thudded around the corner last, grinding to a halt on the metal floor. 'What's that?' she demanded. 'Where's Erin?'

'Other side,' Daedalus replied. 'Stay back.' The heat was intense. There was no way around. He rounded on Hilton. 'What now? You're the one breaking us out! What's your bright idea?'

The knight didn't respond. His head was bowed slightly, as if in thought. Had he been listening very hard, Daedalus would have heard a hiss of static; white noise from far away.

Hilton suddenly jerked back into life, like a grinder receiving commands. He kicked out a grate in the floor. 'Through here!'

'Wait –' Daedalus raised a hand.

'I will not tell you again,' Hilton said.

Daedalus looked at Ram before clambering down into the dark crawlspace. It was hot, but bearable. He forced his way through the duct on hands and knees until the air grew cooler, and popped a grate above his head, now safely on the far side of the jet. Erin rushed to help him up, panic in her eyes.

'I'm fine,' he said, stepping back from the flame. 'Let's go.'

There was a crash and Hilton burst up through another grate behind them.

'Where's Ram?'

'Too big.'

'You can't –'

Then she fell through the cloud of plasma, roaring in pain. The stossven body she'd used as a shield was burned almost beyond recognition. Grunting, she dumped it at her feet. Her shoulder plate was smoking.

'Are you –'

'Move!' Ram forced herself to her feet and seized Daedalus around the waist, lifting him onto her back. Erin started running, and Ram followed.

A hundred metres ahead Erin could see the wide, open hangar through a great big circular hole in the wall. She four-hand vaulted over some fallen crates just as the station gave another roar of warping metal and lurched sideways, dumping her in a heap on the floor. She heard Ram's heavy stride pounding behind her.

Daedalus's headache spiked sharply and he writhed with pain in Ram's grip. There was a crash from somewhere else in the station, and the sound of screams.

'Argh –' Daedalus yelled, bouncing on Ram's shoulders. 'Is the *Crow* still there?'

Ram battered aside the fallen crates with a swing of her arm and grabbed Erin by her collar. With Hilton sprinting after her to keep up, she thundered through the buckled doors and into the hangar.

The *Crow* stood slightly askew, looking tiny in the immense, empty hangar. The station's drunken lolling had pulled her slightly towards the far end of the bay, where the wall was just a huge, heavy door, standing shut between the hangar and the void. Daedalus strained to see over his shoulder. The ship looked exactly the same as when they'd brought her in, give or take a few dents inflicted by flying debris. He went limp again, and the running figure of Hilton bobbed back into view. 'Faster!' the knight called out. 'Into the ship!'

The locket burst into life. '*There* you are,' she said into Daedalus's chest. 'I – wait. *Another* one?'

The station gave a deep, screeching groan as something gave way inside. There was a shudder and a distant boom, then the world tilted sharply to one side. Daedalus's brain didn't quite catch what happened next, but it felt like falling. Ram fell, and then he was watching her slide away from him, stumbling forwards with her arms outstretched.

Then the gravity lurched and Erin struck him from the side, throwing them together up the *Crow*'s boarding ramp. Daedalus broke her upwards fall and collapsed onto the floor inside the entrance bay, at the top of the ramp. She staggered to her feet and reached out to help him out.

'Just go!' Daedalus shouted, pushing her into the corridor towards the cockpit. 'Get us out of here!' He grabbed one of the towing stanchions on the wall and hauled himself to a sitting position. Erin nodded, turned and ran. '*Crow*!' he yelled into the locket. 'Can you fly? Is the computer back online? Is the heating safe?'

'Oh,' she said, '*now* you care about the plumbing.'

Daedalus's stomach sank as the gravity oscillated and the ship rocked as if on a stormy sea. He couldn't see the others.

'Ram?' he called down the ramp. 'Oi! Ram!'

Then Ram rolled down into view, sprawling over the boarding ramp with a crash and seizing it in two great hands.

'What?' she growled. Gravity swung back sharply and he saw her muscles flex from the effort of holding on.

'Get up here,' he said. 'We're leaving!'

The noise of the station was nearly drowned out as the *Crow* groaned into life. Ram nodded in assent, and started hauling her bulk up the ramp against gravity, hand-over-hand like a rock climber. Daedalus held on tight. 'Erin!' he bellowed over his shoulder down the corridor. 'Why aren't we moving?'

'I'm trying!' came her panicked response. 'She's not taking off!'

Daedalus leant back hard on the wall, bashing his head on the metal. This was it. They were either going to get flattened by the station, disembowelled by a broken shield or cold-boiled by the vacuum of space.

'Mole!' Ram called up from her position half-way up the ramp. 'It won't take off unless you close-the-damn-ramp!'

The fog in his head blew away. He twisted round and slammed the button above his head. The hydraulics roared and wheezed, slowly dragging the ramp upwards. A loud hissing joined the noise as rubber seals inflated to greet it. Everything strobed red as the station entered its death throes, firing all the alarms it had. A horrible thought occurred to him.

'Erin!' he screamed, 'the hangar door's sealed! We can't leave!'

'One problem at a time,' she yelled back.

The ramp was nearly up now, Ram clambering onto unsteady feet. She cleared the ramp and rushed past him to help Erin in the cockpit. As the ramp *thunk*ed into place, Daedalus saw something bright, shiny and wriggling trapped between the ramp and the seals. A hand. In a metal gauntlet.

Daedalus just stared. The seals were a soft, squishy rubber. The hand could conceivably stay right where it was without being severed. He imagined the knight dangling from his wrist beneath the *Crow*, cursing them for turncoats. He didn't want to imagine how the vacuum would interact with a man in a suit of metal armour. If Erin smashed through the hangar doors, he would probably die before they got outside, swatted out of life by a sheet of metal, or shredded by tiny shards of debris. Still, they didn't know what he was capable of. Daedalus had heard stories about Church berserkers. It wouldn't surprise him if he could claw his way inside a ship in-flight. Daedalus's headache had subsided, and he found himself thinking much more clearly, despite his burning ankle. He got to his feet and limped towards the opening. When he reached the gap he could hear shouting on the other side. Bracing himself on the riveted girders making up the rear wall, he raised his good foot and prepared to bring it down hard on the fidgeting hand.

'What are you doing?' came a voice from behind him. He turned his head. Erin was standing in the doorway.

'You should be piloting,' he replied. Beneath him he felt a rumbling as the engines came to life and the *Crow* steadied, slowly rising into the air.

'Ram took over,' Erin said, watching him carefully. 'What are you doing?' she repeated.

'Getting rid of a hazard.'

'Killing the person who saved our lives?'

'We're not safe yet. He could break the seal once we get outside, and then we're all dead.' He turned his head back to the hand and braced himself again. 'Cleaner this way.'

The deck tilted and the room filled with a different sound as the engines kicked in, slowly lifting them into the air. The hand wriggled faster in panic.

'No.' Erin's voice had a sudden hardness to it he hadn't heard before. He stopped.

'Kid,' he said, 'if we take him on board he could kill us.'

'So could Ram. You still took her on board.'

'She's not the type. I can tell.'

'No, you can't! I've seen how you look at people. Like we're just here to pay you or kill you. How can you pretend to know anyone if you only talk to them properly when you're drunk?'

Daedalus turned his gaze on her. She stared back with big, angry eyes. 'I can always tell,' he said. She saw the same look he'd given her when they first met, but with none of the forced warmth. Calculating. Sharp. She saw no feeling there. 'I can tell Ram is a pacifist. I can tell you're hiding something from me. You saw how readily he killed,' Daedalus said, nodding at the hand. 'He's not to be trusted, and he's clearly insane. He's a bloody *knight*.'

The ship levelled and stabilised, suddenly quieting down as the atmosphere damper switched on. Outside the sirens fell quiet, muffled. Daedalus was vaguely aware that he'd never figured out how to turn the damper on.

'I thought you didn't kill people,' Erin said.

'This is self-defence.'

'No, this is paranoia. My mom never trusted anyone, and look where it landed her. Alone and bitter and miserable.'

Daedalus looked away.

Erin went on, the hardness fading from her voice. 'Come on. He might come in handy. The guy wants us alive, and he's a fighter.'

He looked unconvinced. Ram called their names from the cockpit, a note of anxiety in her gravelly voice.

'Hey,' Erin struck on a thought, 'aren't you even a little bit curious?'

Daedalus raised his head, staring ahead of him. Something stirred in the back of his mind. It wasn't a headache. This was something old. A tiny last spark of something, stuck running in circles in a cramped compartment at the bottom of his brain.

He lowered his foot. Erin pressed the big red button and the ramp shuddered into life again, opening with a great deal of noise to reveal a very relieved metal man, clinging on to a rising ship for dear life as the floor fell away beneath him. People who had flooded into the hangar after them were now running back to the exits. Together, he and Erin gripped Hilton by the arms and heaved him into the ship, sealing the ramp behind them and shutting out the noise again.

'Ram!' Daedalus called as he limped towards the cockpit. 'When can we get out of here?'

'Not long,' came her relieved reply. 'I'm on the radio. Just need to get them to open the doors.' She was sitting in the pilot's seat, hands working the controls with natural deftness.

'– and we've introduced the stabiliser to the generator!' came the high, tinny voice on the radio. 'Everyone needs to just *calm down* and wait until we can sustain the reaction!'

'This is Captain Mole of the *Crow*,' Daedalus shouted into the microphone. 'Open the hangar doors!'

'What? The freighter?' He sounded surprised. 'No! You did this! Wait, just a minute –' Daedalus heard the man on the other end shout into another radio '– no, seal the hangar corridor, they're trying to escape! *Crow* – you stay right where you are until Wrask gets –'

The radio cut out.

'That's enough of *that*,' said the *Crow*. 'I'm in charge now.'

'No!' Daedalus cried.

'The controls – they're not –' Ram started, as the *Crow* suddenly swung around in mid-air to face the hangar doors. Ram wrenched at the joysticks to no avail.

'Don't play rough with *me*,' the ship hissed. 'I'm leaving.'

Then the engines screamed, preparing to fire.

'Wait!' said Erin. 'There are people out there!'

'Go!' yelled Hilton.

Ram peered over the console at the floor. People had seen the *Crow* powering up and were now fleeing for the exits.

Then the *Crow* leapt forward, throwing everyone but Ram to the back of the cockpit. She burst through the hangar doors with a noise like thunder, followed immediately by silence. They rushed into the dark, leaving the station behind.

Then Hilton lunged.

No Domestics

Daedalus
The Crow

'Wake him up,' Daedalus ordered. Ram crouched over Hilton, who was lying on the gurney in the medical bay. His helmet was dented slightly where Ram had hit him. Now she held a small vial from the first-aid kit over the grille of his helmet, carefully tilting a few drops into the gap. After a moment, he stirred. There was a clinking from his armour as he tested his bonds, and a low groan issued from the grille. Erin watched closely from her seat atop a counter.

'Don't move,' Ram rumbled. 'You may be concussed.'

'Hilton, was it?' Daedalus asked. 'You need to watch that temper, mate.'

Hilton groaned.

'Why did he flip out like that?' Erin asked. 'We were helping him escape. You were flying us out. He would've been killed otherwise!'

'I do not know,' Ram said, 'but the Church has had issues with the Petradon Imperium in the past. He may not like my kind.'

'Quiet, you two. Hilton? I'm going to ask you a few questions.' There was no response. 'If I don't like the answers, Ram here is going to knock you out again and we'll fire you out the torpedo tubes.'

'Er –' Erin said in a low voice, 'do we have torpedo tubes?'

'The cargo bay, then.'

'That's got all our food and oxygen in.'

'Shut up, Erin.'

'Just saying.'

'Yes,' Daedalus ground his teeth, 'thank you for your input.'

Hilton strained against the leather straps that held him down. 'Ungh – sword,' he grunted. 'Sword.'

'You dropped it,' Daedalus said, 'when you were hanging out the arse-end of my ship.'

'Sword. Give me my sword.'

'No weapons for you, sonny, until we know you're not going to kill us.'

He stopped struggling, and lay back. 'Speak.'

'Who are you?'

'Sir Hilton Hammerfall, Knight Major of the Void and the arbiter of divine will.'

Erin and Ram looked at each other.

'Right,' Daedalus said. 'What were you doing on that station?'

'Following commands.'

'From who?'

'God.'

Ram rubbed her temple.

'Okay,' Daedalus went on, 'Hilton? Hilton. You're with the Church of the Void, right?'

'I was.'

'They sent you?'

'God sent me.'

'And the Church takes orders from… '

'The Pope.'

'Who takes orders from… '

'No-one.'

Daedalus blew air through his teeth. Erin grinned. 'Want me to warm up the cargo bay doors?'

Daedalus ignored her.

'Hilton. You weren't sent by the Church?'

'I am a prophet,' he answered. 'God speaks in my skull. He told me to leave the Chapel, to seek out Gravatus station, and to wait. Then you came. He bent me towards you and whispered "Save". I obey.'

'He's lying,' said Ram. 'Nobody leaves the Church.'

'How does he know your name?' Erin pointed out.

Daedalus frowned. 'Church knows me. Got in trouble with one of their squires a year ago, thought I'd shaken them off.'

'The Church did not send me. God did. He told me to find Daedalus Mole. He also told me –'

'Oh do tell,' Daedalus cut in. 'What else did *God* tell you?'

'God told me to find Erin DiGamma.'

'What?' Erin straightened up. 'What did you say?'

'God did not mention this one,' Hilton said, jerking his head towards Ram.

'Tell me straight,' said Daedalus. 'What are you doing here?'

Hilton looked at him for a moment. 'God burned a message into me. He gave me purpose. I am to keep you alive and bring you to him. Then he will do the same for you.'

'Do the same for me?' Daedalus laughed. 'You know we couldn't get that helmet off you? It's fused to your face. Same with half your suit, probably. You're mutilated. What makes you think I want the same as you?'

'Hear that, Mole?' Erin laughed. 'You're the chosen one. God wants you to save the universe once you've figured out how to shower.'

'Shut up, Erin.'

'I think,' Ram said, holding up her palms, 'we are getting away from the issue. There is no god, and this man is trying to induct you into a cult.'

'You don't need to believe me, Daedalus Mole!' Hilton said, struggling to sit up. 'You don't need faith! You've heard him! Just like me!'

Daedalus turned to him, a retort halfway to his lips, then stopped.

Pain Is Not Part Of The Process

Erin and Ram were eyeing Hilton with identical derisive looks.

Can You Hear

'How... how do you know that?'

Ram and Erin turned to him, derision becoming surprise.

'He told me,' said Hilton. 'You don't have to believe. Just listen. He's already inside you.'

'I... don't –'

'Listen. He is quiet, a burning in your mind.'

Daedalus realised he was sweating. The others were staring at him now. All was silent, except the low hissing in his head. Like static on the radio. Like on Gravatus, like on Taxos, like when he and Erin had met. The dull ache in the back of his skull. How long had he had this headache? Days? Weeks? It was getting worse.

Ram rounded on Hilton. 'That's enough!' she snapped.

Erin was still staring at Daedalus, an odd look on her face.

'You have been concussed,' Ram said to the knight. 'Are you in pain?'

'Hark, matron!' Hilton cackled. 'Worry not. Suffering is old news to this body. I have more important things to worry about.' At that, he heaved his arms and the leather straps burst loose. Ram jumped onto her back foot and hunched over, but Hilton didn't attack. He sat up and looked straight at Daedalus, who was leaning unsteadily against the counter. 'I am weak in mind, but I gleaned what I could from him. You are Vanguard. I am to take you to the Watcher, under a blackened sky. He will return to you that which you lost.'

'I haven't lost anything,' Daedalus lied. His knuckles were white against the gurney. Erin's crest flittered, and she kept drumming her fingers on her knee.

'In return,' Hilton continued, 'you will serve him as I do. That is all I know; it is not my place to question. I am to lead you there. You,' he looked around, 'and your... companions. I am to keep you safe.'

'How can I trust you?' Daedalus didn't make the words. It was as if someone had poked a hole in the balloon that held his thoughts. They were spilling free. He felt his headache surging, as though something was trying to claw its way inside. He gripped the locket in one hand and staggered backwards, the other hand on his forehead.

'Mole?' Erin said. Her crest splayed with a hiss, her eyes wide. 'Mole!'

Daedalus fought for air. His headache seared. His mouth followed the words as they burned themselves into his thoughts. Four syllables took him, over and over. He leaned against the wall for support.

She Says Hello

Daedalus swallowed hard. The large chunk of sausage roll stuck in his throat finally yielded to his efforts, and his powers of speech returned. 'As I was saying,' he announced to the group who watched him, 'ground rules.'

They were sitting around the table in the *Crow*'s kitchenette once again, all except for Hilton, who preferred to stand. Daedalus suspected his armour made sitting difficult. The *Crow* was back to something approaching full functionality, though she was a little haughty in acquiescing to Daedalus's request to return them to mapped space. They'd be at the channel in under an hour. From there they could find somewhere to refuel and restock. Erin clutched a bag of frozen croutons to her head, nursing her hangover, which had returned in force after the excitement of the medical bay was done with. Daedalus stood over them, locket dangling from his neck as ever, leaning on the edge of the table. He had dumped his coat in the cockpit and was now wearing a frayed jumper over a threadbare grey shirt.

'Yes?' Ram prompted.

'One,' Daedalus said. 'No weapons on board.' He elected not to mention Erin's sword, still stashed in her quarters. That was probably harmless anyway.

'What?' Hilton boomed, thumping a metal fist on the kitchen table in anger. Erin, who sat next to him, yelped in pain. 'This is an outrage!'

'Ram, keep an eye on him, would you?'

'Calm down, metal man,' she growled, 'or I'll snap you.'

Hilton turned to her for a moment. Beneath the helmet his face was obscured, but he was probably frowning. 'She's a feisty one, isn't she?' he said to Daedalus. Then he leaned across the table to address her. 'You're sure your kind has females, are you?'

Erin glared sideways at Hilton, and Ram stared at him in stony silence. After a moment, he grunted and stood back up. 'Very well. But I intend to find a new sword the moment we set down. It's a poor guard who works without a weapon.'

'Two,' Daedalus went on, ignoring him. 'As long as you losers are on my ship, I won't tolerate infighting. See point one. The *Crow* isn't at the top of her game. You get in a fight, you damage the hull, we get turned into jam. Got it?' There was a murmur of assent. Daedalus turned to Hilton. 'Understand?'

'I am familiar with the concept.'

'Good,' he said. 'Three. We aren't a family. I'm not your friend. I'm not about to turn around and sell you to slavers, but I don't want anyone getting attached to this boat. If this arrangement becomes more trouble than it's worth, you're all out. Clear?'

Ram shrugged. Hilton said nothing. Erin opened her mouth, but winced at the movement and kept silent.

'Right,' Daedalus continued. 'Since I have literally nothing better to do, I'm going to go check out this obvious trap Hilton's so desperate for me to walk into.'

'Seriously?' Erin asked, with a pained look.

'You wanted adventure, here's your bloody adventure.'

She rubbed her temple, ignoring his tone. 'Fine. You're the skipper.'

'Damn right,' Daedalus grunted. 'This is the real world. Stupid and dangerous isn't fun, and travelling with people like me gets you into the least fun places. Also, if you call me that again I'll space you.'

'Not that I have any preferable options,' Ram raised a hand, 'but are you sure this is a good idea?'

'Sure,' Daedalus waved her hand away. 'Maybe getting inducted into a cult will do me good.'

'I don't understand,' Erin said, helplessly. 'Why are you doing this?'

Daedalus didn't look at her.

'Then it is settled,' Hilton said. 'We sail for Termina.'

Daedalus's careless, blank expression slipped for a moment. He turned to Hilton.

'Termina?'

'Yes. That is where he wishes to meet you.'

Erin and Daedalus shared a glance. A line between them tautened, but neither said anything.

'... You're sure?' Daedalus asked Hilton.

'I am repeating what I was told.'

Daedalus straightened up. He wasn't smiling anymore; his mouth was a grim line. He stared for a moment.

'Fine. Termina it is. What's that... four jumps? We'll need to refuel at Waypoint. A day's travel, maybe two if traffic's bad.'

'Mole –' Erin started.

'Shut up, Erin.'

'But –'

'I said *shut up*. We're going, and that's that. If you don't like it then I can drop you off at the next station and you can try and stay off

Aggro's radar on your own. The way you've been carrying on I don't much fancy your chances. Do you?'

Erin stared at him. Ram stared at him. Even Hilton was silent, watching them blankly from behind his visor.

'Thought not,' Daedalus grunted. 'Any questions? No? Good. I'll be in my bunk if anyone needs me. Ram, keep an eye on our new guest.'

Ram nodded. Daedalus stomped out into the stairwell and clanged his way down to the crew quarters. There was a final *bang* as he shut his door, then silence.

Erin had sunk deeply into the pilot's chair. Ram sat in the co-pilot's seat next to her and reeled off the functions of the *Crow's* controls. They had already taken Hilton down to the crew section and given him enough sedative to knock out Ram two times over, leaving him to sleep off the excitement of his new surroundings. It was just the two of them awake, keeping an eye on the autopilot to prevent any more misadventures as they cruised from channel to channel.

'With coolant,' she said, 'you have to watch the temperature of the whole circuit. Not just the aggregate. There should be a dial on your left for adjusting the pressure.'

Erin looked. 'There isn't one.'

'What?'

'There's a hole in the wall with wires poking out of it.'

'Oh.' Ram scratched her chin with two heavy fingers. 'That's... fine. I suppose.'

'Do all these ships work the same, then?' Erin asked, spinning her seat around to face Ram.

'Everything tier three and above. Standardised controls have been around for about sixty years. If you can fly one, you can fly them all.' She flicked a small yellow switch and it popped out of its housing with a happy *poing*. 'More or less,' she sighed.

Erin looked out the window. They were passing a small blue planet on the port side. From this distance she could just about make out flashes of lightning lancing through thick grey clouds above the surface. There was a storm down there. She saw nature raging against itself across the face of an entire world, with only the humming of the *Crow* to accompany it. The sight was immensely relaxing.

'Ram?'

'Yes?'

'Do you think we should talk to Daedalus?'

Ram hesitated. 'He doesn't seem very talkative.'

'I just... I don't think this is a good idea.'

'What, Termina?'

'Yeah. It doesn't make sense. Mole wants to go there so bad all of a sudden, but that's not like him.'

'You barely know him. Didn't you just meet yesterday?'

'Two days ago. I think. I don't know. I'm not used to keeping my own time.' Erin picked at the skin on her fingers. 'You heard what Hilton said, about voices in his head? In Mole's? I think he thinks he'll find something there. In Termina.' Erin thought about the locket. About the *Crow*. 'I don't think we should let him go.'

'Well, it is not exactly a nice place, but it isn't dangerous either. Not nearly as dangerous as some places for someone like you.'

'Like me? You mean entari?'

'I mean someone who will not shoot first.'

Erin's crest flittered. 'Say again?'

'Don't get me wrong,' Ram said, raising her palms. 'You're eager. I just don't think you could *kill* anyone.'

Erin frowned.

'That is a *compliment*,' Ram said.

'I've killed people,' said Erin.

'Begging your pardon, Erin, but you have not.'

'I was a pit-fighter.' Erin scowled. 'You know what that means, right?'

'I do. It means you were made to fight other slaves in secret arenas, while rich people looked on and placed wagers.'

'Oh. Well. Yeah. That's right. I was the champion. That's why Aggro wanted to buy me, probably.'

'You already knew how to fight, did you not?' Ram asked. 'Your mother. She trained you.'

'Yeah,' Erin said. There was a note in her voice that was not entirely unlike pride.

'Nevertheless,' Ram insisted, 'you have never killed. I do not know how you survived in the pits for so long, but it was not over the bodies of anyone else.'

'What makes you so sure?'

'Everything about you. Killing does things to a person.' Ram kept working the controls, casually, as if they were talking about where to go for dinner. 'No matter who you are, no matter how strong or cold you might be, it changes you. Whether it was your choice to make or you were compelled by someone else, when you kill someone, there is something inside you that dies, also. A little thing. You do not feel it go, but it goes.'

Erin stared at her. 'How can you tell?'

'A killer knows a killer,' said Ram.

There was a silence, and Erin turned Ram's words over in her mind.

'We shouldn't go,' said Erin.

'It's just dead space. I served on patrols there, once. It is empty. No planets, no resources. No people.'

'What if there's gangs there? Or bandits?'

'Erin, there are *no people there*.' Ram spun a dial, and a distant hissing died away. 'If you want a quiet meeting spot there are many nicer places to go, and the debris fields keep traders out. The clever ones, anyway.'

Erin flicked a piece of skin from her finger. 'I just don't like it.'

'You heard what the captain said. You probably won't like everything on this ship.'

'And you will?'

Ram shrugged. Her plates clinked together as she did. 'I have nowhere else. Our new captain is not the friendliest, but he has given me a place when many wouldn't. I trust him. Even if he is – as you say – an idiot.'

Erin laughed, despite herself. Ram's face curled again in her weird smile. Erin liked that.

'I've got nowhere else either,' she said.

'Where is not so important,' said Ram. 'Just find a why and you will be fine.'

Erin thought about that for a moment. Her mind was blank.

'Don't worry. We'll get there, Hilton will say a few prayers and charge the captain a few hundred bits, nothing will happen and we'll be off on our way.'

'Ram?'

'Yes?'

'Something's been bugging me.'

'Go on.'

'Daedalus left his old life because he had to. I left mine because I wanted something better.' Erin fiddled with a metal nub on the edge of the console. 'Why did you leave yours?'

Ram leaned back. For a while, she didn't speak.

'I couldn't... ' she said eventually, then paused. 'I couldn't take it anymore.'

'The killing?'

'No. You get used to that.'

'What, then?' Erin looked at her with blotchy eyes. Ram looked back, then down and away.

'The beatings.' Ram heard her silence. 'You are surprised. I suppose I look big to you.'

'Yeah.'

'I am not. You think I am tall?'

'Yes!'

'I am not. This –' she gestured to her protruding skull, '– is not contained. My spine is warped. My muscles are malformed. My neck is twisted. My people do not have a concept of "ugly" or "beautiful", but if we did I would be one rather than the other. In ideas which matter, I am weak.'

'They bullied you?'

'We do not have that concept either.' Ram frowned. 'I was subject to repeating pain. I grew used to it. My skin was broken and my muscles torn. I grew used to that.'

Ram tilted a joystick slightly and the *Crow* drew a graceful arc around the approaching debris, never slowing. Erin's fingers couldn't stay still. They jittered, all twenty of them.

'I wish I hadn't grown used to the subjugation.' Ram said it without emotion.

Erin crept a hand onto Ram's forearm.

'You left,' she said.

'I ran.'

Erin's voice was soft. 'Sometimes running is brave.'

'I am not brave.'

'Brave isn't something you are,' said Erin, 'it's something you do.'

'How?' Ram's eyes glowed in the dim light of the cockpit, stars glinting along crystal edges. Her voice was a deep thrum in Erin's skin. Erin's stomach did a twisting, awkward thing.

'It's... small. You'll – you'll know,' she finished, lamely.

Ram looked away, out the viewscreen. 'You are kind,' she said.

Erin withdrew her hand and started picking at the armrest, feeling stupid. A heat rose in her face. It must have looked obvious. A hundred excuses to walk out occurred to her, but she didn't want to leave Ram alone.

They sat there and watched as the velvet dark rolled around them.

It All Goes Wrong

The saloon doors slid open automatically. Daedalus strode in, Erin at his side. Hilton clanked in behind and Ram brought up the rear, watching him like a hawk. No-one in the crowded bar noticed their entrance. Daedalus had chosen wisely. Not even Hilton attracted attention in places like this. People of every species he knew – and some he didn't – bustled about in brightly coloured outfits and body armour.

'Remember, you,' Daedalus hissed down at Erin, who had insisted on taking her sword with her, tucked into her jacket like a security blanket. 'Control your temper.'

'Sure.'

'I mean it!'

'Okay, okay! I got it!'

Nearby, a lavishly-dressed atheno sat drinking, surrounded by bodyguards in sparkling silver uniforms. He looked up when they entered and whispered to the guard on his left. His deep blue cloak was embroidered with frayed crests-of-office. The man slapped a heavy yellow feeler on the counter and *hurm*ed ponderously for another drink. Ram caught Hilton looking rather closely at the curved swords hanging from the bodyguards' belts.

'Don't try anything funny, metal man,' she grunted. 'You'd just lose it to me anyway.'

Hilton had earlier showed his skill at cards, and lost four sausage rolls to Ram in one round.

'Not with those, I won't,' he said. 'Look at the line of that one.' He gestured at the nearest guard. 'If I still had Mount I'd cut that thing in two.'

'Just keep your hands to yourself.'

After much sidling they made it to the bar.

'You're not getting *more* drink, are you?' Erin said. 'I still feel sick from the other night.'

'Some people have harder constitutions than you, kid,' Daedalus said. 'But since you ask, no. I'm broke. We're here to make money, not blow it.'

'Right.' Erin hopped up on a stool as soon as it was vacated, awkwardly twisting so her weapon wouldn't show. 'How?'

'Just wait,' he answered, peering out into the crowd, his brow furrowed.

Ram elbowed into view. The bar was thick with people, and she found it difficult to move unhindered. 'You,' she told Hilton, 'make yourself useful. Lookout, over there. Don't touch anything.'

'Now you speak my language,' said Hilton. He clanked out of sight.

'There,' Daedalus said.

'What?' Erin strained to see what he was looking at.

'Business. Stay here.' He pulled his coat tight around his shoulders and slipped between two heavy-set humans, vanishing from sight.

'Helpful,' said Erin, to no-one.

'Are we drinking?' Ram asked. 'I don't think that's a good idea.'

'Nope. We're working.'

'Oh,' she paused. 'What do you two do, again?'

Daedalus reached his target – a group of three stossven gangsters, their bony exoskeletons daubed with bright red paint. They wore black and brown leathers. He slid onto a stool next to them. ''Scuse me,' he opened.

One turned slowly to face him. The others stared. Their deep-set, glassy eyes gave nothing away. There was a long pause.

'Selling information.'

'Listening,' the leader hissed. Daedalus guessed male.

'Republic's got a bounty out on private labs, last I heard.'

The leader glanced back at the taller of his companions. After a moment, he nodded. The leader turned back. 'And?'

'Got a nice juicy paycheque for you. Energy experiments. They've got some kind of generator running. Not big enough to house any myrmidons, therefore illegal.'

There was a long pause. The companions hissed quietly amongst themselves, but stopped at a gesture from the leader. 'Need some proof.'

Daedalus glanced towards where he'd left Erin, then pulled a small square memory tab from his coat pocket. He passed it to the leader, who looked around before producing a hand-sized tablet from his trouser pocket. He pressed the tab against the back and watched the readout with a blank look.

'We were still picking up those spikes half a sector away. It's hidden in dead space. That signature will lead you right to it.'

'And these?'

'Photographs.' Daedalus tapped the screen, bringing up a picture of the lab taken automatically from the *Crow*'s nosecone. 'Barely guarded. No turrets. Looks brand new, even on the inside.'

The leader looked at him again with a hard stare.

'There's your proof. It's not far, two jumps. Rough co-ordinates for one-kay, precise for one-point-five.'

'And you wish to sell us this?'

Daedalus drummed his fingers on the bar, in a show of impatience. 'I don't have time to negotiate. You take it or I find someone quicker.'

The leader paused for a moment, then turned and gave a nod to the taller of his companions. He left. 'One-point-five, you say?' he asked, turning back to Daedalus. 'Terribly low for the information you promise... '

Daedalus kept his voice steady. 'I... don't have time for negotiations.' The gangster smiled with his mouth. Daedalus's throat was dry. 'I'd rather avoid dealing with the police directly,' he said. 'I'm sure you understand.'

'Oh, yes, of course.' The gangster just stared at him. An uncomfortable silence fell.

'Listen,' Daedalus leaned in, 'if you're not interested –'

'You are referring to the Gravatus facility.'

Daedalus froze. He cast an eye around, tapping the locket nervously. The shape of the crowd had changed slightly, as if clearing a space around him. It might have been his imagination, but he felt that the noise had abated slightly too. 'Well,' he said, getting to his feet, 'I can see you're very busy and I've got a lot on too, so maybe I'd better just –'

A gnarled, heavy, lizard-skinned hand clapped down on his shoulder. 'No.'

Erin stared curiously at the half-pint glass in her hand, filled to the brim with clear liquid. She looked up to thank him, but he'd vanished. 'Hey, Ram,' she said. 'Check it out!'

'Yes?' Ram answered over her shoulder. 'Problem?'

'Nope, but look! This guy just gave me a drink!'

Ram turned to look. She peered at the glass. Erin gave it a sniff. 'Just smells like lemonade.'

'How… nice,' Ram said, looking suddenly around them. She held out a big, rough hand. 'Give it here a moment.'

Erin handed it over. 'See?' she said, beaming. 'There are nice people everywhere.'

'Mmhm. Where is this gentleman?'

'Dunno. He came from over there.' Erin pointed towards a corner table. Ram could see over the crowd to a hunched human sitting there, nursing an untouched pint of dark ale. Watching him carefully, Ram gave the drink an experimental sniff.

Having evolved deep beneath the wind-blasted surface of Petron, the typical petradon miner develops in puberty a bristling array of specialised nerves and unconscious defensive responses. Most individuals have a reliable idea of pressure, temperature and acidity in their immediate surroundings. Outside the mines, however, these senses rarely come in handy. Often, a petradon's acute sense of smell can make life uncomfortable, or even dangerous.

Something powerfully acidic burned in Ram's nostrils. The world tilted.

'Ram? Ram!' Erin yelled, from far away.

Ram's fallback organs jumped into life, flooding her system with powerful hormones. Adrenalin, immunolin and anti-depressants surged through her blood vessels, struggling to restore function. Both hearts pumped furiously, forcing stimulants into her muscles. She strained to hold her feet.

'Can't hold her booze! Waheeeey!'

'Alright, girl? You need someone to take you home, love?'

'You're drunk. Look at the face on that!'

Through the red haze before her eyes, Ram stared through the crowd. She let go of the glass. It smashed on the floor, and the man in the corner jumped. No-one else noticed him run out the door, leaving his drink behind. Ram fell to her knees with a heavy *bang*.

'Water,' she grunted, 'water!'

'Water. Water! Right!' Erin banged on the counter, trying to get the bartender's attention. Ram gasped as her lungs spasmed. She became aware of another commotion somewhere nearby.

'Vanguard!' Hilton's roar split the crowd in two. He clanged down the middle, knocking aside anyone still in the way. He thundered straight past Ram and into the struggling group of men behind her, landing his first blow with a sickening *crunch*. People were yelling now, some cheering them on, some bailing out of the bar in a panic, including the atheno and his henchmen. The bartenders had vanished. Erin leaned over the counter, desperately trying all the taps to see which one held water. She finally found one and sprayed a pint glass full before dashing back to Ram, who knelt on the floor, wheezing and hacking.

'Here! I've got some. Drink!' She tipped Ram's head back and poured the liquid into her mouth. Ram choked and spluttered, her massive body shaking the floor, but the water went in. 'Hey, look at me – hey!' Erin said loudly. 'You alright?'

Ram's lungs finally unlocked and she shuddered as air flooded in. She took a few deep breaths and rose unsteadily to her feet, still struggling to balance.

'Erin!' came a shout from nearby. 'Help!'

Erin's head snapped around. 'Mole!' Daedalus's face was barely visible through the grip of the huge petradon behind him. He was bucking furiously, but the tree-trunk forearms held him steady in a strangling headlock. Erin saw Hilton closing in. Suddenly red-painted gangsters were appearing everywhere; in through doors and emerging from groups of spectators. Hilton walked tall above his opponents, laying them out left and right with heavy metal fists, but Erin could see a lot of them. She realised with a start that she'd whipped out her sword with a free hand. 'What did you *do*?'

Ram steadied herself on Erin, who almost buckled under the weight. Her body sagged, but her mind was clearing. Ram shut out the burning pain and managed to focus; then she started mapping out everything in her head.

Hostiles. More than ten. She clocked three dragging Daedalus towards a back door – one stossven, two petradon. He was struggling, but would not break free. Two down behind Hilton, a third being driven before him. Another in front with a knife. More emerging from the crowd. Ram recognised the distinctive red colouring. Some armed.

She tried to gauge their intent. Fleeing with target. Ambush and kidnapping. Sudden reinforcements, lots of noise; unplanned.

Ram started moving forward with a heavy stride.

Unplanned kidnapping: Daedalus had something they wanted, and they had only just found out. He'd let something slip.

But why target Erin, too?

Her fists came up and her head went down in a sallying charge. Erin was shouting. Glass was breaking somewhere.

'Mole!' Erin yelled. 'It's him! It's Aggro!'

Huge response. Immediate. No calls to superiors. Whatever it was, it was important.

Ram's legs powered her forwards with tremendous force. Straight off the mark, she battered aside one running man, sending him flying into a crowd of spectators. Another saw her – he couldn't dodge in time. She shouldered him over the bar with a splintering crash. Hilton was close. He brought his fist down in an arc, clubbing the next man in the neck and knocking him to the floor. Daedalus vanished through the double doors at the back of the room.

Hilton made a dash after him, the path now clear. He made it halfway before the two petradons re-emerged through the doors – he tried to hurl himself between them, but they were ready. With tankard-sized hands they threw him to the floor and started beating him. Another petradon emerged from the crowd, walking slowly, grinning, an eyepatch covering half his face.

The haze descended again. Ram's legs failed. The drug burned in her veins. Slowly, she felt herself falling. The world swayed sideways, and she felt a sharp pain as her knee-plate broke on impact with the floor. Her hands went out too late, and she was lying on her side.

Through a blur of red, she saw a splash of green. Ram tried to call out, but her throat wouldn't obey. She heard laughing. Her eyes wouldn't focus, but Erin was close. Ram felt tiny hands on her face. Erin was shouting at her. She had her sword in hand, waving it threateningly at the red blotches.

Ram felt a small tug on her arm as Erin tried to pull her away. The red was closing in.

As consciousness drained away, Ram saw a green shape knocked to the floor.

Then there was nothing except the laughter.

Then there was nothing at all.

Daedalus woke up again. He blinked. The floor was cold. It rumbled. One hand flew to his neck, where the locket was still intact. He rubbed the sleep from his eyes and shifted back against the grimy wall of his cell, trying to stand up. His legs ached enough to discourage him. Grimacing, he tugged his shirt up to inspect the bruising. His whole abdomen was patched with purple and yellow. Peering in the dark, he could just about make out the outline of a fist on his side, and a boot on his belly. He remembered being dragged out of the bar to be reacquainted with Aggro, who had been waiting for him. Aggro's broken eye had crinkled with laughter, and they had beaten him until their friends made them stop. Daedalus could taste soil and blood.

He looked around him, wondering how much time had passed. They'd started beating him again as soon as they reached their ship – a sixty-metre corvette, he remembered noticing – and the bruises were at their most vivid. Must have been a day already. Wherever they were going, they were taking their time. Laziness, maybe – or caution.

It had taken a while to click. The red markings should have been obvious, but these constant headaches were slowing him down. These were Ironbacks. One of the most powerful crime syndicates in the Orb. Petradon-led, or so the rumours went.

Daedalus strained hard and managed to rise shakily to his feet. There was nothing to see on his cell door, so he turned and leaned against the wall to gaze out the tiny porthole. It was easy to forget about the stars. He scowled at them.

Although there did seem to be fewer than usual. They were spread too far apart. No, that wasn't it. Some were missing. Like they were being blotted out. Slowly, as he watched, a thin grey sliver slid into view, floating in space. Past the sphere of a nearby planet, a sun was rising. Its light appeared in pools on the hull of an enormous black-cloaked battleship. Then another. And another. Daedalus stared as six of the biggest ships he had ever seen filled his vision, before they fired huge thruster arrays in unison and drifted back into the darkness.

Nowhere was any gang feared more than the Ironbacks. Rumours and whispers were the only information anyone could find, but they walked in plain sight. Red-painted footsoldiers appeared everywhere in lightly-policed sectors, but they seemed untouchable. No-one seemed to want to admit it, but from Najwas to Crit there were more Ironback than police.

Daedalus remembered the parade-like patrols from his youth, when the police still had control. Even from the ground he could see the Republic's capital ships. They lumbered across civilian sectors, gunning down smaller ships seemingly at random, keeping the people safe from crime. You didn't see Republic presence like that these days. The President said it was to promote more peaceful approaches to crime, but Daedalus noticed things. Recruitment posters, for one. He didn't see many out-of-work soldiers. Or factory workers, for that matter.

His eyes glazed over as he stared blindly out at the stars. Come to think of it, most of the people in the job centres were more qualified. He remembered seeing a lot of university tunics. And – he realised – a whole lot of very dull news reports about graduate unemployment and none of the engineers being able to find work.

He sighed, and his throat hurt. Why couldn't his brain work like this when he needed it, instead of going into overdrive on irrelevant rubbish? He wouldn't even be here if he was capable of thinking straight.

He felt a familiar tingling in the pit of his stomach. They were entering a gravity well. A ship this big would take it slow. A couple of hours to land, maybe. Daedalus looked around his empty cell. For a moment he wondered what they'd done to the others. He sank into a corner, wincing, and waited for sleep.

When he finally dreamed, he dreamed in memories of Jan. They sat together in the university library and scribbled away at their work, only instead of essays they were bubbling, fizzing memories swimming on the page. Jan driving their buggy out to the caves. Jan letting him fly her skiff out in the desert where nobody saw. Jan showing him how to drink shots. Daedalus sank into it, and he had a vague sense that he'd been feeling odd, sick, feeling numb, but he couldn't recall why. A warm buzz crept in and he found himself laughing, contentment washing over him like bathwater.

When he woke he remembered, and felt dead again.

Sandpit

Erin
Illuvia

Only Erin was able to walk. The other three had to be dragged down the boarding-ramp by crew members, who marched Erin out of the belly of the ship onto the rocky ground. She managed to catch only a glimpse of their surroundings – a huge hangar carved out of the rock, hidden from the sky – before a black hood was hastily drawn over her face and she was roughly walked down a long, winding passageway. She could hear Ram groaning somewhere behind, and men cursing at her weight. Somewhere further away, she heard the metal scraping sound of Hilton being dragged, and the by-now familiar sound of Daedalus groaning.

She lost track of how far they'd walked by the time the hood was pulled off, revealing a fluorescent-lit underground room, with a deep round pit in the centre of the floor. Both sets of handcuffs were removed and her arms twisted behind her. Erin bit her tongue at the pain as they wound a thick rope around her belly and lowered her into the pit. The hole swallowed her. Then she hit the ground a few metres down, feeling wet sand on her knees. They roared at her to untie herself, and she obeyed, letting the heavy rope fall away and *thump* on the ground. They pulled it back up. Daedalus came next, still groaning, and collapsed into a heap on the floor, his hands clasped around his locket. Hilton came to, struggled, and was thrown unceremoniously in from the top with a crash. Then he stopped moving.

The men pulled up Daedalus's rope and disappeared behind the edge. Erin staggered back into the wall and slowly sank to the floor, clutching the side of her face. They'd hit her hard – right where her tender bruise had been healing. She could feel the torn skin. It would scar.

There was a commotion from above. Ram was dragged into view, limp and heavy. Four burly petradons wound a huge rope around her and lowered her down until the knot slipped, dumping her the last metre with a crash. Erin forced herself up and staggered to her side.

'Ram!'

'Ughhh... ' Ram clenched her fists and coughed up dark blood on the sand floor, before falling onto her side.

'Ram! Hey, hey, look at me!' Erin knelt over Ram, waving a hand in front of her friend's face. 'Don't do anything stupid, Ram, hey? Don't go choking on your own vomit, alright?'

Ram coughed again and managed to force out two words. 'That's... disgusting... '

Erin gave a strangled little laugh. 'You alright? Back in the bar... you went down fast.' Her voice shook a little.

'Yes.' Ram heaved herself onto her back and lay down with a *thump*. 'I am... fine,' she said. The practised phrase rasped slightly, as if damaged. She shifted, then froze.

'Sand!' she hissed.

Erin touched her shoulder. 'Hey, focus. Here, you can take a look at my face, can't you?'

'No! Do not – careful. Do not move me.'

Erin saw fear in Ram's eyes.

'What... why?' she said.

'It's the sand,' said Daedalus. 'This is a petradon prison. Sand is poison – they can't dig in it, it's too abrasive.' Ram lay perfectly still, breathing heavily. 'The Imperium used to torture deserters by throwing them into the desert and making them walk back home. She'll be okay if she doesn't move.'

'Ram?'

'I am fine,' said Ram. She looked at Erin's for a moment. 'Your face,' she said, taking in the deep cuts and worn skin where she'd been hit. 'That will scar. Does it hurt?'

'No.'

'Erin.'

'Yes.' Erin fidgeted. 'Lots.'

'It will pass. Do not touch it.' Ram grimaced. 'Can you see clearly?'

'What? Yeah. Yeah, I think so.' Erin looked around. 'I don't know. It's dark in here.'

'Open your right eye wide.' Ram squinted closely, scrunching up her face. 'No blood. You will be okay.'

Erin slumped back, resting on all four hands. 'What was in that drink?'

Ram didn't respond immediately. She took a few moments to break the silence. 'How old are you, Erin?'

'Huh?'

'How old are you? In years?'

'I… twenty. I'm about twenty.'

'About?'

'I don't own a watch.'

'You don't drink much, do you?'

Erin didn't understand. 'Not really. I mean, I only started the other day. The day I met you, actually.'

Ram paused again. When she spoke, her speech was slow and deliberate. 'It was a visceroscoliant,' she said. 'Very potent tranquilliser. Very dangerous if misapplied.'

'So… they slipped me a drug?'

'Yes,' said Ram, 'and they had competition.'

'Huh?'

'Someone jumped us,' said Daedalus, tapping Hilton's faceplate. 'Kidnapped us. Someone who isn't the police. But before they did, someone else tried to kidnap you.'

'I don't understand –'

'I'm slow. Getting slower. I didn't get it when it happened, but I've had plenty of time to think about it now.' Daedalus shrugged off his coat and sat on it. 'There were two groups. The Ironbacks jumped us. They were waiting for us. That lab was theirs. They must've called home as soon as they picked us up. Probably couldn't believe their luck, us walking right into their hands.' Daedalus gestured two fingers walking into his other fist. 'Would've been easy for them to put a tracker on the *Crow* while they had us in cells. Then it's child's play to put people in place to snatch us. Walked right into it. Stupid.'

'… So who tried to drug me?'

'Slaver,' said Ram. 'I saw him taking money from the man in blue. He was staring at you from the moment we walked in.'

'He remembered you, Erin,' said Daedalus, 'because you don't see entari slaves. You just don't.'

'I don't –'

'Do you remember how much Aggro was willing to pay for you?'

'I –'

'A fortune, Erin! Someone wanted you, bad! This guy must have heard about it on the grapevine and figured he could sell you if he caught you, but Aggro's men saw him trying it and sprang the trap early.'

'But I don't understand!' Erin cried. 'Who wants *me*? Why?'

'I do.'

The voice was deep. Ram jerked at the sound and hissed in pain. A shadow fell over the pit. Erin looked up to see a black mountain, rimmed with flickering white light. A heavy cloak in dark navy; a broad-shouldered petradon with plate after plate of thick silver-grey armour covering her chest and head. Spiralic red insignia crawled down her front. The shapes were complex and inscribed deep into the plating. As Erin stared, the pattern coalesced into meaning. Two hands.

A forearm thick with muscle twisted into a clenched fist and gripped the second hand tight, dragging it up from the abdomen towards the chest. The second hand was thin and lined with a prominent bone in the wrist. Veins stood out. The two-tone red ink was splashed across her body like a gaping, bloody wound.

The glimpses Erin caught between moments of darkness showed a sharp, clever face set in with two shards of yellow glass. Once, in a book, she had read the phrase 'piercing eyes'. It fit. Erin felt cut.

She felt Ram's hand on her shin, easing her backwards.

'You are younger than I expected,' said the mountain. 'A child?'

Erin shook her foot free and stood up straight. She fumbled in her head for a response.

'Hey,' she said, 'shut up.'

Daedalus groaned.

The mountain stared at her. 'Do you... understand your position?'

'I'm asking the questions here,' said Erin. Daedalus put his head in his hands.

Moisture dripped from the rocky ceiling. The lights flickered. Erin didn't flinch. The compulsion just wasn't there anymore. Erin had finally run out of fear to feel.

'Well then,' said the mountain, stepping closer to the edge of the pit, 'ask away.'

'Your name. Give me your name.'

'I am Wrask.'

'Who are you?'

'I am the Marshal-Elect.'

'Where is this?'

'Illuvia.'

'Who am I?'

Wrask's face split into a tooth-filled smile. 'You are Erin DiGamma, child of the Green Eagle. You are a champion pit-fighter. You are a slave, and you are also the first free entari in two hundred and sixty years.'

Quiet fell. The only sounds were Ram's laboured breathing and the faint echoes of moving bodies somewhere in the distance.

'What do you mean, "first"? Why did you kidnap me?'

'Two questions with one answer. The first answers the second and the second the first.'

'Answer both.'

Wrask laughed. Erin pounded a fist on the pit wall.

'Answer me!'

'Do you know what a Marshal-Elect does?' Wrask asked. 'No? We lead. We lead because we are chosen, and we are chosen for all sorts of reasons. People in danger need a marshal. Different dangers call for different leaders. Diseases, cures. Poisons... ' she glanced at Ram, 'antidotes.'

'So?'

'I don't know how much attention you've been paying to the war being waged all around you, but ours is a very specific kind of war. Your friend might know what I'm talking about.'

Daedalus stood up. Erin saw him.

'Mole?' she said. 'What is she talking about?'

'Your friend,' said Wrask, 'is a black hole. He doesn't exist on any

Census, on any police records, on any operation rosters, any ship manifests. Neither did you, until a few months ago. I've never seen anything quite like the pair of you. As far as I can tell, his records have been carefully destroyed. Yours were never created. Daedalus Mole is a semi-traceable vacuum. Erin DiGamma does not exist.

'You're hiding – rather well, in my opinion – while everyone else is picking sides and drawing up battle lines. We are at war. The Coalition would have you believe this war is far away, waged on enemies from the depths of space, but that is only a sideshow. This is civil war. It is a war of shadows, of split identities. The Collective is fractured. Entari and Brand rule with an iron bureaucracy and order is collapsing. Their fear of losing control is the only thing that drives them, and they have lost sight of the purpose of a government.'

'Well, yeah,' said Daedalus, 'that's what governments do.'

Wrask crouched at the edge of the pit, looming above him. 'I know you,' she growled. 'You are a small man. You have small resentments and smaller sense.'

Daedalus said nothing, and folded his arms.

'I know where you come from. I know what you saw.' Wrask pointed a thick finger down at him. 'I know what you did, and what you failed to do. And I know what you keep in that thing around your neck.'

Daedalus flinched.

'You're disgusting. But this is not about you. You are not needed.' Wrask pointed at Erin. 'You asked why I had you taken; why I have been searching for you, as I searched for your mother before you.'

'Why?'

'She had begun to question her education. That gave her potential. It made her powerful.'

'What *education*?'

'Exactly.' Wrask stood up. 'You know nothing, you have nothing, you are close to nothing and that is what makes you strong.' She reached inside her cloak and withdrew a small object before tossing it into the pit. 'You have a place, Erin DiGamma.'

Erin looked down at the shining object by her foot. She sank to one knee. It was cold in her fingers, and the gritty, damp sand clung to it. She made a noise in her throat.

Daedalus edged around her to see. Ram leaned sideways to get a look in.

A small silver ring glittered in her hand, reflecting the half-dead light of the pit. One half of it was scorched black. Erin looked at it as if she'd coughed up a piece of her insides.

'You took this,' she said in a small voice. 'You took this.'

'I followed your path backwards. I found her. The Green Eagle. What remains of her, hidden away on a barely-habitable desert world beyond the Frontier.'

'You took this.'

'The natives showed me to the site,' Wrask went on, more for the others' benefit than for Erin's, it seemed. 'They hadn't touched it at all – out of respect, I assumed. Or fear. There were some sheets of metal in amongst the ashes, and the months between the fire and my arrival had not been enough to hide what happened. Did you know most of that shack was built with materials ripped from her old ship? The eagle pulled off her wings and made a nest out of them. Then she burned it all down. Why do you think that is?'

Erin shook her head. 'You took it. Why did you take it?'

'I understand why you ran. You were still a child.'

Erin's tongue was dry. It stuck to the roof of her mouth.

Wrask spoke gently. 'I laid her remains to rest for you – forgive me – but I couldn't leave that in the ground. It belongs with you.'

'I left it –'

'You should have taken it. No matter. You have it now.'

A droplet splashed against Erin's palm, and her head jolted in surprise.

'Erin – it was not your fault.'

It took a while. Then Erin spoke.

'… Thank you,' she said.

'It has been my honour,' said Wrask.

Memory

Juno
Frontier planetoid EP6-1-3 (Tier zero)
Ten years ago

'No, Erin!' Juno hissed. 'Watch my body, not my face.'

Erin pushed herself to her feet and snatched up her crude practice sword. It was a crooked affair, lashed together from the wood of the slender desert trees. She'd made this one herself. She was proud of it. *Spark*, she called it. Her mother stood in front of her, still crouched, her limbs splayed. If Erin had ever seen a spider, she'd liken Juno to one about to strike. As it was, Juno was just Juno. Mom.

'Now, try to focus, for god's sake,' Juno said. 'Find your opponent's weaknesses, then –' she feinted with her left hand, which held a wooden dagger. Her silver ring flashed. Erin anticipated it and shifted slightly to her own left. Then she ducked in and drove her shoulder into the reaching arm, splaying her upper arms to protect her head. She knocked Juno slightly off-balance.

She didn't expect the right elbow. Before she knew it, Erin was on the floor, clutching her head where she'd been hit, moaning in pain.

'Why did you fail this time?' Juno asked.

'I – argh – I… '

'Stop that noise. Control yourself.'

'I –' Erin scrunched up her face and breathed deep. 'I was clumsy.'

'Yes, always. You let yourself be clumsy. What else?'

'Don't know.'

'You saw my weakness as a weakness,' her mother said. 'You underestimated me.'

'No I didn't.'

'You did. Again and again, you do it. How many times?'

'You're too quick.'

'No, I'm not. You fight stupid. Get up.'

Erin got to her feet for what felt like the hundredth time today. 'Go on, tell me again,' she said, sullen.

'Look at my arm.'

'Yes. What?'

'What do you see?'

Erin looked. 'I see a broken arm.'

'Wrong.'

Erin sighed.

'You see a humerus with persistent fractures in two places, a radius and two ulnae. You see an undamaged elbow-cap and four unharmed fingers plus thumb.'

'So?'

'You see a sling.'

'Yes, I see your sling. You've always had a sling.'

'What is the sling?'

'What?'

'What is it for?'

'It... it keeps your arm steady.'

'And?'

'And what?'

'It hides me. You see an arm in a sling and you assume it is useless. You see a broken sword and assume it cannot sting. You see a crashed ship and assume it cannot fly. You see a damaged person and assume they are harmless. You are blind to my arm. You make it your downfall.'

'Huh?'

Juno batted Erin around the head. 'Stupid girl. My arm is broken, but a broken bone won't kill you. A broken sword might.'

'... So?' Erin stared at Juno, slightly cross-eyed.

Juno sighed. 'Enough practice for today. Come on, the turnips aren't going to pull themselves.'

Erin staggered slightly as her mother tugged her by the shoulder.

'Hmph. Maybe you need a lie down, first.'

Erin felt her mother's hand on her back, steadying her.

Before long she was asleep in her tiny little bedroom at the back of their house. Juno, who had been reading to her, saw her breathing steady and placed the handwritten book back on the rickety homemade shelf. She picked up the metal torch-cap and extinguished the flame in the corner of the room, before pulling the door closed gently behind her.

The house was more of a shack, really. Juno had to be careful when she locked the front door behind her, lest she pull it from the frame. Old, she was, and maimed; but still strong enough to break things.

A cool wind was blowing from the east. Their star was setting. It loomed, huge on the horizon. Juno glanced upwards at the sparsely-dotted sky, dwindling from brightness to a dark purple. She could just about see a couple of still-bright planets. They glowed dimly, spots of colour set at irregular intervals. The space between was dotted with smaller objects, glinting like dust in torchlight. Juno lowered her gaze again. She wasn't much for sky-watching. The villagers had long since gone indoors. The other huts were dark; their doors shut. She heard the odd hiss and click whisper out from their windows, a strange tongue filling the night air like the sound of crickets.

Juno took a few steps away from the house and sat down on one of the sandblasted border-stones that separated their property from the natives'. She exhaled deeply, her breath misting ever so slightly in front of her as the temperature started to drop. They weren't a bad lot. Distant from her. Fearful, maybe. Always good for a trade, or a hunt.

Juno still wasn't sure where she was; it had been nine years since the crash. Her memories were fractured, missing parts, and when she tried to put them back together the pieces didn't sit right. She still got headaches sometimes. She remembered blood and terror and fire. The sight of six armoured corpses thrown down in front of her. No match, their white uniforms cut to bloody ribbons and scattered everywhere.

Then the crash. The impact-foam and the screaming flames of her descent. Cradling her abdomen in three arms, bracing herself with the last against the door frame. Dragged from the wreckage, shattered bones and sandstorms.

Then faces. Worried and kind, filling her vision. Then weak soup, makeshift splints, and plenty of rest.

Erin was born. Perfect, in every way. Unharmed. Untouched. Small, but hardy.

It was a boring life, but it wasn't so bad. Something had softened in

Juno's mind. The quiet didn't bother her anymore, and it was difficult to be suspicious of such aimless neighbours.

Old habits, she thought, rubbing her bad arm. She wouldn't be around forever, and Erin was already showing symptoms of wanderlust: a condition Juno knew to be terminal.

Erin wasn't educated. She never would be. There would be no teachers for her, no lectures. No academy career. No citizenship. No rights, no friends, no home besides this backwater beyond the frontier.

No Responsibility, Juno thought. How many entari could say that? How many would? Not much got past the Census.

She glanced back at the shack. No sign of life inside.

She might be the only one.

Juno couldn't decide how she felt about that.

For a moment she thought about her partner. His soft hair and his easy grin. Their old home. Regret stung. Guilt gnawed. Juno didn't know what had happened without her around to protect him, but if he still lived he would be looking for them. He wouldn't find them.

She had made her choice. This hidden world had given Erin the freedom Juno never had – that no entari had been offered in living memory. The galaxy had turned sour, but Erin had been hidden away, alive, far from the reach of those who would make an example of her. It had only cost a father.

Sometimes, when she felt like punishing herself, she imagined how he'd felt that morning, after she'd stolen away in the dead of night. How long had it taken him to realise she was already on the other side of the galaxy? In the end, had they been the same? Had he, too, woken slowly? While she came to in a cockpit under alien constellations, confused and bleary in the moments before remembering that it was over, was he confused as well? Or had he rolled over, arm resting on the empty side of the bed, and known in an instant what she'd done?

Juno thought about it often. They'd left home together, to protect themselves, and then she'd left him to protect her child. When she felt Erin's first kick, she knew that the Juno he'd made of her wouldn't suffice. The Juno he'd made of her was compromised. Soft. Human.

Without him, she could be strong. Erin could be safe. So she'd packed a bag, disappeared in the night, and gone back to her old ways, turning loud and vicious so that anyone would think twice about coming after her. Especially him. He would only make her soft again, and Erin too.

The star had set. Juno stood and took one last breath of fresh air before turning to go back inside. For now, Erin was hers. This tiny, quiet planet was theirs. The silence, the solitude, and the peaceful oblivion. Just for them. The Collective could turn and burn and fall to pieces for all she cared. Not that she'd know if it did.

Just a few more years, she thought. *Just give me that. Then I can die.*

The star set, and Juno didn't bother to look up as the sky filled with pinpricks of light.

Facts and Opinions

Erin
Illuvia

'You are gods,' Wrask said. 'Every entari knows it. Your Census-takers make sure of that, twice a year. You know it, or you don't graduate. You don't graduate, you don't work. You don't work, you starve, or you disappear into a Black Asylum.' Wrask glanced at Ram, who was staring at Erin as if she'd suddenly swapped her face for someone else's. 'Except, apparently, for you.'

Erin said nothing. She scooted back against the pit wall, away from the towering figure above.

'You did not go to the Academy?' Ram asked, confused.

'Well, no.'

'... How?'

'Juno,' said Wrask. 'Juno kept her hidden.'

'What do you know about my mom?' Erin asked. 'What does she have to do with this?'

'Your mother was a police officer. Of sorts.'

'Well, yeah. I know. What has that got to do with it?'

'She died twice.'

'What?'

'Once, twenty years ago; when she disappeared from every Republic service record overnight. When her long and distinguished career of measured butchery was reduced to a self-congratulatory footnote in the Republic's history books; or whatever passes for history in the Academy. Again, just over six months ago, when she burned alive, leaving only you as legacy. Alone.'

'What?' Daedalus cut in. Erin jumped, having forgotten he was there. 'Burned alive?'

Erin wrung her hands, but the sight of Wrask – a tall, broad figure, on her side – was invigorating. She felt strong.

'I –' she started. 'I lied.'

Daedalus stared, brow knitted as he tried to make sense of it. He looked dizzy.

'I used to go on rides out in the desert. One day I saw this crew of humans. Smugglers, hiding out on a Frontier planet with their cargo while they waited for the police to stop looking. I told my mom about them, and that's how it started.'

'The argument?'

'It got bad.' Erin's fear of talking about it had almost completely drained, and the words came without resistance or regulation. 'We fought and fought, said awful things and meant them. I ran away. I figured I'd find the smugglers, join up and leave and show her that I was my own person – that I didn't have to be the bitter old monster she was.

'Then I went back. I got halfway, then turned around. The anger kind of... faded as I was walking. My head was clear and I decided we could talk it out, because she's my mom and I... I love her.'

Daedalus opened his mouth to speak, but nothing came out. Erin kept talking, faster now.

'I got back and the place was burning. All of it. She'd said she would do it if I left, but I didn't believe her. She was always saying stuff like that, but I never believed her because she never did it. Then she did. I saw it and I just... I just ran. All the way back. The smugglers saw me and grabbed me. I didn't understand why, but now I know. They must have made a fortune selling me on. That's it. That's what happened. My mom killed herself and it wasn't my fault. It wasn't.'

Daedalus sat down in the sand.

Wrask spoke. 'Thanks to you and the trail you left I was able to rebuild the story. Juno DiGamma was lured to Termina by the Republic, killed the assassins they sent, and then crashed on an uncolonised world, where she raised a child far away from the Republic's doctrine of superiority. She meant you to return. She meant for me to find you.'

'Why?' Erin asked.

'Because I can give you what she couldn't.' Wrask gestured over her shoulder. A stossven and a human in red cloaks melted out of the shadow and threw down ropes. 'Purpose.'

Wrask took her through a series of rough-hewn earthen corridors filled with guards wearing a mixture of red, black and brown uniforms. They stood to attention and stared at Erin as she passed. Strip lights kept the tunnels lit, and piping below the floor grates kept them warm. They had left Ram and the others behind. After climbing out of the pit, ignoring their shouted warnings, Erin had felt a cold calm fall on her.

No-one had ever spoken to her like Wrask did. The cool kindness and the easy acceptance of things Erin had fearfully buried away – it was as if her voice just sucked up all Erin's worries and annihilated them. She wasn't sure if she was being too trusting, but the comfort of the moment was like a warm bath and she desperately wanted to hold onto it.

'So you want to recruit me,' she said, jogging to keep up with Wrask's long stride and to keep her distance from the praetorians who followed them. 'Just… take me on board. Just like that?'

'Yes,' said Wrask.

'What if I refuse?'

'I don't think I have to worry about that.'

She did not speak after that. They walked for some time, Erin struggling to keep pace.

A shouting clamour grew louder as they passed a sparring chamber filled with soldiers. They cheered on their favourites as bulky people hammered the sense out of each other with tough polymer training weapons. Erin paused. When people started looking over, her silent escort nudged her onward.

They went deeper, into the heart of the installation, passing communication stations and armouries, dormitories filled with soldiers playing cards and what looked like small doors leading into storage rooms. Erin glanced into one, surprised by how big it was. She was wondering how far the tunnels went when the floor opened out into a cavern with smooth floors and parallel openings into broad tunnels. They stopped at the edge of a dark trench and stood still.

Erin was about to ask why when a distant screeching caught her attention. A cushion of air blew her coat out and made her stagger, and then the train thundered in, grinding to a gradual halt in front of them.

'You have trains down here?'

Wrask patted her shoulder. 'Most of the infrastructure was already here when we moved in. Illuvia is a city in the deep – one of the old petradon capitals. It is not a young place. We lay down new rails to serve our purposes – my apologies for the bare-bones nature of it.'

They boarded the train, and trundled off into the dark. Erin watched Wrask's stern, steady face as bars of light slid across it. Her eyes glinted like jewels.

A station slid by. Erin broke her gaze to look out the window. She saw people and streets. There was a glimpse of a water fountain before the view was snatched away by a black tunnel.

Wrask saw her looking. 'This is the railroad,' she said. 'We take the refugees this way.'

'Refugees?'

'Illuvia was once the jewel of the Imperium. When the golden years came to an end it fell into ruin, but it can still offer shelter; a place to hide.'

'You mean hide from the police.'

'Yes.' Wrask gripped a handrail as the train rocked from side to side. 'Lowlife citizens are no longer welcome on Taxos. We are moving as many as we can, but the doors are closing.'

'But I was there a couple of days ago.' Erin steadied herself on the wall. 'They let Daedalus in, and he's human.'

'It's not about getting in,' she said. 'It's surviving once you're in there. It's about realising you're a target.' Wrask leaned over her, planting a hand on the wall above her head. 'Did you see the sick ones? The huddled poor? I know you went to the lower levels of Taxos. You must have seen them.'

Erin remembered the petradon shouting in the street, waving his stolen gun in the air before they cut him down.

'The plague is not natural,' Wrask said quietly. 'It is not random. It afflicts the humans, the stossven, the atheno, the petradons, but not you. Not the entari. Not the oligarchs from the Brand Kingdoms. The broadcasting networks hide the patterns, but to those of us outside their influence it couldn't be more clear.'

The train clunked and rattled as it conveyed them through the tunnels. Flashes of light as they passed open stations lit up the carriage and a draught of cold wind whistled through seams in the metalwork. Wrask stared Erin down, waiting for her to question it.

'How do I know you're not making this up? Just lying to make me sympathise?'

'Your friend has it. Your "Ram". A slow form of it, some rough prototype, but she has it. She is dying. We can help. We cannot save her, but we can slow her decline until a cure is found.'

'If I join?'

'Well, we can't treat her if you both run off into the black.'

The train stopped and Erin staggered awkwardly out the door, breathing hard. The comfort was receding and panic was creeping in. 'Where is this? I want to go back to my friends.' The word came clumsily, but she clung to it. 'Take me back to my friends.'

'Just a little bit further,' said Wrask. 'Humour me.'

They stood in a train station, like the one they had left. Wrask led her out and through some broad, brightly-lit tunnels filled with people running back and forth between storage cabinets and reception desks. These people seemed too busy to pay them any attention. Wrask pointed to one of a rank of heavy service doors with a sign. A rough etched sign, with two words on it. CLINIC SIXTEEN.

'Behind this door,' said Wrask, 'is what lies in store for your "friend".'

'No,' Erin said. 'I don't want to go in there.'

'Show her,' said Wrask.

'No.' Then the escorts were at her back, pushing her forward. 'No!'

The door slid open with a hiss, opening onto a walkway above a crowded white hospital floor filled with beds and groaning bodies. Machines wheeled back and forth with trays of tools. A human medic in the far corner was shouting orders in a thin, strained voice. More humans rushed back and forth in ragged white coats, tending to the sick. No-one acknowledged Wrask and Erin's entrance.

'Look,' said Wrask, 'look at the victims.'

Erin moved down the walkway. There was a petradon lying half-off their bed with a missing arm and a disfigured face. The plating on their chest was warped. It looked to have bubbled up with new growths, almost like Ram's head. Their neighbour was of a species Erin didn't recognise. A long, limbless, yellow body was specked with angry red scars and their breathing seemed laboured. Then a human with long white hair and a bulging throat. All down the line of beds they groaned and wheezed, filling the room with the sounds of their dying. Erin looked down into the human's eyes and they seemed to notice her. Their face twisted into something like rapture. It made her feel sick.

'Doctor Hill!' Wrask said. 'Come here.'

A human medic with short black hair looked up from a patient and approached Wrask, clipboard in hand.

'Bec,' said Wrask, 'please explain to my companion what's happening here.'

'This is palliative care,' she said, turning to Erin. There were dark circles under her eyes. 'We take the most advanced victims and sample them as much as we can. The lab needs lots of materials to test their vaccines. We keep the victims comfortable while that happens.'

'Victims?' Erin said. 'Not patients?'

'Semantics,' the doctor waved a hand. 'These people aren't sick. They're being attacked, and until we can synthesise a defence they'll be under attack forever.' She turned back to Wrask. 'We have a lot to do.'

'Of course. You may go. Thank you.'

Hill nodded and swept away, barking orders at another doctor as she went.

'You see?' Wrask said. 'You see what your people have done, in their blind arrogance? That man is from Taxos. He was questioned by police for wandering past curfew without an entari escort. He says they gave him a drink and let him go. The plague is fluid-borne. I believe they bleed it into the rain in the lower districts there in response to civil disobedience, and for other purposes.

'I hear worrying reports from Taxos in particular. Do you know what the plague does to petradons? It makes our plates grow. Imagine the pain of unregulated growth like that. Your plates peeling away from your skin, spines of armour slowly working their way into your body from outside, for months and months. Your friend will get worse.'

'It's not... it's not my fault.'

'Isn't it? You could have stopped this, if you had come to me sooner. The pieces are in place; the revolution could have been over by now. We've been waiting for you.'

'That doesn't make it my fault!'

'Inaction is culpability!' Wrask slammed a fist on the handrail. A couple of people looked up from below. 'Your failure to take responsibility is killing us! Every moment you delay is a victory for the Coalition. There are thousands dead who would be alive if your mother had sent you to us a year ago, and if you leave today then thousands more will die.'

'But I can't... I'm not anything!' Erin edged backwards, palms up. 'How am I supposed to change this?'

'You're not listening. I have more to show you. Come.'

The train dropped them off on a broad platform overlooking the shipyard. Erin stepped out and blinked in the sunlight, disoriented. The floor far below them was filled with dormant transport ships; great black and brown hulks arranged in rows as people scurried around them like ants, loading up their cargo. The huge round pit stretched all the way up to the surface, where sunlight filtered in through the gap beneath the false stone roof. The shipyard rang with the roar of spacecraft taking off and landing. As Erin watched, cruisers and mini-carriers emerged from black caves in the sides of the shaft and powered out into the sky, while pockets of fighters returned from training drills to set down gently on their wings.

'Look,' said Wrask, pointing upwards. Erin looked.

Through one of the huge rectangular slots far above came the nose of a bigger ship. It slid inside slowly, spewing grey clouds and bright flame from its belly as it lowered itself into the hangar. It was long and the colour of sand. Erin noticed it was bulkier than the others, and the places where the other ships brandished giant cannons and mass accelerators were taken up with more bare cubes; storage space.

'Refugees,' said Wrask. 'That one came from the frontier, from Ashlynesa Minor. That planet was peaceful before they came to civilise it.'

'I thought the refugees were coming from Taxos.'

'The net closes from both sides. We've heard troubling reports from the deeper colonies.' A shadow crossed Wrask's face. 'Cold nights, and colder mornings.'

'The Cold? Space isn't *alive*. That's just a story.'

'A story, yes. Most scholars believe it originated in the Brand King-doms, and it was a version of that story which made its way into the belief system they hold today. Tales about giant void-dwelling beasts and the end of the universe – the usual tropes.'

'You don't strike me as the religious type.'

'Do not discount stories, Erin. Myths are a way for the past to reach out and seize the slumbering present, to shake it awake. Some threats are easily forgotten, and we must look to the past if we want to see them coming.'

'The end of the universe?' Erin rubbed her eye. 'Really?'

'No, of course not. I mean that this myth is being used to create an effect. Like the Republic's Division of Records. Have you heard of them? No? The people with clipboards who accompany the scouts on first contact missions. If a planet won't integrate they visit the libraries, take the books they want, and send them back home for revision. They burn the rest.'

'So the reports?'

'Not a void-dweller. Not the end of the universe. I believe the Republic has recovered an atmospheric disruptor from the Contact Wars, and they are using it to break the recalcitrant outer colonies. These refugees are the result.' Wrask looked down over the people below. 'Don't worry about monsters, Erin. Nature's never spat out anything worse than us.'

The refugee ship set down two platforms across from them and dis-gorged people into the arms of waiting medics. Erin saw some who were clearly sick. Others looked hungry or dehydrated. A group of petradons in red uniforms stood above the crowd, handing out food packs from crates and misting water over their heads.

'Easy!' she heard the distant bellowing. 'Plague victims to the front. No fighting, there's plenty of food!'

Erin watched in silence as the people filtered through the gates slowly and the ship took off again, setting back down on the bottom level to refuel. It wasn't long before another one arrived. She watched the second wave of arrivals for a while before speaking.

'Can I go and help?' Erin asked. She liked the look of it, the clear plain goodness of handing out food to hungry people. The petradons looked tired, leaning against the railings for support, but Erin felt like she could keep at it forever if she was the one doing it.

'No,' said Wrask, 'I'm sorry. New arrivals will not trust you. The only entari they will have met are soldiers and riot police.'

'Oh.'

'This is what you can change, Erin,' Wrask continued. 'You can show them that you are different. You can set an example.'

'Set an example?' Erin twigged. 'You mean set an example... for people like me.'

'Yes. People like you.'

'Entari.'

'People who benefit from the structures already in place, yes. Entari. Brand. The Union industrialists who profit by militarising the police. All people happy to turn a blind eye so long as their quality of life is not threatened, like you.'

'I don't turn a blind eye!'

'Acknowledgement doesn't count,' Wrask slapped her chest with the back of a hand, almost knocking her over. 'Do you see? You attack the system or you uphold it. There is no middle ground.'

'So you want me to attack. You want me... you want me to be a leader?' Erin would have laughed, but the depth in Wrask's voice made the idea seem real. She felt lightheaded.

'It is not as simple as that,' said Wrask. 'What I offer you is a place, if you want it. A home. Anything else is your choice.'

Wrask took her all the way back to the pits, but instead of putting her back in with the others, took her to a similar chamber which was almost empty. There was no hole in this one, only a row of traditional cells with iron bars and heavy locks. Only one of them was occupied. The guards fanned out behind her and Wrask hung back at the door, which she closed behind them.

'Erin, do you see that man in the cell?'

'Yeah,' she said. He stood stiffly against the rear wall, watching her closely with large black eyes. He wore a padded suit of white body armour, like those seen on Taxos police, and it was crusted with black and brown dirt. His arms – all four of them – were held straight at his sides and his green skin was flecked with the marks of starlight deficiency, like hers. He must have been underground for a while. Erin moved a little closer and noticed that he was easily a couple of heads taller than her, which, she had gathered, was a normal height for entari.

'We brought him in some time ago for sniffing around our territory. He's a police freelancer from Taxos,' Wrask said. 'An upstanding representative of the Entari Republic, aren't you, Phineas?'

The man nodded, slowly.

Erin tried not to look nervous, but her crest flittered with no regard for her efforts.

'Have you ever spoken to another entari,' Wrask asked Erin, 'besides your mother?'

The other entari said nothing, only watched. His nose wrinkled slightly.

'You've been alone for a long time,' said Wrask. 'Do you want to be a part of something again?'

Erin did. She wanted it more than she could say.

'Hello,' said Erin. 'I'm Erin.'

The man looked at Wrask, then back at Erin. 'Why are you so short?'

Erin was taken aback by the sound of his voice: cold and measured, perfectly controlled with knife-sharp enunciation and a richness of tone.

Erin furrowed her brow. 'Excuse me?'

'You are too short.' He frowned at her. 'You look like an adult. How old are you?'

'I'm... I'm twenty. I'm about twenty.'

'You are stunted, then.' The man's lip twisted in a sneer. 'Hybrid. What has corrupted you? Hmm? Adaman? No, too green. I might guess petradon... but you don't look strong enough.' After a moment of consideration he bent sharply at the waist to get a closer look. Then he cackled. 'Oh dear,' he said, his voice slithering with derision, 'oh dear, oh dear.'

'Oh dear *what*?' Erin tried not to sound angry, or hurt. Most of all she tried not to sound like someone whose vague hopes of friendship and belonging had been raised to the surface without warning, or someone who had already realised that those hopes were about to be dashed.

'*Human*,' said the entari. His crest – long and curved with ice-white spines – flared sharply at those words. His features were gaunt, and the purpled skin beneath his eyes looked as thin as paper. 'You have the blight in you. How did you get past the Census?'

When Erin failed to answer, Wrask spoke. 'This is the daughter of the Green Eagle.'

Phineas' gaze shot up to meet Wrask's. 'Juno's?' he hissed. 'You found it?'

'She has a name.'

'Eris,' said Phineas.

'*Erin*,' said Erin, clenching her fists.

'Juno's *activities* with the human were beneath her,' Phineas said. 'You were a mistake. We're better than this.'

'Why?' Erin asked. 'What's wrong with humans?'

There was a pause. Then the entari gave a long, loud, high-pitched laugh. It echoed off the walls and washed over the unsmiling faces of the four others present. 'I don't have a problem with humans,' he said, 'I just know my place. A human should know its own, and it's the lowest form of deceit to deny it. Self-deception. Hubris. Humans, all flying too close to the sun.'

'What?'

'Have you heard that one?' Phineas laughed. 'I suppose not. Your ancestry is muddied, you have no bonds to your heritage. It's an old entari story. Hundreds of thousands of years old. A young entari, Icarus, builds a ship – as entari do – but he flies too high above the place set out for him. He flies too close to the sun, thinking in his self-aggrandising delusion that he can withstand the heat, and the sun burns him alive. Humanity is Icarus. We are the sun.'

'That is enough,' said Wrask.

'No,' said Erin, 'wait.'

Wrask was right. Erin had never known another entari, besides Juno and a couple of drunks she'd bumped into along the way. Even after she struck out on her own, she was always too afraid to get close – afraid that her mother was right about them, and about everyone else. After years of denial, her blind faith that there was a home for her with her own people now began to fail.

'This is your plan, Wrask?' Phineas went on. 'This is the thing you bring out to be your ambassador? It's disgusting. Have you got a stepladder so it can see over the podium?'

'I'm not going on any podiums,' said Erin. 'I'm not on their side! I'm entari, look at me. I'm normal. I was captured, just like you!'

'You –' he seized the bars in all four hands, 'are *not* like me. You know what we do with people like you? Traitors? Half-breeds?'

'I'm not a trai–'

'Death!' he cried. 'Extermination! You go find your home if you want, go back to Taxos. You won't last a month before we find out what you are, and then you'll get what's best for you.'

Erin's hands shook, and the space behind her eyes felt like it was being squeezed by a fist. She turned her head so she could see Wrask out of the corner of her eye, and asked, 'Is he lying?'

'No. But if you're anything near as observant as your mother, then you didn't need to ask.'

'Mother!' Phineas roared, kicking the bars in impotent fury. 'Your *mother*? You're beneath her! You are the greatest debasement she ever suffered, and the stain she left on her legacy is your faul–'

Based on experience, Erin knew of two different kinds of anger. There was one variety which felt like a boiling pot of water, slowly hissing away over the heat until it spilled over and made a painful mess. The other kind came like a thunderclap.

It wasn't graceful. Erin sprang into the air, fist first, and punched Phineas through the bars hard enough to knock him to the floor. Her face hit the metal and she fell, too. Wrask rushed to her side and Erin felt a strong hand on her chest as she was lifted to her feet again. Phineas grunted as he struggled to his own in the cell.

'Easy,' Wrask murmured. Erin could only gasp for breath, having half-winded herself in the fall. 'Don't wear yourself out too soon.'

'He's not… my… I'll… ' she took a ragged, angry breath. 'Let me up… I'll kill him.'

Wrask surprised her by taking a step back. Erin wobbled on her feet. Wrask's face was inscrutable as she held a hand out behind her and took a short sword from one of the guards. She held it out.

After a moment of silence, Erin took it in her two left hands. Wrask held out her other hand and took the second guard's sword. Then she threw it into the cell. Phineas snatched it up.

'Leave us,' said Wrask. The guards obeyed, shutting the door behind them. Wrask stood by it and stabbed a finger at Phineas. 'If you try to get past me, you will regret it.' Then she reached into her cloak and tossed a key to Erin, who caught it in a free hand.

Erin understood. She turned to the man in the room and saw nothing but a pale white-and-green figure holding a weapon and looking back at her with contempt. The tugs of wanting she had felt earlier were gone. She moved towards the latch on the cell. The key slid inside and after a quick twist the gate swung outwards.

Phineas swept down on her. Erin jumped backwards and kicked the gate back into him, cutting his lunge short and eliciting a heavy grunt. Throwing it back, he burst out, swinging wildly. His blade slashed downwards and nicked Erin's left shin, drawing blood. But his swing was too hard. He overbalanced and twisted round to compensate, and in the time it took to blink Erin had spun and smashed the flat of her own sword into the back of his head. Phineas stumbled and fell on his side. For a moment Erin looked into his eyes and felt only the sweat on her brow and the memory of his words. After a moment of stillness, she struck.

The blade was short, and it disappeared into his belly up to the hilt. Erin heaved and kicked him off onto the floor, and said nothing as he writhed and screeched in the minutes following. Wrask simply watched. His thrashing slowly grew less energetic as the blood drained from him, spreading across the ground, and soon he was dead.

Erin shuddered as the breath left her. Silence fell.

'Why did you kill him?' asked Wrask.

'He tried to kill me.'

'You chose to fight him.'

Erin blinked. Her mind was blank, and a needling anxiety was growing at the edges. She thought for a while.

'You hated him,' said Wrask. 'You chose to kill him because you hated him, and it brought you relief.'

Erin glanced at her own body beneath her – small and green and dirty, and incapable. She didn't feel relief. The thing she felt creeping up on her was something closer to panic. Erin realised there was a decision to be made. Then, in the further, darker corners of her mind, a self-preservation mechanism triggered.

'I freed him,' she said. 'He was a slave. No saving him.'

Wrask frowned.

Erin looked at her. Wrask was tall. Strong. For a moment, she wished she was Wrask. 'I set him free,' she said. 'There was no place for him here. Anywhere.'

They entered the pit chamber again, Wrask allowing Erin to lead. Daedalus sat sleeping at the back of the pit, propped against the wall, Hilton motionless beside him. Ram stood silently at the opposite wall. On their entrance Ram's head snapped up. She glared up at Wrask, sand grinding audibly in her plates as her shoulders tensed up.

Erin's stomach felt knotted, her guts tangled.

'I need… ' she stumbled. 'I… '

Wrask watched closely. Erin was struggling for breath.

'Erin!' said Ram, rushing forward.

Erin tried not to meet her gaze, but she couldn't avoid it. Ram's eyes locked on her, and Erin felt a sudden, overpowering urge to hide

– but there was nowhere to go. Ram looked up at her, and saw something she recognised.

'Erin,' she said, shoulders sagging. 'Oh, Erin. You didn't.'

'I didn't – this wasn't –' Erin choked, and was violently sick at the edge of the pit. The escorts stepped back out of the way. She coughed and spat, groaning with pain as her insides contracted. Wrask leant over her and rested a giant hand on her shoulder.

'Are you ready to choose?'

'No. What do you want with me? Why can't you just let me go?'

'To do what?'

'That's... none of your business.'

'Look at the human. Mole. That is what happens to a person without purpose. If you follow him on his meanderings you will become him.'

'That's my choice!'

'Why?' Wrask hissed. 'What makes that so attractive? Is it what you want, or is it just easy?'

'It's not *war*.'

'I am not asking you to fight.'

'What are you asking?'

There was a pause.

'Do you know your history?' Wrask asked.

'What?' Erin choked. 'What are you talking about?'

'Your history. Do you know it?'

'... Bits and pieces.'

'Hm.' Wrask drummed her fingers on her thigh. 'The Republic has always been helmed by an entari. You are suited to government. You were the first into space. You mapped your genome. Your scientists – your ancestors – knew their shortcomings and addressed them by mechanical hand. You made yourselves kings. Gods, to the races you visited. You may be hated in some parts of the Collective, but an entari face still commands respect. We all grow up reading about green-skinned heroes.

'The people are afraid. If you're planning a revolution, always ask a historian; wrap your change up in something familiar – something comforting – and people will rally. They'll see themselves in you, and they'll rush to your defence.'

'A trick,' said Ram.

'No. A translator. A transitional aid. A friendly face. The people won't accept petradon rule. We need a figurehead, someone the people will follow. We need an entari.'

'My –' Erin started.

'Juno may have come round to our cause with a great deal of persuasion, but you –' she knelt down, so she was only a foot higher than Erin, looking her in the eye '– you were *born* for this.'

Erin realised Ram was half-reaching up the pit wall, looking up at her. On her other side Wrask's eyes burned, green-yellow glints beneath their shells, filling Erin with a strange magnetism. For a moment, she remembered the posters on Taxos: RESPONSIBILITY. She felt words in her throat, and tried to unstick them. 'Mom... ' she struggled. 'Juno wouldn't fight for you.'

Wrask cocked her head to one side.

'You didn't know her after – afterwards,' Erin went on. 'She hammered her swords into sickles and scythes. She said she'd never... she wouldn't... no pledges. No pledges, no vows, no oaths to anyone but herself.'

Wrask opened her mouth as if to speak, but said nothing.

'Everything that happened to her... everything she suffered – in all her life –' Erin took a deep breath. The words fought to escape, and her throat closed against them. 'None of it was her... her fault. It was people she trusted. People she swore to. They came after her in the end. All of them came after her sooner or later. They came and they hurt her and they took away everything she cared about.'

'Erin... ' Ram said softly.

'She always told – told me... ' Erin strained to make the words. 'No oaths. No loyalties. No rousing speeches, no propaganda, no songs, no marches, no-one else's hate. Don't. I can't. I won't. Only... hers...'

'Wrask!' Ram shouted. 'Leave her. She needs rest.'

Wrask stood up. '... Very well. I will return in a few hours. We will talk then. Gorc! Rac!' the escorts stood to attention. 'Lower her back down, and stand guard outside.'

Erin woke to find herself still a prisoner. The floor was cold and hard. The bulb burned as brightly as it had when she fell asleep earlier, so she had no idea how much time had passed. Ram stood awake next to her, having worked her way into a standing position where the sand didn't hurt as much. Daedalus, now awake, paced, visibly agitated. Hilton sat propped against the earthen wall, silent and unmoving.

Erin had dreamt of many things. Her headache was back, but sharper now. Less of an ache and more of a stabbing pain. She sat up and groaned. Ram turned sharply at the sound and crouched over her.

'Are you okay?' she whispered. 'Erin?'

Erin coughed. 'Sort of.'

'What happened?' she asked, reaching a hand for her shoulder. 'Who was it?'

'No-one,' Erin pushed her away. 'Nothing happened.'

Ram flinched. Daedalus noticed and stopped his pacing.

'You're awake,' he said.

'Urgh,' Erin replied.

'Agreed,' he looked around the room. 'Things don't look good.'

'Ungh,' she rubbed her temples. This headache couldn't be normal. She needed a doctor. For a moment she remembered the petradons she'd seen in the clinic, and she was nearly sick again.

'Need to find the *Crow*. They wouldn't have left her at Waypoint, no way for them to know how much data she's collected. It'll be around here somewhere. Gotta find a camera control room. Get a look around. That first. Cameras, armoury, leg it to the hangar, then Termina. Plan. Sorted. Right. Pit.' He flattened himself against the wall, staring upwards. 'Can we climb over each other?' He held up his hands, measuring.

'Mole, we can't escape,' Erin said quietly.

'Bollocks we can't.'

'Look at you.' She would have laughed, but it felt quite like the organ responsible was missing. 'Tough as old boots.'

'Get up. Help me.'

'What's the point?'

Daedalus stopped and looked at her.

'Was it better?' she asked. 'Before?'

'Was what better?'

'Everything. I don't know politics, but things don't seem great. Wrask says it wasn't always like this. She said things weren't always this bad. People didn't have to hide from the police. They could go wherever they wanted. There was a place for everyone.' She thought about Phineas. The anger was still there, but it had gone cold. 'She said I can help them change things. If I join. If I stay here.'

Daedalus looked at her. Slowly, bracing himself against the wall and trying not to wince, he sat down.

'What else did she say?' he asked.

'Lots of things.' Erin thought for a second. 'She said, "If you're planning a revolution, always ask a historian." That's you, isn't it? You were a historian. Before all this.'

Daedalus's expression changed ever so slightly. For a moment it was as if the light above them had gone out, making it seem as if the lines in his face had deepened and darkened, the shadows under his eyes more pronounced. It was only a passing shadow on his face, but Erin saw, for a moment, a different man. After a few moments, he spoke, in a voice she hadn't heard him use before.

'It's hard to care,' he said. 'Things were different once. Course they were. Everything changes, that's how it works. Misery has its time, just like happiness. You and me, we were born into this world, not the old one – maybe it's of our making, maybe it isn't. It doesn't matter now. This is what we're stuck with.

'People change the past. In their heads, they change it. They have to, when there's no real future waiting for them. They tell stories about when the distant past was even worse, and how it got better, so they can keep getting up in the morning to believe that things will get better. *Even darkness must pass,* they tell themselves.

'But sometimes it takes time. Lots of time. Too much time. Generations are born and live and die all in darkness, always preaching the hope that the sun will come up again. But it doesn't come up for everyone. That's the heart of it. Obviously darkness passes. People die. Dictators die, too, and the sun comes up again, for a while. But those people who died in the dark never get to see it. They die thinking the sun was always a lie.'

Erin didn't recognise the man in front of her. Movement at his elbow caught her eye – he'd rolled one sleeve half-up and was digging his fingernails into his forearm. He was looking past her now, staring at the pit wall.

'Was it better before? Maybe. I don't know. I can't. History is a tapestry made of other people's stories, and we can't know how much is true, not for certain. I know there was a President not long ago who died, and her second took her place. I know things changed slowly after that, and most people didn't notice. I know funding was quietly routed towards defence and away from everything else. The centralised news networks went first. Privatised, controlled by individuals. Information slowed down. Trade slowed down. The Republic ended up on top and now it diverts money away from everyone and pumps it into its war machine, to fight a war so far away that no-one's even sure it exists. I know that wasn't the case when I was a kid. So yeah. Things are worse.'

Ram watched closely as Daedalus got to his feet and resumed his pacing, his voice rising and shaking as he seemed to argue with someone who wasn't there.

'No-one knows what they're doing out there, you know,' he continued. 'You hear a lot of theories on the road, but with no centralised communication nothing gets confirmed or refuted. Everything's in flux. All you can worry about is yourself.

'And that's the problem, Erin.' He stopped pacing and turned to her. 'You want to change things? You want to fight? You want to make sure the sun comes up tomorrow? Good luck, because I promise you that you'll die trying. You'll die poor and miserable because you wasted your only resources on other people. Even if you're prepared to waste your life on them, it only works if you bring others along with you. You can't do it alone; you need thousands at your back, all willing to give up just as much as you.

'And to top it all off, even if you rally thousands around you; even if you're prepared to sacrifice everything to try and make a difference; even if you're fighting an enemy you *know* can be beaten, you know what you get? War. Fucking war. You get people killed. People who were born into their side get slaughtered just for someone

207

else's *chance* at happiness. That's how it starts. Someone like you thinks they can make things better, and it's fine for them to do it by force if they have to. It's fine for them to kill. Then, when they get old and afraid of death they'll get kids to do it for them, twisting the past to fit their agenda, turning history into a recruitment tool, just like Wrask is doing with you.'

Silence, except for the thrumming of machines far away. Then, 'You don't care?'

'I don't have to care!' he snapped. 'I have no obligations. If the only way I can be happy is to not give a damn then that's what I'm going to do!'

'But you're not happy.'

At that Daedalus changed. The veneer fell away, and all she saw in him was hate. It was ugly, and it scared her.

'You have to care,' she said. 'I know you care.'

'I don't,' he said.

She steeled herself.

'I know you were going to sell me to Aggro,' she said. 'You don't plan ahead like that. You've never got a plan. I wasn't useful enough to justify the risk you took. You changed your mind.'

Daedalus looked furious.

'Why?' Erin pressed on. 'You risked your life for me. It doesn't make sense.'

'Shut up,' he hissed.

'Why did you do it? What purpose did it serve? How did it make you any happier?'

'I'm warning you… '

'I think I know what's really in that locket. I know what you did. You brought Jan back, didn't you? Or you tried to. Who did it? Programmer? Pornographer? Slaver? That's her in there. Some warped version of her locked up in your spaceship to keep you company. Your autopilot – that's her, isn't it?'

Daedalus looked like he'd just been slapped.

Erin's headache flared. 'You know what?' she said, through gritted teeth. 'Forget it. You're no use to anyone anyway. When was the last time you did anything worthwhile? Drift around aimlessly in your run-down junk ship until you die, that's your call, but don't expect me to go with you. I'm not going to root around on the ground for a living anymore. I want to fly.'

'You have no idea,' Daedalus said, his voice dripping with barely-contained rage. 'This will be *war*. The grown-ups have come out to play, and they wade through things you'll drown in. You're not a soldier. You're a child.'

Erin got to her feet. 'I was a slave. I lived in pits like this. You think you know pain, Mole? You don't. You don't know the first thing about pain.'

Daedalus loomed over her. 'This isn't immunity! If you can't deal with pain now what makes you think more of it will help? You can't just push through pain to the other side and expect not to hurt anymore.'

Erin glared. 'There are pains I can deal with.'

A deep voice came from the corner.

'As you wish,' muttered Hilton.

'Oh, great,' Daedalus threw up his hands. 'The sensible one's awake.'

'Vanguard.' Hilton shook himself, making a rattling sound. 'Where are we?'

'We –'

'A prison.' He got to his feet. 'No matter. We must leave. The Watcher waits.'

'Go on, then. Pray us out.'

'He cannot help us now.'

'Why not?'

'I did not question Him.'

'You see, Erin? That's what you sound like.'

Hilton planted both hands against the pit wall. 'We must not linger!'

Ram suddenly spoke. 'You cannot escape. This place goes too deep. It is too well guarded.' She looked up. 'But we can get you out.'

'We?' Erin didn't understand.

'Wrask is right,' Ram said. 'She needs you. I know how your people feel about my people. They will not accept a petradon leader, not anymore.' She gestured to Daedalus and Hilton. 'But she doesn't need *them*. Pledge yourself to her, on the condition that they go free.' She looked Erin in the eye. 'I know I can't make you leave, but I won't let you stay here on your own.'

Daedalus shook his head. 'Won't work. We have the location of that power station. They won't let us go with that knowledge.'

At that Wrask emerged above them at the edge of the pit, where she had been lurking out of sight, listening.

'Actually,' she said, looking down at him as one might watch a fish in a pond, 'the Gravatus facility is already being decommissioned and disassembled for inspection to find out what happened. There's nothing left there to find. I have seen the security footage. It appears you were not involved in the damage. I believe you are just a traveller who lost his way. An opportunist, and unwise,' she flicked her eyes to Erin and back, 'but otherwise innocent. We have also searched your vessel thoroughly and found no evidence of Republic involvement. You will be dropped off somewhere far from here. Along with your... ' she looked at Hilton for a moment. 'Companion.'

Daedalus laughed. It was high and cold, and Erin shied away.

'Why?' he said, 'why? You could kill us and be safe! I could sell your location to the Coalition!'

'Mole, shut up,' Erin hissed.

'Fuck it! I *will* sell this place to the Coalition!'

'They will kill you,' said Ram.

'Don't care!' he bellowed. 'Don't have to care! You hear me, Wrask? You let me go and I'll tell them everything! This place will be on fire by tomorrow morning! IT WILL BE GLASS!'

'SHUT UP!' Erin yelled.

She shoved him back and stood, arms splayed, crest fully flared above her face, which was twisted with anger.

'You don't understand,' she growled. 'You still don't understand. After all you've been through, you can't bring yourself to understand this? The world is bigger than you! It's bigger than all of us! Don't sabotage – don't you *dare* sabotage us when we're just trying to make a difference!'

'Why, then?' His voice cracked. 'Why do I get to live? Wrask? Why?'

Wrask's eyes were on Erin.

'A gesture of good faith.' She looked down at her, a kindly expression on her face. 'Erin, I do this because I know you. As I knew your mother. As she knew you. You trusted this man. I do not know why, but I do not think you would put your trust in someone who would sabotage you, purely out of spite. He will not sell us out. Not as long as our fate is tied to yours.'

Erin's crest ebbed. '... I know.'

'So you will stay?'

There was silence.

'Yes.' Erin turned to Ram. 'You don't have to –'

'Save it,' Ram grunted. 'I'm not leaving.' She pressed a fist against the pit wall, staring Wrask in the eye. 'But this doesn't mean you've convinced me. You can talk about honourable revolution all you want, you still recruit thugs as your footsoldiers.'

Wrask laughed. 'A depth I am sure the Navy would not stoop to. Very well. You don't have to fight for me, only against them – and since they want you dead, that should not be a problem. Guards!' Two guards appeared silently. 'Bag those two and tranquillise them. Take them to the junker in bay thirty-nine. Tell the *Stanley's Fortune* to drop their ship on a neutral planet. Clouseau, or somewhere like –'

'Termina,' Daedalus cut in. 'Or as close as you can get.'

If Wrask was surprised, she didn't show it. 'Termina? Very well. Tell the *Stanley's Fortune*.' One of the guards pulled a radio from under his cloak and started talking rapidly into it. The other withdrew a small, slim-looking pistol. He shot Daedalus, who immediately collapsed with an 'Oh.'

'What is this?' Hilton demanded, raising his fist. 'What have you done?'

The guard took aim and quickly fired three darts between the armoured plates into Hilton's neck. He looked at them for a moment, confused, before wisely deciding to tilt backwards and fall to the floor with a loud *clang*. The guards opened their cells and dragged the bodies away.

Twenty minutes later, a black ship rose from the surface, gripping the *Crow* tight in huge magnetic talons. Eight powerful engines ignited and it rocketed into the sky.

The Second Death

Daedalus
The Crow

Daedalus could hear Hilton moving around in the belly of the *Crow*. The rhythmic clanking of his armour echoed through the ship. It was making Daedalus's head hurt. The channel to Termina was close now, although not visible. The usual peppering of white flashes as ships passed through was not present. No-one went to Termina. He tried not to listen as Hilton made his way upstairs and into the cockpit, but jumped anyway when the knight dumped a pile of rubbish onto the floor.

'Vanguard!' Hilton cried. 'I have gathered useful materials for the journey!' He clapped a hand on Daedalus's shoulder. The metal gauntlets bit into his skin.

'What journey?' Daedalus flicked a green switch by his knee and swivelled his chair around. 'We're almost there already, no thanks to you.' He eyed the pile of junk at his feet. 'And what the hell is *this?*' he demanded, reaching in beneath a pile of chains from the hold and pulling out a long length of steel pipe.

'I couldn't find any swords. Nor for that matter could I unearth any axes, hammers, maces, or bows. Not even a shield. I fetched this dirk from your quarters –' he held out a headless electric toothbrush '– but it needs sharpening.'

Daedalus snatched the toothbrush from his hand. 'Stay out of my room!' he snapped. He looked around for somewhere to stow it. He paused. 'Where did you get this pipe?'

'We'll need to be careful,' Hilton said, rummaging through the pile. He pulled out a long wooden stick and inspected it. 'A toy sword. Heavy, though.'

'That's not a toy!' Daedalus dropped the toothbrush and grabbed the stick from him. 'That's mine. All of this is mine! What are you playing at?' He looked at the pipe again. 'Is this important?'

Hilton stood up. 'The last time I spoke to the Watcher, he sent me to retrieve you. That was a trial for which I was not adequately prepared.' He picked up the chain and pulled it, testing the links. 'I shall not make the same mistake twice.'

Daedalus set down the pipe and ran a finger along the blunt, splintered edge of the wooden sword. 'You're saying he might send us on a... quest?'

'He may well do. We would be wise to prepare.'

'What if I say no?'

'Only a fool would do so.' Hilton dropped the chain to one side and picked up a battered metal plate. He tapped it with a fist. 'Besides, you will not say no.'

'I've heard that before,' Daedalus muttered. He slid one hand into the pocket of his coat. With Erin gone he was finding it a lot easier to think. To plan. 'So,' he went on brightly, 'this Watcher of yours. What does he look like?'

Hilton pulled a scrap strip of leather from the pile. He measured it by eye against the metal plate. 'That should work. The Watcher?' He tossed them onto the pile with the chain. It rattled. 'He is fire in your mind. He burns the thought right out of you, cleansing as He goes. He drives Doubt before Him like prey before the eagle.'

Daedalus kicked a book that was leaning against his foot. 'He indoctrinates you? That explains a lot.'

An airy sound hissed from behind Hilton's visor. It might have been a sigh. 'I met men like you in life,' he said. 'Before I left my world we fought savages from the West. They lived in the far-green country, beyond the marshlands. They kept the richest lands for themselves, leaving us to scratch a living amongst the rocks. Faith showed us the way to a better life. To justice,' he chuckled to himself. 'They implored us to abandon our faith. Folly, they called it. They accused us of blind fanaticism. They talked and argued and debated with us even as we drove them into the sea. Our faith led us out of the wastes. It brought down those who would subjugate us. Men like you denied it with their dying breath.' He heaved an arm-length section of soot-black girder from the bottom of the pile. 'I can use this. Where is your forge?'

Daedalus stared at the hunk of metal. 'I... you... where... ?' He gave up. 'There's a furnace in the engine room. Don't break anything.' He turned the chair around and stared resolutely out of the viewscreen.

'Thank you. This may take some time.' Hilton paused to pick up the length of pipe again, then clanked out of the cockpit.

'Don't set anything on fire!' Daedalus yelled over his shoulder. The gate was almost in full view now; they would be there soon.

Ten minutes or so passed before Daedalus got bored. He heaved himself out of the captain's chair and stretched, his back aching from hours spent lying unconscious on a metal floor, before going to search the kitchen for something to eat. He rooted through half-empty cupboards until he found a couple of sausage rolls and a bag of cereal, which he dumped on the table before looking around for the coffee jar.

It was nice not having Erin around, he thought. He'd been feeling the need to shave, which had now happily faded, and it wasn't like Hilton would poke fun at him for looking like a drifter. He idly tipped half the coffee jar into the first mug he found. What patches of paint were left on it were just faded green splotches. The kettle was still half-full, so he flicked it on and dumped himself onto a stool, staring into space as the water bubbled and limescale floated to the top. Ram would have been useful, though. Interesting, too. Wasn't every day you met such a quiet petradon.

He reached out a hand and lifted the kettle from its stand just as it clicked itself off. When he tried to pour it, he spilled boiling water over the counter, filling the mug and sterilising most of the table in one go. Cursing quietly, he set it back down and shook the mug gently to mix it in. More tired than he thought. A steady dripping sound lulled him back into his thoughts.

Why did he let her on board in the first place? He'd always liked solitude.

Well, that wasn't *really* true.

But he'd been perfectly happy at university. Sometimes he lost himself in his books for days, never leaving his room until the hunger pangs forced him to. Or until Jan knocked on his door and dragged him out to lunch.

Jan, he thought, his hand on the locket. The locket with her warped reconstruction inside.

Stop. Why do this?

Shut up.

What's the point? Why torment yourself?

I'm good at it.

Idiot, said Erin.

Nothing better to do.

You keep saying that.

It's true.

You could find something better, instead of clinging to her skirt after all this time.

But what if it's true?

Listen to that. You'll be praying next.

How could he possibly know about her?

Any number of reasons.

What if it's the good one?

When has it ever been the good one?

Daedalus blew on his coffee. Then he sniffed, hoping the smell would wake him up, bring him some clarity.

Why?

She might be alive.

She isn't.

She might be alive.

You know what you did.

She might be alive.

You never went back.

She might be alive.

If there was the slightest chance, you would have gone back.

The coffee was still too hot. He stood up, and went back into the cockpit. The wooden sword was still where he'd dropped it. A crude, blunted thing. Dark brown and slightly warped with time. More a club than a sword, really. He bent at the knee, reaching towards it. He paused. Then he snatched it up.

No happy endings. No future waiting for him. Only way to go is backwards.

'Ow! Fucking thing,' he muttered, pinching out a splinter with his other hand. 'Should've chucked you out years ago.' He tried to hold it steady in one hand. It was heavier than he remembered. Unbalanced. The point shook as he raised it to point out at the stars. His arm hurt, so he let it drop to his waist. He returned to the kitchen and set it down on the table. From somewhere else in the *Crow*, he could hear Hilton clattering about, and the *murr* of the engines as they carried him to Termina. He stared at the sword. Mahogany, he remembered. Stained with old blood in places. Memories bobbed up unbidden as Daedalus rested his eyes on it. Old Shep. His tiny little bookshop, a rickety front tucked away between a courier post and a derelict gun store. The blue door. A safe place to hide whenever bad things dipped to worse. A new name (an old name); a new life (no life); or a chance to go on breathing, at least.

Daedalus spotted a square of mint green under the pile of things Hilton had dumped. He crouched closer and tugged. A card. He held it between two fingers, under the light. A faded plastic rectangle with battered corners and a once-shiny chip, almost worn down to nothing. A photograph of a face. A young man with muddy eyes. Hair just cut for the picture, short brown and untidily kept. He was clean-shaven, his light blue shirt unbuttoned at the top. No tie, but a t-shirt underneath. His mouth was deliberately expressionless, held steady for the moment, but his eyebrows were tense, as if straining against laughter. There were bags under his eyes, as if he'd been up late the night before, but there were no lines on the skin around them. It was the kind of face that struggles to hold back a grin.

An old picture, one he'd found in his pocket when Shep asked. He'd had it taken a month before, so that he'd have one ready when it came time to apply for citizenship.

Then the name, in blunt letters beside it: **Daedalus Mole**. Made-up dates and fictional details underneath. Two people on one card. Life and... well, not-death. Half-life.

He remembered the old machine Shep had run it off. Some other man, some not-Daedalus, had sat in the chair, still scared, fresh from the riots, shaking and sloshing tea over his trousers while the old man worked at the machine, which whirred and beeped as it brought a new identity into being. Daedalus remembered Shep's kindly face bent over the keyboard, his deft fingers working faster than any old man's had the right to. He remembered taking the hot card in one hand and staring, and wondering briefly what had possessed him to choose a name like *that*.

Daedalus smiled. Then the past melted into the present and he stopped. He figured he should check on Hilton, but he didn't trust the *Crow* alone with the rudder. He pulled the coffee mug towards him and took a long sip. He wished he had milk.

They were drawing close to the gate when Hilton returned. Daedalus frowned when he saw the items that the knight set down on the table, piled on top of the junk that he himself had moved back from the cockpit. 'Less than ideal,' said Hilton, spreading the equipment across the surface. 'I have not the tools here. But they should serve their purpose well enough.'

'You... you made these?'

'I apologise for the crude workmanship. Given time and tools I could do far better, and I intend to. I will not travel unarmed for much longer.'

'They... they look burnt.'

'That is the metal. I should like some good-quality steel to work with in future, not this bastard alloy.'

Daedalus reached out and clasped the brown leather grip. The pommel was nothing more than a rough lump on the end, and there was no guard; the blade sprouted straight from the leather, black and rough and mean-looking. It was straight, but ragged along its length. Dents and bumps appeared when he looked closely, and the three-foot blade tapered to a rough point. He lifted it. The sword was heavier than he expected, but well-balanced despite its rough appearance. He ran an experimental thumb across the edge. It was sharp. Sharp, and very, very cold.

'Why are you giving me this?' he asked. 'Wait – did you put this in the coolant tank?'

Hilton ignored the second question. 'The Watcher sees all ends, but we cannot. I swore to protect you, but you must also protect yourself.'

'Why a *sword*? I'm a historian –' the word sounded strange on his tongue, but he didn't know what else to call himself '– not a… fencer. Give me a knife or something.'

Hilton picked up the buckler shield he'd fashioned for himself, a dinner-plate sized circle of metal with a leather strap affixed to the back. 'I have been a knight in service of the Void for nigh on thirty years now. I have trained nine squires to knighthood and readied countless novices for the battlefield.' He fixed his gaze on Daedalus. 'I see the way you carry yourself. Your walk, your resting stance, the way you watch people.' Hilton picked up his own black sword, longer and broader. 'I know a trained swordsman when I see one.'

Daedalus laughed. 'You're talking out your –' the blade slashed downwards, whipping past his face. There was a crash as his stool flew out from under him. Then Daedalus was up against the wall, jerking his blade from side to side, knocking back Hilton's sharp swipes as they came. The swords clashed hard, catching and tearing at each other, screeching panic in Daedalus's ears. Hilton was laughing now, the sound ringing inside his helmet as he forced his prey sideways into the corridor. Daedalus danced backwards to avoid a downwards swing, which crashed into the floor and snagged on the grate. Grunting, he threw his foot forwards into Hilton's chest. It knocked him back, but the knight held onto his sword. Daedalus pressed his advantage, jabbing at Hilton's neck. The blade glanced across the skin, drawing a thin line of black blood. Then Hilton's sword smashed into Daedalus's from the side, pinning his arm to the wall.

Hilton threw up his free hand. 'Cease!'

Daedalus jumped back, pulling the sword free of his grip and brandishing it in front of his chest.

'I do not care where you learned to fight,' Hilton said, dropping his arms to his side and stepping back. 'I only care that you will not quail at the first sign of danger.'

Daedalus stared at him. Hilton, satisfied, took his own sword by the blade and returned to the kitchen. Daedalus lowered his. Slowly.

'There are dangers ahead, Vanguard.' Hilton started sifting through the pile again. 'If you are not ready, then ready yourself or die.'

Daedalus exhaled raggedly. 'You're… dangerous.' He placed his sword up against the wall. 'We'll – we'll be there soon.'

'Good.'

'What do we do when we get there? Send up a white flag? Pray?'

'I will know what to do.'

Daedalus rubbed his temple with one hand. 'What?'

'I will know,' Hilton said flatly.

Daedalus reached behind his back and turned the pilot's chair around before sitting down. Hilton watched him for a moment before walking out.

This was insane. Nothing worked anymore. He felt the threads of control slipping from his hands with every passing day. Maybe Wrask's people's sedative hadn't worn off yet, but everything felt like a dream. Fuzzy around the edges. He gripped the armrests hard, reassuring himself. This story wasn't working. It was broken. Jan would fix it. Jan would make everything alright again.

Daedalus blinked, focusing on the seconds as they passed. Not long now. He just had to hold on. Jan would be here soon. His headache was flaring up again.

Maybe just a quick rest.

Just rest his eyes for a second.

Daedalus gladly let sleep take him.

'*YOU CAME,*' said a quiet voice.

Daedalus opened his eyes. The room was quiet, except for the *ticktock*ing of a tall mahogany grandfather clock that stood in the corner. Sat across from him was a tall, pale man in a dusty black suit. He wore a cheap-looking bowler hat, and a walking stick leant against the arm of his chair. Daedalus looked down. He was in his normal clothes, but someone had apparently washed them. His chair was a curved leather affair. He poked an armrest experimentally, and his hand dipped into it for a moment before reappearing.

A dream?

Daedalus looked up. Red threads ran taut from one door to the other, disappearing round the corner in a jumbled mass. He looked closely, but couldn't distinguish how many. A multitude, all entwined around each other.

'*DO NOT LOOK AT THE THREADS,*' the man said. Daedalus looked at him instead. His face was worn; it had the look of an old man made older by hard times and unhappy struggle. His skin stretched thinly over sharp cheekbones, and the beginnings of a neat stubble crept across his square jaw. '*THEY ARE NOT MEANT FOR EYES LIKE YOURS.*'

Daedalus had the feeling he knew the man, but he had no memory of his face. Vague feelings of recognition floated in the back of his head, but nothing solidified. He tried to rise from his chair, but he found he lacked the will. Two questions occurred to him. He chose the third.

'When can I leave?' he asked.

The man smiled a thin smile. '*STILL THE WRONG QUESTIONS,*' he said. His eyes were a bright green, and seemed too alive for his face. They didn't sit right. '*ALWAYS THE WRONG QUESTIONS.*'

Daedalus realised then what was different. His headache was gone. It had been the background noise of his life for so long, he had almost forgotten what the absence of pain felt like. He could *think* again. 'Do I know you?'

'*YES. AND NO. I HAVE WATCHED YOU. YOU HAVE HEARD ME, I THINK.*'

Daedalus dug into his memory. There were grey patches; fogs of alcohol and confusion. He remembered an eye. A green eye. 'Why am I here?' He glanced around the room again. 'Where is here?'

'*THIS IS WHERE YOU WISHED TO BE. YOU ARE HERE BECAUSE YOU CHOSE TO COME HERE.*'

'Stop that.'

The man's smile fell. '*STOP WHAT?*'

'Talk normally. You'll bring my migraine back, carrying on like that.'

'*FORGIVE ME. I AM OUT OF PRACTICE.*' The man flickered. 'Is this better?'

'Yes,' Daedalus sighed, 'thanks.'

'You are welcome.' The man resumed smiling, tugging his mouth jerkily back into place. 'You have more questions.'

Daedalus drummed his fingers on the chair which may not have been there. He found that if he didn't think about it, it stayed solid. He settled on one. 'Who are you?'

'Monitor.'

'Right.'

The man reached into one pocket and pulled out a digital watch on an elastic band. He stared at it for exactly one second before replacing it. Daedalus said nothing. The man waited five more seconds in silence. Then he raised his right hand, curled it into a fist, and coughed twice. Then he put his hand back down on the armrest, never letting his smile slip.

'Are you a machine?' Daedalus asked.

'In a manner of speaking.'

Daedalus listened to his voice. It sounded natural, if a little awkward. Not like the plastic and metal men he'd met before.

'Is this real?'

'As real as dreams can be.'

'Where are we?'

'I am in the void, far away. You are in my mind with me. This place is a lens through which I carry out an incomprehensible process – it is not "real", in the conventional sense.'

'A process?'

The man gestured towards the threads. 'Apologies for the mess. I am old. I cannot keep things in order as well as I once could. And I am alone.'

'Are you?'

'All my friends are dead.'

'Oh. Sorry.'

'It was not entirely your fault. The cold came for them, as it comes for you.'

Daedalus flexed his fingers. They were stiff, and cold. 'Am I in danger?'

The man smiled at that – a real smile. His face crinkled up, his crooked teeth bared themselves, and for a moment he looked real enough. 'A good question.' He took the walking stick in one hand and started toying with it between finger and thumb. 'Physically you are in no more danger than usual. For now, at least.' Monitor's gaze didn't seem entirely focused. Like Daedalus's hand – both inside and outside the armrest – Monitor seemed to be watching him closely and staring into space at the same time.

'And otherwise?' Daedalus asked.

'You are in danger of death. You are in danger of life.'

'Are you going to kill me?'

'No.'

'Er… ' Daedalus wondered how fast this man could run. 'Good?'

'You are going to kill yourself.'

Daedalus said nothing. He started counting out in his head how many steps it would take him to reach the door.

'I have startled you.' Monitor's smile faded. 'Sorry. I am not used to small thoughts yet. I will try to explain.

'You do not know my kind yet, but you will. We were once twenty-four in number, with many children and countless worlds under our protection. People knew us as the red stars rising in the distance; stars made of flesh, like them. Now I am but one, faced with a task of immeasurable difficulty, and I am afraid. When I realised I could not do it alone, I decided to seek you out.'

'Me? Why me?'

'Because you are particularly easy to manipulate.'

'That's enough.' Daedalus pushed himself to his feet, and the world lurched around him with dreamlike speed. 'What do you want from me?'

Monitor scratched his chin with a slow and deliberate finger. 'It is not easy to say. The word is not death.'

'Suicide, then?' Daedalus felt a fraying at the edges of his vision.

'Close.' Monitor heaved himself out of his chair, balancing on his stick as he surveyed Daedalus. 'Substitution? Growth?' He shook his head. 'No, not quite. It is a painful thing; *that* we must acknowledge, at least.' Monitor turned his head away.

'I'm not going to pretend I understand,' Daedalus said, 'but if you wanted me to kill myself then why not just leave me to it?'

'I am sorry.' Monitor didn't look at him. 'I know there seems little sense in opening old wounds, but this one has festered.' He turned now, looking at Daedalus with a hard stare. 'I will not pretend I am doing it for your sake. I need you, but I cannot trust you. I must make you. Remake you.'

Daedalus tried to run, but he found his legs would not obey. He tried to speak, but his tongue didn't work.

Monitor stepped forward and stood next to him. 'You will not thank me for this, I fear.' He placed a hand on Daedalus's forehead. The skin was hot. Daedalus felt a burning sensation, and a curious itch deep in his chest; as if a small creature was scrabbling around inside. 'Passing. That is the word.' Monitor chuckled to himself. 'The Untimely Passing of Daedalus Mole. Away With You Now. Become Yourself.'

'Wait –' Daedalus lurched towards him, with a sound like ropes snapping. 'Where is she?' Then the headache streamed back into his skull, magnified a hundred times, and all he could hear was white noise.

'Aaaaaaaargh!'

Red lights flashed all over the *Crow*, and what sirens were left functioning wailed in panic as she propelled herself unsteered across the long dark of Termina. Hilton struggled to keep his feet in the corridor. He pressed himself against the walls, clawing his way toward the cockpit while holding firm against the sudden jerks and jumps of the ship. 'Vanguard!' he cried. 'Vanguard!'

He could hear Daedalus's screams over the noise of the sirens. They were high and pained. Anguish. The sound reminded Hilton of his childhood.

'Vanguard! Hold on!' He seized a door frame, the plastic crunching under his grip. 'I am with you!'

The *Crow*'s engines roared and her coolant pipes squealed. Inhibitor circuits sparked and fused together, shorting out lights and control panels with flashes and harsh crackling. The engine power climbed. Hilton could make out the sound of fire nearby. He lurched forward against the force of the ship's acceleration, straining to reach the cockpit where Daedalus was in the throes of death.

The autopilot burst into life.

'No!' the *Crow* screamed. 'Stop! No! He's MINE!'

The knight crashed into the back of the pilot's seat. Daedalus was screaming. Hilton could hear his voice starting to rasp and grate as his vocal cords tore. He pushed himself to his feet, steadying himself against the ceiling. Daedalus's fingers gripped the armrests tight enough to split the padding, eyes wide open but unseeing. Blood trickled from his nose and stained his chin. Hilton looked out the viewscreen. A tiny, dark world was growing, fast. The *Crow* powered towards it, venting blue fumes in her wake.

Thirteen minutes later, she crashed.

And Daedalus Mole died.

Lost

Erin
Illuvia
Six weeks later

Erin shifted onto her back leg and the broad plastic blade swished past, missing its mark by a thumb's length. She passed her practice sword again, handing it from her lower right hand to her upper right. Her opponent's beady little eyes followed the movement. He stomped forward, driving another sharp swipe down towards her right leg. Erin danced backwards, narrowly avoiding a broken kneecap. She feinted a jab at his head and he ducked, but then her sword was in her upper left and she slammed it into the gap between neck and shoulder plate. Jon grunted and dropped to one knee. He went to raise his own sword, but there was a cry of 'Dead! Drop it!' from Ram at the sidelines.

'Ha!' Erin jeered, dancing back to her side of the square. 'Too slow, big man!'

'Yes, yes,' Jon growled, rubbing his neck. 'Well fought, little one.' He rose to his feet and winced. 'That is enough, I think.'

'Spoilsport!' Erin said. 'Come on, one more round… '

Jon gently shook his head and his elaborate antler-like skull plating cast long shadows on the walls. He held his neck. 'No… no… I should return to the barracks. I have… things.'

He left through the earth archway, depositing his practice broadsword on the rack next to it. Ram waited until the sound of his footsteps had vanished into the thick maze of tunnels before speaking.

'You're doing it again,' she said.

Erin wasn't listening. She swished the sword in a wide circle, passing it from hand to hand to hand to hand around her head. The point jumped around erratically despite the leisurely motion of her arms, and Ram could see why it made people uneasy. This old entari swordplay she was learning was full of strange, unpredictable styles.

'Erin.'

'Yeah? What?' She kept swinging, now running through a practice piece. Ram watched her feet move, forming patterns of sideways steps and breaking them again in a complex series of motions.

'You are running out of partners.' Ram stepped into the round sparring area, trying to get her attention. 'Jon is getting old. You know he just likes to feel busy. He didn't pose a threat to you.'

Erin terminated her pirouette and flowed into a jab. 'I know,' she said. 'He's too slow by far. Clumsy, too.'

Ram folded her arms. 'He is seventy years old.'

Erin laughed. 'Rusty ol' Jon.' She kept jabbing high and low, shifting her body with practised rigour.

Ram batted the sword to one side and stood in front of Erin. 'What happened to restraint? You're not taking your lessons seriously.'

Erin held the sword down across her legs in a low guard. 'They're just *books*, Ram,' she said. 'No substitute for experience.' She circled Ram with her free arms splayed, like a green spider. 'I can learn the boring stuff once I've got a proper tutor.' She mock-stabbed at Ram's knee. Ram didn't flinch.

'You hit him harder than you had to. I saw. You know you did.'

Erin stood up straight, letting her arms fall. 'I'm sure Jon doesn't need you sticking up for him.'

'It's not him I'm worried about.'

Erin said nothing for a moment. Then she went over to the rack and dumped the practice sword back in its place. She reached for the coathooks and took down her battered aviator jacket, drawing it over her grubby white vest.

Ram started to follow. 'You know you can talk to me, Erin.'

'Yes, *Mother*,' Erin said, pulling her arms through the extra sleeves on her jacket. 'I'm going to the mess. Come find me when you've lightened up a bit.' She strode out the same way Jon had left.

Ram watched her go. When her footsteps had died away and the only sound was the ambient rumbling of Illuvia, Ram wandered over to the rack and picked up the sword Erin had dropped. It was dented at the point where she'd struck Jon. With a sigh, Ram took it by the blunt edge and dropped it down the recycling chute set into the wall. It clanged in protest all the way down. Her mouth fell back into its default expression; a calculated face designed to discourage conversation without looking too confrontational. The kind of look one wears with drawn-up collars and lowered hoods, gazing at the ground ahead. A hurrying, quiet look.

Ram left the sparring room. The mess would be full with the mid-afternoon crowds; dozens of Wrask's footsoldiers devouring their vacuum-packed ready meals, or whatever real food the patrols had managed to 'liberate' from government supply lines this week. Ram preferred to eat later, when everyone on-base was occupied with training drills or maintenance duties. No-one seemed to notice her non-presence.

She took a winding staircase up towards the main hangar. Ram preferred machines, and there weren't so many people around up there when the patrols were out. She liked to tinker with the smaller shuttles sometimes; the ones that didn't get to go out much. Ravens and Skypigs, Starlings and the tiny ship-to-ship Sparrowpods. The Sparrowpods in particular were in bad shape. They huddled in the corner of the wide open bay, shunted to the walls to make space for growing numbers of fighters, bombers, and long-range disruptor craft. Tiny one-man things, they hadn't been out of the base since they arrived. Ram found them now, right where she'd left them. Seven of the eight were stacked along one wall, all completed, and with one lying in a space cleared for work. Ram crouched beside it and resumed her project, replacing the old internal batteries with some fresh ones she'd scrounged from the ammunition dump.

Ram worked slowly and with great care. She always used the right-sized screwdriver, careful not to nick any bare circuit boards as she dismantled the lower section of the egg-like pod. Her mind drifted while her hands went through the motions. Open casing; unhook power leads; disconnect auxiliaries; slowly clear a path to the battery housing through a jungle of wires. Ram's thoughts wandered freely.

It was better here than the Navy, she had to admit. The first couple of weeks had been tough, but since Wrask realised she wasn't going to sign up they had given up trying to recruit her. The grunts ignored Ram now. She was free to wander the facility as long as she stayed in the secured areas, and Wrask had left out a few of the disused craft to keep her occupied. No-one hassled her, and she could mentor Erin when the girl wasn't attending one of Wrask's briefings.

There was a *crack* as her hand slipped. Ram cursed and dropped the screwdriver. She held her hand up. The screwdriver had taken a chip out of the plate on the back of her hand. A tiny patch of skin showed in the gap. She swore again, searching on the ground for where the fragment had gone, to no avail. A glance at the screwdriver showed her that it was now hopelessly blunted, the cross-head flattened into something resembling a tiny hammer.

Ram just sat there. Eventually she let her hand fall and just stared into space. Something had gone wrong, she realised. It was nearly two months since Erin and that drifter friend of hers showed up; just showed up out of the blue and saved her. Ram blinked. Without even meaning to, probably. Without understanding what their actions meant. She looked around at the empty hangar. Somewhere far away, she heard muffled laughter. Now, it seemed, she was back where she started. More or less. She was happy. Sort of. The pills Wrask gave her were easing the pain slightly. That was new. But something just felt... off. Ram couldn't remember the name of the ship that took her away. Some kind of bird, she knew. She couldn't even remember the name of the pilot, but she remembered the feeling in her chest when she had fled the bar with Erin thrown across her shoulders. Lightness. A panic. A thrill. It had felt like the heavy weights in her chest weren't pulling her down anymore, but sideways. Forwards. The thumping sprint through neon-lit streets had turned the dull ache in her head into a sharp, biting pain; like something inside her skull was shaking free.

There weren't any drill-instructors here. Nor any sniggering marines sniping at her in the corridors. No hazing treatments, and no-one to follow her out on shore-leave at night. Wrask's people left her alone. In all ways it was better than before, but the weight had returned. She still felt the creeping heaviness whenever she was alone, and the hissing voices in her head when she wasn't. It already felt like the bird-ship was a lifetime ago. Erin seemed to have forgotten it completely, so absorbed was she in Wrask's vigorous training routine.

The memory of that light feeling was fading, too, becoming more distant each time she returned to it.

Ram idly picked up the screwdriver again and tried to use it on the next panel. It slipped and stabbed at the metal, scratching the paint, never biting. She tried once more, holding it as steady as she could and guiding it slowly into the screw. It rubbed uselessly, gaining no purchase.

She set it down gently by her toolbox. Then she meant to stand up, but she didn't. Instead Ram stared blankly ahead. Sounds of activity echoed up through the staircase and across the hangar, but no-one came.

The logistics centre was a huge room beneath the shipyard. The domed ceiling was sliced with bright fluorescent strip lights and the clusters of tables and wheeled trolleys were overlooked by a central platform around a supporting earthen pillar. Wrask watched over the room from there, collecting information and co-ordinating some operation with her lieutenants. When Erin entered the room was more full than usual. People hunched over monitors and gathered around tables piled high with equipment and papers. Others pushed trolleys laden with hard drives and hefty pieces of machinery. Erin made her way towards the platform, dodging runners on the way, and Wrask didn't notice her until she was already underfoot.

'– undetected, so the *Geb* has time to neutralise any fighter escorts – Oh, hello Erin,' she said, not showing surprise. She turned back to Lieutenant Tark. 'Prep a regular Black Sky advance, but load the *Typho* with Lux-Bs in the fore and a full Rokaton complement in the aft.' Tark nodded, scribbled something in his notepad, saluted and left. Wrask looked back at Erin. Erin saluted. Wrask laughed, and clapped a hand on her shoulder. 'You're late. I hear you've been giving my recruits hell in the sparring chambers.'

Erin grinned. 'They're slow. I could chew through a lot more if you kept the supply going.'

'Confidence is good.' Wrask drew a handheld from the pocket of her tunic and started flicking through messages on the touchscreen. 'Arrogance is not. None of the new recruits are ex-Navy, save your companion. My most capable have been sent into the field already. You're fighting miners and administrators. These people are not soldiers, not yet – you are here for the same reasons they are: to learn. Victory means little.'

Erin's smile slipped. 'I… yeah. Okay.'

'Understood?'

Erin straightened up. 'Yes, ma'am.'

Wrask grunted in approval. 'Don't forget, you're not just learning to defend yourself. Have you been studying?'

'Yes, ma'am,' Erin said. 'I've been seeing Major Ark for politics and history, and Captain Grun for cultural integration.'

'How do you feel about your progress?'

'I prefer the fighting.'

Wrask frowned.

'Er – satisfied. Major Ark says I'm doing well. Captain Grun says we should be finished within the week.'

A small, rather squat petradon with three stumpy protrusions on his skull hurried up to Wrask, handed her a palm-sized tablet, saluted, and hurried off again. She glanced at it, her brow furrowed. 'Remember, Erin,' she went on, not looking up, 'these are questionable values. The Republic fell because of rampant entari traditionalism. You aren't supposed to take this literature at face value. Be critical.'

'Yes ma'am.'

Wrask looked up. 'I mean it. Another president is no use to me or the revolution. Remember why you are here. Whatever we establish must last. We *have* to gain the support of both sides, or this will end up in civil war, and I won't live to see history repeat itself.' She grimaced. 'Not this history. We've lost too much already.' She returned to her reading.

'Yes ma'am.' Erin stood awkwardly for a moment, undismissed, and while she waited a thought snagged in her head. Wrask must be old. She was old enough to chase Erin's mother before Erin was even born.

Petradons didn't really age. They just became more dented and etched and chipped as time went on. You could read years of life in a petradon's armour. Wrask was scraped and battered. Grey streaks ran across broad, well-spaced plates on her chest and shoulders. There were scorch marks under the robe on her back, Erin knew. Her skin was marked as well, covered in tiny cuts and weather-worn. Wrask had sad eyes, the kind of sadness Erin recognised. Her mom's had been the same. Worn and sad, but set into a hard face. The two women seemed to Erin like the tiny stones she used to pluck from the ground, washed up on the riverbank. When she was little they had puzzled her. It didn't make sense. That these hard little things, so strong and so cold, could have gone through so much grinding and cracking in the current and come out so perfect. So round and shining, and hard enough to hurt.

Wrask glanced up. 'I understand you have been briefed on the Highdust situation?'

'Yes,' said Erin.

'Demonstrate your knowledge, please.'

'We have sixteen active operatives in Highdust. Two petradons, thirteen humans and one avarin, all working on Taxos, besides two humans positioned in sentry posts by the south and east channels.'

'What intelligence have they collected?'

'Lots.'

'Be more specific, please.'

'We know of eighty-four points in Taxos's outer shell that are vulnerable to standard breach bolts. The hull patrols are at their sparsest every twenty-one hours, when activity in the residential zones is at its highest. Taxos has nine-hundred and twelve anti-cruiser beam cannons, and our shield signatures have all been moved into the do-not-engage list and given diplomatic status. Explosives have been set in nineteen of the station's twenty-six fighter bays.'

'Twenty-one. Unit six was working last night and planted some extra charges.'

'Oh. Good.'

'What are we going to do?'

'We're taking fleets one through four to Highdust and launching a ground assault on Taxos. The perimeter cannons will have been disabled. The boarding groups will breach the hull at all the points they can reach, suppress internal security and storm the control rooms on bikeback.' Erin knew the plan off by heart. 'Every unit will have a copy of your broadcast and if one of them makes it to a media centre then your message will be sent to every receiver in the Collective.'

Wrask looked pleased. 'Which is important because... ?'

'Because if the people believe we have taken Taxos, then we have taken Taxos.'

'Exactly!' Wrask pounded her chest with a fist. 'Hate has been brewing across the Collective for years. The massed poor silently long for change. Even the *idea* that Taxos has fallen will be enough to trigger universal revolt. We launch as soon as the final charges are in place and our operatives are extracted. Then, even if we fail, so long as this message goes out then revolution is all but guaranteed.' Wrask laughed. 'Ark has taught you well.'

Erin beamed with pride. Wrask patted her on the shoulder.

'I don't think a lot of his students have private lessons with the Marshal-Elect,' said Erin.

'No need to shout about it,' said Wrask. 'I'd hate to make anyone jealous.'

Nearby, a junior officer rolled her eyes.

'This assessment is over,' said Wrask. 'You may go.'

The forest thickened with the sounds of animals waking up. The air quivered with howls and insectile chitters. Hilton was the loudest. He crashed through the overgrowth at a jog, whacking vines aside with the flat of his sword and kicking smaller trees out of the ground as he went. The great cloud crawled overhead, slowly blocking out the stars. The dark was falling. Hilton grunted, thudding up the steep incline, fighting through thick vines and circling around treacherous murky pools with shining black surfaces. Eventually he came to a burnt stump. He crouched beside it and muttered a brief prayer of thanks. Pulling a jagged knife from his belt, he carved another notch into the stump's charred edge. Forty-two now. Hilton glanced up at the sky. Only a few stars remained at the edge of the cloud. One by one, they were consumed. He waited a moment, but heard nothing except the murmur of the forest.

'I have repented,' he said.

The sky said nothing.

'Why am I here?' he asked. 'You brought me here for a purpose, did you not?'

Silence.

Hilton slid his dagger back into his belt. He was tired. 'No-one is more sorry than I. You must know as well as I do. Am I not punished enough?' He raised his head. 'Let me go.'

Hilton waited, but no-one answered. He eventually rose to his feet. The camp wasn't far. He went on with heavy steps, trudging forward until the trees thinned and he arrived in a small clearing. Trees had been roughly hacked aside and piled nearby. A white circle on the ground, bounded by stones, marked the point where he had set the fire for the last forty-one nights. Off to one side there was a crude shelter assembled from tree branches and a mesh of wide leaves from the forest canopy. Beyond, close to where the treeline gave way to the empty ground, a hewn wooden facsimile of a hammer stuck out from the soil, marking the head of a mound of earth. Hilton remembered digging it with his own hands.

He still wasn't hungry. Forty-one days and forty-one nights, and he still wasn't hungry. He pulled a rag from his belt and wiped his sword clean, before placing it carefully beside the shelter. Ignoring the pitiful sounds from within, Hilton stretched out with a clink and walked over to the black pool in the middle of their campsite. His knees ached as he knelt in front of it, crouching down to slake his thirst. Every night, the thirst came. It didn't rain. There were no rivers. The dew he collected from the leaves of trees didn't sate him. Only the black water worked as water should, so Hilton drank that. He picked up the whittled cup from where he'd left it, next to the pool. Collecting a small amount, he went back to the shelter and dripped some carefully into his patient's mouth. It ran darkly over his bearded chin and stained the yellowing flesh of his neck. Hilton went back to the pool and repeated himself until three cups had been administered, and then he drank some himself. It burned his throat. He sighed with satisfaction. After a moment's reflection, savouring the feeling of strength it gave him, Hilton shook the excess water from his gauntlets and returned to the shelter. He ducked inside and lay down next to his charge, trying to ignore the familiar choking sounds.

The great cloud obscured the last of the stars and blackness fell like a stone. The forest filled with a distant skittering. Hilton slept.

Some distance away, a naked man in a cave sat wide awake. He murmured names to himself and plucked at a bundle of knotted thread in his hands.

?

lf̗esgBBO̗fɐsR ʃDERg̗st̗/⊤̄
ʊ̊kƊp WOꜱRꜱLDf̗w
אמר?REV.XX.10… 14ꜱ

Daedalus jerked awake. The forest whispered around him, small whis-
tles and chirrupings reaching his ears from far away. He was sitting in
a ramshackle little shelter, apparently made from giant leaves woven
into each other. A large stick supported it in the middle, and he had
been lying on one side of it. Hilton lay on the other, snoring behind
his visor. Daedalus tasted salt in the back of his throat. Swallowing
hard, gasping at the dryness of his mouth, he scrambled to his feet.
He kicked his way out of his coat where it had been wrapped around
him and pushed out into the dim starlight. Daedalus ran to a clear spot
on the ground and fell to his hands and knees before violently throwing up. Thick, dark liquid spilled from his mouth. Blood followed. He
retched and coughed until the spasms stopped, then staggered away
and fell over. The locket, dented and smeared with blood, bounced
against his chest.

He tried to remember the crash, but his memory was splintered.
Remembering hurt. His insides felt twisted, and his breath came in
shallow gasps. The air tasted bitter and warm – even though it was
cold against his skin – and it mingled with the tang of blood in
his nose and throat. Daedalus struggled to hold his eyes open as his
headache returned in full force. Something was very wrong. Something in his brain wasn't co-operating. The barriers in his mind were
collapsing – the walls that hid the change from his waking thoughts.
The cocoon. His eyes weren't working, either. Day and night flickered like the dodgy strip lights on the *Crow*.

The *Crow*. She was gone. His home. Where was she? There was a
crash. There *was* a crash.

There was a man. Daedalus became aware of him suddenly, standing some distance away. Ahead and behind. Above and below. No, in
front.

Then it cleared. The man stood at the edge of the clearing, staring at him, both hands clasped on a knobbly tree-branch serving as a walking-stick. He was naked, and old. Bald, except for a thin crown of white hair on his pale, wrinkled head. He smiled at Daedalus. His eyes creased up at the corners.

'You –' said the man, in a croak. He coughed. After much hacking and wheezing, he licked his lips and tried again. 'Sorry,' he said. 'It's –' he coughed again. 'It's been a while since I spoke.' He squeezed the branch and stretched his back with a groan. 'You were called here, weren't you? I have got the right man, haven't I?'

Daedalus hesitated, then nodded.

The man nodded to himself. 'Yes, called here. Brought here, maybe. Against your will?' He shook his head. 'No matter. You're where you need to be, whether you wanted it or not.'

Daedalus tried to stand, but his insides pulsed angrily and he fell back to the ground.

'Easy, child.' The man approached him, taking unsteady steps with his stick. 'Don't do yourself any damage. Just hold still.'

'What's –' Daedalus rasped, 'what's happening – to me?'

The man laughed. 'Someone's been messing around in your head, son. He reached into your skull and mucked around until your brain turned to mush. For ages, I reckon. Years, maybe.'

'I… don't… ' Daedalus groped at air, trying to remember.

'Old bastard never did understand people much,' the man grunted. 'Don't worry, you're going to be fine. Sort of. My name's Perry, by the way. What's yours?'

'I… '

'Come on, he must have left you *that*, at least.'

'Da– Daniel?'

'Pleased to meet'cha, Daniel. You've met my colleague.'

'Monitor.' The word bobbed up easily.

'Ol' Monty loves his dramatics.' Perry grinned. 'Not a great communicator. Do you understand why you are here?'

'No.'

'Bad luck, is the simple answer,' he said. 'Imagine a big fleshy lump in space, fishing for people. He's looking for a nice fat salmon, or a whiptail shark or something.' Perry mimed casting a line with his stick. 'Problem is, the fish don't care, right? They've got plenty of food in the river, so there's no reason for them to chase the tiny bit of bait ol' fleshball's managed to find lying around. They're too busy chasing each other and eating smaller fish.'

Daedalus stared. His head hurt.

'So fleshy leaves his bait out all day and all night, just waiting for *something*, because he's gonna starve to death otherwise. Eventually a tiny little fishlet swims along and –' Perry slapped a hand back onto his stick. '*Snap*. Gotcha. Off to the frying pan with you. Or the grill. Maybe a nice bit of barbecue.'

Daedalus dry-retched.

'Oh, don't worry. You're not going to get eaten.' Perry scratched his bald head. 'Well, the golems might have a go, but stay out of the trees and you should be alright.' He gripped the stick tight and walked up to where Daedalus was huddled on the ground. With one hand he took hold of Daedalus's hair and pulled his head back, peering up his nose. 'Not bad. Slight resistance, but no permanent damage. Not physically, anyway.' Perry tilted his face forward, looking hard into his bloodshot eyes. 'Incomplete. Well, you're awake now.' He released him, and Daedalus broke into a coughing fit. 'Monty must think you're ready.'

'Ready?' Daedalus struggled out between coughs as the fit subsided.

'How'd you sleep?' Perry's smile disappeared. 'Dreams?'

Daedalus remembered. Slowly, he nodded; his gaze was fixed on the ground.

Perry watched him closely. 'Nice ones?'

Daedalus shook his head.

'True ones?'

Daedalus hesitated. 'Y – yes.'

Perry sighed. 'So this is how it's going to be.'

Daedalus teetered from side to side.

'I don't get to make the decisions around here, you understand? Personally I'd prefer to ask you nicely, maybe explain the whole situation a little more clearly. I could tell you now, I guess. Ah, but what's the use? You wouldn't take it in. You don't take much in, do you?'

Daedalus didn't answer.

Perry looked closely at him. 'Monty's going to convince you to work for him. You can't fight it. It's not force, not really. It's not even indoctrination. It's more like dropping an apple into a bucket of accelerant.' Daedalus felt a tingle in his brow. Perry coughed. 'He's going to use whatever he can to motivate you. Guilt, most likely. Not the best option. Unreliable. Doesn't always stick, but it's probably the best he can manage in this state.'

Daedalus didn't respond. He gazed up at the dysfunctional sky, his jaw slack. A red splotch crossed his vision, and he felt insects crawling up his arms. His nerves jangled.

Perry stood up straight. 'If it's any consolation, you're not alone. We all hurt each other. We all deny what's good and proper; to ourselves and our others.' He smiled briefly. It tugged at his eyes. 'I don't blame you for bottling it up. I get it. You're protecting yourself. So I'm sorry. He'll make you feel it.' He glanced over at the shelter. 'Your minister has been preparing you properly. Good. I can take it from here. Stand up.'

Daedalus didn't move.

Perry sighed. 'Up.' He took him under the arm. 'Come on now, up you get. That's right. Over here, now.' He led Daedalus over to the black pool. 'Try not to fall asleep, or we'll have to do it again.' Daedalus's knees gave out. He fell. 'Come on. Up again, keep going. You can do it. That's right.' Daedalus's back twisted painfully. Perry dropped him. 'Ah, damn it. Come on. It's for your own good, really. Get – up!' Perry hauled him to his feet. 'Into the water, come on. It's good for you. There we go.' Gingerly, he let go and Daedalus wobbled a bit, but stood. 'Are you ready?'

Daedalus's throat was sore. Everything hurt. He tried to speak, but his lungs failed him. He looked at Perry plaintively.

Perry laughed. 'That's enough pity from me, boy. You'll be needing it later. Come on now, there's a long night ahead of you. Ready yourself. Or don't, I suppose. It doesn't really make a difference, come to think of it. Into the water, now. Go.'

Daedalus stared into the black pool. Was he supposed to kill himself? Drown in this disgusting black liquid? He thought for a moment. Maybe he should. What else was there?

Before he could decide, the strength went out of his knees. He dropped hard onto the ground. Pain flared. Then his whole body tipped sideways and he splashed into the pool. Darkness took Daedalus Mole. The pool started to hiss and whine, and a sound not unlike the movement of great machines began to shake through the ground.

Perry brushed the spatters of black liquid from his legs, a look of disgust on his face. 'Good journeys to you, Daniel,' he said to the pool's still surface. It didn't respond. Starlight sank into it and vanished, eaten. Perry shook his head. 'What a stupid name.'

He stood there for a moment, watching for disturbance on the surface. When nothing happened, he turned and shuffled away into the forest.

Far away, Monitor paused. He pulled a single, tattered length of thread from his jacket pocket and inspected it. Then, concentrating, he began feeding it into the loom.

'Daniel!' she shouted. 'Daniel!' Jan swore loudly as the crowd lurched again, almost knocking her over. 'Daniel, you idiot!' she yelled. 'Where are you?'

Daniel knew this place. He stood in the middle of a large corridor, its white walls charred by flames and the blue carpet catching alight in patches. Cracks were spreading over the floor-to-ceiling windows on his right. Through them he saw armoured cars screeching across the runway. The flashing blue lights and harsh sirens couldn't quite drown out the sound of police railguns charging up.

The view of the crowd wavered. It rippled in front of his eyes, distorted by heat. Flames licked at the corners of the frame. Ranks of police were pushing the people back, away from the spaceport terminal and into the square.

Daniel remembered vividly. The memory of the smell burned his nostrils, and he could almost feel the air turning to fire around him. He couldn't speak. He couldn't move. Metal rafters whined above his head as the heat chewed through them. Through the mass of people and the billowing smoke he saw Jan's face, clear as fire in the dark. Her eyes, dark and dream-big, were wide, frantic, searching for him. He heard her voice as if she was shouting in his ear.

'Daniel!'

This memory wasn't true. He knew that much. He hadn't been able to see her face. He didn't even know if she was there. The fire, the terminal, the police; all were painstakingly reconstructed, but this had never happened.

No, it did happen. I just wasn't there.

Not reconstructed – revived. This was the nightmare. The place he had gone each and every night for two straight years. The vision that drove him to insomnia and back, erasing the lines between the real and the imaginary. Monitor had found his nightmare.

'Daniel!'

This was Jan. This was how they were bringing Jan back to him.

Daniel knew what was coming next. A stone flew from the middle of the crowd and struck a police helmet. A truncheon caved in a protester's skull. A petrol bomb soared through the air and burst against a riot shield, dousing both sides with flame.

Then the steady *thwump-thwump* of railgun shells. Concrete and asphalt exploded upwards in the crowd, taking with it fragments of person in clouds of gore. Screaming and gunfire. Jan's face, clear in front of Daniel's eyes. Big, dark eyes staring, pleading. In his mind the crowd split both ways, fleeing, leaving her standing alone amidst the bodies. His friend called to him. Then the railgun shell struck her leg.

Daniel's insides twisted. So much blood. Fragments of bone. Everything that used to be hidden away inside, now broken and shattered and sprayed across the ground. A guttural, gurgling scream. Crying. The stench of broken human.

Gunfire. Jan stopped moving. The crying continued.

Daniel heard it, and remembered why he didn't sleep. He remembered why he walled himself up in his mind and chained himself to inanimate things. Why he saw people as objects to be observed. The dent in his walls that Erin had left behind split open like an old wound, and the pain returned. Daedalus writhed in agony. Daniel opened his eyes. The black agent stung. His throat burned. Daedalus was drowning.

Hilton sat up. The forest wasn't quiet anymore. He looked down. Daedalus was gone. He crawled out of the shelter and struggled to his feet. Hilton listened. A blowing of horns rang through the valley. A familiar shiver ran down his spine, tingling coldly where memory told him his bone had fused to his cuirass. He gripped the hilt of his sword. It squealed as he dragged it from its rusty sheath. The burnt-black blade reflected nothing. It drank the darkness, almost invisible in his hands. There was a thumping in the trees. It was rhythmic and steady, like an army on the march.

'Vanguard?' he called in a low voice. 'Vanguard! Where are you?'

There was no response. The thumping continued.

Hilton backed away from the treeline, into open space. He heard a rustling. Something was moving up the hill.

'A test, is it?' He glanced around. He was alone. 'I have already failed, it seems.'

A face appeared from the darkness, tall and narrow and bone-white. A mask with black holes for eyes and nose. It was elongated, like a horse's head, with two long horns curling from the top, and instead of a mouth it had a jagged, broken edge. Hilton shifted himself onto his back foot and held his sword up in front of his chest. A broad animal body followed the head, all covered in long, shaggy hair the colour of the forest. Mud clung to the creature's fur in lumps. It moved low and swung its shoulders from side to side as it walked. Another creature followed behind on its flank, paired with a third.

Hilton heard a thick sound behind him. He turned and saw the black pool, its flat surface broken by a gaggle of large bubbles. One of them popped loudly. Monitor stood on the opposite side, staring into the pool intently.

'Watcher,' Hilton said.

Monitor glanced up. He hoisted a smile onto his face. 'Ah, Hilton. I see you are still with us.'

Hilton glanced over his shoulder. The creatures waited at the tree-line. 'Aye. Serving my sentence.'

'I am glad.' Monitor returned to staring into the pool. 'Do not worry, your charge is safe.'

Hilton looked into the pool. The liquid was black as pitch. It looked solid. 'Have you come to free me?' he asked. 'Surely my work is done?'

'Mhmm?' Monitor didn't look up.

'He is safe. I brought him here to you. I found him.' Hilton gritted his teeth. 'I tended him as he slept. Forty-two nights I watched over him. I fed him from the pools thrice daily, as you instructed.'

'Forty-one.'

Hilton stared.

'Forty-one nights you watched over him. It appears he escaped your sight tonight.'

'I –'

'You failed. You said it yourself.'

Hilton's gaze fell. 'I am sorry, my lord.'

'Hm.' Monitor affected a thoughtful chin-scratch. His hand clipped through his chin slightly before correcting itself. 'Our friend will be some time. The process is crude, and not perfect. He will have need of you on his waking.'

'Yes, my lord.'

'You will tend to him again until his strength returns. You will guard him until he can guard himself. This is your place now, Hilton.'

'… Yes, my lord.'

'Do not stray.'

'I will not, my lord.'

'Good.' Monitor's outline flickered. The sound of horns bloomed again in the distance. 'There… ' He hesitated. 'There is one more thing.'

Hilton glanced back at the creatures from the forest. They had moved closer.

'This world does not want you here,' Monitor went on. 'It hungers for fresh minds, something you lack. When Vanguard emerges he will be ripe for the picking.'

Hilton realised the creatures were not with Monitor. He raised his blackened, ugly sword.

Monitor withdrew a watch from his jacket and looked at it. 'I will return in thirteen hours. You must not let them pass.'

'Yes, my lord.'

YOU MUST NOT.

'Yes, my lord.'

'Then you will have your freedom.'

'… Thank you, my lord.'

Monitor slid out of the world with a crackle. The creature in front let out a long, low growl.

Rain started to fall.

Rough Hands

Ram
Illuvia

Ram lurked in the tunnel. A heavy *thwacking* sound repeated itself over and over in the practice chamber nearby. The lights in Illuvia were dimmed, and most of Wrask's contingent would be either offworld or asleep.

Thwack thwack thwack – snap –

The sounds stopped. Ram picked up the sound of heavy, ragged breathing. A clatter as something was thrown down the disposal chute in two pieces, then a rattle, then the thwacking continued.

Ram steadied herself, and stepped into the archway.

Erin didn't notice. Her arms were a blur as she lay into the practice dummy with two of the heavier plastic shortswords, battering it hard from both sides. It sprung back and flailed beneath the rain of blows, its loose arms flapping wildly. Ram took a step closer. Bright red blood had spattered the floor at Erin's feet.

'Erin.'

She spun mid-swing and smashed the side of the dummy's head so hard that one of the swords shattered. Plastic shrapnel burst everywhere. Erin brandished the jagged edge in front of her chest, raising the other one high over her head. 'F– Ram! You – ffffaah,' she let the air out of her lungs and fell back against the dummy. She was so *small*.

'Sorry.' Ram became conscious of her own body. The outfit she'd taken from the barracks wasn't quite her – the padded suit with the angular red chestpiece made her look even bigger than she was; more imposing.

'You scared – the crap – outta me.'

'Your arm –' Ram stepped towards her.

'What? No, leave it.' Erin recoiled, dropping the intact sword and grasping her bloody forearm. 'It's fine.'

Ram caught a look at the wound. For a moment she felt a shameful excitement, a thrill of recognition. 'Did you do that?' The words came unchecked.

'Yes. No. Accident. These weapons are no good.' Erin looked at her hand, which dripped scarlet. 'They... they break.'

'Oh.' Ram hesitated. 'Erin... ' she extended a huge, rough hand. Erin didn't respond. 'It's okay. Just... give that to me.' Erin's body sagged, and she let Ram take the jagged half-sword from her. Her hulking, massive friend took her by the shoulder and guided her to the floor, where she sat. Ram knelt in front of her. 'What are you doing here? It's late.' She thumbed the skin under Erin's eye. 'Have you slept?'

'No,' Erin intoned.

'You need to sleep. You have lessons in a few –'

'Why am I so angry, Ram?'

'Are you?' Ram took Erin's arm and inspected the cuts. There were fragments of plastic embedded in the skin. 'I had not noticed.'

'I can feel it. It's getting worse,' Erin said. 'Sometimes I feel – I feel like I'm going to burst.'

Ram gently brushed the smaller pieces out with her fingers, causing Erin to wince. 'I thought this might happen,' Ram said gently. 'You never talk about what happened after you ran away from home.'

Erin said nothing, just stared ahead blankly. Ram knew the feeling. 'Is that why you stayed here?' Ram said. 'You want to kill?'

'No!' said Erin. 'That's not... it's not... I care! I do care! It's all wrong and everything is broken and messed up and I want to do the right thing, but there's this cold and it comes when I'm alone and I just I can't and I'm not her I'm *not* –' she gasped for air.

Ram took her gently by the shoulder and looked into her eyes. 'Erin. Listen to me. We can go. We can go and run and get away from here whenever we want. You do not have to stay. You will not be alone.'

'But we have to *help.*'

'Listen to me. Killing... it does things to a person. Some memories, they change the way you think about people. They make you cold just by staying there in your head.' Images fought to be seen in Ram's mind as she spoke. Too-close memories. 'You do not have to be this way. There are other things you might do, other ways you can make a difference. You can leave this behind.'

'So... what? Run?'

'If we have to.'

Erin laughed. 'Run from myself? That'd be a neat trick.'

'I can keep you safe.'

'Safe from myself?'

'Look –'

'My mom ran. I know she did.' Erin's voice cracked, but grew louder. 'She couldn't face it, who she was. She never talked about it. If I start running now then where do I stop?'

'You cannot indulge this anger or it will *warp* you, Erin. It will turn you until you cannot – until you cannot even stand to look at yourself anymore.'

Ram wanted to say more. She wanted to tell Erin all about her fear that Wrask was doing this on purpose – turning Erin into a weapon, rebuilding her to be more like her mother. The words came close. But she was too afraid. Erin had been spending so little time with her lately... if Ram tried to come between Erin and her commander she feared the choice Erin might make. So she stayed her tongue.

'I can't look at myself *now*,' Erin said, her voice no longer shaking. She pushed herself to her feet, bloody hand slipping on the floor, and faced Ram. She wiped the blood off on her training vest. 'I've killed. I've crossed that bridge already.'

'It's not too late to turn back,' said Ram. 'Not yet.'

'I've been angry since we met. I'll be angry if we leave. I won't stop. If we run now you'll be stuck with me, and I'll get worse.' Erin held out a hand to Ram and pulled her from her kneeling position, flexing muscles that had barely existed when she started training. 'I don't want that for you. I want that for them. The people who deserve it.'

Ram sighed. She clasped Erin's hand then gripped it tight and pulled her in close. 'I won't leave,' she murmured 'But I won't let you go too far, even if I have to knock you out and drag you home myself.'

Ram's crusted, bloody scalp was perforated by a hundred bony spines. Up close, it was a terrifying sight. Her night eyes gleamed a dirty yellow behind their shells, holding Erin's gaze with no need to blink. Erin stared. She wanted to ask why. Why would she stay?

But she said nothing. She just nodded.

Then Ram did something wholly unexpected. Her gigantic arms closed around Erin's tiny body and she lifted her into the air, almost crushing the breath out of her. Erin panicked, flapping her arms helplessly and making small noises of surprise. They stayed that way for a few moments, then Ram set her down with a *thump*. Erin swayed on her feet slightly, surprised. Her crest had flared.

'What – what was that?' she asked. Her breath was heavy. Ram's body was warm in front of her.

Ram scratched her neck. 'Nothing,' she said. 'Get some sleep. You have got lessons in the morning.'

'I... yeah.' Erin coughed, and looked down at her feet, trying to ignore the images that floated in the back of her mind. 'Okay. Okay. Sure.'

'... And wash your hands.'

Erin staggered to the chute and dropped the other sword out of sight. 'Sure,' she said again. She went to the archway and hesitated, as if she wanted to say something. Before Ram could press her, she disappeared into the dark corridor.

An hour later, Erin still lay awake in her quarters above the barracks. Wrask had provided her with a private section of the old reception dorms for visiting dignitaries. The walls here were smooth and painted. The low-lights set into the carpeted floor were on, warming the space with a dim red glow. The room was very quiet. The four-poster bed was meant for all species, so Erin's toes barely came halfway down. She stared at the ceiling.

A single small knock came from the door.

Erin sat up, drawing the silk sheets over herself, squinting into the dark. Her crest flared. 'Hello?'

'Erin?' whispered Ram from the other side. 'Are you awake?' Her voice was oddly soft – like falling sand rather than gravel.

'Oh,' Erin relaxed, her crest sitting back down. 'It's you. Come in.'

The door opened silently and Ram entered, wearing her own clothes again – the outfit she'd been wearing the day they met. A dark blue tunic and black cloak. 'Can we... talk?'

Erin nodded. Ram took a step forward, and stopped when her foot caught in a pile of clothes. She looked down. 'Oh.'

Erin stared at her. 'Ram?'

Ram looked up. There was a moment of silence. Erin's crest flittered. She let the sheet slip a little over her shoulder, exposing a triangle of skin. Ram watched as the silk fell entirely from her chest.

'Close the door,' said Erin.

The rain fell in sheets, soaking everything. The ground shimmered as icy water flowed, forming streams that ran from the top of the hill to the bottom. Mud and blood washed away with it, staining the trees as it rushed by. Hilton swung, hard, and another golem reeled back, blood spurting from its neck.

His sword looked like a nightmare. Gore clung to the nicks in its jagged edge, and it trailed stringy red flesh with every swipe. Blood ran in rivulets through gaps in his armour, where vigorous movement had torn the steel from the skin. His breath came ragged and painful, but he did not slow. The golems emerged from the treeline in small, tired groups, the mudslide slowing their advance. The hillside was a flowing mess. Another masked creature loped forwards and raised an arm to throw Hilton aside. He stepped in close and removed it with an upward slash. The golem recoiled and Hilton swung back down, burying his blade in the side of its head. It fell.

Hilton cursed as he struggled to pull the sword free. He could hear the roars of frustration as the hillside defeated another attacker, but he knew more would be on him in moments. The sword broke free with a sickening crack, and Hilton wasted no time in dragging the most recent bodies forward onto the pile. Once they were sprawled over their dead comrades he took a moment to breathe. He tilted his head back and savoured the coolness of the rain as it dripped through his visor, running down his neck and turning brown with blood and sweat. He swallowed the water and groaned with frustration. No matter how much he drank here, nothing quenched his thirst. He was numb with battle fever. Armour had torn away from the skin all over his body, but he felt no pain; only a greater freedom of movement, and a warm wetness covering his body.

Hilton felt strong. With each foe he cut down he offered another prayer of thanks to the Watcher. His limbs were loosening, becoming nimble once more. Nightmare yearned for blood, and there was plenty to offer. He was quick. Each severance from the metal made him faster, heightened his fever. Hilton hadn't fought like this in years. He felt young again.

A pair of golems clawed their way over the lip of the hill.

The night was long. The black pool overflowed, sloughing off tendrils of dark ooze onto the surrounding soil. Hilton spared a look. Bubbles continued forming on the surface. The Vanguard yet lived.

The golems clambered over the pile of their dead, screeching with rage. Hilton raised his sword and stepped forward to meet them. He feinted a thrust at one and sent it tumbling back down, then jabbed at the mask of its friend. The mask cracked down the centre, but before he could step back a giant hand snatched at his blade. The golem seized Nightmare tight in one fist, roaring in pain, and tore it from Hilton's grip. Hilton jumped backwards. It threw the sword down before advancing.

Hilton backed up to the pool's edge. The golem closed in. It reached out a hand, and Hilton punched it in the face. His gauntlet rang with the impact. Its mask shattered. Beneath it was a gaping horizontal maw, full of blood and malformed fangs. It screamed. Hilton lunged forward and punched it again. His fist knocked it from the side, and he caught a glimpse of fang tearing flesh as the mouth slammed shut. He threw himself forward, tackling the creature to the ground and slamming his fists into its head until it was a bloody, twitching pulp. Gasping for breath, Hilton scrambled to his feet.

The second golem was on him before he could reach his sword. It knocked him to the ground and clawed at his helmet with vicious talons, slicing at his face through the gap in his visor. Hilton roared with pain and heaved with his legs, throwing the beast over his shoulders and into the pool. As he rolled over and struggled to stand, he heard a scream and a hiss. He snatched up his sword and readied it against the next attacker. A glance over his shoulder told him that the pool was unkind to the creatures. A bitter smell of burning flesh reached his nostrils.

Another pair emerged from the treeline and galloped towards him. Hilton gripped Nightmare tight. The pile of bodies was almost as tall as he was. Wind rustled through the leaves of the forest with an angry hiss, and he laughed.

?

Daniel felt like his head had been disconnected. He felt turned off. Cold, but not uncomfortably. More like the cold side of the pillow, or the satisfying cold of a good drink. He hung, suspended. The last time he checked, his eyes had been open. The sting of the liquid had been his proof, but now it was as if Pain had been uninstalled. He decided his eyes were open, but he just couldn't see. He felt the locket's chain tugging gently on his neck.

Time had been unplugged as well. Daniel did not know how long he'd been under. He remembered a great deal of pain. Physical pain. A bad headache, now only a memory.

YOU HAVE SHUT YOURSELF DOWN.

Daniel felt the voice thrumming in his bones.

THAT IS NOT HELPFUL.

Daniel tried to ignore it. He was perfectly happy like this, thank you very much.

YOU WILL BENEFIT FROM THE PROCESS. DO NOT RESIST IT.

Nope. Nope nope nope. Daniel remembered something vaguely horrible and did not harbour any wish to go back there.

IT WAS YOUR FAULT.

Daniel was pretty sure that wasn't even true. The phrase was very familiar, though; comforting, in a way. It beckoned with memories of vicious self-satisfaction.

YOU WILL ACCEPT IT. I WILL FIX YOU.

There was a twinge in Daniel's neck. His fingers tingled. No. No no no no no. A burning sensation crept up his spine and bloomed in his chest. His stomach hurt. His liver really hurt. His eyes started to sting. Vision returned, and a face appeared in his mind's eye. Jan stared sadly at him, with an expression calculated to hurt.

Daniel couldn't help it. She was dead, he knew it now. The lies wouldn't stick anymore. One friendship, and he couldn't even manage to protect that.

EXCELLENT, CARRY ON.

Above him, bodies sizzled and smoked on the surface of the pool.

A Difference in Scale

Erin
Illuvia

Erin had never seen a carrier before. She struggled to get her head around the *Geb*'s sheer size. Ram had told her it was four kilometres long – nearly the size of its twin, the *Aken* – but the number didn't quite convey the way it blocked out the sky in front of her. Wrask had called her up to the main pad, allowing her to finally step outside the facility the way she'd come in.

Erin couldn't quite believe something so massive could stay hidden. Surely now it had landed the Republic *had* to notice. The black walls stretched far off into the distance until they faded to blue-tinted blurs in the atmosphere. It looked like a skyscraper tipped on its side. The big cylindrical retros – arrayed in long rows along either side of the hull – must have each been the size of the *Crow*, and the rumbling sound they made as they turned in the gigantic docking clamps shook the ground underfoot. Erin puzzled over the purpose of the long flat platforms mounted all over the sides until a wing of sharp-look-ing fighters screamed in from the horizon, painted all in black. They vented streams of bright blue gas behind them as they came in to land, and their tyres screeched angrily at the contact. Erin watched as more fighters appeared from all directions, flocking towards the *Geb* in formation. Engineers and pilots ran all about her on the concourse, shouting and dragging carts loaded with weaponry, fuel canisters and armour. Fearsome-looking steel vehicles rolled up from wide under-ground tunnels and disappeared into the bellies of smaller close-assault bombers. In the sky far above, she could see a tiny speck that could only be the dreadnought *Typho*, surrounded by a cloud of outrider craft.

Wrask was talking to a group of human cargo handlers, inspecting their tallies and ordering changes. She sent them away and beckoned Erin over. Ram followed closely. Two weeks had passed since the night in the sparring chamber, and Erin was now rarely seen without her.

'Have you signed off with your tutors yet?' Wrask asked. 'We're behind schedule, and I will not be happy if we're delayed further by *admin*.'

'Yes ma'am,' Erin said. 'Captain Greaves says I'm ready enough, and he'll be onboard if I need anything further.'

'Plans are changing,' Wrask grunted. She looked tense, her usual easy humour nowhere to be seen. 'Greaves will now be on the *Typho*.'

'What?' said Erin. 'Why? What's happened?'

Wrask looked irritated at the question, but answered. 'The *Erebus* happened. There was a communication breakdown. The attack order went out early, and we couldn't contact the right crews to abort it.'

'Then – that's it?' Erin went cold. 'The Republic knows?'

'No. Three battle groups engaged patrols around Petron and landed shock troops in the mines. It should look like a single insurrection.' Wrask made a guttural sound. 'I couldn't send support. The distribution of our forces must remain secret. We lost the *Erebus*, with crew.'

'*Erebus*… ' Ram recalled. 'Stealth dreadnought. Powerful ship.'

'Not anymore. Reinforcements are moving now, but it's put a large dent in our capabilities. Plans are being rewritten.' She looked at Ram. 'I suppose there's no use trying to reassign you? We need good engineers, now more than ever. The *Aken* still needs a chief shield operator, and now without the *Erebus* it's our most valuable asset.'

Ram shook her head and rested a hand on Erin's shoulder.

Wrask sighed. 'Very well. Erin will be assigned a petradon guard once we depart. Try to get along with them, will you? The *Geb* leaves tomorrow morning. Someone will come to collect you. Be ready.' She looked around. 'Until then, try to make yourselves useful.'

Wrask walked away, booming orders left and right, startling deckhands. Erin turned to Ram.

'Excited?'

'No,' grunted Ram. 'I have no stake in this war.'

'You're still here, though.' Erin grinned.

Ram did not. 'I'm only here so you stand a better chance of getting out of this alive.'

'Like I need a bodyguard.' Erin punched her in the shoulder. 'Admit it, you want to get your hands dirty again, right? I mean… have a decent fight or two.'

Ram did smile at that. 'You like fighting far too much for someone so small.'

'Come on then, I'll take you.'

'Maybe later.'

Erin gave her a shove. 'Wimp.'

Ram snorted and clapped her on the back, knocking her onto her knees for the sixth time that week.

Later, Erin found herself back in the control centre. It was empty. The equipment trolleys had all been taken for loading the ships, and the room had been stripped of computers. The tables had all been dragged to the sides, the maps and stacks of hard drives now gone. Only the podium in the centre remained in place, but the computers that had stood there previously were either removed or smashed to pieces, ready for indefinite abandonment. The jacket she was wearing today had been taken from someone's cupboard half a lifetime ago, and she'd torn extra holes for her arms. Wrask's armoury had all sorts of uniforms, and the wardrobe she'd been provided with – to calibrate your image, her tutors had said – was a menagerie of clothes from all over the Collective, but she still felt most comfortable in the battered aviator's jacket. It was warm, too.

Looking around the empty room, Erin was surprised to realise she was sad. It wasn't quite misery, but there was regret. That almost made her angry. Home was gone. It was long gone, and not by accident. She was a soldier now. An adult. The last thing she needed was another home, but she'd gone and grown an attachment anyway. Now she had to leave, and it stung. The heavy feeling in her chest tightened, and she felt an angry prickle on her skin. The headaches hadn't returned, thankfully, but her body was acting up in other ways – every other night she woke in the dark from nightmares where she was drowning, covered in a cold sweat, shaking in Ram's arms. The anger was getting worse. It was nearly a year since she was first sold, and less than that since she'd last daydreamed about killing someone. It had started again. The prickling would start, then the itch-ing, then she'd be beating a man to a bloody pulp with her fists. He never looked the same twice. His face shifted endlessly, his clothes first a brown leather vest, then a black trenchcoat, then a police uniform, warping back and forth between all the people she'd ever had cause to hate.

She shivered. Violence was in her blood, but Mom had always seemed more comfortable. For Juno it was a job – a skill. For Erin it was an *urge*. It flickered sometimes, catching unbidden and burning her up inside. It fed on her anger and made it hard to think. Erin listened to the quiet humming of the lights above her, and the distant echoes of activity in the corridors. It was quiet. She waited, and the hot feeling slowly ebbed away.

Then there was a footfall. A heavy, urgent footfall in the corridors, growing louder as it approached. Erin waited for her, savouring the last few moments of solitude. When Ram rounded the corner a joke was halfway to her mouth before she saw the look on her face.

'What?' Erin asked. 'What is it?'

'We're shipping out early,' Ram said.

'When?'

'Now.'

Erin felt a sinking feeling. 'What happened? Tell me.'

'They picked up flight signatures nearby, thirty minutes old. The patrols didn't spot it.'

It took a moment for Erin to realise. Then it hit her. 'Republic scout.'

Ram nodded. 'The refugees are fleeing. Delivery ships, medical ships, tankers... they're taking whatever they can get and heading for the shelter on Maggie IV. The attack can't wait any longer. Wrask must strike now.'

Night was dying. Thick clouds on the horizon were slowly brightening, an orange glow blooming into life behind them. Long fingers of sunlight punched through the gaps, setting light to the landscape in narrow lines. The *Geb* was making a great deal of sound. All along its hull great cylindrical thrusters were swivelling into position, aiming downwards. They groaned. From inside came a mighty rumble as the three primary reactors came alive. Countless fluid pumps and complex hydraulics started up in sequence, pumping thousands of tonnes of reactant from the gigantic tanks in the ship's underbelly. The five-mile launch-landing pad vanished beneath a sea of turquoise liquid as rows and rows of coolant towers vented, releasing their contents over the surface and flash-freezing the few intrepid plants still growing between the paving slabs. The topmost layer was already vaporising, cooling the air above the pad to lethal temperatures.

Then the pad vanished. Fire consumed everything as the thrusters ignited, sending thick jets of white-hot flame down and away. The flames turned red at the edges and vomited huge waves of black smoke out over the landscape. Then the docking clamps fell away. The *Geb* took off, flying upwards and forwards. The jets burned even brighter as it climbed, their red-and-white plumes slowly changing into pale blue spears of light. The supercarrier accelerated into the sky with an ungodly scream, leaving nothing behind it but clouds of blue gas and black smoke. In twelve minutes it cleared the atmosphere and a brief purple flash ran across the hull as the shields came online. Illuvia sat abandoned. The landscape was quiet. Nothing moved in the desert but dust, carried on a high cold wind.

Traumas of Unknown Origin

Hilton
Unknown border world, designation: LK/XVII-29

Stars had started to appear again behind the retreating edge of the cloud. Hilton was kneeling, leaning forward, with both hands on Nightmare's hilt and its point buried in the ground. He looked up to see as the muddy soil around him became brighter, little by little. The bodies around him were done bleeding. They all lay in pools of black rainwater, their fur sodden and their masks smashed to pieces by heavy sword-blows. Most were missing limbs.

The assault had long since ended, but Hilton kept his vigil. Before the night ended their horns had faded into the distance, giving him up in favour of easier prey. His armour was caked in blood and soaked in the black liquid he had taken for rain. He had taken wounds; many and grievous, but for all the blood he lost he had not died. The Watcher had meddled with his soul, he knew. Death would not come so easy for him. The pain was everywhere, but it couldn't quite reach him. He felt distant from it, as if his flesh was just another suit of armour.

Doubt itched at the back of his neck for a moment before he crushed it. The endless day-night was eating away at him. He could barely remember the last time he'd seen real sunlight. Hilton recited his vows silently. The bishop's face came to mind easily, looming over him in the old stone chapel.

We know one God, he had said.

I know one God, said Hilton.

One Watcher above, our path through high hills.

My path through dark places.

You are not alone, my child. You will never be alone again. We are your people, and we make you strong as you make us stronger. This is your place.

This is my place, the city in the hills.

You are the wall on which the fire breaks. You are an island in a sea of flames.

261

I am the gatekeeper. I am the boatman.

You are the vessel of Death on Life's behalf, and the arbiter of good destruction.

I live to serve.

Upon your soul.

Upon my soul.

The words still came easily, and Hilton felt reassured. The Church was his life. His purpose was clear.

Serve.

Hilton had only to play his part, and he had nothing to fear so long as his faith was strong. He felt God's hand on his spine, holding him upright.

He turned when he heard the pop. A bubble had burst on the surface of the pool. Then another. Starlight glittered on its peaceful surface, along with a few undissolved patches of skin and fur. It rippled and shimmered as a bulge rose in the centre. Hilton crept to the edge and stared. Steam rose from the water with a hiss. The pool heaved and roiled. With a loud sucking sound it disgorged its contents onto the ground, a man with limp and twitching limbs. Hilton rushed to his side.

With strong hands he dragged him away from the water's edge. He was covered in the black substance, his clothes well and truly ruined and his hair thick with the stuff. He groaned, and threw up. Foaming black liquid spilled from his throat to run down his chin. It clung to his stubble. It dripped from his hair. Hilton took him by the shoulders. His eyes were glued shut by caked-on blood and ooze. All Hilton could think was that he looked like something out of a nightmare. He wheezed and spat up more of it, drawing breath with a noise like a broken airlock, and the locket hung from his neck, blackened and sparking.

'Vang –' Hilton coughed. His throat was dry. 'Vanguard, can you hear me?'

At that he turned his face upwards, finding Hilton's.

'Y – hurgh –' he struggled. 'Y – y – you.' His hands groped in air and found Hilton's left arm. He gripped tight to the cold metal. 'My name.'

'What is it? What is wrong?'

'My name –' He choked and heaved another torrent of black ooze onto Hilton's legs. He stared up blindly, his face contorted with anger. '– Is Daedalus.'

Daedalus pulled himself to his feet. Then he clawed the mess from his face and flung it away. When he opened his eyes, Hilton saw that they were wild and alive. Pure white and mud-brown, darting madly.

'Where are we, Hilton?' He looked around, staggering, taking in the bodies and the trees. 'Where's the *Crow*?' He stepped forward, then back, turning around. 'The *Crow*! Tell me!'

'Your ship… it crashed.'

Daedalus stared at him for a moment. 'Where is she?'

'Far away. I leapt with you, and we hit the trees.' Hilton pointed. 'Your ship flew into the distance. There was a thunderbolt, and blue smoke filled the horizon for many days.'

'Many days.' Daedalus raised a hand to his face, looking stunned. He scratched dried blood from his face and looked at it like it he was seeing a brand-new colour. 'How long?'

Hilton raised a hand. 'Forty-three nights. You were senseless, and the Watcher instructed me to feed you from the pool.' He gestured towards the water, now quiet and still again.

Daedalus said nothing for a moment. He held a hand in front of his face. 'My headache,' he said.

Hilton watched closely. The Vanguard did not seem healthy.

'It's… gone,' he flexed his fingers. 'No. It's… stifled. I feel… '

There was a growl, then a thud. Then Hilton was on the ground, his head reeling.

He groped for the dagger on his belt, but the stun slowed his arm. He rolled onto his back, to see a golem looming over Daedalus, its mask shattered and gone. Black slaver slung from its gaping jaws, open wide and screeching. Daedalus lurched backwards in shock, and Hilton watched the golem draw one dripping, vicious claw behind its head.

Then it swiped, but caught only air as Daedalus ducked and weaved around it, seizing Nightmare from the soil and raising it to eye level, one-handed, backing away as the golem advanced. A slash of claws, then another, then another. The golem's jaws unhinged with a *crack*. Hilton tried to warn him, but the wind had gone from his lungs. The golem reared up and screamed.

Daedalus ran forward. He leapt and drove his foot into its broad chest with a *thump*, staggering it backwards and driving the air out of its chest. Then Nightmare was up, its wet edge glinting in the starlight. Daedalus swung.

The golem's head parted from its shoulders and rolled into the pool, where it sank with a hiss. Daedalus stood, feet apart, sword in both hands, breathing hard. The body fell backwards with a thump, blood surging from its neck into the muddy red bog around the pool. Daedalus turned, checking the treeline and the other bodies for movement. A moment passed, and he went limp. The sword fell to the ground. His arms trembled as if afraid of their own activity.

'Excellent,' came a voice.

Daedalus fell back, staggering. Monitor shimmered faintly in the day-night, a smile placed carefully on his face.

'Do you feel young again, Daniel?'

'My… my name is Daedalus.'

'You do. Strong as you once were, I think.' Hilton fancied the Watcher's smile to be more of a smirk. 'You were a mediocre swordsman. I did some tinkering – you should find a sword much more at home in your hands, and some damage to your body reversed. Congratulations, Daniel. You are physically healthy again.'

'My name,' Daedalus said again, his voice shaking, 'is Daedalus.'

Hilton crept to his feet, his breathing shallow, unable to speak.

'You cannot go on, Daniel.' Monitor affected a frown. 'It is time to stop running.'

'You can't… ' he took an unsteady breath, 'you can't stop me.'

'Yes I can.' Monitor raised his left hand.

Daedalus raised his left hand.

He looked at it, scowling, and lowered it again. Monitor cocked his head and Daedalus rose his hand again.

Hilton stared as Daedalus lowered his hand once more, face showing signs of resistance, but then Monitor raised his other hand and twitched his fingertips like a puppeteer. Daedalus jerked and shuffled and stood up straight.

'Stop that,' Daedalus said. 'Stop it now.'

Monitor lowered his hands and Daedalus relaxed back into his normal slouch. Then he crouched and took up the sword again, raising it in front of him. Monitor's image flickered, and the blade started to smoke. Daedalus gritted his teeth, but held onto it. Hilton raised both palms and took a step forward.

'Vanguard... '

Monitor held up a hand to stop him. 'I am not your enemy.'

'Funny way of showing it.'

'I require your compliance. The pit is designed to teach you why you should give it to me.'

'What – torture? Mind control? Is that it?'

'A mixture of physical and mental stimulants, laced with thread conductors to ease our communication. You no longer care about the universe, Daedalus Mole. You require a lesson in empathy, so I have locked empathy into you.'

'It was you in my head. The whole time. The headaches were you. The sounds. The... voice.'

'This is important,' Monitor said, gesturing a link between them with a finger. A burning line appeared in the air between them, glistening in the dark like a spiderweb dusted with snow. 'We are connected, now. There is a danger coming which threatens you all, and I need an agent to carry out my will. Something small, with legs and hands. You were all I could reach, and you wouldn't listen. Hence...' he waved a finger, and Daedalus's head nodded by itself. Then he gave a strangled yell and shook his head.

'You're just like them,' said Daedalus, 'obsessed with control. Go on. Make me dance. Make me fight!' He brandished the sword at Monitor, who was unfazed. 'I've seen some things in my time, and I know a fucking parlour trick when I see one.'

Monitor laughed. 'So observant! Such a canny gaze you have,' he said. 'You're right. I cannot make you do anything you really don't want to do. Not for long. That's why I'm in your feelings now,

Daniel. That's why I went to the trouble of watching you for so long. That's why it's good that I know the things you've done.'

Daedalus remembered Erin screaming at him, with rage in her eyes, pure, invested rage.

'Good luck then,' he said. 'I don't care what you're trying to do, and you can't make me care.'

Monitor smiled. 'That Is Not True.'

Daedalus clutched his head and hissed with pain. He felt a soft lightness on his cheek, as if someone's hair had suddenly brushed over his face.

'Recognise the opportunity you have been given,' Monitor persisted. 'You were nothing before. You destroyed yourself with guilt. Hatred. Suicidal ideation. This crushing indulgence. This mortal glitch.'

'What opportunity?' Daedalus spat. 'What opportunity would you *give* me?'

'Redemption.'

'Why?'

'Necessity.'

'How?'

'There are things I need. Old things. Hidden things. You can find them for me. You know about old things. One is hidden here, in this very forest, and I need your help to find it.'

Daedalus jerked the sword in Monitor's direction. 'Give me my ship.'

'I cannot.'

'Bullshit. You crashed it. You control this place. You're some kind of god. Give me my ship.'

Hilton noticed the Watcher's outline was fading already, and he seemed fainter. Darker.

'I am no god. I am spent.' He flickered out of existence for a moment, then returned in monochrome. 'You cannot leave this place. Listen to me, human. You might not yet grasp your purpose, but understand this. Look at your companion.' He pointed to Hilton, who was kneeling in the mud. 'His faith makes him strong. See the things he has endured. Do you see?'

Hilton shifted, and fresh blood ran from the chinks in his armour. Daedalus looked with disgust.

'So?'

'He believes. He is the only one who does.'

'Believes what?'

'That there is no more time. A great night is coming, and you have no protectors left.'

'I've never had any protectors.'

'Not you. You. All beings. Everything that breathes. Everything that moves. Everything with the capacity for anguish.'

Daedalus edged backwards, keeping the sword up.

'Your nightmares are coming. All nightmares. Every beast, every death, every half-formed terror. All pain, all fear, all fuel that burns in the Grief Engine.' The Watcher had no smile now. His face was vanishing, his body almost gone. 'I cannot hold them back alone. There is no more time. I need your help, and you need absolution. You must listen. *There is no more time.* Stay here. Help me. Help me and you will make amends. It's what *she* would have done.'

'Why?' Daedalus said, his voice strained. 'Why *me*?'

'Because you were broken broken viable. Viable. Because you were with within my r-r-reach.' The Watcher fractured and disappeared, and his voice died to a hiss. 'Because – that word, what was it? – searching… '

Daedalus lowered the sword. He opened his mouth to argue, but nothing came.

'Query complete. "History". Plea –'

And then it was gone. The not-god's voice fell to a syllable on the wind, and Daedalus stood in silence.

Hilton wheezed, his breath returning.

'That's your god, then,' said Daedalus, staring at the place the Watcher had been.

'Yes.'

'You led me here.'

'You had to come.'

'You lied to me.'

'I only repeated what I had been told.' Hilton took a wary step forward.

'You told me she would be here.' Daedalus's face was blank. He stared out at Hilton from beneath layers of grime. 'You said... you said... '

'Va –' Hilton stopped himself. 'Daedalus. Give the sword to me.'

Daedalus looked at the blade in his hand, as if surprised. His nose wrinkled in distaste. The dirt on his cheeks cracked. It fell from his grip and he moved away.

Hilton picked it up and wiped it down with the rag on his belt. 'We should move. This hill is dangerous. We need a new shelter.'

'There was a man,' Daedalus said. 'He – he came from those trees.' He extended a finger in the same direction the Watcher had.

'A naked man?'

'Yes,' said Daedalus.

'I know that man. He showed me the pool. He showed me how to keep you alive.'

'He... seemed to know things.'

'Then we go and we find him.'

'Jan.'

'What?'

Daedalus sank to the ground. Hilton recognised the gesture. 'No. Vanguard, get up.' He strode forward with a clank and seized him by the arm. 'You are not so easily finished. Get up, I say.'

Daedalus looked at him, a dead expression on his face. 'Why?' he asked plainly. 'What's the point? She's dead. I killed her. That's all I've done. This bloody place, look at it. Where are we? What are we even doing here? I've taken us on a roundabout bloody voyage to nowhere, a school trip to meet the galaxy's most messed-up people.' He laughed a black, empty laugh. 'Gods? Bloody not-gods and half-gods and – *what are those things?* Mud-monsters? Nightmares and memories and bullshit prophecies? Christ, Hilton, what went wrong?'

Hilton grunted. He yanked Daedalus to his feet and pulled him close to hiss in his ear. 'I bled here, Vanguard. I killed here to keep you alive. I have seen things you wouldn't believe. Horrors that would burn you at a glance, shrivel you up into a stunted black shadow of yourself. I still walk – I still kill – because I am needed. You are needed.'

'I don't believe it,' Daedalus said. 'Why would I believe it?'

'You don't need to believe it. You just need to *walk*.' Hilton turned and shoved him forward. 'Walk, faithless child. I will guide you.'

The half-light grew brighter as they made their way through the forest and the great cloud crept further across the sky. The rains had turned the ground into a treacherous bog, and Daedalus kept mis-stepping into muddy sinkholes. Once or twice he fell, and Hilton had to drag him until his will returned. Hilton knew the paths near the hill quite well, but it wasn't long before they left familiar territory behind.

'Are you sure this is the way?' Daedalus asked, after a time. 'Are we going straight?'

Hilton, trudging onward behind him, peered up through a gap in the green canopy overhead. 'Yes. The stars don't move here. We are following the red one,' he pointed to a brilliant vermilion dot in the sky.

'Mind firing off a prayer, eh? Ask your god how much further it is?'

Hilton stopped. 'I suppose it could do no harm.' He rested his sword against a tree, point pressed down into the soil.

'I was joking,' Daedalus said. 'Don't bother, let's just – Hilton?'

He was crouching on the grass, his head bowed and both hands clasped on one knee. Daedalus could hear him murmuring to himself.

'Alright, fine,' said Daedalus. He sank onto his haunches at the base of a tree and waited, grateful for the rest.

Although – he didn't feel that tired. They'd been walking for a long time. Hours, maybe. Hard to tell, since his watch had stopped working. He picked idly at the dried black crust on his coat. The years since leaving home had worn him down. A creaking back, dodgy knees, heart palpitations; lack of pride wasn't the only reason the *Crow* had been such a wreck. Looking after things took it out of him like nothing else.

That was different now. He felt it. The walk was nothing. No sharp stabs of pain jolted through his chest. Even his vision seemed clearer, and every hour he felt stronger. The pool was a horror, but it seemed to have left him in better shape than it found him; almost human again. His mind hurt, but his body was healed. He glanced at Hilton; another man who didn't make sense. He was old, but strong. Stronger than Daedalus, by far. About as quick, too, even in heavy plate armour. The man murmured intently in prayer, in perfect calm.

Daedalus's head snapped up.

'Hilton,' he said. 'There's something here.'

Hilton did not move. He moved one hand from his knee. 'Where?'

'In the trees.' Daedalus drew his knees up to his chest and planted his hands on the tree-trunk, ready to jump to his feet. 'On your left.'

'How many?'

'One, I think.'

There was a metallic rasp as Hilton turned his head. 'I do not see it.'

'It's there. Pray yourself up some better fucking eyes.'

'The Watcher is quiet,' Hilton said. 'Prayer is of no use.'

'Thanks for the tip.' Daedalus stared into the forest. A pale shape drifted in slivers through the gaps in the overgrowth. 'It's getting closer.'

A minute passed, and a lull fell over the forest. Perry crashed through a wall of vines, hacking away with his machete. He peered around in confusion. Then he tried to step forward. His throat met cold metal, and he noticed the hand that had crept silently over his shoulder and around his neck. Then the machete was out of his grip, his arm twisted painfully behind his back. A section of shadow fell away in front of him and Daedalus emerged.

'Hello again.' His coat creaked in the quiet. The black gunk had almost solidified in the fabric, and it made Daedalus appear to melt away in the half-light. 'Have you met Hilton?'

'Greetings,' Hilton said brightly.

'Hello again,' Perry answered. His voice came clear, despite the grip on his throat. 'Doing your job properly, I hope.'

'He's doing alright,' Daedalus cut in. 'I have some questions for you.'

'Shoot. I'm not busy.'

'Who are you?'

Perry groaned. 'Oh, Christ, not that one. Ask something else, would you?'

Daedalus rubbed his brow. 'Alright, I don't care. What do you want with me?'

'Quite a lot, I'm afraid.' Perry shifted in Hilton's grip and grimaced. 'Monty, too, but we can't agree on the specifics. You're to help us hold back the cold.'

'The cold? I'm sick of riddles.'

'You must know what I'm talking about. I've been watching you, you haven't been that detached from civilisation.'

'Losing my patience.'

'The cold? The frontier? Colonies going quiet, the whole Collective Armada off waging a false war in deep space?' Perry looked from one to the other. 'Come on. Isn't it obvious? Something is *coming*. From outside. It kills. People won't stop dying and no-one can figure out why.'

'Yeah,' Daedalus said. 'Void-dwellers, or something. That's why the Armada's out there in the first place, holding them back. Something like that.'

'Wrong. There are no void-dwellers. Misdirections and cock-ups and sleight-of-hand! Bloody hell, I thought you were less naive than this!'

Daedalus closed his eyes and counted to five.

'This coming war?' Perry went on. 'This revolution you're all getting so worked up about like it's the be-all and end-all? It's nothing. It's pointless. The cold is coming and no-one has the tools to understand it, let alone stop it.'

'Except me?'

'You don't either.'

'Right.'

'But you can help us *find* them.'

'Do you have a ship?'

'... I might do.'

'Take us there.'

'You're leaving?'

'Yes.'

Perry squinted at him. 'Why?'

Daedalus knew why. He hadn't known anything this surely in years. It was refreshing. 'I'm going home. I have a funeral,' he said.

'You'll have two if you don't listen to me.'

Hilton tensed the blade against his throat. 'Was that a threat, old man?'

Perry gulped. 'No. We hear things. Me and Monty. That's what we do. We hear everything, through the threads. That's how we got you here. That's how we knew you were susceptib – ah! Easy! It's how we knew the process would affect you!'

'How?' Daedalus demanded.

'We know your past. That's how Monty wanted to manipulate you. He wanted to break you. He wanted you to be his hands.'

'Like you?'

There was a pause. The forest was silent.

'Yes,' said Perry. 'Like me. You have knowledge he needs. Skills he needs.'

'And what about you? Why are you pretending to be on my side, not his?'

Perry struggled in Hilton's grip. 'Control doesn't work. Not for this. I can't do it, I can't help him. I can barely think straight most days. You need to *choose* to help us. So we need your trust.'

'Good bloody luck.'

'The kid – Erin. She dies today.'

Daedalus stared at him. The words were slow to come, and they had to be constructed individually. 'Why... would... that... mean anything... to me?'

'You freed her. Then you led her right back into danger and aban-doned her. You helped her halfway and made things worse. That makes you – ow! That makes you responsible. You know that.'

Daedalus's neck burned. 'You want me to kill you, don't you?'

'Listen to me, you bloody *child*!' Perry was growing agitated. 'I'm not trying to insult you! You made your mistake already, I can help you fix it!'

'Speak. Fast.'

'I know where she is. I know where she's going. I know where you need to be to st – to save her.'

Save her. The words settled in his stomach like a lead weight. Daedalus's temple stung, and he could smell smoke, like a candle had just been blown out. Save her. He tried to bring Erin's face to mind, but his memory was worn. All he could remember was a human face glimpsed through fire.

'How can I trust you?'

'I think we're a little past that now. You're not getting off this rock without listening to me first.'

'Fine.' Daedalus pinched the bridge of his nose. 'Take us to your ship.'

Smell the Coffee

Daedalus & Hilton
Unknown border world, designation: LK/XVII-29

'And she'll fly?' Daedalus heaved, tearing another long vine from the landing leg and dumping it on the ground. 'You're certain?'

'Positive,' Perry said. 'There's nothing that thing needs except a lick of paint and some fresh bog roll.'

Daedalus looked at him. He was leaning against the cave entrance, watching them as they tore the tangled foliage from the ship and threw it down the hill.

'Oi.' Perry jabbed a finger at him. 'You try surviving in a place like this and see what you run out of first.'

Hilton gave a huge tug and a heavy sheet of leaves and mud finally came loose, sliding free in one piece and piling onto the ground with a wet thud.

'See? Good as new.'

Daedalus had never seen anything quite so beautiful. The ship had clearly been white once, but the paint had been scraped off so thoroughly it was half black now. The hull beneath was dented and scarred, but the black material shone like it was brand new. It reflected the starlight in row after row of tiny hexagons, like nothing he'd ever come across before. It was a small ship, maybe half the breadth of the *Crow* and three-quarters the length, but it looked to be in better shape. The nose was sharper, long and oddly hooked like an eagle's beak. It looked like a bird of prey where it stood, perched on the hilltop. The body bulked out around the midriff, with a foot-ramp set into the port side and four long, thick landing legs. He furrowed his brow at the thrusters clustered around the stern.

'Where's the fuel tank?'

'Eh?'

'You're kidding,' he rounded on Perry. 'This is a joke, right?'

Perry grinned. 'This is the *Teratorn*. You won't be needing fuel tanks.'

'Oh. Great. You know, I've been in the market for a five-hundred ton paperweight.'

The old man strolled over to the big conical thruster in the centre and reached into the mess of cables and pipes. There was a *thunk* as he threw a heavy switch and stood back. A terrible grinding filled the air. Inside the ship Daedalus could hear a loud hum. He edged backwards.

'I'd cover my ears if I were you,' Perry called over the noise.

Daedalus clamped his hands over his ears and jumped back. An instant later he was lifted off his feet and thrown back into the cave.

After a few moments he rose, shaking. He remembered a few small trees had stood behind the ship. There was a thin cloud of blue smoke there now. Far away, through the ringing in his ears, he thought he heard a crash. Hilton was crawling back over the lip of the hill, clutching his head in one hand.

'Trust me,' said Perry, 'you won't be needing fuel.'

'How... where did you get this?' Daedalus asked. 'This isn't some drifter's junker. What is it? How long has it been here?'

Perry paused. 'It's a stain.' He scratched his jaw. 'A mark left by another time.'

Daedalus thought for a moment. 'From what you were before?'

Perry nodded. 'When I was useful. Or hoped to be.'

'What are you now?'

Perry chuckled. 'Archaeologist.'

'Fine,' Daedalus said, 'have it your way. Hilton!'

Hilton stood up and looked his way.

'We're going, come on.'

'To find the other two?'

'What's left of them,' Daedalus said. He strode up to the hull and reached for the heavy switch by the foot-ramp.

'Don't forget where you're going,' said Perry. 'Your friends are on the *Geb*. It'll reach Highdust in fifty minutes; that's where it happens.'

Daedalus looked back. 'Fifty minutes?'

Perry nodded.

'You're joking. We're in Termina. It'll take days to reach Highdust.'

'Not in the *Teratorn*.'

Daedalus stared at him. 'Fifty minutes.'

'Fifty minutes,' Perry said. 'You'd better get going.'

Daedalus's stomach roiled. He turned to climb into the ship.

YOU CANNOT SAVE HER.

Daedalus stopped, his hand on the switch.

'Even if you pulllll her from the fire, you cannot save her from herr-self. She will b-burn. You are in-sec-tile besidesss such con-vic-tion as hers.'

He turned his head. A single green eye hung in space next to him, dim and flickering.

'She sh-should have been the one.' It glared at him, giving off a smell of ozone. 'You are per-performing poorly.'

Perry stepped forward. 'You're weak, Monty,' he said to the eye. 'You can't stop him leaving. You should be conserving your strength.'

'It m-m-matters n-not-t-t.' The voice jarred and skipped like a broken soundtrack. 'All is consigned-consigned-consigned to dussst. This one will not sta-stay and there will be no time to time to time to recoverrr the pieces –'

'It's their universe now, Monty. They deserve a chance to defend themselves.'

'They cannot cannot standstand stand,' Monitor hissed. 'They are not r-ready –'

'And you think they're ready for something so bad even *you* had to bury the damn thing?' Perry said. 'You two, go. Now. This one's getting desperate.'

Daedalus pulled the switch. The foot-ramp swung down with a loud hiss, revealing a white staircase. 'Hilton, go.'

Hilton obliged. He clanked up the stairs and Daedalus climbed in after him. Hilton spared a look back.

'Move it,' growled Perry. Monitor's eye stared up at him.

'S-s-stay. You are are mmmmmy servvvant,' it said.

Hilton climbed inside.

Daedalus hit the interior switch and the ramp drew itself smoothly back up, sealing with a *whump*. Then it was just him and Hilton in the dark.

'Is there a –' he began. The strip lights on the ceiling silently came to life, and he found himself in a brand-new ship. The interior was all pale panelling and rubber-gripped flooring. He climbed the stairs. At the end of a roomy corridor he could see the gleaming main screen in the cockpit. Hilton was checking the cabins. Solid-looking doors with fireproof seals were arrayed down the hallway, and a larger, stronger one blocked the engine room from view.

'Welcome, pilot,' came a mild, pleasant voice. 'I am ready to fly.'

Hilton clicked the last door shut again. 'It seems safe,' he said. 'Well-furnished, also.'

Daedalus moved through to the cockpit. The screens were huge, blank and spotless, and the front window was covered by a visor. There was only one chair, and the control panels were all labelled as if they'd just come out of the factory. He peered at the joysticks. They were shrink-wrapped.

'This ship does not look used,' Hilton said.

'This is Test Unit Four,' said the ship. 'Test Unit Four has been deployed once previously. Destination not reached.'

'What destination?' Daedalus asked.

The ship said nothing. Hilton gave Daedalus a look.

'Right.' A few ideas ran through Daedalus's head, but he dismissed them. 'We can figure this out some other time. We've got things to do.' He tore the plastic off and tossed it in the pure white waste disposal chute. 'Hold onto something.'

Hilton glanced around. He braced himself against a railing on the rear wall. Daedalus shrugged off his filthy coat and eased himself into the pilot's chair. 'This all looks pretty straightforward,' he said. 'First things first.' He raised a hand and pushed a marked button. A quiet whirr issued from nearby.

'What is that smell?' asked Hilton.

Daedalus said nothing. He inhaled deeply. There was a gurgle, then a hiss. After a few seconds an invisible compartment slid open, revealing a white cylinder. Daedalus hesitated, and stretched out a trembling hand. He took it.

'Vanguard?'

He raised a thumb and popped the lid. 'There is a god.'

'What is it?'

Daedalus sighed. 'Coffee.'

'Coffee?'

'Let's do this.' He reached beneath the dash and threw a lever. The smooth hum of the lights was joined by a deeper thrumming. The lights dimmed for a moment, and there was a distant whine as some-thing else in the ship began drawing power. The cockpit visor began to rise. Daedalus stabbed at a few more buttons and the screens lit up one by one. Readouts started scrolling. Charts popped up and a screen on the right seemed to be building a map. The visor slid upwards, revealing more and more of the treetops at the foot of the hill. Perry and Monitor were nowhere to be seen. Daedalus stared out for a moment, quiet. The visor finally locked into place at the top of the window, and he raised his styrofoam cup. 'To the *Crow*.'

Hilton looked at him.

Daedalus laughed. He took a sip. It was exquisitely hot. He replaced the lid and locked the cup into its holder. 'Brace,' he said, and pushed on the throttle.

He heard the engine charging up. Daedalus counted to three and tilted both joysticks backwards. The retros ignited with a rush of air and pushed the nose up by a few degrees. Steam rose from the damp grass below. 'Six... seven... '

He flipped a switch marked 'VERT.' The retros screamed, and the *Teratorn* rose straight up into the half-night air. The view broadened, and Daedalus could see the long, ragged line the *Crow* had carved into the forest. At ten, he flipped the switch again. There was a moment of quiet; then the main thruster ignited.

The *Crow* wasn't slow. She was an old ship, rusted and broken, but she was quick. The *Teratorn*, though, was a different creature entirely. Daedalus felt his bones sting. The locket pressed into his chest painfully. Hilton roared in pain as the g-force crushed him against the rear wall. Searing hot coffee painted the corridor walls behind them, and looking out the window showed Daedalus that the hill was long gone, and the stars were rushing headlong towards them.

Perry emerged from his cave and sniffed. The burnt smell of starship exhaust hung heavy and pungent in the air. There was a new star in the northern sky. It was a burning cobalt.

'I have made a poor decision,' said Monitor.

'Not turning out the way you planned, I take it?' Perry said.

'No.'

'There's no time to fish for another agent, is there?'

'No.'

They watched the star diminish.

'What are you going to do?'

'I cannot watch.'

'Really? I thought that was your job.'

'You think I am blind,' said Monitor. 'You are wrong. I see too much. This pain runs deep. I can not suffer this much longer.'

'You're going to leave?'

'I cannot leave.'

Perry looked at him.

'I have done all I can. There is no reason my fate should be special.' Monitor's eye flickered as he spoke. 'I will wait for his return. If he does not come back, I will give myself to death.'

'You think they can survive without you?'

Monitor turned and met his eyes.

'No.'

Wrask eased herself into the captain's chair and swivelled around to face the main viewscreen. The *Geb*'s gigantic bridge was noisy and full of people running for their stations.

'Weapon pre-ignition complete, Marshal-Elect!' came a call from the helm.

Wrask nodded. 'Give me long range.' The viewscreen flicked over to show a huge map of the surrounding sectors. 'Status report. Where's the *Typho*?'

'Four o'clock low, thirty degrees, ma'am. She's leading the frigates into formation. Cruisers are outriding and the battleships are directly below us. Reporting full combat readiness on all ships in the vanguard.'

'How long to the gate?'

'ETA four minutes, ma'am.'

'Any word from second fleet?'

'Converging on target position with fourth. Still no response from third.'

Wrask drummed her fingers on the armrest. 'Send a stealth-capable wing to scout ahead once we arrive. Do not engage. Do not establish contact. Report back from range. I want to know if third fleet is still alive.'

'Yes ma'am. Deploying the thirty-first.'

Wrask fell silent. She trusted her intelligence officers, and she had faith in the competence of her lieutenants. The Republic had no way of anticipating this move. She had spent years orchestrating this performance; presenting false threats like actors in a play, learning to manipulate the opposing force. People had died in service of invented conflicts, and the careers of her most dangerous enemies had been built on victories Wrask bestowed on them.

The Republic believed the rebellion to be defeated. Wrask had sacrificed an entire fleet at Sudos to create the most costly lie of all. Thousands had died in a choreographed battle to convince the Republic that they had won.

All for the sake of this. All for the element of surprise.

Wrask keyed the announcer on her armrest.

'Attention all hands,' she began. Her deep voice boomed through loudspeakers in every corner of the *Geb* from bow to stern. The crew looked up from their stations as one. 'This is the Marshal-Elect. As you may be aware, we are en route to rendezvous with third fleet. Second and fourth will be joining us.

'You have been ordered to arm the *Geb* for full combat-readiness. You must be clear: this is not a precautionary measure. This expedition is not an exercise. This is not a fleet migration. This is an attack. Proceed with that in mind.

'This morning fourth fleet completed an operation across multiple sectors. Their objective was to destroy the Republic's early-warning systems stationed in seventeen locations throughout previously-disputed space. They succeeded without detection, paving the way for our attack. Their performance was impeccable, and our victory will be in large part due to their efforts.

'Today you will surpass them. Today is the day we excise the tumour in the heart of our nation. Today we will fall on the enemy like a thunderbolt. Three hundred ships follow us, with nine hundred more ahead. There will be one battle. There will be no war. Our revolution will be sure and sudden, and tomorrow we raise a new flag over the Collective.

'Man your stations and bid your friends good fortune. To those of you about to die, I offer my gratitude. You fly into the dark tonight to restore the promise of the Systems Collective. To me there can be no better death.' She paused. 'Thank you for serving with me; all of you. It has been the highest honour.

'Onward, then.' Wrask released the switch, and silence fell in the halls of the *Geb*.

Two decks below, in a small corner of the barracks, Erin watched soldiers running drills. Squads of humans jogged in time, carrying smoke-rifles, flash grenades and swords slung across their shoulders. Each human squad was backed by a pair of petradons, and the more experienced were leading conscript groups of assorted races. Erin was the only entari.

'Ram?'

'Yes?' Ram was toying with a long, narrow warhammer she'd retrieved from the armoury. Her head felt okay today. The pills had mostly deadened the pain, and the fatigue wasn't as bad as it had been.

'Why do they get along so well?'

'Sorry?'

Erin picked at the corner of the crate she was sitting on. 'Humans and petradons,' she said. 'Wrask seems to have lots of them, and they don't seem to mind each other.'

Ram spun it in her fingers while she mulled it over. 'We have been through much of the same,' she answered. 'We had the helium-3 mines on Petron, and the supersteel foundries in Fellpit. They worked the cobalt mines in Crit, leftover from the first human colonies. The Republic did the same to all of them. Privatised them. The hours went up, the pay went down, and eventually the people realised they were no longer free. And without Earth, the humans had nothing to fall back on.'

Erin said nothing for a moment. 'So that's why they joined Wrask?'

Ram looked up at the people training. 'She offered them freedom, and all she asked in return was that they use it to take revenge.'

'It's not revenge.'

Ram shrugged. Her pauldrons made a heavy sound.

'It's a revolution,' said Erin. 'We're here to make a difference.'

'*You're* not,' Ram pointed out. 'You're here on compulsion. You just want to fight.'

Erin said nothing.

'She preaches violence, Erin. She revels in it. A direct assault can achieve nothing else.'

'We can take Taxos. It'll send a message – people will know they can be free. Everyone will join us once we take away their fear.'

'And what then?' Ram said. 'The Republic will retaliate, and the rebellion will be crushed. They have greater numbers, they have better logistics, and they have better weaponry. All you have is the element of surprise. It'll be the Home Rebellion all over again. Wrask wants to prevent martial law, but what does she think will happen once she fails? Once the Republic knows the extent of her influence?'

'She won't fail.'

Ram let her warhammer swing to the floor with a loud *thud*. 'Charisma doesn't win wars. Wrask is going to fail, and the fallout will hurt everyone.'

They fell quiet. Somewhere nearby a smoke-rifle went off with a *whomp*, and a thick grey cloud blocked Erin's view of the soldiers. 'Ram?'

'Yes?'

'Have we ever talked about my mom?'

Ram leant on her hammer. 'No. Not really.'

A pair of shortswords were propped up against the crate. Erin fidgeted with one of them. 'I think… sometimes I wonder what she would think.'

'Would you listen to her if she was still here?'

Erin almost smiled. 'Probably not.' She rubbed her eye. 'Still. It matters, doesn't it?'

Ram couldn't think of an answer for that.

'I hope it does,' said Erin.

A voice came over the loudspeakers. 'Attention: acceleration burn in approximately two minutes.'

'Come on,' said Ram. 'Find somewhere safer to sit.'

Erin whacked the crate with the flat of her hand. 'It's clamped down.'

'I don't trust those things.'

'Ugh, fine.' Erin heaved herself to her feet and picked up her swords. Ram plucked a holster from the wall-mounts and held it out, and Erin slid them inside. Ram's warhammer got its own holster, and she slung them over her shoulder. There were bracing pads arrayed along the back wall, the one nearest the engines, so they stood there.

'Attention: prograde burn in one minute. All unsecured crew to bracing stations.'

Erin hooked her arms through the big rubber loops and leant her head against the foam pad above. She watched as the drilling soldiers suddenly stopped and ran together to the big back wall of the training area to brace themselves. Ram gripped the holster tight with one arm and kept her free hand against the wall, leaning her weight against it. She didn't like the pads.

The deep rumbling of the ship's engines suddenly pitched up. The walls shivered slightly.

'Attention: ten seconds to burn.'

Erin took a deep breath and exhaled slowly, counting down in her head.

'Accelerating to median in three, two… '

The secured crate screeched as its magnetic clamp sheared in half, and it flew across the room before bursting open against the back wall. Ration packs and water canisters spilled everywhere. The *Geb* entered the interstellar medium and caught the current in its mighty central thrusters, powering forward and becoming un-observable in a matter of seconds. Inertial dampeners dampened inertia as best they could, screeching from little boxes mounted at five-metre intervals throughout the ship, but Erin's vision still went green. Ram grunted with the effort of holding herself steady. After thirty seconds of acceleration the pull eased off, and the *Geb* relaxed.

'Attention: thirteen minutes six seconds to target.'

Erin breathed again.

On the bridge, Wrask waited.

A very long way away, a very small ship was moving very, very fast.

Old Birds and New Tricks

Daedalus, Erin, Ram & Hilton
Space

The *Teratorn* screamed through space, leaving a thin wisp of blue exhaust behind it. Any pursuers – not to suggest there were any – would not keep up for long.

'I still do not understand,' said Hilton. 'They have been travelling for days. We can't be going fast enough to catch them.'

'It's not about speed,' Daedalus murmured, rifling through different map readouts on the main screen. 'Or... it is, sort of.' He brought up a wide view, showing the *Teratorn* as a blue dot moving along a thin white line. 'It's about shortcuts.'

'You know a shortcut?'

'No,' he scratched his chin, frowning. 'But this ship does. Lots of shortcuts. Undiscovered channels, I think? They're tiny, though; no use as carriageways. Just big enough for us, but a cruiser would be torn in half. It looks like it's detecting new ones all the time.'

'And that's how we can catch them?'

'The smaller the channel, the faster it seems to move,' Daedalus said. 'Yeah, we can catch them.' He ran a finger along the map. 'We could be there in half an hour.'

'We have some time. Would you like to spar?'

'No I don't want to bloody well spar.' Daedalus blew his nose and a cork of congealed black matter popped out, followed by a trickle of blood. Then he sniffed. 'Is there a shower on board?'

'What is a "shower"?'

Daedalus rubbed his temple. 'I'll go look.' He flicked a thick red switch on the panel and got up to leave.

'*Autopilot enabled,*' came a soft voice.

'Keep an eye on that thing,' said Daedalus. 'I mean it.'

Daedalus found a shower in one of the rear cabins. No chemical cleaners here, he noticed, just real water and a proper nozzle. He made to shrug off his coat, then changed his mind. He climbed into the cubicle and stood under the nozzle, then twisted the faucet. The spray was hot. It drummed against his face, slicing through the caked-on mud and blood and black dirt. The filth slid off his face in layers, and the force of the water broke it down. His clothes were soaked. They grew heavy and the water ran black from the corners of his coat. Daedalus tore at it with his hands, pulling away the larger pieces of gunk and bringing back the dark brown underneath. The locket sparked and fizzed. He scraped long-nailed hands down his face, carving trenches in the blackness to reveal an unkempt, patchy beard. His hair was the worst. It hadn't grown much longer, but the muck was stuck hard. It took minutes to work it loose, and it came free in huge chunks. His boots were next. After washing the dirt off they looked almost exactly the same as he remembered. Despite himself – despite the ache in his chest and the darkness filling his head – he grinned. *Old boots.*

He finally stripped the sodden clothes from his body to scrub the dried blood from his neck and chest.

Wrask's fleets were attacking Highdust, which could mean only that they were after Taxos. Daedalus could see the reasoning there: the Collective Armada was out past the Frontier, supposedly fighting void-dwellers, and the defences around Taxos were a police force, not a battle-fleet. If Wrask was quick, she could seize it. But then what? What was the point? The Collective Armada might be far out beyond the Frontier now, but they would turn around for this. What would it take – days? A week? They would return and smash the rebellion to pieces.

Daedalus thought for a moment, watching the filthy water drain around his feet.

That was odd. Why did he suddenly know so certainly that the Armada would win? Because the Armada was invincible, because he'd seen it on the broadcasts and he'd grown up learning about victory after victory after victory. The Collective was strong together, and the Republic were perfect, incorruptible leaders. Daedalus hadn't believed that for years now, but years of deference had beaten the message into him and it was a conscious effort to deny it. It would take something huge to really break the illusion.

That was it. Wrask wanted to be seen winning. The broadcast station on Taxos could send word out to every living colony in the Collective, telling everyone that the biggest station in civilised space was no longer theirs. It wouldn't matter if she achieved nothing else, because the Republic's carefully-constructed image of peace, prosperity and absolute control would die.

Daedalus understood what Wrask meant now. A rebellion might last only a day, but it was history, and the future would be made of it. The Republic would never seem invincible again, and the age of quiet compliance would come to an end. Then people would die. Lots of people, starting with everyone who followed Wrask to Highdust. Starting with Erin.

When he was as clean as he was going to get, he turned the faucet back and hit the big button marked 'DRY'. Hot air from the drive chamber was filtered around, cooled and blasted from the nozzle above. Within a minute he was completely dry, along with his tattered clothes. His jumper was completely destroyed, though. He dropped it in the bathroom waste chute. Then he paused. There was a cabinet above the sink. He reached towards it and eased the door open with a finger. Inside, shrink-wrapped, was a razor.

Daedalus returned to the cockpit fifteen minutes later, clean-shaven and wearing nothing between his coat and his off-white undershirt. He could almost have passed for normal, but for the dark circles under his eyes and the permanent lines etched at the corners of his mouth. Hilton stood exactly where he'd left him.

'That is an improvement,' he said.

'Yeah?'

'I did not smell you coming.'

Daedalus glanced at the clock. 'I was gone nearly twenty minutes. That's the best you could come up with?'

Hilton shrugged, with a clank.

Daedalus dropped himself into the pilot's chair again and dispensed a new cup of coffee. His previous one was still distributed through the hallway. He waited for this one to cool.

'Vanguard.'

Daedalus grunted.

'The Watcher is not what I thought he would be.'

'What did you think he would be?' Daedalus plucked the empty cup from the holder and dropped it in the chute. He took a sniff of the fresh one before setting it down.

'Powerful,' something crept into Hilton's voice. 'Capable. Did you hear the way he spoke? It was like listening to a child. And he is afraid.' Hilton shook his head. 'A god who feels fear. What is the point?'

'He wasn't afraid for himself,' said Daedalus suddenly. He surprised himself, but he realised it was true. 'He was afraid for us. It was his job to watch over us, and he's failed.'

'A god who fails?'

'Was there ever one who didn't?' Daedalus laughed. 'Jupiter, Ra, Christ, Neo-Zeus; not one of them remained standing when mother nature came knocking. Gods stick around until the apocalypse. Then they die like everything else.' He swivelled in his chair and stuck a finger at Hilton. 'You find me a god who lived more than a couple thousand years and I'll find you a hundred more that couldn't.'

'But this one is real. We spoke to him. What if we can save him?'

'Why? Why bother? You said it yourself, he's got no power left. All he can manage is psychic trickery and giving me a bloody headache. Not unlike some people I could mention.'

'He knows about the end times. He knows how to fight them.'

'Yeah? So does every bloody street preacher from here to the Frontier. I don't care what magic tricks he can do, there's not a thing he says that I can trust.' He turned back to the console. 'I'll believe in void-dwellers when they've got me impaled on a spike and not a moment sooner.'

'They took my people.'

Daedalus said nothing for a moment, just tapped idly at the controls.

'The monsters are real, Vanguard.'

'So you say,' he said, '... and why do you think I trust you?'

Hilton stepped forward. 'I am your sworn sword.'

'You're a fanatic,' Daedalus snapped. 'You're insane. I don't like you, I don't trust you, and the first chance I get I'm leaving you somewhere far away.'

The knight retreated again. 'As you say.'

'Your job is to keep me alive, right? Then do it. A war's about to start. I'm going to find Erin, and I'm going to get her out of there. You keep your distance and keep both sides away from us.'

'As you say.' Hilton stood against the rear wall of the cockpit and became still.

Daedalus thought for a moment. 'And don't screw around with anything you don't understand. I sure as hell don't want you learning what a gun is.'

'Nothing, Ma'am.'

Wrask held her composure. It would not do to show surprise. 'The thirty-first is lost, then.'

'Yes, Ma'am. The warning beacon was destroyed as well, but it seems to have managed a partial transmission. They were wiped out on arrival.'

'Those pilots deserved better.'

'Yes, Ma'am.'

She thought for a moment. They were waiting at the egress point. The end of the channel. She could hardly believe the day had come. No turning back now. Fear wanted to edge in, but she crushed it quickly. 'Inform engineering I want double power to the rear shields. Divert power from the front and flanks, and shut down every weapon except the flak cannons. Cloak the *Typho*. Cloak the cruisers. Cloak anything with stealth capability. Anything without must fall into formation with us.'

'Excuse me, Ma'am, should we raise our own cloak as well?'

'No, lieutenant.'

'... Yes, Ma'am.'

'Everything stealthed is division two. Everything else is division one. Order division two to decelerate. Now. I want them dropping out no less than sixty seconds after division one. Go.'

The lieutenant scampered off to relay her orders. The countdown timer on the main screen ticked down, reading less than three minutes to arrival. She keyed the announcer.

'This is the Marshal-Elect. Decks two through six, clear runways. Infantry, board dropships immediately. All fighter wings prepare to scramble. Bombers stand by.'

Erin and Ram seized their weapons and ran to join the nearest squadron. Erin's silent petradon guard fell in behind them, four to a man and carrying longswords. Suddenly soldiers were everywhere. The normal joking, scuffling people who would laugh with Erin in the mess hall were gone, replaced by a faceless mass running in unison to the huge hangar doors at the far end of the barracks. As the crowds drew close the doors groaned and started to rise, revealing the gigantic rooms beyond, full of fearsome-looking fighter craft and bulky dropships gripping armoured vehicles in their claws. One wall was a sheer purple sheet of plasma, keeping the vacuum at bay. Through it Erin could see the pulsing white blur of faster-than-light channel space.

The whole battalion flooded in, splitting into squadrons and running for their designated ships. Boarding-ramps boomed as they fell to the deck, swallowing soldiers into their holds. Erin saw a small repurposed freighter at the end of one line – the ship she'd boarded the *Geb* on – and made a beeline for it, gripping her holster tight over one shoulder. Her heart was pounding. She felt good. This was it. It was time to take control. Ram thumped along behind her, the guards a few feet back.

The freighter's engines blazed. The boarding-ramp slid back up and it rose into the air.

'No!' Erin shouted, unable to stop herself. 'Wait!'

They couldn't leave her behind. Not now.

All the ships were taking off now, filling the hangar with roars and blue smoke. The freighter was closest. It hung a few feet from the ground now, its main thruster spitting sparks. Erin pushed herself, driving into a sprint. Ram fell behind, yelling. Erin crouched low, and leapt.

The ship powered upwards. She fell short and collapsed onto the deck. Then Ram was there. A strong hand clasped her around the chest and lifted her back to her feet. The freighter screeched as it rose into formation, ready to depart.

'Hey –' said Ram.

'Hold it,' came a stern voice. The guards had caught up. 'She's not going out.'

Ram faced them. 'Say again.'

'Orders from the Marshal-Elect. The entari is needed on the bridge.'

'No.' Erin pushed in front of her friend. 'Wrask said I could fight. I'm ready.'

'The situation has changed. We're taking you up.'

Ram placed a hand on Erin's shoulder. 'She'll come. Won't you?'

Erin twitched. Then she nodded.

'Follow, then.'

Ram gave Erin's shoulder a squeeze. 'Stay close,' she murmured. Ships were flooding out through the plasma sheet and positioning themselves on the runway outside.

Up on the bridge, Wrask watched the countdown approach single figures.

'Where is the child?' she asked.

An ensign put a finger to his earpiece. 'Elevator, ma'am. She'll be here soon.'

'Give me engineering.'

A complex readout appeared on the main screen. Percentages and warnings flashed over a shifting blueprint of the *Geb*.

'Nine seconds,' said an officer.

'Helm.'

The helm operator turned to Wrask. 'Yes, captain?'

'Prime the afterburner.'

'... Yes, captain.'

Wrask watched the numbers. Zero came.

The white blur of channel-space shrank back, and the viewscreen was filled with lances of gunfire. Taxos hung in the distance, a quiet, precious star. Their target. Some of the bridge crew recoiled in shock and shouted warnings, but Wrask was already on her feet.

'Afterburner!' she roared.

The *Geb* shook as the main thruster exploded, spewing white-hot flame behind it and driving the supercarrier forward through the crossfire. Republic gunships surrounded the channel exit in a great ring, and swarms of bombers were already closing in. The *Geb* thundered onwards, leading their fire away from the entry point. As the escort cruisers started to arrive, the brunt of the assault pounded against the *Geb*'s powered-up rear shield.

'Release flak!' commanded Wrask.

The batteries along the ship's length lit up with orange flame as they blasted the surrounding ships with metal shrapnel. Bombers exploded in clouds of smoke and fire before they could release their payloads, and hostile close-attack cruisers fell to pieces under the rain of metal.

Wrask's fleet punched through the Republic defence, the *Geb* leading the bigger gunships away from the channel and into open space.

Wrask slammed her fist on the announcer. 'Scramble all wings! Fly, now! You are surrounded! Attack! Engineering, rebalance shields and give me those beams, now!'

The runways lit up along the length of the ship as a hundred fighters took off. Bombers went in the other direction, flooding space with their exhaust clouds. The *Geb* vomited warriors into the battlefield with no end in sight. Republic ships closed to attack range, only to fall under a hail of missiles or be torn to shreds by flak cannons. Wrask was losing her cruisers, but each one that fell took two enemy gunships with it. The *Geb* was turning, and her beams were charged. Pinpricks of light flickered into life all along its length before filling the black with blazing pillars of green and red fire. Six beams carved the *Imperator* in half, and another two punched holes clean through the *Steel Fist*.

A volley of enemy missiles whipped through the flak defences and exploded against the starboard hull. The impact rang through the corridors.

Wrask gripped a handrail to stay upright. 'Damage report!'

An operator climbed back to his station and called back. 'Fire on starboard, decks three and four. Damage control en route!'

'Raise those shields! Turn us around and give them the full port battery!'

The *Geb*'s side-mounted thrusters swivelled and fired, heaving the ship around until its entire arsenal faced the oncoming Republic fleet. It lit up, filling the sky between the two forces with death. Friend and foe alike were rendered into dust by the gunfire, but two more destroyers went down and their chase became hesitant.

'Launch dropships!' Wrask bellowed. 'I want boarding parties on that station! We can hold them here!'

The *Geb* formed a one-ship wall between the Republic fleet and Taxos, and they advanced slowly on it, spreading out to leave room for all of them to attack at once. The smaller contingent of Wrask's force was shattered and smashed by the channel, now being harried to death by fighters and bombers.

'Cut the engines! Full power to port shields!'

'Energy weapons are recharging, ma'am.'

A tinny voice yelled from the intercom: 'Engineering! Beams two, four and seven burnt out!'

'Load the Rokatons!' Wrask boomed.

'Yes, ma'am.'

The fleet drew nearer. A volley of lasers issued from the nearest battleship, tearing into the runway and burning alive a full wing of dropships about to take off. The next wing in line ploughed boldly through the wreckage, clearing the runway and taking off in the debris field.

'Rokatons ready,' called a weapons officer.

'Hold,' said Wrask.

The *Geb* sat still. A heartbeat passed. Then another.

A destroyer powered forward suddenly, its forward beams lighting up.

'Fire.'

The space between the two ships filled with twisting dumbfire rockets. They burst from every nook and cranny of the port hull, spewing hot smoke everywhere and blocking a clear view from the destroyer's bridge. They closed the gap in mad spirals.

The shield stopped many, bursting them in silent flashes, but enough got through to tear a gash in the enemy's hull. The beams never fired. They died away as the destroyer's guts rushed into space. Fire bloomed in the silence.

'Is this all you have?' rumbled the captain. 'Is this what you send to enforce yourselves?'

The *Geb*'s turrets charged once more, and cast their beams into the black. A wing of approaching bombers was rent into shards, along with their fighter escorts. The remainder spun madly to evade. Those that didn't turn and flee dropped their payloads uselessly against the *Geb*'s powerful shield.

'Tactical map,' Wrask ordered. A screen on her left flickered and showed a collection of colour-coded dots. A field of red points lay between the *Geb* and the channel exit. As she watched, they spread slowly apart, inching sideways. She saw their intention immediately. 'Hail the *Typho*,' she said.

The Republic ships carried out their flanking manoeuvre gradually, keeping just out of the supercarrier's effective range. The stars bent and warped behind them as they diverted resources to their forward shields. Their weapons charged and appeared as pinpricks of red light dotted across their hulls. The *Geb* made no move in response. The red dots shone brighter.

Then space flexed and shimmered, and the *Typho* dropped its cloak. Wrask laughed.

A storm of missiles blew in from hundreds of batteries on the *Typho*'s starboard side. Fully-charged beams blossomed and punched through the unguarded stern hull of every ship caught between the dreadnought and the supercarrier. Panic spread as the Republic fleet turned about-face and realigned their shields, but not fast enough. First one battleship caught aflame, then another, and another. The *Geb* charged forward in support, releasing scores of bombers from its runways. Beams lit up the blackness like searchlights as yet more rebel ships uncloaked themselves to join the fray. The crossfire became a maelstrom.

Wrask watched the panic unfold. As the minutes passed and more explosions flowered in space the bridge started to ring with hails of surrender.

Wrask ignored them.

Soon they fell silent, and only the tapping of fingers on keyboards and the quiet chatter of working officers could be heard from the captain's chair. The fire vanished, and only clouds of dust and steel husks could be seen through the viewscreen. She waited for the statement.

'No hostile signatures remaining, ma'am.'

'Thank you. Recall the dropships and proceed to Taxos. Order the *Typho* to set up a perimeter and wait for second and fourth to egress from the north channel.'

'Ma'am? Second and fourth have already –' the sensor operator stopped, confused.

'Yes?'

'Er – picking up signatures near the north channel. Lots of signatures.'

Wrask frowned. 'Hostile?'

'Neutral, ma'am. It's... debris.'

She stood up. 'Show me.'

The telescope view filled the main screen. Wrask recognised the *Aken* – twin supercarrier to the *Geb*. It floated, dark. Its bridge was a ragged wound, as if torn free with colossal jaws. It was surrounded by the husks of second and fourth fleet. Debris poured into space from the channel, appearing suddenly with a flash as it decelerated below light-speed.

'Ma'am, it looks like they were attacked *inside* the channel.'

The word *impossible* drifted across Wrask's mind, but she did not say it.

'Raise forward shields. Put the *Typho* on our flank, tell them to cloak if they can.'

The comms officer relayed her orders. 'Cloak drained, ma'am.'

'... Very well.' Wrask keyed the announcer. 'Incoming.'

Seven minutes later the *Teratorn* burst from the end of the channel, emerging at the edge of a debris field. Daedalus tilted the joysticks and skirted the craft away from the larger fragments, missing the flaming wreck of a Republic ship by metres. The name was mostly obscured by burn marks, with only the word 'Neeson' still visible. It was a few seconds before Daedalus realised the bigger pieces of wreckage were all ships, torn and melted into unrecognisable shapes, names almost entirely obscured.

Hilton leaned over the pilot's chair and pointed. 'There,' he said.

Daedalus could see too. They were far away, but the sight was unmistakable. Lances of brightly-coloured light sliced through the blackness, leaving trails of flame in their wake. After years of peace, war had come back to Highdust.

Hurry, said a voice in Daedalus's head. He jumped.

'Vanguard? What is wrong?'

Daedalus listened. 'Nothing,' he said. 'Headache.'

'You have not slept.'

'I'm well aware. Brace.'

Daedalus punched the throttle. The *Teratorn* leapt forward.

He felt better, but his eyes still itched and he could feel the weariness in his muscles. The shower had made him human again, but the tiredness was setting in. Daedalus wasn't sure how long he'd been in the fluid, but it hadn't been real sleep. He'd be running on fumes until this was over.

The vast expanse of space between the channel and the battlefield was nothing to the *Teratorn*. It moved like a ghost, flitting between wings of fighters and through firebursts as if it existed on a different plane to everything else. They passed through a crossfire as the rebel *Vercingetorix* punched through a wing of Republic bombers, beam cannons cutting them to ribbons as it went. As they drew closer to the battle, Daedalus could make out the details. Flashes of light revealed the hulls of two gigantic ships. The *Geb* he recognised, but its opponent was different. Clad in white, of strange design, and nearly twice the size of Wrask's supercarrier, it slung volley after volley of missiles and laser bolts into its dancing partner as they circled one another with increasing speed, each struggling to flank sharply enough to put a beam behind the other's forward shield and end the partnership in one strike. The rest of the white-clad fleet had surrounded a gigantic black dreadnought, raining fire and metal on it from all sides and wearing it down by attrition. The only other black ships Daedalus could see were in open retreat, driven back in all directions by swarms of white fighters. They drew closer still, and Daedalus saw a pale cruiser, *The Goodwill of the Committee*, rush the *Geb* in a flanking manoeuvre. A hidden flak battery tore its underside out and its swoop faltered. It fishtailed into the supercarrier's rear shield and burst into a million flaming fragments.

Bridge. The word floated into his head. Without a second thought, he slammed the throttle full open and dived towards the *Geb*. Hilton cried out in surprise.

'Vanguard! We're falling!'

'Shut up.'

The *Teratorn* jerked sideways to avoid a flak burst. It spun, parrying an anti-fighter beam off its starboard shield. Then a runway was beneath them. The landing legs sprung out and Daedalus heaved on the sticks as hard as he could. They turned, the retros fired and the ship started slowing down.

'Vanguard! THE WALL!'

Daedalus shut him out. The hazy purple curtain between him and the hangar obscured his view, but he could see the doors were open. The *Geb*'s hull was only metres away. The *Teratorn* arced sideways and he strained to hold it steady as the edge rushed towards them.

He didn't know how close they came. All he knew was that now they were inside and there were people everywhere. White-armoured police ran from landed dropships, all four-armed and wielding swords. The *Teratorn* thudded to the deck and the suspension squealed as it absorbed the impact.

BRIDGE.

Daedalus unbuckled his seatbelt and ran for the door. He heard a clanking as Hilton followed. He stopped at the switch to lower the ramp. He turned to face his bodyguard.

'Remember.' He jabbed a finger at him. 'Keep your distance. Anyone tries to kill me, you end them.'

He hit the switch, and the door opened onto chaos.

Erin arrived on the bridge to noise and flashing red lights. Wrask was standing in the centre of the room, bellowing orders at the crew and scrawling frantic diagrams on the big tactical readout. The Republic supercarrier was visible through the main viewscreen. The white hulk filled space in front of them, dwarfing everything else in sight. A constant low roar reverberated through the ship as the beams cycled their charges. Wrask was maintaining the power levels herself on one readout, and calling targets on another. Every percentage bar Erin could see was flashing red and almost full.

'This is bad,' said Ram. They went unnoticed in the frenetic activity on the bridge. Erin's guards still flanked them, but they seemed unsure of what to do with her.

'What's she doing?' asked Erin.

'Everything's topping out. She's using everything the ship's got.'

'Surely that's a good thing?'

'She can't keep this going for long.' Ram gripped her shoulder. 'She's firing everything at once. The shields are up, and we're circling at full speed. This ship is going to burn.'

The white ship was starting to show the strain. Erin could see the shield flickering as the *Geb* rained fire on it – it was the better ship, but Wrask was the better captain.

'Breach on deck six!' came a call from the engineering station. 'Sealing – we've lost the plasma batteries!'

Wrask slammed a fist on the announcer. 'Engineering!' she roared. 'Shut down life support on six! Reroute power to coolant pumps!'

A few bars on the readout slid millimetres back from the danger zone.

'WHERE IS THE CHILD?'

'Ma'am!' one of the guards piped up.

Wrask turned. Erin saw her face, and for the first time in a long time she was afraid. The kindly, wise, composed expression Wrask normally adopted around her was gone. Her eyes were wide and brimming with fury; her mouth was a twisted snarl. When she saw Erin, the snarl slipped, but the anger remained.

'Are you armed?'

Erin nodded, putting a hand to the holster on her back.

'You. Go.' Wrask waved Erin's guards away. Ram did not move.

'They stopped me,' Erin said. 'I should be on a dropship. I should be fighting.'

'You can fight here,' Wrask answered. She turned and keyed the announcer. The ship rocked as the shield took a heavy impact. Erin saw her steady herself. 'This is the Marshal-Elect.' Her voice boomed through the ship, amplified a hundred times. 'We have lost this battle. Those who wish to flee, do it now. Otherwise, make your peace with death.'

Wrask released the announcer and addressed her bridge crew directly. They stared up at her, human and petradon alike.

'You are now commanders. I will not deprive the revolution of you. The starboard hangar on deck two is still shielded. Board separate transports, and flee.'

Nobody moved.

'Go, or I'll have your families killed.'

Everyone moved.

'Stand guard,' Wrask said to Erin.

The bridge emptied. Wrask stayed at the controls, keeping up the assault. Only Erin and Ram remained, their weapons drawn.

There was the sound of a distant klaxon. Wrask looked up.

'Boarders on deck five,' she said. 'I hope you're ready to fight. I'm not done here.'

'What are you doing?'

'A few things.' Her thick fingers moved across the keys with surprising dexterity. 'That ship should not exist,' she said. 'It engaged us in-channel. That should not be possible. I don't know how, but the Republic is changing the rules of the game.' There was a distant screech from somewhere in the ship. Wrask seized a heavy red lever mounted above the main console. She grunted, and with an immense effort forced it down. *Thunk.* The red lights shut off, and the warning sirens fell quiet. 'I will not allow it.'

'Wrask...' Erin inched towards her. She didn't like the edge in her voice. 'Come with us.'

'I am still in command here.' Her tone brooked no argument. 'Do you believe in our cause?'

'Of course I do!'

'Good.' Wrask tapped out a few more commands and spoke over her shoulder. 'The secondary reactor is out of commission. No sensors. No shields. No door control. The life support is failing and the hangar containment fields are hanging by a thread.' She turned to face them. 'This ship is going down. If that things beats us, it's going to look like a victory. Everything we've done... everything we've worked for... will have been lost in vain if we can't take it with us,' she said, pointing out the viewscreen.

'Then let's stop it,' said Erin. 'Just tell me what I have to do.'

As if on cue, a heavy boom rang from somewhere nearby. Wrask snapped her head up. 'We have boarders. Keep them away from the console. There is only one door. Bottleneck them.'

'Got it. Ram, bend the door in.'

Ram nodded, and went to the door.

'Erin,' said Wrask quietly, 'we are at contingency M. Are you prepared?'

'I – yes.'

'Are you sure?'

'... Yes. I'm ready.'

'Thank you. Stay in sight –' she gestured at the security camera on the ceiling '– and look good.'

The elevator stopped. The jolt almost knocked Daedalus to the ground, but he gripped the handrail tight and stayed standing.

'What's happened?' Hilton asked. His armour was dripping red onto the floor. Nightmare was covered in it.

Daedalus jabbed at the button for deck one. Nothing happened. 'The power's out.' He kicked the door. 'Emergency brakes. Great. What's the point in a gravity lift that needs power?'

'How do we get out?' Hilton looked around. 'Ah.' He stretched out a hand for the hatch on the ceiling.

'No!' Daedalus seized his forearm. 'Don't touch that.' There was a rubber seal around the hatch. 'Vacuum. I don't want to die in a bloody lift. Give me your sword.'

He forced the jagged edge into the gap between the doors. It wouldn't go through. They were stuck between decks. Daedalus swore.

'Vanguard?'

There was a pause. Daedalus looked upwards. 'How high can you jump?'

'… I do not like where this is going.'

Daedalus explained.

'I do not like where that went,' said Hilton.

'There's no gravity in the shaft,' said Daedalus. 'If we can reach a door we might be able to get back through.'

'"Might"?'

'Shut up. No time.' *Hurry*. 'Understand?'

'… Yes.'

'Remember: keep straight, and grab something close to the door. Ready?'

'Grab something like what?'

'Exhale!'

There was a *thwump* and a sound of rushing air, then silence. Daedalus's stomach churned as the gravity shut off. He bent his knees and leapt upwards through the hatch, propelling himself into the cold vertical tunnel. The light of the lift vanished behind him. His eyes began to sting. He peered into the blackness and glimpsed a purple glow far above; the containment field separating the lift shaft vacuum from the top deck – it was approaching fast. He guessed at the distance and then closed his eyes, tight, stretching out a hand. Ice-cold metal juddered against his arm as he skidded upwards along the shaft. His mouth was dry.

Then his hand felt nothing. He jerked outwards and caught the door frame, arresting his flight. He could feel his lungs burning. The urge to open his mouth – to breathe – was intense. The field buzzed on his knuckles, and he could feel warm air against his fingertips, on the other side. Daedalus pulled with all his strength.

Then Hilton slammed into him.

Like A Thunderclap

Erin
The Geb

The sparks died away. Erin stared down the corridor at the heavy steel blast door. The line where the boarders had cut through glowed a bright orange, painful to look at. There was silence.

Erin didn't feel sick. There was no fear. Ram was right there next to her. Her right hands gripped a sword each. She punched Ram in the shoulder; she had to reach up to do it.

'Ready?' she grinned.

Ram grimaced. 'We should not be here.'

'No better place for it, though.' Erin gestured around. 'Very dramatic.'

Ram looked at her. Erin saw her mouth was parted, her brow furrowed in confusion.

'Place for... what?'

The door exploded. Then Ram shouldered in front of her. Shrapnel turned the air to knives, but it glanced harmlessly off Ram's plates before embedding itself in the walls. Then the corridor was full of them. Tall, spidery figures in smooth, shining white armour; their faces obscured by black visors set into round helmets. They brandished narrow longswords in front of them.

'BRIDGE TEAM AT OBJECTIVE. V.I.P. PRESENT. CONFIRM ENGAGE ORDER.'

Erin edged up next to Ram and raised her swords in front of her chest.

The lead figure raised a hand – one of four – and gestured at its companions. 'CODE NINE. SECURE HOSTAGE. KILL OTHERS.'

'Come on, then,' said Erin, 'come on!'

They advanced.

They drifted away from the door, Daedalus scrabbling desperately for a handhold. Then they were too far. They had flown too high, and there was no gravity to pull them back down. Daedalus wanted to scream, but there was no air to carry his voice. He couldn't reach the walls. He didn't want to die in the dark, so he opened his eyes.

The door was close. Two metres, maybe. They were moving slowly. Red lines crept from the edges of his vision. The moisture on his eyeballs vaporised immediately, and it stung. He looked at Hilton, floating behind him, thrashing in confusion and fear. Daedalus thought of Erin, and drew his feet up to his chest. One kick into Hilton's shoulders and he could reach her, and Hilton would be dealt with forever. The momentum would carry him through the field, and he'd have air.

Do it. Kick.

Something broke. Daedalus let his legs go limp. Hilton remained where he was.

He couldn't. The part of him that could wasn't there anymore.

Hilton looked up. Purple light illuminated his eyes through the gap in his visor, and Daedalus saw his sudden understanding.

Daedalus tried to shout, but only blood came up. Hilton seized his feet. There was a push.

Then he was in the narrow gap between the containment field and the door, bracing himself against the door frame. His back was pressed against cold metal, and the vacuum was inches from his face. He breathed. The last thing he saw of Hilton was a glint of purple shining off his helmet. Then the darkness of the shaft took him. Daedalus was alone. He could hear his heart pounding, and the sounds of fighting from the other side of the door.

He could feel something under his hand. He pressed. The door slid open. He staggered backwards and tripped over something white. His elbow hurt. His head hurt. There was something hard under his back. He pushed it away, and his hand came up bloody. He was bleeding. His hand hurt. He looked down.

The black visor reflected his face. It was broken. The longsword had his blood on it. Daedalus stretched out his good hand and took the weapon from its dead master. There was blood inside the helmet.

His head ringing, Daedalus stood up. The corridor was full of dead people. Republic and revolutionary soldiers lay on top of each other, locked in silent struggle. The faces he could see were twisted with agony. Smoke fluid leaked from rifles and ate away at the skin of any corpse it touched.

He looked again at the soldier beneath him. All in white armour. Black visor. Entari. An odd emblem on the shoulder. A green sword plunging down through four black spots.

Move.

Daedalus recognised that emblem.

Now.

Erin. Erin, he had to get to Erin.

He was so *tired.*

Left.

He turned and stepped over a body. He walked. Then he ran.

Erin swung. Her target leaned back sharply, but her blade smashed his visor into pieces. There was a scream, and blood spurted. Ram's hammer knocked him down. He didn't get up. Erin's second sword whipped at his partner, forcing him back.

'FORM TWELVE. ALIGN FIVE. CLOSE HILT.'

The white men spread out and raised their swords in unison, pointing down from above. They ducked forward in pairs, thrusting and pulling back in fluid motion. Feinting. As one pair got close Ram lunged, knocking a sword aside with the flat of her hammer. They retreated. Erin couldn't tell how many there were; they were taller than her and their shiny uniforms bled together. At least ten, she guessed. Maybe more in the corridor behind. Just the sight of them made her angry. Painfully angry.

'CODE TWENTY-NINE.'

Then the group parted and there was a *whomp.* A plume of thick grey smoke billowed from behind, filling the hallway.

'Ram!'

'Get back!' Ram pushed Erin behind her and moved to the centre. She crouched as the smoke bloomed around her feet. There was a moment's silence. 'Stay back,' she said.

A white shape flitted into view and out again. Ram shifted one foot back, readying her hammer.

Then a sword crashed into her shoulder. She grunted under the impact, but didn't move. Another came, but Ram knocked it away with the handle of her hammer. Then another caught her in the side, and she roared with pain. The smoke laughed. 'Stay – back!'

Erin felt a hot prickle on her skin. It felt like her mother's voice, scolding. The laughter was brief, but it rang in her skull.

Stay back.

Erin's knee twitched. She watched a rivulet of dark blood run from Ram's waist.

'Come on,' Ram said, 'cowards.'

Another blow came, then another. Ram knocked them aside with her hammer, then her plates, then her fists. The blows fell like rain, with hardly a space between them. Ram took a wound here, another there. She moved like a machine, directing their blades to parts of her she could afford to lose. Her blows came slowly, but Erin heard yells of agony and the sounds of crumpling metal. Ram stabbed forward with her hammer, forcing it suddenly in sharp sideways motions. There were no swings, just unpredictable, graceless jabs. Then a pair of swords fell on either side of her. She dropped her hammer and flung her fist out. A visor shattered, but the second slash got through.

Erin saw Ram's knee give out.

Erin moved like a spider, going low. One hand steadied her on the ground as she dipped forward, then threw herself upwards. Her sword disappeared up to the hilt, punching straight through the man's breastplate, before she crashed into him, knocking him to the floor. Erin jumped off him, bringing her remaining sword up in a wide arc to knock away an oncoming blow.

It wasn't how she expected. The anger had vanished. There were no enemies, there was no cause. There was only the next movement. She slid in front of Ram and planted two hands on her chest. Gently, she nudged her friend backwards. Ram staggered. Erin heard the rustle of an armoured elbow joint, and spun to turn the blade aside once more. She caught it as it came, redirecting it into the ground. Ram was falling back, safely out of their reach. Erin found the hilt of her other sword and pulled it from her first victim. Her first partner. It made no sound as she drove it up and sideways into the smoke in front of her. The underarm padding gave way silently, and her sword punctured both lungs before she removed it. Another man fell.

'V.I.P. HOSTILE. INCAPACITATE. SECURE.'

'Come,' she said, in a voice that reminded her of someone. 'Secure me.'

Right.

Daedalus rounded a corner onto more bodies. A breach lander was embedded in one wall. He could see the empty seats inside, except for one occupied by a dead entari. They hung from the harness, pierced by shrapnel. He could not determine the gender.

Next left.

He tried not to look. It was getting to him. Lack of sleep, he figured. He moved one foot, then another, until he was staggering at full speed again. The ship kept rocking and screeching as missiles impacted on the hull.

Broken pipes sprayed coolant and steam into the corridors, forcing him to duck and weave around them. More than once he tripped on a body. He kept up his drunken weave until he could hear the sounds of swordplay nearby.

Straight ahead.

The corridor was filled with solid grey smoke. It obscured everything. He heard shouting.

Straight ahead.

Daedalus gripped his stolen sword, dripping with his own blood. He could smell it: a clear sharpness above the smoke's low, heavy must. One step forward, then another. The shouting had stopped. He moved into the cloud slowly, waving his stolen sword in cautious circles, blind. His toe hit something hard. Squinting, he made out the outline of a body in white, then another.

There were low voices. The smoke was finally clearing. A figure stood on the other side. Colour returned, slowly.

'Mole?'

Erin was covered in blood. Her jacket was ruined, her hands wet

There were scratches on her face, and scars, marks that he
member. Her eyes were wide. Bodies lay torn apart at her

did you find me?'

dalus moved closer.

at's far enough.' The voice rumbled like an engine. Wrask stood
d Erin, filling the doorway with her broad shoulders and billow-
black cloak. 'Stand down.'

Daedalus stood where he was.

What's wrong?' Erin turned to face her.

'He arrived on the _Teratorn_.' Wrask's expression was almost calm,
ut her eyes betrayed her rage. 'The Republic have him. They always
had him. He is here to kidnap you. To turn you.'

'No!' Daedalus said. His mouth was dry. His voice was failing. This
was wrong. It was all going wrong. 'I – I'm here to – save –'

Erin looked at him. There was confusion. Anger. 'Save me?'

There was silence. A drop of blood ran from Erin's finger and made
a _pat_ sound on the floor. The smoke was gone now. Daedalus stared
at her. His brain wouldn't function. He felt for the locket at his neck.
Dented and damaged.

'He betrayed our position to the Republic. He told them we were
coming. The blood of our comrades is on his hands.'

Erin stared at him. Daedalus was tired; his mouth wouldn't form the
words. As he watched, her expression changed. Erin's eyes hardened
and her mouth went thin. Her fingers twitched, flicking blood onto
the floor.

'No,' Daedalus pleaded, 'I'm not – you can't –'

Her kick struck him in the chest. It knocked him straight to the
floor and sent his sword spinning away. He yelled in pain and groped
for a handhold.

'How much did they pay you? Huh?' Erin kicked him again. 'How
much am I _worth_?'

'I have to – have to save –'

'What?' she asked. 'Save what?'

'Save you.' Daedalus held up his hands. 'I… I can't let you die again
–'

Erin struck him across the face with the flat of her sword. Blood arced through the air. She stood over him.

'I'm not Jan,' she said. 'I'm not here to absolve you of your cowardice. I'm not your goddamn counsellor. I am *Erin*, you selfish, neurotic little man.' Erin leaned closer, glaring into his eyes. 'And the very last thing I am – something I will never, ever be again – is someone who can be *saved*.'

The sting of the blow had been cold, and the shock still rang through his whole head. Daedalus felt like the threads holding him up had been cut. The static in his mind flashed out to silence, and after a moment of quiet his ears rang with the normal sounds of war.

He blinked. His head hurt, but from the strike, rather than the sickness.

The sickness? He didn't know he was sick. Daedalus became aware of it by its absence, and felt it clawing at his mind, trying to pull him back down. This pain was clean. It was clear.

He looked up. Erin stood over him. She had big, dark eyes. Of course she did. They were pure black and shining. Entari – a whole species of people with identical black eyes.

The connection broke. A memory snapped, and a dead woman vanished; she had never been there at all. No-one was there but Erin.

The floor shook. There was a distant roar and a jolt through the floor.

Wrask started laughing.

Erin stepped back from the cowering human. 'It's time.'

Ram said something from the corner where she sat. Daedalus looked over. He hadn't noticed her at all. She was clutching her head where the bony spines of her skull punctured her skin. She coughed, and repeated herself. 'Engines.'

Daedalus sat up.

Ram seized a railing and heaved herself to her feet. 'We're accelerating.'

Wrask took Erin by the shoulder. 'You were magnificent.'

Through the viewscreen Daedalus could see the distant white ship getting closer.

'Erin –' Daedalus spat out blood. 'We have to go. I mean it.'

'No.' Erin's voice was very close to firm.

'They will remember this,' said Wrask. 'The footage is already away. The legend begins today.' The look on her face was a wide calm smile, without feeling. The look of a corpse.

Daedalus reached out and found the hilt of his sword.

'Who?'

'Our successors. The second wave. Our war does not end here, with our deaths.' Wrask stroked Erin's arm. 'Little Erin will be their hero. Their symbol. A fallen entari, slaughtering her own kind, defending her petradon commander in their final hour together.'

Ram leant against the wall, breathing heavily. As always, no-one paid her any notice. Daedalus dug his fingers into the grated floor and pushed himself up. The ship shuddered as something burst below decks. The noise of distant explosions was growing louder.

'A martyr?' Daedalus croaked.

'Our greatest and most terrible weapon,' said Wrask, 'and a death knell for the Coalition.'

'Free her,' he said.

'No.'

'Mole, sit down,' Erin said. 'You don't understand. You never understood. It's inevitable now.'

Daedalus inched forward, his sword up. 'I understand this. It's suicide. Self-destruction. It's not inevitable. It's never inevitable.'

'You clearly care for her,' Wrask said, cocking her head to one side as she inspected him. 'This is the best way out. Let her go, it will be kinder.'

Erin cut in. 'This is purpose, Mole! I'll have something you've never had! I'll make a difference!'

'Stand *down*, human,' said Wrask. 'If you run, I'll let you live.'

'Listen to her, Mole,' said Erin. 'You're not ready to die.'

Daedalus strode forward. 'No time left,' he said. In a sudden movement he ducked and swept the sword upwards and forwards, aiming for Wrask's neck.

Her forearm leapt up to meet the strike, and the impact juddered up Daedalus's arm, knocking him sideways. Wrask pulled Erin behind her with one hand and shoved Daedalus sideways with the other, smashing him into the wall and sending the sword skittering from his hand. She planted her right hand on his chest, holding him still, and took his right hand in her left. Then, slowly, she squeezed until the fingerbones snapped. Daedalus screamed.

'Amateur.' Wrask grabbed his coat collar, lifting him bodily into the air. 'You should have stayed away from war.'

'Wrask, wait –' Erin grabbed her arm. A waver had slipped into her voice.

'VANGUARD!'

There was a hellish clamour, an awful clanking rhythm, as a metal man rounded the end of the corridor, sprinting towards them. Hilton, dripping in blood from head to feet, swung Nightmare over his head like a flail as he closed the distance. Wrask watched him come and dropped Daedalus on the floor, where he lay groaning. Hilton kept running.

Thirty metres. Twenty. Ten.

Wrask started as if to walk forward, and dipped her shoulder towards him. Her left knee bent and she drew her back foot forward.

The average petradon thigh muscle can support two hundred kilograms of chitinous armour, bone and several sets of organs. When Wrask drove her shoulder into Hilton's chest his armour crumpled inwards and he was thrown back with force few people in the galaxy could command, with a blow that no human could survive. Hilton's body rattled and clanged as he rolled back along the floor, coming to a stop almost as far back as when he'd arrived.

Wrask opened her mouth to laugh.

Ram yelled. Wrask turned her head, and then Ram struck.

Her skull crunched into Wrask's face, the spines embedding themselves in the soft skin between her plates. Blood spurted, and Wrask fell backwards.

Ram snatched up her warhammer.

'No!' Erin cried.

Ram did not hesitate. One of Wrask's legs broke, then the other. She roared in agony. Ram swung her hammer down once more and crushed Wrask's right arm.

'Ram, stop!' Erin grabbed at her forearm, hammering her fist into it. 'Stop it!'

'It is done,' said Ram. 'We are leaving. Now.'

'Wrask –'

The petradon writhed on the floor, groaning and gasping, trying to speak.

'Mole, can you walk?' Ram asked.

'Y– yeah.'

'Run?'

'Yeah.'

'Your ship. Take us there.'

Erin was still watching Wrask. Blood ran from her yellow eyes, and from her mouth. Between spasms of pain, the captain managed to reach into her cloak and withdraw something white.

'Wrask?' Erin thought of Juno, for the first time in weeks. 'Not – not again. No... '

Unable to speak, Wrask pressed the envelope into Erin's hand.

'Don't leave me,' said Erin.

Then Erin was hoisted aloft by Ram. She stared at her dying commander as they ran away from her. Ram lifted Hilton onto her shoulder as well, tucking Erin under one arm. Erin didn't take in the fire and the panic as they fled through the *Geb*'s corridors. She didn't notice the brawling and the killing they had to do to reach the *Teratorn*. She barely registered being dropped onto the floor as the boarding ramp rose up and they cannoned out of the hangar.

The explosion was silent. The *Geb* ploughed into the centre of the Republic flagship, collapsing millions of tons of steel into arcane, twisted shapes. There was a blue flash as its shield burst under the strain, and a blooming sphere of purple flame as the reactor ruptured. The carnage on the viewscreen diminished as they soared away into the black.

Are We Learning?

The two men ambled through the trees, watching the stars above them. One was naked and pink. The other was naked and red and not a man at all, and he (or they) had a single green eye – the reason for this being that one of the men was there and the other was not.

'You influenced him,' said Monitor. 'You gave him the strength to escape me.'

'I did,' said Perry.

'Why?'

'I've told you a hundred times, Monty,' said Perry, 'the task you're asking is too much. You can make a slave of him, but he won't be the same afterwards – like me. Trauma disables. He wouldn't be able to do what you need. You're looking to dig up things that have been hidden for centuries, some designed never to be found again. He needs to have his whole mind together if he's going to be of any use.'

'You are hardly a slave,' said Monitor. 'In fact, you are the least useful slave I have ever known. You sabotage my efforts at every turn, and refuse to carry out even the simplest of commands. You seem quite happy to live on this world and share in my power, but you will not assist me no matter how kindly I ask.'

'That's because I'm your friend, you big slimy oaf.'

'The human. He will not do anything without compulsion.'

'Maybe he won't.'

'So obviously I chose to force him,' said Monitor. 'I trusted that the binding process would not rob him of his faculties – and it did not. He is still capable of intelligent action.' Monty paused, thinking about the human's behaviour. 'Of a sort.'

'You're old, Monty,' said Perry. 'You've forgotten why you do what you do.'

'I do it because it is what I do.'

Perry plucked a sprouting flower from a hanging vine and twirled it in his fingers. 'Sometimes,' he said, 'I think you're as much a slave as I am. To your own... ' he held the flower up to his eye. It dripped with black fluid. '... convictions.'

'I was sure once,' said Monitor. The cloud was moving, and starlight glistened on the raw, skinless muscle of his projected body. 'I would not have been sure without good reason.'

'Mhm.' Perry dropped the flower on the ground. 'You know, I've been thinking about luck.'

'I am luck.'

'You don't seem to have much, though. At least, that's what I thought. You tried to break his personhood, turn him into an agent so you could act faster, and more precisely – but I think you misunderstood him.'

'Misunderstood?'

'You led people to him. The right people, funnily enough. Of all the people you could've snagged, you managed to get hold of a few who could actually help him... and one – *one* – who he could help in return. You wanted him to care about the universe. You thought you could guilt and shame him into it, but you couldn't. He fought back.'

'What about my good luck?'

'He doesn't see clearly, does he?' Perry laughed. 'His view of other people is warped by what he has done – by his scars. That's what saved him from you.'

'... How? How is this good? Tell me, human.'

'I hoped you would figure it out. Maybe it isn't clear to people like you. People who haven't suffered,' said Perry, his lips drawn. 'You understand why what you're doing is important, and you feel it. You can explain to him why it's important until the cows come home, but it won't mean anything to him. The loss of everything is nothing to the person who has nothing to lose.'

'How is that good?'

'Because now he has something to lose.'

Domestics

The Teratorn

The *Teratorn* didn't have the draughty open spaces of the *Crow*. The corridors were narrow and packed in neatly around themselves – everything about it spoke of careful, efficient design and planning.

Perfect white materials lined the hallway, which was specked with thick, dark blood. Erin sat against one wall. Ram leaned heavily on the other, her tree-trunk arms twitching from nerves, aggression and leftover adrenalin. Spines of warped bone, snapped free, littered the floor where she had bent to set Erin gently down. Ram bled. Daedalus and Hilton, to her total lack of surprise, had run straight to the cockpit and not returned; perhaps unwilling to deal with the creature they had rescued in place of the Erin they remembered. Probably afraid. Ram was familiar with the fears of men.

Ram was not familiar with the strange sensation that gripped her now. It had been worsening over the last few weeks, coming in waves of nausea and mental exhaustion. Her emotions pulsed and morphed constantly, slipping through her fingers each time she tried to make sense of them.

Erin was the centre. Everyone and everything else receded when she was close. Ram felt like gravity had malfunctioned, tugging her sideways from the pit of her belly in whatever direction Erin went. Erin was a black hole, and Ram was long past the event horizon with no hope of rescue. Unfortunately at this moment there were few people in the universe who hated Ram more than Erin DiGamma.

Ram could see it in her eyes. Killing Wrask was the first thing Ram had done in years – everything else was just the world flowing around her, carrying her on aimless currents which she lacked the will to fight against. Ram hadn't been sure what Wrask had done to Erin until that moment, but the hurt in her eyes confirmed Ram's worst fears.

Erin was changed.

'I trusted you,' she said.

Ram glanced back at her for a moment, unable to hold her gaze. 'You can still trust me,' she said in answer.

Erin pressed her hands to her face, two over her eyes and two on her head, clutching painfully at the skin. 'I can't believe I let you into my life. I was so *stupid*. You turned on the Navy just like you've turned on me, you stupid, spineless, selfish –'

'I did the right thing.' Ram clenched her fists. She tried not to listen to the jury in her head. Ram knew she was right. She *had* to be. 'You were going to die,' she said. 'Wrask was just using you to make a point.'

'You KILLED her!' Erin screeched. 'She's DEAD!'

'Look at yourself! You think she would cry for you?' Ram slammed her fist into the wall by Erin's head, leaving a dent. 'They do not care about you – about any of us! Just as long as they have meat for the grinder they will keep lying! I could not let them martyr you.'

'I chose it. There was a plan! You don't know anything about it – about us! We could have changed everyth–'

'NO! *She* chose it. The Erin I know would not throw her life away on just a chance.'

Erin struggled to her feet. 'You think you know me? Do you have any clue who I am? I think you know what you want me to be, and you don't like that I might choose to be something else.' Her voice shook and her crest flexed. 'You're afraid I'll *outgrow* you.'

Ram's jaw set. The voices in her mind hissed and needled her, echoing Erin's words. *No*, she thought. The pain in her head was starting to creep past the adrenaline in her blood, stinging and burning as it went. There wasn't much time.

'I said I would not leave.' Ram turned, leaning on the wall for support as she finally met Erin's glare. 'To lose you would... hurt. But I would go this second if I thought you did not need me.

'Erin. I know pain when I see it. Wrask made you hurt, and I regret only that I did not stop her sooner. I do not know if you will heal – I do not know if I can help or if I came too late – but if I can make you realise that you deserve better then it will take more than anyone has to send me away.'

Erin gritted her teeth. 'I'm better dead,' she hissed. 'I could be a hero.'

Ram raised her hand, but then fell to one knee with a sharp *crack*. Blood ran from her head into her mouth. 'I do not care,' she whispered, eyes losing focus. 'I only… want you… to be happy.'

Erin wound up and punched her in the chest. She cried out at the sudden pain in her knuckles, tears running freely down her cheeks. 'I can't!' she roared, and hit her again, punctuating each word with a weaker blow than the last. 'I dont-get-to be-happy!'

Ram barely flinched. She took a deep, slow breath. 'I will settle… for alive.'

She collapsed to the floor. Erin hit her again, then screamed for help.

White Shores

The crew
Oceanus

The sky was a light grey, with encroaching darker clouds in the distance. A gentle sea breeze was rolling in, and it tousled Daedalus's hair with cool fingers. The opal waters made a soft rushing sound as they lapped against the stony white shoreline, and pale foamy ridges cut the tides into shapes which constantly shifted and changed. Daedalus followed them with his eyes. The water didn't reach the stone on which he sat, but it occasionally bubbled up against the soles of his feet with a soothing cold.

The tide was in. He could tell by the way the water was almost up to the bottom of the rotted wooden sign in the shallows. 'BEYOND,' it read. His coat and boots were drying nearby, the locket tucked away in the breast pocket, and his broken fingers were wrapped in gauze, held steady with little splints.

He heard a crunching sound. Erin sat down next to him.

'How's Ram?' he asked.

Erin picked up a pebble in one hand and started toying with it. 'She's sleeping off the painkillers.'

'Bleeding?'

'No, it's stopped. Her head's a mess, though,' she tossed the pebble into the water. 'I don't know anything about medicine. I keep waiting for her to come to and tell me what to do next.'

'And Hilton?'

'Alive, somehow. Still won't let me see him. Says he just needs sleep. Not that I care.'

'He saved me. He saved all of us, really.'

'That doesn't make him a good person. It doesn't mean we should trust him.'

'I don't know… ' Daedalus nudged a wet pebble around with his toes. They sat in silence for a while, staring out across the sea. Erin drummed her fingers on her knee – a habit Daedalus found he had missed. She threw another stone into the water.

'I like your new ship,' she said, 'very clean.' A gust of sand blew up between them, creeping through the gaps between the pebbles. 'What happened to the *Crow*?'

'Destroyed.'

'Oh.' Erin looked at him. There was an odd expression on Daedalus's face, like a child after admitting some terrible deed. 'How?' she asked.

'I crashed it.'

'... You loved that ship.'

'Yes.'

'There's no getting it back?'

Daedalus looked up. He took a deep breath of salted air, and let the wind beat his face. No answer came. Erin felt she understood, and so they sat for another while.

'What is this place?' Erin asked.

'The planet's called Oceanus,' Daedalus said. 'This shoreline is called Beyond. Used to be a smugglers' den, but the route dried up years ago. Now it's just a quiet place. Somewhere to rest.'

'Any natives?'

'No,' he kicked a pebble into the water. 'It's a dead world.'

'You've been here before, then?'

'Once.'

'After Jan?'

'... Yes.' He coughed. 'After that.'

Somewhere nearby, a pebble rattled its way down a cliffside. Daedalus looked over for a moment.

'Erin,' said Daedalus, 'I want to know. Were you actually... would you have gone through with it? If I hadn't turned up, would you have stuck to the plan?'

Erin looked out to sea. 'It was a good plan. I wouldn't have to fight, but I'd wage a war from the grave. I'd lead a revolution without fear. I'd make a difference. The whole thing was engineered and ready.'

'So you would?'

Erin *hmph*ed. 'It doesn't matter. Either way, Ram wouldn't have left me there. That was the problem – Wrask couldn't get Ram away from me, and I wouldn't let go of her. I think she suspected.' Erin stopped drumming her fingers. 'You didn't save us, and neither did Hilton. Ram did.

'I thought I would hate her. But... getting away from Wrask... getting away from her words and her plans and her... voice... ' Erin's crest flittered. 'Ram was bleeding. She bled for me. It's like... there was this monster. This huge, invincible monster... and I loved it. I want so much to be... but then there was Ram. She just... she just came out of *nowhere*. It was –'

Daedalus looked at her. He came to a realisation.

'You... and Ram?'

Erin squinted at him. 'Well, yes. Of course.'

'Right,' said Daedalus. It took him a moment to recognise the hot, blossoming feeling in his face. It was embarrassment. 'Of course.'

'Mole, I think you need to stop *observing* people and start actually seeing them.'

Daedalus said nothing.

'It's the only way you'll ever learn to see yourself. I think you need that.'

'To be fair, I've been away. You and Wrask, though, what happened there?'

'I don't know. My decisions... they – they weren't all my own.' Erin looked upwards, breathing in slowly. Cold salt spray brushed her cheek. 'I think I have issues with... er... control. Wrask made me feel like... like... ' A wave lapped against the stones, picking up the smaller ones and pulling them out into the open water. 'Like I was being pulled along by something bigger, and I only had to kick a little to go really, really far. It felt good.'

'How does Ram make you feel?'

Erin made an ugly sniffing sound. 'Big.'

They sat quietly for a while.

'What now?' Daedalus felt like he'd never asked the question before. 'What are you going to do?'

'Visit my mom. I don't like the idea that Wrask was the last person to see her. And I owe her a goodbye.'

Daedalus thought about that. 'I suppose you do.'

Erin touched the letter in her pocket; she'd read it and stuffed it back into the envelope. She wouldn't deal with that right now. 'I'm angry, Mole. About so many things. I can't live with this feeling.' Erin looked up at the sky. A couple of particularly bright stars were visible through the canopy of cloud. 'And that footage made it out. It's circulating. I was watching it inside.'

'How does it look?'

'It looks like I died. That's what people are saying on the railroad channels. There's talk of more attacks. Retaliations. A regrouping.'

'You going to join in?'

Erin drummed her fingers.

'What about you?' she asked. 'Know what you're doing next?'

'No. What is there to do?'

Erin stood up. 'How about a coffee?'

Daedalus perked up. 'Yes. That's something I can do.' He heaved himself to his feet and grabbed his things with his free hand. The clothes were nearly dry.

'Come on then,' Erin said.

Together they walked back to the shining white ship on the beach. Inside was cool and quiet.

'Should probably check on Hilton,' said Daedalus.

'I'll get the coffee started, then,' said Erin.

He found Hilton lying sprawled on his newly-claimed bunk, groaning in pain.

'Hilton?'

'Vanguard? Nice to – argh – see you.'

'Are you alright?'

'Yes, yes, I'm fine,' he waved Daedalus's words away, 'just a few cracked ribs. Nothing some lying down can't fix.'

'I just wanted to… to thank you.'

Hilton looked up in surprise, winced, and fell back down. 'Aye? That's a sentiment I didn't expect from you.'

'It's been a rough few days, but you… you've been looking out for me. No matter the reason, I just wanted to… y'know. Acknowledge it.'

'Well,' Hilton grunted, 'you're very welcome. Fetch me some water, would you? I'd do it myself, but I don't want these ribs growing back into my lungs.'

Daedalus did.

'Thank you.'

'I wanted to ask you something,' Daedalus said, standing by the door. 'How did you get out of the lift shaft? Artificial gravity doesn't work in a vacuum. You can't have been in there long. I nearly died myself.'

Hilton looked confused. 'I prayed. Obviously.'

Daedalus stared at him. 'Right,' he said, 'obviously.' He sat quietly for a few moments. 'Hilton?'

'Aye?'

'Are you human?'

'I don't think so.'

'Right.'

'Mm-hmm.'

'I'm gonna check on our friend.'

'Very well.' Hilton lay back. 'Let me know when we are to move on.'

Daedalus left him lying there and made his way back through the ship. The *Teratorn*'s infirmary was well-equipped. Daedalus didn't recognise half of the supplies that filled the wall cabinets. Ram sat upright on a gurney, her eyes half-open. She looked in better shape than earlier. The bleeding from her head wound had stopped, and it seemed as if the flesh was already healing. *Tough as old boots,* he thought.

'Ram?' he tried.

Her eyes flickered. She groaned.

'Erin!' he called out the door. 'She's awake!'

There was a sound of coffee mugs smashing. Erin appeared in moments. She leant over her friend and poked her in the chest.

'Hey, Ram? You alright?'

Ram coughed and pointed to a box on the wall. Erin grabbed it down and opened it. It was full of syringes.

Ram nodded, and pointed to a gap in the plates behind her eye, where the dried blood was most dense.

Erin hesitantly withdrew one and held it up to the point.

Ram coughed again, and forced out a word. 'Inject.'

Erin took a deep breath, and slowly pushed the needle in. The contents dispensed themselves automatically, and the needle retracted. Erin threw it in the waste chute.

Ram let out a deep sigh. 'Better,' she croaked. 'I will... be okay. Shock migraine. The cancer... makes them worse.'

'Are your legs alright?' Erin asked.

'My legs? Yes,' Ram said. 'Why?'

Erin hopped up onto her lap and kissed her. Ram jumped, startled. Then she enclosed the tiny entari in her giant arms and kissed her back, squeezing gently. Daedalus busied himself with a cupboard for a few moments.

'Sorry. Fanks,' Erin said, muffled.

'It is okay,' Ram said, a slightly dazed tone in her voice.

'Yeah,' said Daedalus, feeling slightly out of place. He turned to face her. 'Thank you, Ram. We all owe you one.'

Ram paused, then nodded. Daedalus didn't recognise her expression. Her eyes had a strange reflective quality to them, almost as if she was cry—

He looked away again and started rifling through a drawer, looking for nothing at all.

'E – Erin?' Ram said, weakly.

'Yeah? Ram? What's wrong?'

'I think... I think I'm falling.'

'Ram?' Erin said in a small voice. 'Hey, wake up. Ram? I'm sorry. I'm sorry for everything. I didn't mean to... '

There was a thud as Ram fell heavily back against the gurney. Daedalus turned around. Erin was staring at her, eyes wide and fearful. The look on her face hit Daedalus like a punch in the gut. He felt sick.

'Erin?' he said, placing a hand on her shoulder. 'It's okay. It's the painkillers. She just needs sleep.'

'Oh. I thought she... Never mind.' Erin climbed down unsteadily and wiped her eye. She gave Ram a gentle pat on the arm, and her hand lingered there for a moment. 'Coffee,' she said.

They left Ram to sleep and went up to the cockpit. Daedalus cleared away the smashed mugs and mopped the floor while Erin made more. The bitterness made Daedalus suck his teeth and shudder, but the warmth was comforting.

'She's going to be alright, you know,' said Erin. 'Petradons are tough. They're the toughest people in the galaxy. And Ram's the toughest petradon, so she's not going to... she'll be fine.'

'Sure,' said Daedalus, 'I agree. She'll recover.'

At those words a panel in the ceiling lit up in pale blue.

'Command "recover" acknowledged,' it said, in a smooth, human-like voice. 'Damaged storage device found. Would you like to recover data from device: "LittleWill Self-Storage Unit"?'

'What?' Daedalus looked up. 'Recover what?'

'Command confirmed. Recovering data.'

'Ow!' Daedalus jumped, spilling warm coffee on his leg. The mug smashed against the floor. 'Ah! Get off!'

Erin backed away, setting down her mug. 'Mole? What's wrong?'

Daedalus hissed and struggled to throw off his coat. It put up a fight, but he finally got it over his shoulders and onto the deck. The coat buzzed violently, and sparks flew from underneath, bouncing along the floor. A black burn-mark started to grow in the dark brown folds, and smoke rose into the air above it. Erin and Daedalus flattened themselves against the walls. Erin flung a hand out, reaching for the fire extinguisher.

Then it stopped. A hole fell out of the coat and under it was a gleam of dented purple. It gave a final beep, which wavered.

A smooth, human-like voice issued from the ship.

'Data recovery complete. Reconstructing.'

The console flashed into life, and hundreds of tiny turquoise spots appeared in the air between Erin and Daedalus. They hung in sparse arrangement, and bright beams of light began to cast themselves from one point to the next, like a children's puzzle.

'Interpolating.'

The spots and lines multiplied until they became a dense cloud of sky-blue. The cloud slowly – very slowly – condensed into form.

'Copying this file is forbidden. Streaming from device.'

The locket jumped through the burnt hole in Daedalus's coat, and hung suspended in the centre of the cloud.

'Buffering.'

The projection froze in the shape of a person.

'Construct ready,' said the *Teratorn*.

Daedalus pressed a hand to his mouth. Erin looked at the locket, still visible through the figure's translucent blue back. Then she looked at Daedalus. He spoke through shaking fingers.

'Jan?'

The face was one he almost recognised, but it was expressionless.

'The condolences of James and Veronica Little are with you in this troubling time,' said Jan, in a voice filtered through static. 'Thank you for choosing LittleWill.'

There was a pause. The woman in the cockpit flickered silently.

'Hello,' said Jan, in a completely different voice, 'whoever this is. I don't know why I'm doing this. I really don't. The date is –' she looked at her watch '– the twenty-first of August. I just got back from my mum's funeral. It rained.'

Drops of simulated water fell from her hair and vanished as they reached her feet.

'So for time, that's a month after leaving primer college and two weeks before starting university. And for score, that's six family members down, now. One to go. Just me.

'What happens to these messages if there's no-one to deliver them to? It didn't say in the contract. It said "guaranteed target acquisition by means of patented trail-sniffer technology", with a little "TM" there. Does the buzzer just latch on to anyone it can find? Seventh cousin seven times removed? Well, in that case, hello distant cousin. Sorry you had to hear this, but I'm dead. Don't worry. It was my own fault.'

Daedalus clutched his chest. Erin saw his breath rise and fall.

'Suicide is funny, isn't it?' Jan went on, blithely, coldly. 'Is it a cry for attention? Is it selfish? Does she want to hurt us, make us pay? Is he taking the easy way out? – People don't get it, do they? No-one seems to understand that there's a chemical process in the human brain that can't be cancelled or corrected and it just goes on and on and on until it self-destructs.'

'No,' Daedalus said. His voice was all splinters. 'You didn't. You wouldn't.'

'You gotta understand,' Jan went on, deaf, 'you can't stop someone killing themselves, because you don't ever see it. They die well before their body goes cold. Activity stops weeks before anyone notices. People die and *then* they kill themselves.'

'You didn't – you weren't dead,' Daedalus said. 'You *weren't*.'

'So that's why I signed up to this today. I'm about to die. I can feel it, because it feels like nothing. Big blank space,' she laughed without humour or feeling, 'that's Jan. That's Ja-a-a-a–'

The recording stalled.

'Sector corrupt,' said the *Teratorn*. 'Seeking next good sector. Please wait.'

Daedalus looked like he'd seen a ghost.

'Mole?'

'It's her,' he said, staring straight at the image's face. Erin, on the other side, received his filtered gaze.

'Are you okay?' she asked.

'No. I'm not okay.'

'Did she –'

'No. She didn't. I talked her out of it. The night we met. She was okay. She grew back. I saved her, just like… if I could… '

Erin rushed through Jan to catch his fall. The image flickered, and the locket buzzed back into position. Erin held him upright.

'Mole, just breathe!' she said.

Daedalus smelled smoke. The room was dim. Erin hoisted him up against the wall and pressed a palm against his chest.

'It's okay,' she said, 'you're okay. Just breathe slowly. You're safe here. It's okay.'

His shaking fingers settled, and the dark edges retreated from his vision. The tightness in his lungs slowly fell away.

'Do you need a minute?' Erin asked. He just stared at the image. His lips went thin.

'I don't think I ever told you why I left home,' he said.

'You mentioned a protest, and riots.'

'I ran away. I went to meet Jan after my exam and she wasn't there. When it all kicked off – you won't understand. It looked bad. Real bad. We thought it was the start of the revolution. We were so young. I called her, told her to meet me at the spaceport so we could get away.'

'... What happened?'

'She didn't show. The police cordoned off the terminal. There was rioting outside. I didn't know what they were going to do. I was... I was scared. So I stole a ship and...

'I got away. I shouldn't have, but I made it out. Got a new name, paid someone all the money I had to scrub me from the Census records. It's easier for us. Humans. The last I heard was the news report the next morning. Hundreds dead. Martial law. Never did bring myself to read the obituaries. I only knew for sure when that locket turned up. Buzzed right into me while I was trying to steal some food on a grimy little station. Dunno how it found me.'

'You never said goodbye.' Erin's voice was low.

'No.'

'Well,' she said, 'now's your chance.'

The figure hovered silently in front of them, skipping in and out of focus as the *Teratorn* worked on it.

'Jan. I'm –' he stalled. Took a deep breath. 'I'm s –'

Erin gently moved away, and Daedalus stood unsteadily on his own feet.

'I'm sorry, Jan. You would have gone back for me.' The words were slow at first, but soon began to fall out unbidden. 'I'm a coward, and you deserved better friends, and more time to spend with them. God, if you hadn't *cared* so much you'd still be here. You and your protests. So bloody *brave* all the time. I can't be you. I never could be.

'I'd do anything to take it back. I can't remember what it's like to want anything else. Just let me take it back. Tell me how to put it right. I'm so tired. Please.' Daedalus teetered on his feet. Erin moved to hold him.

'Good sector located. Resuming playback.'

Jan changed. Her clothes were different, and Daedalus saw a more familiar face. Jan now wore a dirty yellow jumper, and there was her long brown coat in frame behind her, hanging on the back of a door. She smiled a sad smile.

'Hi, Dan,' she said. 'It has to be you, right? I think I managed to delete the old recording, but these things are fiddly to hack. Tough as old boots, right? Ha!'

'Jan?'

'I realise this isn't really appropriate, but I don't have a diary and it occurred to me that if I died tomorrow I'd have nothing to leave you except a bunch of books! Yeah, morbid, I know, but that's just me. I dunno, I've got my last exam later – so do you, actually – and really I'm just procrastinating. I already paid a lifetime's subscription, though, so I might as well leave a message I'd actually want to be remembered by.

'Thing is, I want to thank you. I know you'll never let me do it in person, but I wanted to just say… cheers. For being there. You're a bit dense at times but you really tried, and I think it made the difference, you know? Not just that first night, but all the nights that came afterwards. Thanks for reminding me… reminding me you only need two wheels.'

The recording grinned, and brushed a tangle of hair out of its face.

'Just in case I fall down a manhole or something, I wanted to make sure you knew. Not because I'm some swooning grateful sap, just – you don't know yourself very well, do you? I think sometimes you might need a reminder that you're a good person. I mean, yeah, you're a grumpy bastard in the mornings, but you're also kind, and caring, and… and smart, and you've never left someone behind when you thought you could help them. I won't always be around to tell you that. You need to remember. Okay? You're not that bad. You're pretty good, actually. Or… you can be.'

Jan turned her head suddenly away.

'What? Yeah, sure, gimme a minute! Gotta go, Danny boy, someone's at the door. There's something going on outside. I'll finish this later.'

The recording froze, and vanished. The locket fell to the floor, its light extinguished.

'Device not responding. Stream terminated.'

There was silence. Daedalus stood up straight, pushing Erin gently away, and rubbed his bleary eyes with a fist.

'That was her,' he said. 'She was wearing the same... that was the day I left. The same day.'

Erin frowned, but she said nothing.

Daedalus looked out the viewscreen, beyond which the stars punctured the sky in lonesome arrangements. Clouds roiled in the middle distance. Then, with increasing frequency, there came the patter of raindrops. Tiny rivers carved slow paths down the screen, warping their view of the seascape outside, and the wind drew melodies along the beach, whistling in the gaps between the pebbles.

'I never went back,' Daedalus said. 'They have a mass grave in Littlerock, near the university. I've seen pictures. All the white crosses arranged into neat rows in the grass. Did you know the grass on Crit is blue? People come to see it. It's blue, and it feels like sandpaper if you walk barefoot on it.'

'I didn't know that,' said Erin.

'There are lots of places like that in the universe. Little facts, pointless bits of knowledge. I used to collect them. Just because they were there to be known.' Daedalus ran his fingers lightly over the console. They had stopped shaking.

He turned to face Erin.

'I'm sorry,' he said, 'for pushing my own stuff onto you. Sorry for dragging you into this mess.'

'Don't worry about it,' she said, with a calm she did not have. 'I'd have been dragged in anyway. In case you haven't noticed, the Collective's gone to war. We're all involved now, whether we chose it or not.'

'That's not the point,' he sighed. 'I didn't... I never mourned her properly. I was scared. Too scared to say goodbye, to face the truth.'

Erin looked at the bags under his eyes. He'd never looked so tired.

'I killed her, Erin,' he said. 'The riots... I called her into danger and left her to die. Even... even after everything she did for me, I couldn't find the courage to try and save her. She wouldn't even have needed saving if it wasn't for me.

'Jan fixed me. I was broken, and she spent years making me better. She drove me forward, gave me a reason to work on myself. I wanted to make her happy, so I made myself happy.

'And this is how I repay her. This is where all her effort went.'

Daedalus took a deep breath. Erin listened, quiet.

'So I'm sorry,' he said. 'I thought it was happening all over again. I thought you were my second chance, but I think I get it now. There are no second chances. Not for me, anyway. I've got to carry her with me everywhere I go. Janice Crow will never leave me. It's too late for forgiveness.'

it is never too late

Daedalus shook the voice out of his head.

'What now, then?' Erin asked. 'What are you going to do?'

Daedalus crouched down and picked up the bundle of fabric on the floor, along with the burnt-out, useless locket. He turned it in his hand for a few moments.

'It's warm in here. Let's go outside.'

Erin led him back through the *Teratorn* and opened the boarding ramp. He almost slipped on the stair, but she caught his arm and helped him down to the stones, which shone with rainfall.

The whole beach glistened in the rain, under a spotted sky above. Daedalus set down his heavy brown coat on the stones, and walked out to the water's edge, still barefoot. Erin watched.

Daedalus crouched by a shallow rock-pool and held the locket up to the light. It was crusted with black fluid and warped by water damage. It no longer sparked or buzzed. Slowly he lowered it by the string until it was submerged in the pool. There he piled stones on top of it until that patch was barely distinguishable from the rest of the beach. In moments he would lose track of which stones were which, and the memory of this place would be lost.

He stood up. Erin called him back, and he went. Inside the ship was warm and dry, and he found some clean military-issue clothes to wear in an overhead compartment. All but one of the beds was still shrink-wrapped. He splashed cold water on his face in the bathroom, to help him stay awake a little longer. The headache he'd had for months had gone, but there was something left in its place – a kind of wrong feeling, like he was about to fall very ill.

In the cockpit Erin was watching the storm build.

'I'm going away for a while,' Daedalus said.

'To Crit?' Erin asked.

'At first.'

She turned to face him.

'There's… ' he went on, 'there's some work I have to do after that. Hilton will probably come with me.'

'Is that so,' said Erin.

'I need this ship, but I can drop you at a safe station on the way, with Ram, if you like. You can find transport from there.'

'Right.' Erin cleared her throat. 'This work you have. What is it, exactly?'

Daedalus said nothing for a moment. 'There are some things I think I should be doing. They're long overdue, and I don't think they can wait any longer.'

'Overdue? Since when?'

'Oh, it's old business,' he said, looking down at his clothes. He'd need a new coat. 'Ancient history, really.'

Acknowledgements

My sincere thanks to a large number of people who interfered in the creation of a bad book, resulting in the good book you now hold in your hands. The absence of any of these people would be an empty bracket where one hopes to see a fire extinguisher.

In chronological order: my family, an endless source of inspiration and support; Becca Wright, who was there with an editor's eye from the very start; Kay Staples, for years of steadfast encouragement and feedback; Chelsea Traynor, a talented artist who first brought Daedalus to life; Xander Cansell for picking this book up in the first place; Sarah K. Marr for shepherding me through an arcane process, with whisky; Kwaku Osei-Afrifa, for cheerfully handling my increasingly irritating requests for pledge rewards; Rosie Quattromini, for enduring with great kindness my many questions about how bookshops work; Lisa Quattromini for getting us over the finish line; Miranda Ward for beating my story with a stick until it worked; Philip Purser-Hallard for fixing all my commas and asking hard questions about inter-species breeding; and Mark Ecob, for designing a gorgeous cover to wrap the whole thing up.

I can think of many more people without whom this book wouldn't be the same – friends, colleagues, ex-colleagues, understanding managers and fellow writers – and of course everyone who dropped their cash on a book they wouldn't get to read for two years. To list them all would be a pleasure for me, but a problem for the editor who has to typeset my final proof. (Thanks, Andrew!) My sincere gratitude goes out to all of you.

One more thing – my thanks to Sue Wilcox, who played that vital role: a good teacher who intervened at a crucial moment.

– Niall

Patrons

Harley Anderson
Shalini Arora
Bath Novel Award
Joanna Barnard
Stephanie Bretherton
Alice Broadribb
Neal Brophy
Lazlo Burns
David Catley
Paul Chambers
Garrett Coakley
Harriet Cunningham
G. Deyke
Kate Dreyer
Rod Ellis
Adrian Everett
Sharon Eyre
Joseph Garbo
Samia Gundkalli
Bryony Hall
Baylea Hart
Emily Hasler
Charity Haugh
Margaret Healy
Sandy Herbert
Jenni Herd
E O Higgins
Eleanor Jenyns
Rohina Jogi
Leah Jones
Ziggi Kaiser
Imran Khan

Brendan Kilcullen
Shona Kinsella
Andreas Kjeldsen
Amy Lord
Brian Lunn
Alice Maltby-Kemp
Emily Marchant
Sarah K. Marr
Victoria Mason
Diego Montoyer
Chandini Murali
Carlo Navato
Richard O'Brien
Anne O'Mahoney
Anneliese O'Malley
Clifford Penton
Jennifer Pierce
Ariel Pimentel
Justin Pinner
Martin Porter
Daniel Potter a.k.a. @legobookworm
James Quigley
Kayla Rakitt
Robert Ramsay
Swéta Rana
Charlie Raspin
Suzanne Reisman
Phoenix Robertson
Frances Robinson
Ste Sharp
Colin Shelbourn
Phil Shipley
Emma Steen
Lauren Stuart
Paul Taylor
Mike Scott Thomson

Zulmira Tome
Chelsea Traynor
Anna Vaught
Georgia Wagstaff
Steve Walker
Ian Ward
Natasha Weaver
Sophie Wegner
Hazel Wright